# ESREVER
# DOOM

# TOR BOOKS by PIERS ANTHONY

**THE XANTH SERIES**
*Vale of the Vole*
*Heaven Cent*
*Man from Mundania*
*Demons Don't Dream*
*Harpy Thyme*
*Geis of the Gargoyle*
*Roc and a Hard Place*
*Yon Ill Wind*
*Faun & Games*
*Zombie Lover*
*Xone of Contention*
*The Dastard*
*Swell Foop*
*Up in a Heaval*
*Cube Route*
*Currant Events*
*Pet Peeve*
*Stork Naked*
*Air Apparent*
*Two to the Fifth*
*Jumper Cable*
*Knot Gneiss*
*Well-Tempered Clavicle*
*Luck of the Draw*
*Esrever Doom*

**THE GEODYSSEY SERIES**
*Isle of Woman*
*Shame of Man*
*Hope of Earth*
*Muse of Art*
*Climate of Change*

**ANTHOLOGIES**
*Alien Plot*
*Anthonology*

**NONFICTION**
*How Precious Was That While*
*Letters to Jenny*
*But What of Earth?*
*Ghost*
*Hasan*

*Prostho Plus*
*Race Against Time*
*Shade of the Tree*
*Steppe*
*Triple Détente*

**WITH ROBERT R. MARGROFF**
The Dragon's Gold Series
*Dragon's Gold*
*Serpent's Silver*
*Chimaera's Copper*
*Orc's Opal*
*Mouvar's Magic*

*The E.S.P. Worm*
*The Ring*

**WITH FRANCES HALL**
*Pretender*

**WITH RICHARD GILLIAM**
*Tales from the Great Turtle*
(Anthology)

**WITH ALFRED TELLA**
*The Willing Spirit*

**WITH CLIFFORD A. PICKOVER**
*Spider Legs*

**WITH JAMES RICHEY AND ALAN RIGGS**
*Quest for the Fallen Star*

**WITH JULIE BRADY**
*Dream a Little Dream*

**WITH JO ANNE TAEUSCH**
*The Secret of Spring*

**WITH RON LEMING**
*The Gutbucket Quest*

# PIERS ANTHONY

# ESREVER DOOM

A TOM DOHERTY ASSOCIATES BOOK

NEW YORK

This is a work of fiction. All of the characters, organizations, and events portrayed
in this novel are either products of the author's imagination or are used fictitiously.

ESREVER DOOM

Copyright © 2013 by Piers Anthony Jacob

All rights reserved.

Map by Jael

A Tor Book
Published by Tom Doherty Associates, LLC
175 Fifth Avenue
New York, NY 10010

www.tor-forge.com

Tor® is a registered trademark of Tom Doherty Associates, LLC.

The Library of Congress Cataloging-in-Publication Data is available upon request.

ISBN 978-0-7653-3136-6 (hardcover)
ISBN 978-1-4299-4661-2 (e-book)

Tor books may be purchased for educational, business, or promotional use.
For information on bulk purchases, please contact Macmillan Corporate and
Premium Sales Department at 1-800-221-7945, extension 5442,
or write specialmarkets@macmillan.com.

First Edition: October 2013

Printed in the United States of America

0  9  8  7  6  5  4  3  2  1

# Contents

1.  Arrival . . . . . . . . . . . . . . . . . . . . . . . . . . . . . . . . . . . . . . . . 11
2.  Mission . . . . . . . . . . . . . . . . . . . . . . . . . . . . . . . . . . . . . . . 31
3.  Castle . . . . . . . . . . . . . . . . . . . . . . . . . . . . . . . . . . . . . . . . . 49
4.  Partner . . . . . . . . . . . . . . . . . . . . . . . . . . . . . . . . . . . . . . . . 68
5.  Zap and Yukay . . . . . . . . . . . . . . . . . . . . . . . . . . . . . . . . . 88
6.  Illusion Fields . . . . . . . . . . . . . . . . . . . . . . . . . . . . . . . . . . 109
7.  Hades . . . . . . . . . . . . . . . . . . . . . . . . . . . . . . . . . . . . . . . . 132
8.  Dragon . . . . . . . . . . . . . . . . . . . . . . . . . . . . . . . . . . . . . . . 152
9.  Demo Derby . . . . . . . . . . . . . . . . . . . . . . . . . . . . . . . . . . 176
10. Alter Ego . . . . . . . . . . . . . . . . . . . . . . . . . . . . . . . . . . . . . 194
11. Bomb Sniffer . . . . . . . . . . . . . . . . . . . . . . . . . . . . . . . . . . 211
12. Ghost . . . . . . . . . . . . . . . . . . . . . . . . . . . . . . . . . . . . . . . . 230
13. Trap . . . . . . . . . . . . . . . . . . . . . . . . . . . . . . . . . . . . . . . . . 249
14. Bogeyman . . . . . . . . . . . . . . . . . . . . . . . . . . . . . . . . . . . . 268
15. NoAmi . . . . . . . . . . . . . . . . . . . . . . . . . . . . . . . . . . . . . . . 287
16. Bomb . . . . . . . . . . . . . . . . . . . . . . . . . . . . . . . . . . . . . . . . 307
    Author's Note . . . . . . . . . . . . . . . . . . . . . . . . . . . . . . . . . . 327

# ESREVER
# DOOM

# 1
# ARRIVAL

Kody woke when the nurse came into his hospital room. He felt awful. "What happened?"

"Ah, you're awake," the nurse said. "The doctor will be with you shortly. Now if you will just sign this admittance paper, your insurance will cover it."

"What happened?" he repeated as her hand guided his numb fingers for the signature.

She glanced at him sympathetically. "You don't remember?"

"I don't," he agreed.

"You were in an accident. A bad one. But they got you here in time."

"In time for what?"

"The doctor will explain. Meanwhile this will relax you."

"Don't—" But she was already giving him a dose via the IV hooked to his arm. He had no choice but to fade out.

When Kody woke again, he was cautious about speaking. He wanted to know more about his situation before they dosed him. He had been in an accident? It must have been a bad one, because his whole body felt washed out. Had a drunk driver hit him? Then what about his car? Was it suffering similarly?

The nurse, morbidly attuned, knew he was awake. "Just in time for the doctor," she said briskly, as if that was all that mattered.

"I just want to know—"

"Not now," she said with impersonal efficiency. "He's here."

So much for any preference he might have. This was, after all, a hospital; they had better things to do than chat with patients.

The doctor was brusque. "You face some serious surgery, Mr. Kody."

"My name's not—"

"Don't be concerned; we'll put you out for the duration. It's called an artificial coma. When you emerge, the surgery will be done and you'll be well on the way to recovery."

"Surgery? What for?"

"So glad you understand." Already the nurse was doing her thing with the IV. He had only moments of consciousness remaining.

"There may be some disorientation," the doctor explained. "It's a known side effect of the anesthetic. A sense of floating, perhaps some temporary mood reversal. Nothing to be concerned about, Mr. Kody."

Mood reversal? He didn't want his mood or anything else reversed. But it was too late to protest; he was going under. Only the doctor's last words lingered. Mood Reverse. Mood. Reverse. Mood reversed was Doom. That did not sound good.

"Boom! Doom!" the ogre cried, hurling the poor creature at the shimmering wall.

Kody reacted before thinking. He put out a hand and intercepted the victim just before it collided. He brought it in to him, unharmed, as the ogre tromped away.

Ogre? Where *was* he?

It got worse. He looked at the creature he had just rescued. It was a bird. No, a cat. In fact it had the head and wings of a bird, and the body and tail of a cat.

The creature, briefly stunned, recovered. "Cheep?" it said.

"You're welcome, I think," Kody said. "I don't know where you were going, but it didn't look healthy."

"Cheep!" The creature looked at the wall, which shimmered in response. The wall was translucent, with an open meadow beyond, but there was a sinister cast to the scene. Kody didn't like it.

"Can you run or fly? I think you need to go home before you run afoul of another ogre."

The thing seemed to understand him. It sat up in his hand, spread its wings, and flapped. It flew up, made a circle in the air, then departed, flying over the jungle.

"You're welcome," Kody repeated, bemused.

Now, exactly where was he? Not in the hospital! This seemed to be some sort of fantasy land, with ogres, catbirds, sinister walls, and who knew what else. Kody really wasn't into fantasy; that was his friend Joshua's department. He was at a loss to explain how he had so suddenly come here; the last he knew, he was being put under for some sort of surgery. The doctor said there would be disorientation, maybe mood reversal, and his disoriented mind had translated Mood to Doom.

Could that phrase Mood Reverse be translated into Esrever Doom? That would make about as much sense as the rest of it. He was doomed to be caught in reversal.

And there had been the ogre crying "Doom!" Kody had arrived just in time to rescue a composite creature from likely doom. An incredible coincidence.

But maybe not. Maybe he was in the coma, suffering some sort of mind reversal, and this was a dream deriving from that word. No coincidence at all, if he was imagining it.

Well, he might as well enjoy it while it lasted. He feared he would not enjoy whatever had happened to him in the real world.

He saw a speck in the sky. Something was flying in, and it did not look like a regular bird. Was the composite creature returning? No, this one was rapidly looking larger as it approached. It was the size of an eagle, no, a turkey, no, a horse.

A horse?

It looked like a large winged horse. With the forepart of a man. A—a flying centaur.

The creature landed neatly before him and folded his monstrous gray-brown feathered wings. His muscular human portion was taller than Kody, which was unusual. "Hello, stranger! My friend the catbird tells me you rescued him from a fate worse than death." Now Kody saw that the small creature was perching on the centaur's broad equine back, between the wings.

"I don't know—" Kody said, somewhat at a loss for words.

"Of course you don't know me," the centaur said. "I am Griff the Hipporoc, son of a male centaur and a female roc bird. My parents splashed into each other at a love spring they took for a normal pond. You know how it is; these accidents happen all the time, and account for many interesting crossbreeds. So I share their characteristics, and can speak avian dialects as well as human ones. That's how I came to know the catbird."

That hadn't been exactly what Kody was saying, but it would do. "I'm Kody, from—" He paused, uncertain whether his origin would make any sense to this fantasy creature.

"From Mundania, of course," Griff said. "You have that civilian look about you. Did you die?"

"Oh, I don't think so," Kody said, startled. "At least not yet. They put me in a coma, and I seem to be having a really weird dream."

"Well, that's one way to come to Xanth," Griff said. "We do see Mundanes here every so often, and dreams are important. Look, I really appreciate the way you saved my friend from the Void, so I came to tell you that."

"The Void?"

"The Region from which there's no return," Griff said, gesturing at the wall. "That's the event horizon. If the catbird had gone through that, he would have been lost."

"Oh, I see," Kody said, not really seeing.

"So I think I owe you a return favor. Why don't I take you any-where you want to go, so you don't have to stumble through the dangerous jungle? Air travel is much faster and safer. You'll soon get eaten by a dragon otherwise."

"I appreciate that," Kody said. "I don't know whether getting eaten by a dragon in a dream would affect me much, but I'd rather not find out. But I have no idea where I want to go."

"Good point." Griff considered favors.

Two micelike creatures ran along the ground between them. "Oh, bleep!" Griff said. "Don't let them touch you."

Bleep? "Those mice? Aren't they harmless?"

"Hardly! Those are vices. A cross between a vole and a mouse. See those letters on their backs? The one is an AD, the other a DE. If the ADvice touches you it will make you do bad things. Then you'll have to touch the DEvice to become nicer. Better to stay clear of them entirely." He stomped a front hoof. "Get away from us; we don't want any vices." The little creatures scurried away.

"Uh, thank you for the ad— uh, the clarification," Kody said.

"That's not enough of a favor. You saved my friend's life."

The catbird chirped.

"Now that's an idea," Griff agreed. "I'll give him the check her board." He looked at Kody. "Do you play check hers?"

"Well, I—"

"Or cheese. It's adaptable. But it doesn't matter. Just refocus and you'll see the scenes. Touch whichever one you want to go to." He produced a small object and handed it to Kody. "We have to be going now, but thanks again for what you did." The centaur spread his huge wings, trotted along the ground, and sailed upward. In one and a half moments he was gone.

One and a half moments? Evidently that was how time was kept here in Xanth.

He looked at the object. It was a folded mass that unfolded re-peatedly to show a checkerboard (check her board?) with the check-ers painted on the squares. Each one resembled a buxom young woman in a circular skirt. He touched one, and she moved forward to another square, jiggling.

Intrigued, he touched another, but she didn't move. Then he touched one of the opposing checkers, which resembled a handsome young man in a kilt, and he did move. It was necessary to take turns. Soon Kody was in a game with himself, seeing the check hers jump each other and disappear. When each one jumped, skirt flaring, the other piece looked up, froze in place as if seeing something forbidden, and faded out with an audible huff. They were checking each other out! Thus Check Hers and Check His. This was one naughty magic board!

But checkers was a relatively simple game. Too bad there were not chess pieces. And as he thought of that, the chess pieces appeared, each a little marvel of statuary carved from hard cheese. Which must be why they called it cheese instead of chess; it wasn't just a typo. When he touched a pawn, it stepped forward two squares. Other pieces moved in their traditional ways. So he could play chess on this board.

But what about the pictures Griff had mentioned? Kody focused, and refocused, and in a moment got the range. It was like looking at a 3-D picture; focus was everything. Once he had the pictures, they were fascinating. Scenes of assorted magical creatures and things. And if he touched one he would be there?

Better experiment cautiously, because some indeed were dragons. So he oriented on an appealing castle with pleasant foliage and turrets. That should be safe to visit. He touched it.

Nothing happened. Ah, well. He folded the checkerboard, tucked it in a pocket, and looked around.

He was standing before the castle. The change had been so smooth he had not realized it had taken place.

So the game board worked. He could go where he wished, in this fantasy land. There were sixty-four scenes in all; surely one would serve his purpose. If he could only figure out what his purpose was, in this dream.

The front gate of the castle opened. A stunningly lovely young woman stood there, svelte and blond, evidently the mistress of this castle, as she wore a petite crown. "Why, hello," she said, surprised.

"I apologize for intruding," Kody said. "A centaur gave me a magic device that enables me to travel, and I was trying it out. I think I can as readily depart as I came here."

"First let me touch you," the woman said, approaching him. He stood bemused as she came and touched his hand. "Oh!"

"You see, I'm not from this region," he said. "I don't know the geography or the customs."

"You are Kody, from Mundania," she said. "You were in some sort of accident, and woke in a hospital, where they drugged you, and you find yourself here in Xanth. You think it's all a dream."

Kody's mouth opened, but no words came out. How could she know that?

She smiled, and it was like the rising sun. "I am Princess Dawn. My talent is to know everything about anything living that I touch. You need my help. You must have been guided here. Come in." She turned and reentered the castle. Her back side was just as impressive as her front side.

Kody followed. He kept being surprised by this dream!

"This is Caprice Castle," Dawn said as they walked. "It has marvelous properties you will discover soon enough. A number of us live here. We gather puns for storage, so that Xanth is not infested worse than it has to be."

"Puns," Kody said. "I believe I have encountered some of those."

"Indeed, it is hard to avoid them. It's a real problem."

"Yes," he agreed. But puns were the least of his concerns at the moment.

"Picka, dear," Dawn said, not loudly.

A spook-house animated skeleton appeared. "Yes, dear," it said.

"This is Kody, from Mundania. He needs help."

"We'll help him," the skeleton agreed. It came forward to shake Kody's hand. He tried not to recoil at the touch of the bare bones. "I am Picka Bone, Dawn's husband. And these are our children."

For two small figures had appeared. One was a walking skeleton, the other a cute little girl.

It seemed this crazy realm was destined to keep surprising him. A walking skeleton could marry a princess, and they could have children? Obviously so.

"I'm Piton," the little male skeleton said.

"Hello, Piton," Kody said. "You look a lot like your father."

The boy giggled, complimented.

"I'm Data," the girl said.

Kody realized that Piton was a P name, surely because of his father Picka, while Data was a D name, after her mother Dawn. It seemed that in Xanth men had sons, women had daughters. "Hello, Data. You are lovely like your mother."

The child blushed with pleasure. Kody had not realized a small child could blush. But of course this was a magic land.

There was an awkward pause. Then Dawn approached. "I need to touch you again."

"Welcome," Kody said. "I never mind being touched by a lovely lady." That made *him* pause, because it was not the kind of thing he had ever said before.

Dawn touched him. "It is true. You see us as beautiful."

"Doesn't everyone?" Kody asked, perplexed. "I'm no expert, but if you are not one of the loveliest women extant, and your daughter a beautiful child, this is the most remarkable realm imaginable. Or is it considered bad manners to say the obvious? Have I given offense?"

"No offense," Dawn said. "Far from it."

"He sees you as beautiful?" Picka asked, as if not quite believing it.

"He does," Dawn said. "And Data as really cute."

"Then he's immune!"

Dawn considered. "Not exactly. He's just not reversed in the same way we are."

"Then can he fix it?"

"I don't know. Kody is not completely real, here."

Picka looked at her, perplexed. "Not?"

So did Kody. A walking skeleton found him perplexing? "I don't really understand any of this."

"Come and sit down," Dawn said. "This may take some explaining."

Soon they were ensconced in an appealing living room. Data, thrilled to be appreciated as pretty, came to sit on Kody's lap. But the surprises were not through. For a moment she became a little skeleton, startling him. It was definitely her, because now her dress hung loosely on the bones. She was just as cute in that form as when she had flesh.

"We can change," Data said, her voice emanating from her little skull. "It's part of the magic of Caprice Castle." She reappeared in human form, and squirmed to get her sagged dress to fit properly. "Do you really think I'm cute?"

"Yes, definitely," Kody said.

"That's great!" She leaned forward to hug him.

"Here is the background," Dawn said in a businesslike tone. "About a week ago the Land of Xanth was affected by a malign spell of reversal that caused people to perceive others as the opposite of what they are. That is, handsome or beautiful folk are perceived as ugly, while ugly folk are seen as handsome or lovely. Those in the middle range are affected less, becoming moderately the opposite of what they were. So, for example, others now see me as a hag, while seeing true hags as beautiful. We of the sightly persuasion find this distinctly awkward. We would like to have the old order restored, but we don't know how to do it. The Good Magician Humfrey says that only a person unaffected by the spell has any chance to nullify it. But all residents of Xanth are similarly affected, at least to some degree."

Kody's head was trying to spin. "This is not a literal change? Just one of perception?"

"Correct," Picka said. "I see Dawn as I always have. But now I am repulsed. That complicates our relationship."

"So it's really a mood reversal," Kody said. "Your sight has not changed, just your appreciation of what you see." Esrever doom, he thought: mood reverse. It was almost starting to make odd sense.

"Exactly," Picka agreed. "Even when she assumes skeletal form, I see her nice bones as ugly sticks."

"I don't like being seen as ugly," Dawn said candidly. "No woman does."

"While I, being Mundane, am not affected," Kody said, getting it straight.

"Not exactly," Dawn said.

"I'm not exactly here, yes, as it seems I am dreaming. But apart from that, I see things as they are."

"Not exactly," Dawn repeated.

"I'm not following you."

"I think I need to demonstrate." She glanced at Picka. "With your acquiescence, dear."

The skeleton shrugged. "Of course."

She faced Kody. "Stand."

Data got off his lap, knowing what was coming. He stood, perplexed.

She came to him, put her arms around him, drew him close, and kissed him. He felt almost as if he were floating off the floor. Her wonderful bosom was pressing into his chest, his hands were somehow on her marvelous bottom, and the contact of their lips was sheer rapture. She was an utterly mesmerizing creature. In that moment he loved her, despite knowing that she was not and would never be his. Not only was she a magic princess, far beyond his station, she was a thoroughly married mother of two. He had no business reacting romantically to her.

She drew back, knowing how well she had impressed him. Now it was no mystery how she had conquered a walking skeleton. She could seduce the dead, if she tried. "You liked that."

"God help me, I did," he admitted, shaken. "Please don't do it again."

"So you are reversed."

Now he appreciated her point. "I guess I am."

"Reversed?" Picka asked. "He's a perfectly normal man."

"Indeed he is," Dawn agreed.

Picka and the two children looked at her, puzzled.

Kody changed the subject. "So it may be that I am here for a reason: to get this spell of reversal turned off. So that Mood Reverse is no longer Esrever Doom."

"It may be," Dawn agreed. "The Good Magician will know."

"Who is this Good Magician?" Kody asked.

"He is Xanth's most respected Magician of Information," Picka said. "Anyone who really needs to know something can go to ask the Good Magician. But it isn't easy."

"Not easy?"

"He doesn't much like to be bothered," Picka said. "He is chronically Grumpy, so much so that he has five and a half wives who rotate month by month, a new one stepping in when the old one is worn down. He makes his castle difficult to get into, so that most querents are discouraged and go away without entering. And when he does Answer a Question, he charges the person a year's service, or an equivalent service. Even then, his Answers are seldom obvious; it takes time to figure them out."

"That does seem to be discouraging," Kody agreed. "Obviously I don't want to ask him anything."

"Yet you must," Dawn said. "The welfare of Xanth may depend on it."

The welfare of a purely imaginary magic land he was dreaming about. Yet she surely knew it better than he did. What could he do, but agree? "I must."

"We will have you here as our guest for a few days," Dawn said. "You need time to acclimatize, to get to know more about Xanth. Then we will send you to the Good Magician's Castle."

"But if I am here only a few days, there won't be time for me to do anything, regardless."

"You will be in Xanth as long as you need to be," she said with certainty.

"So be it," he agreed. "But you won't need to help me get there. I have the chessboard." He touched it in his pocket.

"It is best not to depend too much on such artifacts," Dawn said. "Some of them are limited, so that if you use it when you don't need to, you may not be able to use it when you do need to."

"Point taken," Kody agreed.

"Tweeter will show you to your room. You can clean up, then go out to talk with Bryce."

"Tweeter? Bryce?"

"Tweeter is a bird who knows what's what," Picka said. "Bryce is an old Mundane who arrived here last year. Princess Harmony is courting him."

And there was a small nondescript bird hovering in the air before him. "Good to meet you, Tweeter," Kody said.

The bird flew out of the room, and Kody followed. It was apparent that animals were not just animals, here; they were people. They proceeded up winding stairs to a rather nice suite on an upper floor, complete with a made bed, dresser, bathroom, and shower.

"This is all for me?" Kody asked.

"Tweet."

Kody washed up at the sink, noting that the mirror showed him as unchanged from life. Then the glass flickered, and Picka's skull appeared.

"Dawn said you should eat before you go out, as it might be a long afternoon," the skeleton said. "Tweeter will show you where."

He needed food in a dream realm? Evidently so, because he was getting hungry. "Thanks. I'll be there," Kody answered. Then he glanced at the bird. "A magic mirror?"

"Tweet," Tweeter agreed. He was evidently a bird of few words.

In due course they reported to the dining nook, where the meal was already laid out: a sandwich in the shape of a realistic submarine complete with a pickle periscope, and a glass of what looked like root beer. The two children were there. "Yours," Data said expectantly.

He bit into the sandwich, and it was excellent. Then he sipped the drink, and jumped. It felt as if something had kicked him in the rear, though that was impossible, as he was sitting. Both children giggled, and Tweeter made a laughing tweet.

Something was up. "Okay, what's the joke?" he asked them.

"It's boot rear," Piton said. He looked to be barely two years old, assuming skeletons aged at the rate of fleshly folk, but could speak well enough.

Kody contemplated the drink. Root beer, boot rear. A pun that was literal. A kick in the ass. But it was nevertheless tasty and satisfying. "Thank you. I did get a kick out of it."

Children and bird laughed again.

It seemed that this dream realm had a character of its own, and humor was a significant part of it. He could live with that.

After lunch he departed the castle with Tweeter, on his way to find Bryce. The landscape was a hilly jungle with odd-looking plants and trees. He spied what had to be a pie plant, because it was growing pies, and another growing assorted shoes.

There was a path curving around and through the scenery, meandering as if enjoying itself. The air was pleasant.

Then Tweeter paused. "Tweet!" That sounded like alarm.

"What is it?"

Instead of answering the bird flew to a large tree by the side of the path, and perched on a massive lower branch. He made a gesture with one wing as if beckoning. So Kody carefully climbed up to join him there. But immediately Tweeter flew to a higher branch, and Kody followed again. Before long they both were on a high branch, peering down at the path. It was a fine view, but what was the point?

There was a motion behind the trees, accompanied by a sort of snuffling. Then a large dark creature, a vastly oversized lizard, came walking down the path, its long body sinuously handling the curves.

"Is that a dinosaur?" Kody asked, amazed.

"Tweet." That was negation.

"Then it must be—a dragon!"

"Tweet." Agreement.

The dragon heard them. It angled its head to peer up the tree. A puff of smoke emerged from its snoot.

"A smoker!" Kody said. Somewhere he had heard that dragons came in several types, one of which was the smoker. If that thing chose to rev up its smoke it could make a cloud around the tree and literally smoke them out. He understood that in house fires, more people died from smoke inhalation than from direct burning. This thing was dangerous!

Then the dragon shrugged and moved on. It had concluded that they weren't worth the effort. It would have required a lot of smoke to surround a tree this size.

"But if you hadn't warned me, I'd have run right into it on the path. It could have smoked me with one puff, and swallowed me whole."

"Tweet," Tweeter agreed.

"Well, look who's climbing trees!" a female voice screeched.

Kody looked, but didn't see anything.

"A silly tweety bird and an ignorant Mundane oaf," the voice screeched.

Now Kody saw the source, perched in a distant tree. It looked like a vulture, except that it had an ugly human head.

"That's a harpy!" he exclaimed, amazed.

"Tweet," Tweeter agreed.

"Lo, the light dawns!" the harpy screeched. "I'm Sniper, mistress of the long-distance verbal attack! What are you two doing there—making love?"

"That's one foul mouth on that creature," Kody remarked.

"Get it straight, idiot!" the harpy screeched. "I have a fowl mouth, not a foul mouth!"

Kody was getting annoyed. "And your face is uglier than your mouth."

This set the harpy back. "Ugly?"

"Repulsive," Kody clarified.

"But since the Curse I've been beautiful!"

Curse? Then Kody caught on: the reversal that made lovely women seem ugly, and ugly harpies seem beautiful. "Too bad, Sniper; I see you as you are."

Tweeter was amused. "Tweet!"

"Oh, yeah?" the harpy screeched. "Well, you're another!" Then she spread her motley wings and took off, evidently overmatched.

"Tweet."

"You're right," Kody said. "That was sort of fun."

They dismounted from the tree and resumed travel along the path. Now Kody appreciated his need for a competent guide. It wasn't just a matter of finding a man, but of knowing what dangers to avoid. The bird knew.

They came to a bushy clearing. Tweeter flew ahead, then returned. "Tweet."

"Right. Go this way." He followed the bird to where a young man was kneeling before a melon.

The man glanced up. "Hello. Tweeter tells me you're Kody, a fellow Mundanian, newly arrived, and you want to compare notes."

"Uh, yes, in essence," Kody agreed, taken aback. All that from one tweet? Well, maybe it did fit within 140 characters.

"I'm Bryce. Just let me capture this pun, and I'll be with you."

Now Kody saw that the melon had legs, head, and tail. It was a sadly fat little dog! Bryce opened a bag and put it over the creature. When it was safely inside, he closed the bag and stood up. "That's a melon-collie, a gourd dog. More pun than guardian, I fear. We're trying to capture the most egregious puns first."

"So I see," Kody said.

"So how did you come to Xanth, Kody?"

"I was being anesthetized for surgery, and they warned me there could be side effects, such as mood reverse. I got mood backward and it came out doom. Esrever doom. Things seem to have regressed from there."

"Could you have died?"

"Not that I know of. I'm in a controlled coma."

"So you should return when they bring you out of it."

"Yes. Then the dream will end."

Bryce smiled. "Funny thing about dreams. Some turn out to be true. Take me: I'm eighty-one years old and in ill health."

Kody repressed a smile. "You don't look it."

"I know. I was magically youthened when I came here, and now am twenty-two, physically, and absolutely healthy. And being courted by a princess. For some men, that would be the stuff of dreams."

"For some men," Kody agreed cautiously.

A lovely teenaged girl approached, accompanied by several young dogs. "Did I hear my name?"

"Princess Harmony," Bryce said. "Kody Mundane."

Harmony smiled, lighting the area. She had lustrous brown hair under her pert crown, glowing brown eyes, and wore a shape-fitting brown dress. "Kody," she repeated.

"Princess Harmony," Kody said. "You look ravishing."

She seemed surprised. "I do?"

He laughed. "I can't think when I've seen a prettier teen, princess or not."

Harmony turned to Bryce. "What do you see?"

"You are the ugliest creature I have ever seen," Bryce answered matter-of-factly.

She looked again at Kody. "Do you want to rephrase your answer?"

"Tweet!"

Harmony looked startled. "True?"

"True," Kody said. "I am not suffering that particular reversal. I see people as they are, and you are almost as beautiful as Princess Dawn."

"Thank you. I think I was, before the gross reversal." She frowned, frustrated.

"So you're here for a reason," Bryce said. "To abolish the Curse."

"I'm not sure about that. I think I'm here by coincidence, or pure imagination. But if I can help, I will."

"I need that Curse to be abolished," Harmony said seriously to Kody. "You heard him say how I'm the ugliest creature he's ever seen. That means when the Curse goes, he'll see me as the loveliest. Then maybe I can nail him. A kiss or two could do it. Certainly a night in the hay. Then he'll have to marry me."

"Stop it!" Bryce said. "You're only seventeen. You know I won't touch a child."

"I know you'll *try* not to touch a teen. But you're weakening."

Kody shook his head. "You're trying to seduce him, and he's resisting?"

She made a cute moue. "He has this foolish Mundane thing about being my grandfather's age and not robbing the cradle."

"I *am* your grandfather's age!" Bryce protested.

Harmony turned to Kody. "See?"

Kody shook his head. "There must be more of a story here than I know."

"There is," Bryce and Harmony said together. Then they laughed. They had evidently been over this ground many times. Obviously they knew each other well, and were probably in love even if they didn't admit it.

"Maybe I can help you collect a few puns while we talk," Kody said. "I need to know more about this land of Zanth."

"Xanth," Bryce said, somehow hearing the spelling. "And yes, you do need to know more about it, if you're to abolish the Curse."

Harmony conjured (perhaps literally) a pun bag for Kody, and they reoriented on the pun-collecting chore. "Woof!" a puppy barked.

"Show the way, Wolfe," Harmony said.

"Wolfe's the son of Woofer, Tweeter's friend," Bryce explained.

"He and his sister Rowena are working with us today. Their mother, Rachel, crossed into Xanth last year with me, found romance, but returned to Mundania. Woofer was pretty broken up about it, but the pups are doing well."

Kody saw that the male pup had a W name, the same as his sire. The female one had an R name, the same as her mother. "Woofer? That sounds like a loudspeaker."

"Precisely. There are three of them, Woofer Dog, Tweeter Bird, and Midrange Cat. They came to Xanth with a Mundane family, and now live here."

"There seems to be a lot of Mundania here."

"Right around here, yes. Not elsewhere. That's probably why Dawn sent you to me. Mundanes understand Mundanes better."

Wolfe barked. There was a huge-trunked tree that looked like nothing so much as a giant beer mug. Small side branches held out steaming hot dogs and mugs of what had to be beer.

Bryce held up his bag. "Now if we can just fathom the pun."

"Frank 'n Stein," Kody said before he thought.

The monster mug shimmered, dissolved into smoke, and flowed into Kody's pun bag.

"You're a quick learner," Bryce said as Kody stared.

"I had no idea!"

"You could make a good pun catcher," Harmony said. "Of course, it is considered hard labor because it drives people crazy."

"But about this Curse," Kody said as they resumed their quest for puns. "I understand I'm supposed to go beg a favor from a certain Good Magician, who will tell me how to go about it. But that he charges outrageously. I don't see why I should do it."

"Because if you don't, you'll be stuck here forever with pundigestion," Harmony said. "Watch where you're stepping. That's crab grass."

Now Kody saw the little green pincers orienting on his feet. He quickly put down the bag. "In, crabby." And the grass wavered into smoke and flowed in.

Wolfe barked, signaling another pun. A woman was walking toward them. She was of indifferent appearance, which meant the reversal had little effect, but her bosom was curiously cloudy. In fact it was roiling, as if live things were trying to escape. The effect was both fascinating and alarming.

"What is that?" Bryce asked. Kody was similarly perplexed.

"A storm front," Harmony said. "If you men weren't so fixed on bosoms . . ." She opened her bag, and the front dissolved and entered it.

"Ah, here are some nuts," Bryce said. But when he took one it unwound into a wad of paper money. Wolfe barked.

"Cashews," Kody said. "So money really does grow on trees, here." But he was concluding that they were right: he needed to get out of this punfest before it rotted his brain. "How do I get to the Good Magician's Castle?"

"We'd take you there," Bryce said. "But we're pretty busy here, as you can see. We don't want any of these puns to escape, lest they reproduce. Any we don't get today will be lost. But Harmony may be able to help."

"Yes," the princess agreed as she grabbed a vat of tea that had books floating in it. "Novel-tea." It dissipated and was duly captured. "I can mark a path there. But you'll need a steed, and some protection. Here there be dragons."

"True," Kody agreed, remembering the one he and Tweeter had encountered. "And harpies."

"I will talk to Dawn about it tonight," she said. "I'm sure we can arrange something."

"You could just point the way, and I can go there. I have a good sense of direction."

Both Bryce and Harmony shook their heads. Tweeter tweeted negatively. Even the dog barked No. Apparently they had little confidence in his traveling ability.

Kody sighed. "What must be, must be. I will accept the help I need."

Bryce nodded. "You're learning."

Harmony punched him on the arm. "Now if you were as fast a study, you'd learn that age is irrelevant here in Xanth. Then you'd marry me."

"Unfortunately I'm not that fast a study," Bryce said.

They all laughed.

# 2
# MISSION

S o it came to pass. Kody had a good night at Caprice Castle, and in the morning Picka and Dawn took him out and showed him the marked path, which consisted of a floating blue line winding into the forest. But something was wrong.

"The scenery," Kody said. "It's not the same."

"To be sure," Picka agreed. "It is the nature of Caprice Castle to travel. It soon gets bored with any particular locale, so it moves."

"The castle moves? But I didn't feel anything."

"It does it in its own fashion. It fades out at one place and fades in at another."

Now Kody understood why they had needed to get all the puns of the locale harvested yesterday; they were no longer there today. That was also why they couldn't point him in a direction: it changed overnight.

"I believe a steed was mentioned," Kody mentioned.

"Yes. Unfortunately he can't come to the castle. But the path will lead you to him. Your guardian will be with him. You should be safe enough."

"Guardian?"

"Normally, living folk travel on enchanted paths that are guaranteed to be safe," Picka said. "But there's no such path here, so Princess Harmony had to mark an alternate route that avoids most hazards. But considering your unfamiliarity with the land, we thought some additional protection was warranted. It would help if you had a magic talent, but fresh Mundanes generally don't."

"Let me check," Dawn said. She touched his hand. "Why yes he does! It seems to be another aspect of the reversal. Kody, your magic talent is to summon chips of reverse wood. Do you know what that means?"

"No."

"Reverse wood reverses things, often in unpredictable ways. Presumably it won't affect you; that would be part of your talent. It's marvelous stuff. If a dragon threatens to toast, steam, or smoke you, you can conjure a chip and flip it at the creature, and it will suffer an awkward reversal of some sort. So you should be able to defend yourself, once you get the hang of it. You can practice during your trip to the Good Magician's Castle."

"Shouldn't I practice here, before traveling?"

"Not in my castle," she said firmly. "Reverse wood is tricky; there's no telling what harm you might accidentally do."

"Not here," he agreed. "How do I summon one? I promise not to flip it."

"Just hold out your hand and will the chip to appear."

He held out his hand. "Like this?" And a chip of wood appeared.

"Like that," she agreed. "Now get rid of it before it reverses something and causes a problem."

Kody willed the chip to vanish, but it didn't. "I don't seem to be able to banish it, just to summon it."

"Oh, that's right," Dawn said. "Yours is a one-way talent. You have to use what you fetch."

"I'll put it in a pocket." He tucked the chip in his left front shirt pocket.

"That would not be wise. That reversal is struggling to take effect, and it might start affecting you."

"Already," Picka said, looking at the pocket.

Kody looked. The pocket was inside out, having been reversed, and the chip was on the ground, where the dirt was turning into mud. Its solidity had been reversed. He quickly picked up the chip, and the ground solidified. "I guess I need to use it on something."

"Touch me," Picka said. "I can't be hurt."

"I'm not sure of that," Dawn said warily.

Kody touched the skeleton's hip bone. Suddenly it was clothed in flesh. In fact his whole midsection had become a bare human posterior. His dead bone had been reversed to living flesh.

"Now that's a real ass-et," Picka said, amused, flexing his nether cheeks. "When I first met Dawn, I wasn't attracted to her, because her nice bones were covered in awful flesh. Since then, I've grown more tolerant."

"Get it out of here!" Dawn said sharply. She was definitely not amused by the exposure. It seemed that she liked her men as flesh or bone, not a mixture.

Kody hurled the chip into the forest. It struck a large, heavyset, serious tree. The tree guffawed, floated up, and sailed into the sky.

"That was a gravi-tree," Picka said. His midsection had reverted to normal white bone. "It became a whole lot lighter in weight and mood. That was a powerful reverse wood chip."

"So it seems," Kody agreed, impressed. "Now I appreciate why you don't want me to play with chips in the house."

"Exactly," Dawn agreed severely.

It was definitely time to move on. "Thank you for your hospitality," Kody said.

"You're welcome," Picka said. "It has been fun."

Dawn seemed to be suppressing a glare. "Do try to get the Curse reversed."

"I will." Kody walked away from the castle, following the blue line.

After a few steps he paused to face back and wave, but stifled it, because the castle was gone. There was only untrammeled rock and gravel where it had been. Caprice Castle had made sure he would not return.

He entered the forest, which seemed pleasant enough. But now he knew there could be serious dangers, like demons or dragons.

A shape loomed up before him. "Well, now," it said.

Kody realized that he had been subvocalizing, and in this magic land it was dangerous to name something lest it consider itself summoned. This looked like a demon, but it was cadaverous. He hoped it wasn't hostile. "Hello. I'm Kody."

"How would you like to join me, Kody?" the demon said.

"That depends on where you are going."

"It's not a place, exactly, but a state of being."

"I'm already in a state of being. A dream state."

The demon laughed cavernously. "Ho ho ho! And in that state of death, what dreams may come?"

Kody was not easy with this. "I think I'll pass on your invitation, thanks all the same."

"It wasn't an invitation. It was a threat. I am Demon Ceased. D Ceased for short."

"A demon pun," Kody said. "I get it: deceased."

"Most of us are puns," Ceased agreed. "D Mension contracts to provide the rest of us with length, width, and depth so that we can function here in Xanth."

"Dimension," Kody agreed.

"Not to mention D Mention," the demon agreed. "But enough of this dull, boring, and pointless social chitchat. Now come along, Kody; I love company." He reached for Kody's arm.

Kody snatched it away. He wished he had been given the talent of persuasion, so that he could talk the demon into departing peacefully. "I don't really like threats."

"Now be reasonable. If I gave everyone his choice in the matter, who would ever keep company with me? I must insist." He reached again.

Kody summoned a reverse wood chip and flipped it at the demon. D Ceased caught it, having surprisingly fast reflexes for one so near death. And changed.

Now a vibrantly alive man stood there, the reverse of the original. "What have you done?" he demanded. He did not seem to make the association with what he held.

"Just given you a boost," Kody said. "Have great time." He walked on.

But now a dragon appeared, the other creature he had inadvertently named. It was a large fire-breather; Kody could see the flickers of fire around its red-hot lips. It inhaled, ready to blow out a blast of flame. Kody knew that if he didn't act swiftly, he would soon be toast.

He conjured another chip and flipped it into the open mouth.

The dragon closed its mouth, formed an O shape, and blew out a fierce volley of—

Ice cubes. They struck Kody on the chest and bounced off harmlessly.

The fire had been reversed.

"Have a nice day," Kody said, and walked on. He was coming to like his magic talent. But for it, he could have been dead twice in the past few minutes, or at least extremely uncomfortable.

Soon the path led him to mountains. The first one abruptly rose up from the level ground, slanting at a steep angle toward the sky. It would be difficult for a man to navigate that slope, and worse for a horse.

And there was his steed. He was somewhat like a deer, and somewhat like a bull, with a brown coat and rabbit ears. But there was something odd about him. After a moment Kody realized what it was: the creature was standing level on the slope. The legs on the upper side were short, and on the lower side were long, so that he was perfectly balanced. The blue line went right to him.

"Uh, hello," Kody said uncertainly. "I am looking for a steed."

The creature glanced his way, then nodded his head toward himself. He was, it seemed, the steed.

"I'm going to the Good Magician's Castle. Can you carry me there?"

The creature nodded.

"You made a deal with Princess Dawn to help me? Why?"

The animal shrugged. Apparently he just liked to help people.

"There's supposed to be a guardian, too."

The creature flicked his head forward. Then he made a mooing call. In barely more than a moment there was an answer. "You found your rider, Guy? I'll be right there." It sounded like a woman.

It wasn't. It was a, well, it had the head and tail of a dragon, large wings, the body of a horse, silver hooves, and gold talons. And somehow it talked. Kody was ready to summon another chip, just in case.

The creature paused. "Oh—you must be the one. I'm Hadi the Alicenagon. I'll be your guardian this trip."

"I'm Kody Mundane. Uh, alicenagon?"

"My parents met at a love spring. Drek Dragon and Karia Centaur. I inherited from both of them. You know how it is."

Kody remembered Griff the Hipporoc. It seemed that those who met at love springs developed sudden passion, regardless of species, and their offspring were mixtures. Miscegenation was evidently no problem in Xanth. "Yes."

"And this is Guy Guyascutus, commonly known as a sidehill hoofer. I can understand him pretty well. We're both going to see the Good Magician, but didn't have a feasible route to get there. We can't use the enchanted paths."

"You can't?" Kody was happy to have her do the explaining.

"Guy is great on mountain slopes, but can't walk effectively on the level, so he's limited. I am barred because of my ancestry. Dragons aren't trusted among ordinary folk." She laughed. "For pretty good reason. I guess I could find the Good Magician's Castle if I searched long enough, but it's really much easier to have a marked wilderness trail."

"So the three of us have a common cause," Kody said. "To go to see the Good Magician."

"That's it. Guy contributes transportation, I contribute protection, and you contribute the marked route."

"I'm going there because I have a mission to perform. If I may ask, why are you going there?"

"Guy wants to find a way to cross flat spaces without getting hopelessly fouled up. I want to find a suitable mate. I'm the only one of my particular kind I know of, but there's got to be another somewhere."

"I met a hipporoc named Griff," Kody said. "The son of a male centaur and a female roc bird who also met at a love spring."

"Oh, he sounds perfect! But can you tell me where he is?"

"I encountered him near the Void, but I'm not sure he lives there. He gave me a really nice check her board."

"Sorry, I don't play that naughty game."

"It's not limited to games. It has sixty-four pictures, and when I touched the one showing Caprice Castle, it put me there. Maybe it could put you in the vicinity of Griff."

"Now that intrigues me. Let's see it."

Kody brought it out. "You have to refocus to see the pictures."

She peered at the board. "Ah, yes. Got it. No, no hipporoc in sight. But maybe the Good Magician will know. Thanks for the lead, anyway."

"Maybe he will," Kody agreed.

He mounted Guy, who had no saddle but was surprisingly comfortable, and they set off following the blue line, which obligingly remained close by the side of the mountain. It must have been charted to do that, for the benefit of the sidehill hoofer. Hadi navigated it by half flying, half hoofing it, touching the slope with the two feet on the upper side. Kody thought that must be quite a trick, but evidently she was used to it.

In due course the blue line diverged from the side of the conic mountain, and cut across to another. Guy followed it, stumbling briefly at the level base before telescoping his two left legs to be long and his two right legs to be short. Then he moved confidently along the new slope. Certainly he was handling it far better than Kody could have, and they seemed to be making good time.

"We need to eat," Hadi said. "Keep moving. I'll fetch something and catch up with you." She took off into the sky and was soon lost to sight.

"She's very helpful," Kody remarked.

Guy twitched an ear in acknowledgment.

Now that he had time to himself, in a manner, to think, Kody was half bemused to think that here he was in a wild fantasy land, riding a weird fantasy creature, while a part-dragon foraged for them. Was any of this to be believed? He doubted it. But in dreams all things were possible, and this was the Dream of all Dreams. He was amazed at his own imagination.

Meanwhile, what was happening to his body back in the Mundane hospital? He still could not remember the accident. Maybe a rogue car had hit him, and he had never seen it coming, hence no memory. Just how bad were his injuries? The nurse and doctor had been singularly uncommunicative. That was not a good sign. Well, there was little sense in worrying about it, since he could do nothing. He would just have to wait and see. At least this Land of Xanth was not boring. Far from it!

Hadi returned, carrying a package in her hands. She had four feet and two hands, in the manner of a centaur. Add in the wings, and that was eight limbs. Kody was pretty sure he had never imagined such a creature. So how could she be here in his dream?

"I found an egg plant with assorted ripe eggs," Hadi said, handing Kody a leaf folded into a bag. "Hardboiled, deviled, poached, fried. I hope you like them."

Eggs grew on plants? Evidently so, here in the land of puns. Kody looked into the bag, and the eggs did look good. "I'm sure they're fine."

"And a boot rear float," she added, handing him a leaf bottle.

Boot rear. He had encountered that before, and knew to be cautious. He tried a small sip. The kick he received was so hard it made him sail up off the hoofer and into the air. Fortunately he floated, not coming down hard. He was able to scramble back into place. So when it was a float, it was literal.

"And some cookies. But they may be too tough."

Kody tried one. But when he tried to bite it, it formed a little arm and fist and punched him in the mouth. It was indeed one tough cookie. He left the rest in the bag.

"And for you, Guy, a barrel of crackers," Hadi said, presenting a barrel-shaped feed bag to the hoofer. "Water, tsoda, but watch out for the—"

A cracker exploded in Guy's mouth, and smoke puffed out.

"Fire crackers," Hadi finished. "They're not strong enough to do any damage, but they have a bang-up taste."

So it seemed. Guy looked startled but unhurt. He quickly bit into a water cracker, and the flood of water washed out his mouth.

"And some more of those for me," Hadi said. "They'll help stoke my furnace." She bit into a fire cracker herself, evidently enjoying it. "And I found some gin rummy we can play when we camp tonight. But we'll have to watch it. You know how it is."

"I don't. How is it?" Kody asked.

"The more you play, the more drunk you get. Gin is strong stuff."

Oh.

They moved on, and soon enough dusk approached. There did not seem to be much danger here on the conic mountains, perhaps because few creatures were comfortable on the steep slopes. The blue line led them to where a spreading butternut tree provided cover and buttery nuts to go with a nearby pot pie bush. The pies were in the shape of pots, of course, and hot and delicious. A nearby stream had clear, clean water. There was even a blanket bush with fluffy clean blankets.

They played some gin rummy, with Kody dealing the cards for the others, but it was true: they all quickly became intoxicated and had to stop. Tongues loosened, they talked. Kody explained how he had found himself here in this extended lucid dream, now committed to finding a way to turn off the Curse affecting Xanth.

"But it doesn't affect you," Hadi said. "That's curious."

"I may have been selected for this mission because of my immunity," Kody said. "If it's not just chance. Princess Dawn implied as much."

Guy bleated.

"He says he wouldn't care what a female of his kind looked like," Hadi translated. "But any that exist must be on mountain ranges not connected to this one, so he can't meet them anyway. That's sad. At least I have a chance to meet someone, if I find out where to look."

Kody washed, and settled down on a blanket for the night. Guy, in the manner of a horse, slept on his feet, and so did Hadi.

Kody woke to see a small cloud hovering nearby, visible because there were flashes of lightning within it. "Say, you're an ugly one," he remarked conversationally.

The cloud huffed up larger, and more internal lightning flashed. It was almost as if it had heard him. Kody was amused. "Was it something I said, foggy-bottom?"

The cloud swelled further. Now there was thunder to go with the lightning.

Hadi woke. "Oops. That's Fracto. Did you annoy him?"

"The cloud can hear and understand me? Then I guess I did."

"Bad move. Now he'll pee on us."

"A stupid cloud? A little rain won't hurt us."

"But a lot of rain will. We'd better get out of here."

"In the dark? That's not feasible."

She sighed. "Maybe not. Let's hope it blows over."

It did not blow over. The cloud quickly expanded to fill the sky between the mountains, emitting so much lightning that the whole area was illuminated and the thunder was deafening. Wind whipped up, swirling into brief funnels. Then came the rain. It blasted down like a waterfall. Soon the crevice between the mountains flooded, and the water continued to rise.

"This is mischief," Hadi said. "I can't fly in this weather; I'd crash and break a wing. Guy can't travel; the water washes out his traction. And you—can you swim?"

"Yes. But this is becoming rough water. I'm safer clinging to the tree." He moved to grab on to a low branch.

"Do that then, until we ride out the storm."

"I'm sorry. I didn't realize—"

"You didn't know. Fracto calls himself the king of clouds, and he's extremely sensitive about being dissed. Just be glad it wasn't a volcano you saw."

"Volcanoes have feelings?"

"Everything has feelings. Some are more touchy than others. When someone irritated Mount Pinutuba it went ooom-pah! and blew out so much ash it cooled all Xanth by one degree."

"I will watch my mouth around volcanoes," Kody said.

The storm continued, and the flood rose rapidly. Hadi took hold of another branch, and Guy moved upslope. Still the water rose, coursing around the mountain. Was there no end to this?

There was a light. Kody stared. It looked like a ship! That was of course impossible.

The ship floated closer. It was a luxury liner with portholes along the side. "Ho!" its captain cried.

"Ho!" Kody called back. "We're in danger of drowning here. Can we come aboard?" Though he wasn't sure how Guy would make it.

"Are you old retirees?"

"No, just ordinary folk."

"Sorry. This is a Senior Citizen Ship carrying residents to a retirement community. No ordinary folk can board." And the ship moved on.

Kody stared after it, appalled. A ship that refused to rescue folk in a storm?

Then another ship appeared. This one looked feminine, with curtains in the portholes and prettily painted decks. "Ahoy!" Kody called. "We need help!"

"Are you a mother?" the lady captain called.

"No, just three people in danger of drowning."

"Then you may not board. This is a Mother Ship, and only

Mothers are allowed on her, or Maidens for their Maiden Voyage." It moved on.

There was the third ship, but this one turned out to be a Father Ship, limited to fathers.

Meanwhile the water was still rising. They were in trouble.

Guy bleated.

"Are you sure?" Hadi asked. "It's dangerous!"

He bleated again.

"All right," Hadi agreed dubiously. "Kody, catch hold of my tail, quick, so you won't be washed away."

Kody was doing all right treading water, but didn't argue. He could see her well enough because of the constant lightning in the background. He got a good hold on her serpentine tail.

The sidehill hoofer let go of the slope and swam away. He could swim well enough, because the length of his legs was less important. What was he up to?

There was a thudding sound. "I hate things that go bump in the night!" Hadi said.

Kody agreed. They were in enough trouble without some new threat developing.

Then the water swirled, dragging on them both. Hadi spread her wings and lifted partly out of the water, fighting the sudden current. Kody was glad for her support, because she was right: he would have been washed away.

Somehow the water was draining down. Before too long they sank back to the land, and Kody was able to stand again. He let go and braced himself against the slippery slope. The rain was still pouring, but the drainage was more than keeping up with it.

"Now I'd better see how he's doing," Hadi said, and flew away.

Soon she was back, and Guy was following her.

"What happened?" Kody asked.

"Guy kicked out a section of the bottleneck," Hadi said. "That let the water flow through faster. See, here's a fragment." She held up the broken neck of a large bottle.

"But with all that water backed up, he could have been carried away with it," Kody said.

"Yes. That's why I was concerned. He took the risk so that you and I could be safe. Fortunately he was able to brace himself with his uneven feet and hold his place."

"That was a brave thing to do."

"Yes. I am impressed. He knew what to do, and had the courage to do it."

At last the storm was abating. The lightning faded and was replaced by moonlight. They had survived the storm, were wet and bedraggled. Their blankets had been washed away.

"I know it's still night," Kody said. "But I don't think I will sleep well now. How do you feel about going on?"

Guy bleated, and Hadi nodded. "We feel the same. We'll travel until dawn. Then we can clean off some of the mud and harvest new clothing for you."

They trudged on, in their fashions. They were rewarded when dawn came, discovering a marvelously clear lake beside a sloping meadow. There were assorted shoe trees and shirt trees and pan-trees with pants. Guy set to grazing the slope, while Hadi flew out over the water to hunt for edible fish. Kody washed in the clean water, then scrounged for fresh clothing. Refreshed, he realized he was hungry, and the one thing this meadow lacked was pie trees. What could he eat?

A woman appeared, walking from the other direction. She had a nymphlike figure. "Hello!" she called. "You look hungry for—"

"For food," Kody agreed.

She paused. "That wasn't exactly what I was going to say. But I know a man whose talent is summoning fish. Will that help?"

"It might," Kody agreed. "If I got some fish, Hadi could roast them for me."

She frowned. "Hadi? Oh. So you have a girlfriend."

For some reason Kody was cautious. "Not exactly, but she'll do."

"Just my luck. I'm Nymph Ophelia Maniac. O for short on the first name."

"I'm Kody Mundane." Then he realized the pun in her name: Nymph O Maniac. A woman with an insatiable sexual appetite. Now he was glad for his caution.

"Hey Dave!" O called.

Soon a nondescript man appeared. "No, I won't try to do it any more," he said. "You've worn me out."

Just so.

"Kody here could use some fish."

Dave looked at Kody as if aware of him for the first time. "Oh. Sure. I'll call some." He knelt by the water, holding a fishnet Kody hadn't noticed before. "Hey, fish fish fish!" he called.

Suddenly there were fish practically leaping out of the water. First there was a group of grouper, then bass sounding low notes, a complaining carp, irrelevant red herrings, dogfish and catfish chasing each other, skating skates, perching perch, and an en garde swordfish. In one and three-quarter moments there were several suitable fish on the ground.

Hadi returned. Dave and O drew back in alarm, but Kody reassured them. "She's with me."

"Your girlfriend is a dragon?" O asked.

"Not exactly. We're just friends."

Nevertheless Dave and O decided to move on, and were gone by the time Hadi landed. "Oh, you found some fish!"

"Yes. If you care to roast them for me . . ."

"Immediately." She breathed fire and the fish roasted.

"Thanks. You saved me some awkwardness."

"Oh?"

"The woman was Nymph O Maniac. I think she had her eye on me, until you showed up."

She laughed. "You do have to be careful whom you take up with."

There were more roasted fish than Kody could eat, but Hadi was happy to consume the rest of them. Guy got his fill of grass and foliage. Then they resumed their trek.

The sloping meadow gave way to a sloping forest. The terrain became irregular, with many dips and crevices. The trees thinned into thin stems that formed a mat above. Then they abruptly ended as if receding, and what appeared to be a farm commenced, with cabbages and head lettuce growing abundantly. "This is one weird landscape," Kody muttered.

"The blue line knows the best route," Hadi said. "We had better stick with it."

"Yes. We need the perpetual slopes, for Guy."

"So it seems." She oriented her snout on the hoofer. "Have you been in a region like this before, Guy?"

Guy bleated No.

"So this is new territory. Maybe there's a lady hoofer here."

The hoofer shrugged.

"Isn't that what you want? If you found her, you wouldn't need to ask the Good Magician."

Guy did not respond. Hadi didn't push it.

The stems abruptly ended, and they were by a remarkable curving outcrop that seemed more like leather than rock. "This is weird," Hadi said. "It looks almost like a—"

"A giant ear," Kody finished.

The three of them paused together. "Uh-oh," Hadi murmured. "I think we had better get quietly away from here."

"Before the giant wakes," Kody agreed.

They were too late. The ear shuddered and lifted, and they dropped into the void below.

Only to be caught by the giant's hand. It cupped them and held them before the monstrous face. "And what are you three assorted creatures doing here?" the giant boomed.

Kody spoke. "We are traveling to see the Good Magician," he called. "We are following a blue line the Princess Harmony made for us to show us the way. We didn't mean to intrude on your slumber." Would that be enough? "I am Kody from Mundania, and these are Guy and Hadi." Named folk might be less likely to be eaten.

"Princess Harmony? The one who took up with an old Mundanian?"

"That one," Kody agreed. "She's still courting him while they
gather puns."

"It won't be long before she lands him."

"Surely not," Kody agreed.

"Well, Kody, the princess surely had a reason to route you past
my cranium. I am Intella-Giant, a huge repository of knowledge. I
trust you admired my re-seeding hairline; the local farmer gets
excellent crops. I will be taking your data now to add to my data-
base. Then you may proceed to the Good Magician's Castle. Tell
him I sent a significant fragment of a greeting."

"We will," Kody agreed, relieved.

"*You* will. Guy and Hadi will not be joining you."

"Not?" Hadi asked, alarmed.

"You are about to realize that Guy has fallen in love with you.
That's why he is no longer looking for a lady sidehill hoofer. Since
you also realize that he is a worthy creature, you will return to his
native slopes with him."

Now she was clearly taken aback. "But—"

"All you need to do is shop for an accommodation spell," Intella said. "Then your love will be complete. You should produce
an interesting crossbreed, just as your ancestors did." It seemed the
giant knew all about her background.

"Um, yes," Hadi agreed, looking at Guy with a new appreciation.

"Accommodation spell?" Kody asked.

"Such a spell enables any two creatures to breed, even if they
are not in a love spring. It is useful when there's a need."

"Oh. Thank you."

"I have no background data on you, Kody," Intella said.

"Well, I—"

"No need to speak. Just touch my hand."

Kody squatted and touched the surface of the huge hand with

one finger. Immediately he felt a flow of information passing from him to the giant.

"You are an interesting one indeed," Intella remarked. "So you are tackling the reversal Curse. Possibly you will succeed in nullifying it."

"I will try, at least."

"And you are less real here than you appear to be. In fact this stay in Xanth is your dream."

"Yes, so it seems."

"One thing you need to get clear. You may be dreaming, but the rest of us are not. You did not imagine Xanth. You merely visit it via the mechanism of the dream. What you accomplish here will endure for the rest of us, even if it has no permanent effect on you."

"Uh, thank you for that clarification," Kody said uncertainly.

"And though you are dreaming, you can be hurt here. If a monster chomps you to death, your dream will end in death. That is one permanent effect on yourself you can accomplish. So it behooves you to take care."

Kody had pretty much assumed that death here would simply eject him from the dream, but this made uncomfortable sense. He was in surgery; if something went wrong . . .

"I wish I could get a CAT scan or something, so I'd know my condition," Kody said. "Not that that relates to Xanth."

"Oh, but it does," the giant said. "There is a magic cat who can tell exactly how healthy a person is. Unfortunately it's not around here at the moment."

Yet another pun. Kody sighed internally.

"We are trying to convey him safely to the Good Magician's Castle," Hadi said.

"Which is close by," Intella said. "Fortunately. So we don't have to discuss the prose and cons of the route."

"Prose and cons?" Kody asked, wondering how he could hear the spelling.

"Prose is ordinary dull unpoetic language," Intella explained patiently. "Cons is short for conventions, where fans of particular enterprises go for camaraderie. Writers attend prose and cons. You can afford to bypass this."

Kody wasn't sure how much of this was humor. "Thank you. I'm sure that's best for the time being."

"No, the Time Being is more of a scientist," the giant said. "He doesn't attend Fan Cons because he can't stay long enough to get to know anyone well."

Kody shut up.

The giant set them down on the blue-lined path where it resumed, and they traveled on. Soon there was a fork in the line, with one marked PROSE & CON. There were notebooks and kegs of beer lining it. "That's the writer's convention," Kody said. "We can skip that."

They did, and a few steps farther was a castle. The Good Magician's Castle.

"We have arrived," Hadi said. "Now you must proceed alone. There will be three punnish Challenges for you to navigate before you can enter. Good luck!"

"Thank you," Kody said, a bit weakly.

"Come on, Guy," Hadi said warmly. "Let's go catch that convention before all the beer is gone." The two of them moved back along the path.

# 3
## CASTLE

**K**ody walked down toward the Good Magician's Castle. He knew he was on his own, and wasn't at all certain he was up to the mission. There was just so much wild and punny magic in this Land of Xanth!

The castle had a moat, with a drawbridge crossing it. He headed for the bridge. There was a path through the tall foliage leading up to it. He rounded a corner.

"Savvy, stranger!"

Kody jumped, surprised; he had not seen anyone here. It was a dusky young woman holding a rounded mass of fur. "What kind of stranger?" he asked before realizing how stupid that must sound.

"Discernment, appreciation, recognition, salutation, greeting—"

"Hello?" he asked.

"Whatever," she agreed crossly.

"Hello," he repeated. "I'm Kody Mundane, come to see the Good Magician. Who are you?"

"Who do you think I am? Philip who fills things up? Nora Nos-noora who stops anyone from snoring? Onomatopoeia, who makes the sounds she writes so others can hear them? I M Bigbucks, the man made of money?"

Kody refused to play this ludicrous guessing game. "None of the above, I'm sure. Is there a reason you intercepted me, you intriguing creature? If not, I think I had better be on my way before I lose it, in more than one sense."

That evidently satisfied her. "I'm the Demoness Metria, here to stop you from getting in."

"You're a demon? You don't look like one."

"I don't?" She frowned. Then little horns grew out of her head, and a tail grew out of her posterior. "How about now?"

"You *are* a demon!" he said. "You looked so—so fetchingly female I just didn't believe it before."

The horns and tail puffed into vapor, which drifted away. "A demoness can look like anything she wants two."

"Two?" he asked.

"It's a homophone."

"What kind of phone?"

"It sounds the same but spells differently."

"Ah. So you can look like—"

"Anything I want too," she agreed.

He laughed. "Close enough. Is that speech impediment natural, or is it part of the Challenge?"

"Mixed. I got stepped on by a sphinx long ago and it affected my articulation. It also fragmented me into three parts. My other part D. Mentia is a little crazy, and Woe Betide is a child who must live by the Adult Conspiracy."

"The what?"

"The Adult Conspiracy to Keep Interesting Things from Children. It frustrates the bleep out of them."

"Oh, I see. We have something similar in Mundania."

"You should. It's a parody of Mundane attitudes, one of many."

"That surely explains a lot of what I have been seeing here."

"You called me fetchingly female. Not ugly."

"You are definitely not ugly," he said.

"Then what about the expletive?"

"The what?"

"Oath, swearing, whammy, nemesis, bane—"

"Curse?"

"Whatever." Her decolletage descended and the hem of her skirt lifted to show enticing flesh at either end. "Don't you suffer from it?"

"I don't suffer from that particular reversal." Indeed, it was difficult to keep his eyes from locking onto her exposure.

"What's your secret?"

"It may be that because I am here only in my dream I am not affected the way you natives are."

"You're dreaming?"

"I seem to be."

Her clothing shrank further. His eyeballs threatened to glaze over. "Well, I can fulfill your dream. Take off your trousers."

He did not trust this. "Um, no thanks. Such a distraction would surely prevent me from reaching the interior of the castle."

"Oh, bleep!" she swore. "You caught on."

"If that's all, I'll proceed to the next Challenge."

"Oh, no you don't, dummy! This was just chitchat. I have not yet begun to Challenge you." Her clothing faded out entirely. Her body was almost impossibly luscious. He was surprised by how seductive it was. "Last chance to have at me before this gets serious."

"Sorry. I can't forget that you're a demoness rather than a real woman, appealing as you are. It could be dangerous to touch you." He did not add that he wished he could risk touching her.

"Bleep!" This time the word appeared in a speech balloon, with smoke rising from it. Her clothing re-formed. "Very well then, idiot. Figure out the Challenge."

"What Challenge?"

"The Challenge the Good Magician is making me perform, in return for the inconsequential minor little favor he did me," she said crossly.

"What favor was that?"

"He Answered my Question."

"Isn't that what he normally does?"

"Yes. But it was such a stupidly simple obvious Answer that I shouldn't even have had to Ask it. So now I'm serving for nothing, really."

"I appreciate the frustration. I hope it's not the same with me when I get my Answer."

"It's not the same. You're here to save Xanth."

"I'm here to see if I can reverse the spell that makes pretty girls ugly."

"Same thing. If it's not reversed, who will want to signal the stork?"

"Do what?"

"When folk want a baby, they signal the stork, and months later the stork brings it. No stork signaling, no babies. The population will crash."

Oh. Storks were literal too. "So what was your Question?"

"It all started innocently enough. I was passing by this village, and there was this village lout, so naturally I flashed him with my panties. I mean, that's what a girl does with a village lout; she flashes him and he freaks out and by the time he recovers she's long gone and he is frustrated as bleep. More fun!"

"Let me be sure I understand. Just the sight of a girl's panties freaks out a man? Puts him into some kind of stasis?"

"Exactly. It's a great weapon in the battle of the gendarmes."

"The what?"

"Police, officer, guard, grammatical, sexuality—"

"Genders?"

"Whatever! So there I was, doing what comes naturally, and this lout just stares and doesn't freak. Can you imagine a worse disaster?"

"Well, considering that I am of the lout persuasion myself—"

"Never mind. It really beetled me."

This time Kody refrained from asking for a clarification of the term; he already had a fair notion. "Understandable."

"So I finally went to the Good Magician, and he told me that the girls had developed a panty shield that generates a local field that shrouds their panties and prevents louts from peeking at them. All they see is a fogged-out outline, a fuzzy blob. That's no good for freaking."

"No good," Kody agreed. "They do that with Mundane TV when there is too much exposure."

"Then one oaf got hold of a shield in a panty raid. At first he didn't realize what it was, as it looks much like a panty. Now he's using it to get into young women's homes and steal more panties. They can't freak him out. So my assignment is to recover that panty shield so it can't do any more damage. Only problem is that I don't know where it is. The villain strikes by night, and by the time I learn of a raid, he's long gone. So I have to work here until I recover that shield."

"That seems fair enough. But I find it hard to believe that the mere sight of a girl's panties can freak a man out. I have never been freaked that way."

"Oh? Look at this." Metria turned and hoisted her short skirt.

Fingers snapped near his ear, and he came out of his reverie. The demoness was no longer standing in front of him, but beside him. "What happened?"

"You freaked out," she said with satisfaction.

"But I was aware of nothing."

"Here's a repeat, in slow motion." She stood before him and hooked her fingers into her hem, slowly lifting it. First her well-fleshed thighs showed, then the bottom line of her panty.

Kody's breath quickened. His eyes locked in place, starting to glaze. "I . . . see . . . your . . . p-p-"

"Panty?" She lowered the hem a fraction so he could recover enough to speak clearly.

"P-p-point. I do freak out. But is it really the panty? You have a remarkable bottom."

"It's the panty. Here, I'll show you."

"Don't do that!"

But her panty line had already dissipated into smoke. Now she hauled her skirt up to show her bare bottom.

Kody was impressed, but he didn't freak out. She had a most evocative bottom, but he could look at it without his eyes glazing.

"So you see," she concluded. "Panty magic."

"Panty magic," he agreed.

"All of which is beside the point. I wouldn't waste time like this if I didn't like flashing men. I won't let you by until you figure out what I'm doing." The mass of fur reappeared in her hands; it had faded out during their dialogue. She plucked at it with her fingers, and an awful screeching emerged.

"You're torturing an animal."

"Not exactly." She plucked again, and the sour notes formed a crude melody.

"You seem to be playing what appears to be the corpse of a hairy little monster."

"Not exactly," she repeated.

"Actually it's in the rough shape of a guitar. A guitar made of hair."

"So?"

He got a notion. A little bulb actually flashed over his head. This was a pun. "A hair guitar!"

"An heir guitar," she agreed. "Or an heir band." The guitar shrank and changed to form a band around her head, holding in her lustrous hair. "Folk who expect to inherit like to play this instrument." Written musical notes rose from the band and floated away.

Had he really gotten the pun? The spelling was starting to confuse him. How could he hear a sight pun? "Hair" and "heir" were not pronounced alike. "I'll be moving on now."

"The bleep you will," she said. "You haven't gotten it yet." The hair guitar was back.

Kody sighed inwardly. He was afraid of that. What was he to make of this nonsense? "So you're not exactly playing a hair guitar, or an heir guitar. But you are playing something."

"Something," she agreed.

Kody got a wicked idea. "A noted tool!"

"A noted what?"

"Notes on a puppet, supply, process, device—"

"A musical instrument?"

"Whatever," he agreed crossly.

"Bleep."

"And in your distraction you let the heir guitar fade out. Now you're playing nothing." Indeed, her hands were empty.

"Double bleep."

"In fact what you're playing is an air guitar."

"Triple bleep!" she swore, and turned into smoke, which in turn drifted away.

He had finally gotten it. He took a step forward toward the next Challenge.

"Are you sure you don't want to be abstracted?" a wisp of smoke inquired, forming into winsome curvature. "I'll wear transparent panties so you can have the best of both views without quite freaking out."

"I'm sure I don't want to be distracted," he said firmly, and moved on.

"Quadruple bleep!"

What bothered him was that he had actually been tempted. Once the Challenge had been passed, it was probably all right to dally with a sexy willing demoness, but such a prospect had never interested him before. What was there about this particular demoness that encouraged foolishness? Or was it simply that he was in a dream, and normal cautions did not apply here?

The next scene was of a small field with dry wheat growing, surrounded by green fir trees. A young woman with flame-red hair sat in a chair reading a book. Kody saw the title: *Fahrenheit 450*. "Is that number correct?"

"It is for me," the woman said. "One degree more and the paper will burst into flame and I won't be able to read it."

And here where things tended to be literal, even a book title needed to be circumspect. "I see. I presume you represent the next Challenge."

"Of course I do. I'm Burnice from Burnsville. I can set fire to anything I focus on." She oriented on the wheat in front of her, and the dry stalks burst into flame.

"So I see. So I guess you won't be flashing me with your panties."

"You must have me confused with that floozy demoness next door."

"Who you calling a floozy, hotbox?" a wisp of smoke demanded.

"Maybe I was," Kody said quickly. "I'm new to this Challenge business."

"It's simple," Burnice said. "You have to get through this field to the next setting. But I will burn any path you try to take. So you have to deal with me to get through."

"I see. I don't suppose I can sweet talk you into dousing your flame?"

"Hardly," Burnice said, returning to her book.

"So you see, you might as well dally with me," the smoke wisp said. "I can give you a hotter time than she can."

"Get your smoky butt out of my scene!" Burnice snapped. She focused on the smoke, but nothing happened.

"You can't set fire to smoke," the demoness said smugly.

"But I can tell the Good Magician you're interfering."

"No need," the smoke said, and faded out.

Kody would have been amused by the interaction if he had time for it. But right now he needed to get a handle on this second Challenge.

"There's always a way, have you but the wit to find it," a tiny wisp of smoke wisp-erd in his ear.

"Confound it, tart, begone!" Burnice yelled. "One more word and I'm reporting you!"

"Wordlessly gone," the wisp said, fading.

"Sorry about that," Kody said. "Maybe I encouraged her by talking with her."

"Unlikely. Metria always pokes into things that aren't her business. The only way to get rid of her is to ask her to do something useful."

That might be useful information. The demoness had, however, done him a favor by advising him that there was always a way. What was a way to douse a fire, in a setting like this? Dip water from the adjacent moat? He was pretty sure it wouldn't be that easy. For one thing he saw nothing to dip with. Still, there could be a bucket or something hidden under the water.

He stepped toward the moat. Immediately the grass before him burst into flame. He hastily retreated.

So much for that. Burnice had not needed to say a word.

Then she spoke. "What are you planning to ask the Good Magician?"

"I need to find a way to save Xanth from the reverse Curse."

"And he's making you go through the Challenges?"

"So it seems."

"That doesn't seem right."

"He must have his reasons."

"Actually the Curse hardly affects me, because I'm a plain girl, neither beautiful nor ugly." She was speaking the truth; she was quite ordinary. "But I think it best that it be ended."

"So do I, though it doesn't affect me either."

"Well, good luck."

"Thanks." Did this mean she would not try hard to stop him?

He stepped toward the far side of the setting. Fire formed before him. He retreated again. So much for Burnice not trying. She was still doing her job. He respected that.

He stood and looked around. The scene was unchanged except for the dying blazes. Burnice still sat in the middle, and the fir trees still lined the setting, forming a large U-shaped area with the moat across the U. There simply seemed to be nothing to douse a fire.

Then he got a notion. It wasn't enough to make a bulb flash over his head, but it might be worth exploring. If there was always a way through provided, and the firs were the only other feature of the setting, maybe they were the key. What kind of firs were they? It was hard to make out details from this distance, but they seemed to be fruit-bearing, which was odd for such a species. He thought he saw little bottles hanging from their branches.

Then suddenly the bulb did flash. They were Aqua-firs! Trees growing water. A pun on aquifer.

So maybe he had the answer. But he still had to get to the trees to get the water, and Burnice would naturally try to prevent him. He didn't blame her; it was her job to do, just as his was to save Xanth if he could.

Still, now that he knew where to go, he could figure out a way. He took another step toward the moat. Fire blazed. He took two steps back. Then, feigning desperate courage, he took another step forward. The fire strengthened, and he took two steps back.

When he had backed himself all the way across the setting and come up against the line of trees, he suddenly turned and grabbed a branch. It came off in his hands, the bottles tinkling and breaking, dropping their water. He hurled the whole branch into the fire, and it dissolved into water that made the fire sizzle and retreat.

Well, now! He grabbed another branch, holding it carefully, and a third. Then he walked toward the far side of the setting, staying close to the trees.

Fire blazed up before him. He threw a branch into it, and it sizzled angrily out, allowing him to walk through. Another fire appeared, and he tossed the second branch, drenching it into nothing. When a third fire appeared, he grabbed another branch and doused it.

Then he was at the exit. "Adieu, Burnice," he called. "I have to move on now."

"I'm glad you made it," she called back.

He was sure she meant it. "Thanks."

Beyond the line of trees was . . . a nursery room. There was a rather pretty young woman and a two-year-old child, who was also pretty. This was a Challenge?

"Hello, pretty ladies," Kody said.

Both looked at him, startled. "Do you really think so?" the adult asked.

Ah. "I do not suffer from the Curse. I see you both as you are. So yes, I really think so."

"Can you share your secret, so we can nullify the Curse?"

"No, because I do not know it. I am Kody Mundane, and I am dreaming; I'm not really in Xanth. If my immateriality here is the reason, it won't do you natives any good, I'm sorry to say. But my mission is to locate and nullify the Curse so that things return to normal."

"That will be wonderful," the woman said. "I am Lyre, and this is Ione."

"Hello, Lyre. Hello, Ione."

"I am babysitting Ione, who is the daughter of Princess Ida and Prince Hilarion. She might have been named Iona, but that seemed too common, even if it fit better."

"Fit better? I'm not sure I understand."

"In Xanth, men generally have sons, women have daughters," Lyre explained. Kody refrained from saying that he had already figured that out. "So she's an I name, with the end of her father's name added. But Ion isn't female. So she's Ione despite there being no E in Ida's name. It's only a minor awkwardness."

"As long as she is satisfied," Kody said. "I'm not much into the science of names."

"Names have magic, not science. It's important."

"I am new to Xanth, and still learning the conventions." Kody took a breath. "I gather this is a Challenge, but it does not seem like any kind of a threat or riddle. Am I in the right setting?"

"You are," Lyre said. "To get through you must solve my problem. Otherwise the ravening monster just beyond here will pounce when you try to enter the castle."

Just so. "And what, if I may ask, is your problem?"

"I am a compulsive liar. Only here, in this setting, for this introduction, am I telling the truth. One day a demon was inconvenienced by a lie I told and cursed me to lose a memory for every lie I told thereafter. The result was that I have lost much of my mind. I can't even remember how I came here, but think I must have asked the Good Magician for help, and this is how he is handling it: by making me a Challenge."

"Why don't you just stop lying?"

"What part of 'compulsive liar' do you not understand?"

"Ah." And even her name, which he had taken to be a musical instrument, identified her, in the punnish way typical of Xanth. "So I have either to find a way to stop you from further lying, or to restore your lost memories, or get the demon to lift the curse on you."

"Something like that," Lyre agreed. "All three would be better."

"All of which options seem impossible. But there must be a way, because this is a Challenge. I just have to figure it out."

"That's all," Lyre agreed.

Kody looked around the room. There were dolls, a teddy bear, marbles, a picture book, a little mirror, assorted hair ribbons, and a cute little hat. Things a child liked. He doubted any of them could abate a demon's curse. What else was there? An open window overlooking the moat, an odd little plant on the windowsill, a child's bed, and an open closet with several hanging little-girl dresses. Those did not look promising either.

So it must be something else. With the Demoness Metria it had been her speech impediment leading to the identification of a pun. With Burnice it had been the surrounding Aqua-firs. What was there about this setting that could facilitate the kind of magic that would deal with a curse? He had the suspicion that he was missing something obvious.

He needed a new approach. Maybe he simply needed to learn more about this setting. "May I talk to the child?" he asked.

"Yes," the little girl replied.

"Hello again, Ione."

"Hello again," she agreed, smiling prettily.

"Please tell me about yourself. Your history, your likes and dislikes, and why you are here in this setting instead of home with your mother."

"I'm too little to have much history," the child said, speaking well for her age. "I like eye scream, I don't like bathtime, and I'm here because Mother is busy at Castle Roogna today so I need a babysitter even though I came on a mission of my own."

"You seem to have a very good understanding of your situation."

"Yes. I am very mature for my age."

"What is your mission here?"

"I want to learn my magic talent."

Her magic talent. Could that relate? "And what is your talent?"

"I don't know."

"The Good Magician wouldn't tell you?"

"Yes." Ione grimaced cutely. "So now I'm stuck here for the rest of the day until Mother picks me up tonight."

"Are you sure you have a magic talent?"

"Yes."

"How can you be sure?"

"Because all people in Xanth, except Mundanes, have magic talents. And the Good Magician told me I did. A really good strong talent, maybe even Sorceress level. He just wouldn't tell me what."

"That seems unkind of him."

"Oh, he has a reason. He always has a reason. But it's frustrating."

So far he did not seem to be learning anything useful. "Tell me about your mother, Princess Ida."

"She's great! She can make anything true, just by agreeing with it. Only—"

"Only?"

"The one who says it mustn't know her talent."

That was odd. "She can use her magic talent only if someone doesn't know it?"

"Yes."

"Then how does she ever use it?"

The child focused. "When someone says something, like maybe the sky is blue, and she wants it to be true, she agrees."

"But the sky *is* blue."

"Yes. It's a great talent."

Kody took stock. Was the child confused, or did her mother really have magic strong enough to change the reality of the color of the sky? It was becoming more important to know how these things were.

"How is it your mother has such a great talent?"

"Way, way, way long ago, Great Grandpa Bink helped the Demon Xanth, and he made all of Bink's descendants Magicians or Sorceresses. Ida is a Sorceress."

"All of them? Then you must be a Sorceress too."

"Yes, maybe."

"I gather there are different levels of talents, and a Sorceress is at the top. Princess Dawn has a really powerful talent, knowing anything about any living thing she touches."

"Yes. Aunts Dawn and Eve are Sorceresses. Eve knows about anything not alive."

"I wonder if part of my Challenge is to figure out what your talent is? That might explain why the Good Magician wouldn't tell you."

The little girl pursed her lips, considering. "Maybe so."

"Because maybe you can help me solve Lyre's problem."

"Yes!" Ione agreed eagerly. "Figure it out now!"

But Kody was cautious. There could be some better reason why the Good Magician had withheld the information. Maybe he didn't want the child to have to serve for a year. Or maybe—

He began to get a glimmer.

"I saw it!" Ione said. "I saw the bulb flash! You got an idea!"

"I think I did," Kody agreed. "But it's complicated."

Her little face clouded. "You won't tell me?"

He felt like a heel, yet he had to follow through. "Not yet."

"Why not?"

Maybe he could explain that much. "Because I think your talent resembles your mother's talent. It works only if the person with you doesn't know it. So if I told you, you wouldn't be able to use it. At least that's my assumption. That would explain why the Good Magician wouldn't tell you. So it's for your own good."

"That's what Mother says when she makes me take a bath! I hate it!"

"I understand your frustration. Let me see if I can make your talent work, then I'll tell you. Is that a fair compromise?"

"You'll tell me before you go?"

"I will."

"Promise."

"I promise."

"Okay," she agreed grudgingly.

"Now I think I need to talk privately with Lyre."

"You're pulling the dread Adult Conspiracy on me!" Ione accused him wrathfully.

"I am not. This isn't about se—" He paused. "Signaling the stork. This is about your talent."

"Oh, all right." Ione stalked off to gaze out the window.

Kody joined Lyre. "I am gambling that this will work if she doesn't know her talent," he murmured. "You will have to know it, to make this work."

"She can reverse curses?"

"No. But we may, with careful management, be able to have a similar effect."

"You're not making much sense yet."

"Here it is: I suspect she can do the same thing her mother can, creating reality."

"No, she can't."

"How can you know that?"

"Because talents never repeat. At least, not in the same generation. Not unless you're a Curse Fiend. They all have the same talent of cursing."

Kody smiled. "Many men in Mundania have that talent also."

"Real cursing. Making bad luck."

"Anyway, this is different. A variation. What I think she can do is convert a lie to a truth, provided a key person doesn't know her talent."

"And I'm a liar!" she breathed. "But that isn't enough for me. I need to recover my lost memories, so I can function normally."

"Here is the key. Suppose she converts a past lie to the truth? What happens to your memory?"

She worked it out, her face showing awe. "I think—I think it should undo the memory loss. Restore the memory."

"And if she continues to convert lies to truths?"

"I'd get a string of memories restored! Oh, that sounds wonderful!" She stepped into him and kissed him. Xanth women seemed to do that. He wasn't used to it, but did not care to make an issue. Not at all. "Thank you!"

"Don't thank me yet," he warned, shaken by the kiss, which he had enjoyed. He simply wasn't accustomed to being so readily moved by strange women. "It is only my theory, and I still don't know how to implement it."

"I have a notion. I'll tell her the lie, and—" She broke off.

"And she'll know her talent," he finished. "That's the tricky part. For this purpose we need her not to know it. After this session I will tell her; then there will have to be another person who doesn't know."

"Maybe Burnice, next door," she said. "She's a nice person. I can feed her statements to relay to Ione."

"Well, let's give it a try," Kody said. "What's the last lie you told?"

"About the ravening monster next door."

He laughed. "And I believed it!"

"My lies are persuasive. That's why they cause so much mischief."

"That's another thing: after you get out of this, you've got to stop lying! Otherwise you'll soon be back in the hole."

She gave him a canny look. "Maybe I know the right lie to start. About my curse."

"About your curse? But she already knows about that."

"We'll see." She faced the girl. "Ione, we're done with our nasty secret dialogue."

"About time!" the child grumped. "The only secrets I like are the ones I make myself."

"Of course, dear." Lyre took a breath, nerving herself for the effort. "I'm going to tell you something, and I hope it doesn't make you too mad."

"What, that you lied about how we'll have eye scream after this is over?"

Both Kody and Lyre repressed smiles. "Oh, no, dear! I wouldn't

lie about an important thing like that. No, this is different. It's about myself. You see, I told you how I'm a constant liar, and am cursed to lose memories because of it."

"Sure. That's why Kody's here. To fix it."

"Well, here's the thing. I'm not really such a liar. I hate lies, and never want to tell one. I had to pretend to be a liar so there could be a Challenge for Kody, but it's not true. He figured that out, and now I have to come clean, even if it does spoil the Challenge."

Ione digested this. "You lied about lying?"

"Yes, dear. Can you forgive me?"

"Oh, sure. As long as you didn't lie about the eye scream."

"I didn't. So you believe me now? That everything I say will be the absolute truth?"

"Yes, sure. I don't much like lying anyway."

A peculiar expression crossed Lyre's face. Kody realized that she was feeling the curse of lying depart, which would in turn stop her memory loss.

So had she recovered a memory? Kody thought not; for this change in status she merely was not losing one.

"And that ravening monster next door," Lyre said. "That was not exactly—"

"I'm sure there is one," Kody said. "Otherwise I might just pass on through without winning the Challenge. Maybe we should take a peek to be sure." He offered his hand to the little girl.

"Okay," Ione agreed. "As long as we don't have to get too close to it."

Lyre looked perplexed, then caught on. Ione's talent was to convert lies to truths, so calling them lies now would not do it.

They walked to the edge and peeked. There was the ravening monster.

Kody had never been happier to see such a thing. It meant he had solved the problem.

They turned back. "I recovered a memory!" Lyre exclaimed, thrilled.

"So now we can tell Ione her talent," Kody said. "She will

surely be happy to help you with other memories, as long as Burnice does not know."

Ione's brow wrinkled. "Does not know what?"

"That your talent is to make lies become truths," Kody said. "As long as the person discussing them does not know your talent. That's why the Good Magician did not tell you right away."

"To make lies truths? Isn't a lie a lie no matter what?"

"Not necessarily," Kody said. "Not when there's a Sorceress present."

She remained understandably perplexed. "How can a lie become truth?"

"Maybe I can show you," Kody said. He walked to the side. "Burnice! We can use your help."

"I'm not allowed to help you with your other Challenge," Burnice protested.

"My Challenge is over. This is something else."

"Very well." Burnice walked toward them.

"Now do not say a word about your talent, Ione," Kody whispered. "It won't work if she knows."

"Okay," the child said doubtfully.

"I am going to tell Burnice a lie. Lyre will agree with me, even though she knows it's a lie, because she wants to help you understand and use your talent. That's not the same as lying for personal gain or to make mischief. Lyre is not doing that anymore. You must agree with me also. Can you do that?"

"Sure. For a good cause." The child was quick to catch on.

Burnice arrived. "What's this about?" she asked.

"There is a big tub of chocolate eye scream under your chair. May I fetch it for Ione? I'm sure she'll share."

"There is no such thing!" Burnice protested. "It would melt!"

Now came the key part. If this didn't work, the whole effort was lost. "I say there is. Are you calling me a liar?"

Burnice opened her mouth, plainly wanting to do just that. But she decided to be diplomatic. "Ione is welcome to anything you find under my chair."

"Thank you." Kody marched out across her burned scene toward the chair. There was the tub! It really was filled with ice cream, however named. He picked it up and brought it back. "See? It was the truth."

"I'm truly amazed," Burnice said, truly amazed.

So were Lyre and Ione. And Kody, if the truth were told.

"Now there may be other things you girls would like to discuss," Kody said. "But I believe I have business in the castle with the Good Magician."

"You surely do," Lyre said. "And that's no lie."

"Now can any of you explain how that tub of eye scream got under my chair, unmelted?" Burnice demanded as Lyre served out portions.

Lyre smiled. "We will in a moment. But first we want to amaze you with some of the fun things hidden around here, like a case of bottles of boot rear."

"And piles of candy," Ione agreed.

Kody left them to it as he walked to the edge. The ravening monster was gone, because it was no longer needed. In its place was a path leading to a door into the castle. He was at last gaining admittance. He hoped.

# 4
# PARTNER

A pleasant woman was waiting for him. "Hello, Kody," she said. "I am Wira, the Good Magician's daughter-in-law. We have been expecting you."

"Hence the Challenges," he said somewhat wryly.

"It is the custom. The Good Magician needs to be assured that you are serious and will not be readily dissuaded from your mission."

"Folk who aren't serious come here?"

"Oh, yes. It's amazing how many people seem to want something for nothing. They think they can somehow finesse the Challenges, get advice from the Good Magician, then renege on their commitment for service. Just last week there were twins, Barbar and Barbara. His talent was to make folks' hair shorter, hers to make it longer. They didn't need any advice, they just wanted to see if they could get in to see the Magician and waste a bit of his time."

Kody appreciated the problem. There were folk in Mundania like that. "How did you handle it?"

"The first Challenge was to get past a pool containing a kraken, a ferocious seaweed monster with thousands of hairlike strands. Making a few strands grow longer or shorter didn't help; it only annoyed the kraken. They gave it up as a bad job."

"But isn't there always a way through a Challenge?"

"Yes. All they had to do was offer to style the kraken's weed-hair attractively. But they were afraid to come close enough."

Kody was amused. He decided not to argue the case further. "I may not be in Xanth long, so probably need to get on with it."

"Of course. The Good Magician will see you soon. This way, please."

They came to a narrow, winding stone stairway. But a woman puffed into existence on the bottom step, barring their way.

"Metria?" Kody asked, surprised.

The features coalesced into an unfamiliar face and form. "Hardly. That nuisance is not allowed inside. I am Dara Demoness, the Good Magician's Designated Wife for this month." She turned to Wira. "Humfrey's not ready yet. Something about a conflict of schedules. I'll entertain the querent in the night room."

"I will check with the Good Magician," Wira said. "I will come for you in the night room soon, Kody." She started up the staircase.

Kody realized there was probably a pun there: day room, night room. Puns were endemic in this crazy land; no wonder they needed to be cleaned out. He followed the demoness as she floated slightly off the floor, leading him to a dusky chamber. Stars shone in the dark walls and ceiling, but it was light enough for him to make his way without faltering.

"Zosi, this is Kody from Mundania," the demoness said. Now he saw that there was a young woman standing in the chamber. She was rather pretty, with shoulder-length gray hair to match her gray eyes.

"Hello, Zosi," he said.

"Hello, Kody," she answered shyly.

"I think Humfrey—that's the Good Magician—did not realize he had a scheduling conflict," Dara said. "So both of you got set up to see him at the same time. Wira will set that straight. She's the only one who could. Sit down, both; I'll bring refreshments." She faded out.

They sat on opposite sides of the room. Kody couldn't help noticing that Zosi sat with her knees parted so that her legs were visible under her skirt. She did not seem to be a flirt, so it was more likely that she was distracted and careless. He could understand that, if her situation was remotely like his own. Which of course it couldn't be, unless she was another dreamer.

There was an awkward pause. Kody really did not know how to make small talk with a woman he didn't know, but it seemed she was similarly limited. So he made the effort.

"The— I'm new here—new to Xanth—and I don't know what's what. Can you tell me what 'Designated Wife' means, and why Wira is the only person who can set the Good Magician straight about a scheduling conflict?"

Zosi smiled. That made her surprisingly warm. "It—it's a long story, maybe dull."

With luck it would last until Dara returned with the refreshments. He smiled back. "I'm a fair listener, and reasonably dull myself."

She smiled again, appreciating the attempt at camaraderie. "The Good Magician is said to be really old. Over a century. He takes youth elixir to keep his physical age around one hundred. In the course of his life he outlived six wives—technically five and a half—that's complicated—then finally went to Hell to get one back. Instead he got them all back at once. That was awkward, because in Xanth a man is supposed to have only one wife at a time. So now one wife is designated each month and the others remain clear. This month it's Dara Demoness, who is a rare demon with a soul, making her decent as demons go. But the person who remains full time to handle castle details is Wira, Humfrey's son's wife. She seems to be the only individual he really likes, and indeed she's just about the nicest woman in Xanth. He can't say no to her. Normally he is insufferably grumpy, but never to her. So they let her handle anything awkward."

"Ah, now I comprehend. Very nicely put, Zosi."

She paused. "Oh, my! I'm blushing. I don't know how to handle that."

A simple routine compliment made her lose her composure? "Don't be concerned. Please. This is what girls do."

"I'm not exactly a girl."

Now he paused. "I don't want to be offensive, but to me you look exactly like a girl."

"It's— I shouldn't have said— It's supposed to be secret— Oh, bloop!"

This was getting curious. So he focused on the least of it. "Bloop?"

"I mean bleep. I'm not used to swearing. I'm all flustered."

"Zosi, chances are we'll never meet again. If something's secret, I promise I'll never tell."

"I don't know. I was afraid I would mess up, and I'm doing it already." She wiped her face. "Now I'm crying."

What could he do? Kody got up and crossed to her, putting a hand on her shaking shoulder. "Would it help if I told you how messed up *I* am?"

"I don't know," she repeated miserably.

"I'm from Mundania. If I understand it correctly, I'm asleep there while my body recovers from some bad accident, and this is all a dream. That is, it may be real to you, but not to me."

"You don't mind touching me?"

He was surprised yet again, then realized that might be the effect of the Curse, making a pretty girl ugly. "I see you as you are, a pretty girl. I don't mind touching you."

"Oh!" she wailed, putting her face against his hip.

"I'm here to find out how to reverse the Curse of perception, so that Xanth can revert to normal."

"Oh, I want to revert!" she said.

He found himself sitting beside her, one arm around her shoulders, comfortingly. "With luck, it will happen."

"Not that."

She was just one surprise after another. "I don't think I understand."

"I've got to tell you, though you'll hate me."

"I won't—"

"I'm a zombie."

He must have misheard. "A what?"

"A zombie. The living dead, with rotten pieces constantly falling off. Nobody can stand to be near us."

Kody shook his head. "But you're warm and firm and soft. No rot."

"Not now. But usually. When I revert to my true nature."

A dim light was beginning to show. "You are normally a zombie? Changed for this occasion?"

"Yes. I haven't been fleshly long, only a few hours, and I'm not used to it. I hate having to eat and peep and all."

He was about to ask about "peep" but then realized that it must be another accidental vowel substitution, like "bloop" for "bleep." "Living folk do."

She shuddered. "Yes." She took a deep breath. "So now you can recoil away from me. No one wants to touch a zombie."

It was a sentiment he understood in a rather different context. "But you're not a zombie now."

"Oh, I am, inside. A zombie in living human form."

That might be, but he repressed his urge to cast her abruptly loose. It would not be kind. "If I may ask, what prompted you to change state and come to see the Good Magician?"

"Xanth is running low on zombies, and needs more."

The surprises just would not stop coming. "I should think Xanth would want to be rid of zombies."

"No, Xanth needs zombies. We do important things, like serving in bad dreams, and of course we guard Castle Roogna from harm."

"Castle Roogna," he repeated. He had heard that name before.

She took it as a question. "That's the capital of human Xanth, where the king lives. It has to be protected, so we zombies do it. If there's a bad threat to Castle Roogna, we will rise out of the ground and deal with it. No living army wants to fight us."

Kody appreciated why. "I'm sure you are effective."

"We are. But we don't last forever. We wear out and fade out. So there needs to be fresh zombies to take our places. But since the Zombie Master retired there have been no new zombies made. So we are getting thin. So to speak."

"Now I see the problem."

"So we drew rotten straws, and I got the short one, and had to take the treatment to become alive for a month or so, so I can go among living folk and find a way to replenish the zombie stock. That's why I'm here. But if anyone knows I'm really a zombie, they won't help. That's why it's supposed to be secret."

"I will keep your secret," he repeated gallantly.

"Oh, thank you!" she said. Then, impulsively, she kissed him.

And recoiled. "Oh, I didn't mean to do that! I'm so sorry! You must be sickened."

He had made it a point not to flinch. Actually the kiss, sincere and fleeting as it was, had been nice. "Not at all. You're fleshly now."

"Oh, that's right. I forgot."

Dara returned with the refreshments. "I see you two have gotten to know each other."

Kody and Zori quickly disengaged. "We have been talking, yes," Kody said.

"More than that, I think. No matter. I brought tsoda pop fresh from Lake Tsoda Popka, and hot cross buns."

Kody picked up a bun. It was quite hot, and the expression on its surface was indeed cross verging on angry. Maybe it didn't like to be eaten.

Zosi hesitated. He realized what her problem was: she hadn't eaten before, in the living state, and was wary of the digestive complications. "Take small, ladylike bites," he suggested. "Chew carefully and swallow. It takes several hours for it to, um, reappear."

"You're telling her how to eat?" Dara asked. "What presumption!" Obviously she did not know the girl's origin.

"Oh, no, he's right," Zosi said quickly. "I had a—a complication, and feared making a mess."

"A complication? In my day they called it flirtation."

To forestall further questions, Kody asked Dara one. "How is it the Good Magician came to marry a demoness?"

"Oh, that goes way back over a hundred and sixty years. I was his very first wife, if not his first love." She continued with the story, as he had hoped, and asked no further questions of them. Zosi squeezed his hand appreciatively, understanding what he had done.

Then Wira reappeared, interrupting the romantic narrative. "It seems the scheduling was not a mistake," she said. "The Good Magician wants to see you both at the same time. I apologize for the delay."

"That's all right," Kody and Zosi said almost together. Both of them were glad they had had a chance to get to know each other, whatever Dara might think.

But why did he want to see them together? They had quite different missions.

They followed Wira up the winding stairway, Kody bringing up the rear. Zosi stumbled and he quickly put his hands to her narrow waist, steadying her. He realized that zombies wouldn't much care if they stumbled, as their substance was already well beyond damage, so she might not yet have the reflexes.

They were ushered into a dingy little study filled mostly by a giant open tome on a desk, with a very old little gnome of a man perched almost over it. "Here are the querents, Father," Wira said.

Querents? Kody decided not to ask. There was something about that word he didn't much like.

The sour countenance quirked into what for want of a better description might have been taken as a smile. "Thank you, Wira."

Then his grumpy gaze fixed on the intruders. "The two of you have complementary qualities," the Good Magician said. "You will enable each other to complete your separate missions, each of which is important. Your Services will consist of assisting each other. You, Kody, are unaffected by the Curse, so see people and things as they are. That is your asset. You, Zosi, are familiar with the general layout and history of Xanth. You are also affected by the Curse. Those are your assets. Work together to achieve both your objectives."

"I don't get it," Kody said. "She has to find more zombies. I have to reverse a Curse. Those are two quite different things."

"Different things whose solutions may nevertheless be found in one particular area. Your main challenge will be to locate that area."

"How can we do that?"

"The effect of the Curse intensifies near its origin, which is the Mood Reverse Bomb that someone discovered by accident, an ancient or foreign artifact, invoked and left on, heedless of the mischief."

"How is that possible?" Kody demanded. "The effects seem to be highly noticeable to everyone except me."

The Magician's ancient eyes oriented on Kody with a disturbing intensity. "In much the same manner as a careless camper in Mundania may fail to put his fire out completely, leaving it to smolder into activity that then burns an enormous area. The camper may mean no actual mischief, but his carelessness wreaks a havoc that affects many others."

Kody nodded. "Now I understand that aspect. But how can my immunity to the Curse enable me to locate it?"

"You are immune. Zosi is not. The effect is increasingly intense in inverse relation to the distance from the Bomb. The closer you come to it, the greater the effect. Therefore the contrast between your two views will increase. That is what will provide you with the direction."

"And Zosi's replacement zombies are in the same area?"

"Not exactly. You try my patience," the Magician grumped. "Begone."

"But—"

"Please don't linger after you have been dismissed," Wira said hastily. "That will only annoy him." She urged them both out of the chamber.

"You're right," Kody said. "He *is* grumpy, and not very communicative."

"That's the way he is," Zosi said. "But his answers are always accurate."

"It seems to me he could have said more."

"There's always a reason."

He thought of the way the Good Magician had not told the child Ione her magic talent. There had indeed been a reason. "Well, I hope so."

"I am sorry you must travel with me," Zosi said. "I did not know he would require this."

"Oh, I don't object to you," Kody said quickly. "You're a nice girl. I just wish we could set out on our missions with more assurance that we can succeed in achieving them. This is extremely thin."

"You can succeed," Wira reassured them. "The Good Magician knows."

"At least we'll proceed on that assumption," he agreed wryly.

They returned to the night room, where Dara and the refreshments remained. "Now you have your marching orders, as it were," she said briskly. "It's my job to see that you proceed competently and don't suffer any avoidable mishap."

"Mishap?" Zosi asked.

"Like getting toasted and eaten by a dragon."

"But dragons don't toast zom—" She cut herself off. "Oh, I forget I'm alive now."

"You are indeed, dear," Dara said. "Any dragon worth its fire would consider you delectable."

"I can help there," Kody said. "My talent is to conjure chips of reverse wood. They can have a peculiar effect on dragons."

"Such as reversing their fire," Dara agreed, laughing. "Never-thenonetheless, it is better to avoid them when possible."

Neverthenonetheless? But this was Xanth, where words had their own domains. "We will try to avoid dragons," Kody agreed.

"And what is your talent, Zosi?" Dara asked.

"That's right, I did have one when I lived," Zosi agreed, surprised. "I never had much use for it as a zombie. It is conjuring peanut butter and jelly sandwiches."

"Well, at least you won't go hungry," Dara said. "But I'm not sure how that talent would protect you from a dragon. Could you make a big one? So big it would block the dragon like a boulder?"

"No, only regular size. It's nothing special as a talent. I was nothing special as a person."

"If I may ask," Kody said, "how did you become a zombie?"

"That's a long and dull story."

"Not dull to me."

"It may be necessary background," Dara said. "If the two of you are to work together, it should help to know each other reasonably well."

Thus encouraged, Zosi plunged into the narrative. "I was delivered to a nice family in the South-South-West Village and grew up as a normal village girl. But just as I came of age to marry, the trolls raided the village. A troll snatched me up and carried me away. I screamed, of course, but he stuffed a wad of leaves in my mouth, and anyway I probably couldn't be heard in the confusion of the raid. He took me to a dark cave, where he ripped my clothing off. I knew he was going to eat me, or something. But then a gob of goblins raided the cave, and started to carry me off. I knew this would be even worse than what the troll planned on, and I fought them, but their horny hands grabbed on to me every which way, especially my chest and bottom, and dragged me away. The troll fought them savagely, but there were too many of them. They took me to their goblin mound, which looked like a giant anthill. I knew the moment I entered that I was doomed. But then an ogre appeared, attracted by the commotion, and pounded his great hollow chest with a loud booming sound and said, 'Give mee bare shee!' I didn't understand the words the goblins replied, but they set the nearby brush on fire. I think they referred to something impossible the ogre was supposed to do with his anatomy. That made the ogre mad. He picked some goblins up and flung them into orbit around the moon, and rammed the heads of some through hardwood knotholes, and stomped some into paper-thin pancakes, and the rest were less fortunate. Meanwhile in the distraction I fled again, but in the darkness stumbled into a pit full of nickelpedes. Their awful pincers started gouging out nickel-sized chunks of flesh, five times as bad as the little stings of the centipedes, and I screamed and fought my way out. Scrambling blindly, I smashed into the trunk of a tree, and died, because it was a Mortali-tree. The troll, goblin, ogre, and nickelpedes couldn't touch me because any contact with the tree would have killed them too. Then the Zombie Master came, and reanimated me, and I became a zombie without pain and served at the Castle Roogna graveyard ever since, for I don't know how many years. It didn't seem all that long, because mostly I slept, not rousing unless there was a threat to the castle. Until we held a meeting to discuss our dwindling numbers, and I drew the short rotten straw and had to invoke the spell of reanimation and go to ask the Good Magician what to do about it. So here I am."

Kody exchanged a glance with Dara. That was quite a story! Was it true?

"We are so sorry you had to go through that," Dara said sympathetically. Obviously she accepted it, and she surely was better informed about such things than Kody was. "We know that reanimation is a terrible fate for a zombie."

"It's awful!" Zosi said. "I'm away from all my zombie friends. When I stumble I feel pain! When I don't eat I get hungry! And now that I've eaten, before long I'll have to—to expel the refuse." She burst into tears of revulsion.

Kody had never viewed the living process in quite that manner. So it was the living state that Zosi detested, not the zombie state.

"It's not something we demons properly understand, as we don't have to eat either," Dara said. "But look at it this way: your companion is subject to the same messy processes. You won't be alone in your misery."

This was not precisely the type of encouragement Kody had been thinking of. But it seemed it helped.

"Yes, if he can stand it, maybe I can too," Zosi said. "At least long enough to complete my mission."

"Very good," Dara said. "Now let's go to the courtyard and practice dragon repulsion."

"I would also appreciate a clarification of the process by which we will locate this Bomb," Kody said. "The fact that there is contrast between our two appreciations doesn't mean we'll know where the thing is."

"That, too," Dara agreed. "It will be simple enough in practice. The greater the contrast, the closer you are. So you must keep traveling until the contrast is intense."

"Ah, a form of triangulation," Kody said.

Dara glanced at him. "You know that magic?"

"We don't consider it magic, in Mundania."

She shrugged. "Perhaps you wouldn't. I have heard that Mundanes don't consider perspective to be magic either."

"We don't," he agreed. "What's magic about it?"

"Isn't it true that when you move rapidly, the things close by allow themselves to be left behind, but the more distant things race to keep up?"

"That effect is more apparent than real. It looks that way only because—"

"Of the magic of perspective," she concluded. "And you probably doubt the rainbow is magic, too, though it can be seen only from one side and moves or vanishes when you try to see it from the other side, like a one-way path."

"Well, the refraction of the sun's rays by water droplets—" He saw the blank stares of both women. He was trying to talk Science to folk who did not believe in it. He surrendered. "Magic."

"Now assume I'm a dragon about to toast Zosi," Dara said, puffing into smoke and forming the outline of a small dragon.

Kody lifted his hand, conjuring a chip of reverse wood. He flipped it at the dragon.

"Ooof!" it exclaimed, collapsing back into Dara, the chip on her head. With one change: she was now male.

"It reversed your gender!" Kody said, amazed.

Dara caught the chip in his hand and hurled it away. He reverted immediately to female. "I've never suffered that transformation before," she said, evidently shaken, because her outline was fuzzy and her halter was across her hips. That was an interesting sight in more than one sense. In a moment she firmed and was fully herself again.

"But I guess it would stop a dragon," Zosi said, repressing a smile.

"When I reversed a dragon before," Kody said, "it went from fire to ice."

"Reverse wood is unpredictable," Dara said. "There are many different types of reversals. But Zosi is right: that would stop a dragon."

"But what about when he's not watching?" Zosi asked. "I'm not used to being careful about my body."

"True," Dara said. "You need to sit with your knees together, and try not to bang into things."

"Knees together? How will that keep me safe?"

Dara hesitated, so Kody answered. "So nasty goblins can't peek under your skirt and maybe see your panties."

"Oh!" Zosi said, and clamped her knees together though she was standing.

"Maybe we can adapt your talent," Dara said. "There are different kinds of peanut butter, and different jellies."

"I don't understand."

"I think I do," Kody said. "What about jellied gasoline?"

"I don't know what that is."

"Just conjure one," Dara said. "Carefully."

Zosi's face tightened in concentration. A sandwich appeared in her hand.

Kody sniffed. "I smell gasoline. Set it down. Carefully."

She did so, putting it on the ground, and backed off.

"Can you make a fire?" Kody asked Dara. "To emulate a dragon?"

"Yes." The demoness pointed at the sandwich. Her arm dissolved into smoke. A small jet of fire shot from it to the sandwich.

There was an explosion, and they were peppered with flying peanuts and balls of butter. Black smoke roiled upward to form a barrel-sized mushroom cloud, surely not from mushroom jelly.

"That was gasoline," Kody agreed. "It would have blown apart the mouth of any dragon that tried to eat it."

"I never realized," Zosi said, taken aback.

"And the right kind of pee-nuts would make it a real stinker," Dara said. "If you just wanted to repel a stray monster. I think you can defend yourself, Zosi."

"Maybe I can," the girl agreed in wonder.

"It is just a matter of learning to make the best use of your talent," Dara said. "Many people don't realize what they are capable of. I understand that in Mundania someone figured out how to make colored spots appear and disappear on a screen, and it became a whole entertainment industry."

"Television," Kody agreed. "Illusion magic, to you."

"I have so much to learn," Zosi said. "It really was easier being a zombie. I did not have to use my mind much."

"Many living girls don't use their minds much either," Dara said. "Why bother, when the boys aren't using theirs?"

Was she teasing him? "Now, about locating the Bomb," Kody said. "It seems we will have to do a lot of traveling. That will take time."

"I believe you have a traveling device that will serve."

"The chessboard! I had forgotten about that. How did you know?"

"The Good Magician knows everything he cares to. He mentioned it."

Kody brought out the packet and unfolded it. "It's a regular game board. You have to look at it in a special way to evoke the pictures."

"Of course," Dara agreed. "Simple folk see only the jumping women or carved cheese. The pictures seem to cover a wide sampling of Xanth. You can begin by trying them randomly, then orient on the direction of greatest contrast."

"How will we judge the contrast?"

"You will need to view people or scenes. You will see them as they are, but Zosi will be most avidly repelled by the most attractive. You may need to develop a system of ratings to determine the intensity."

"Let's do that now. Zosi, on a scale of zero to ten, with ten being the most appealing, how do you rate Dara?"

Dara stood up straight, posing. Her hair whirled about her in a dark cloud and her figure threatened to burst out of its inadequate restraints.

Zosi was abashed. "Oh, I wouldn't say a thing like that."

"Be honest," Dara said. "We do know about the Curse. That's what Kody's here to solve."

The girl gulped and said it. "One. You look repulsive."

"Which would be a nine in ordinary times," Dara said. "Do you agree, Kody?"

"Yes, a nine. You're a fine-looking woman." He was aware that a demoness could look any way she chose, and those who associated with human beings preferred to resemble starlets, but it was true.

"But if we were closer to the Bomb, you would have to go beyond ten, and Zosi would have to go into negative numbers. There's your scale."

"There's our scale," Kody agreed. "So we can travel to a random site on the board, and rate someone, and judge whether we are closer to the Bomb."

"You've got it," the demoness agreed.

"I remain unsatisfied," Kody said. "I don't like depending on the chessboard to travel. Suppose I lose it?"

Dara eyed him again. "You're hard to satisfy."

"Thank you."

She laughed. "I've been around a few centuries. Let me ask a friend. Some demon is bound to know the answer." She faded out.

"She's very helpful," Zosi said.

"I suspect it is to make up for the gruff obscurity of the Good Magician. Someone needs to be sure the querents are able to use the Answers they get." He still didn't much like the word, but it seemed that that was what they were: folk who questioned the Good Magician.

"Yes." She took a breath. "May I confess something?"

Confess? "What is on your mind?"

"All this is so new and different to me, I'm sure I would mess it up on my own and fail in my mission. I'm glad you will be with me. You seem to have more sense than I do."

"But you're the one who knows Xanth, Zosi! I'm just here in a dream. *I'm* depending on *you*."

Now she laughed, weakly. "We're depending on each other."

"Perforce," he agreed. "Maybe it's not coincidence. The Good Magician knew we'd need each other, to succeed at either mission."

"That must be it," she agreed.

Dara reappeared. "Let's see that bored."

"That what?" Kody asked.

"Blase, uninteresting, tired, world-weary, lumbering, plank, timber—"

"Board?"

"Whatever," she agreed crossly.

"You're welcome, Metria."

The demoness puffed into smoke. "Free Fudge and Popsicles! What gave me away?"

"Just a lucky guess," Kody said. "I thought you weren't allowed in the castle."

"This isn't the castle. This is the open courtyard."

So she had found a loophole. "What are you doing here, Metria?"

The smoke shaped into dusky lusciousness in a halter that would have been eye-popping if there had been enough of it to assess. "I am insatiably attracted to anything interesting, especially if it's anything I'm not supposed to know about. What's this about the board?"

"It's a magic artifact I was given that enables me to jump to different sections of Xanth. But I worry about losing it and maybe getting stuck somewhere I wouldn't like."

"Like the embrace of a tangle tree?"

"What's a tangle tree?"

She re-formed into a small tree whose foliage consisted of green tentacles. "Touch it and it grabs you, and . . ."

Curious, Kody touched it. "And?"

"And gobbles you down." The tentacles whipped to wrap around him and haul him in to the trunk. Before he could resist the trunk formed lips and gave him a smacking kiss on the mouth. "Fortunately I'm not a real tangler."

"Fortunately," Kody echoed weakly.

"Oops, gotta go." The tree turned smoky and dissipated.

Dana appeared. "I smell brimstone. What happened?"

"Demoness Metria was here, emulating you," he said, rubbing his mouth.

"And you kissed her?"

"Not intentionally."

"Because if you thought it was me, you had no business kissing a married woman."

"No business," Kody agreed.

"It wasn't like that," Zosi said. "She became a tangle tree and hauled him in."

"You kissed a tangler? This is not normally considered a safe thing to do."

"I appreciate that," Kody said.

She smiled. "You're fun. Now here's the word on the board. It has a few extra pieces, checkers, pawns, go-markers, or whatever. Take one of those and rub it into your palm. Then the board will know where you are at all times."

"But if I lose it, *I* will need to know where *it* is, not the other way around."

"Not so. You may simply summon it and it will come to you. So you can't really lose it."

Kody nodded. "I like that. But how do I get a pawn when it's only an image?"

"Just take it."

Kody set the board down on a table. The chess pieces appeared, properly set up for the game. To the side, he now saw, were two spare pawns, one white, one black. He put his thumb on the white one. "Come to me."

He felt nothing, but when he lifted his thumb, there was the picture of the pawn on it, smelling faintly of cheese. He pressed it into his other palm. It transferred there, then faded out.

He left the board on the table and walked away. "Come to me," he repeated.

Something nudged his hand. It was the board packet, tightly folded. The magic worked. He had bonded with the board.

"That must be wonderful," Zosi said enviously.

"Take the other pawn," Kody said. "That way you will be able to summon it too."

"Oh, I couldn't!"

"If we are to work together, we need to be sure we can't get separated from each other without recourse," Kody said. "This board can protect us from that. Take the pawn." He proffered the board.

She did not protest further. She opened it out and set it on the table. She put her thumb to the black pawn. In half a moment she had it, and in the other half moment it was sinking into her other palm.

"Test it," Kody said.

She walked away from the board, as he had, then paused. "Come to me."

The board quickly folded itself and flew to her hand.

"I believe that does it," Dara said. "You may spend the night here, and start on your missions tomorrow morning. I wish you every success in abolishing the Curse." She grimaced prettily. "So that Humfrey does not wince when I kiss *him*."

They all laughed.

"Oh, one other thing," Dara said. "Sometimes when there's a difficult Quest, there is Demon involvement. You need to be aware of that, just in case."

"What's with the capital D?" Kody asked.

"There are two primary levels of demons. The great majority are lowly garden-variety types, like Metria and me. But a few are supreme types, like Demon Xanth, from whose incidental body radiation all the magic of Xanth derives. Demon Earth governs Mundania, providing the magic of gravity, and others like Demon Mars and Demoness Venus have their own domains. They are incalculably more powerful than anything else. Their interest is mainly in vying with each other for status points. Sometimes they levy wagers on random things, such as whether a given mortal will do a certain thing. They don't normally intervene, they just watch. But you can never be sure. So keep in mind that your Quest just might be a Demon bet, rather than a routine chore. It might make a difference."

"But if these super-powerful things don't intervene, what's the difference?"

"Perhaps none. But there could be special aspects that make no sense unless it is a stricture set by a Demon. In any event, do not take any Demon's name in vain; there could be consequences."

"Like disrespecting an ugly little cloud?"

Dara smiled. "Exactly. Only infinitely more so."

"I will be properly respectful."

"That is best." Dara faded out.

So it seemed they were ready to go. But Kody remained doubt-ful. Were they really equipped to tackle such formidable missions? Surely there were dozens of other folk better qualified than a dreamer and a living zombie. Unless some Demon had a twisted sense of humor.

Well, no matter. They were the ones who had been assigned, and they would do their best, hoping it was good enough.

# 5
# ZAP AND YUKAY

K ody had a pleasant, quiet night alone, glad to catch up on sleep. This remarkable realm just kept throwing new things at him, and he needed time to assimilate them. He had pretty much given up wondering why he needed to sleep when he was already in a dream state.

In the morning he joined Zosi for breakfast. She looked nice, with her gray hair neatly brushed, and she kept her knees together. She was relearning the living mode. Then, armed with knapsacks full of knickknacks, they departed the castle. "I hope you have a forthright notion how to begin," Zosi said.

"I was hoping *you* did."

She smiled ruefully. "It has been some time since I was alive, and I've never been on a Quest. But I understand there's always a Protagonist and several Companions, plus lots of challenging Adventures. So maybe we should start by seeking some Companions. Maybe they'll have better ideas how to proceed."

"Why do we need Companions? Won't they just slow things down?"

"I think it's mostly Tradition. But there must be a reason. I suppose Quests are more likely to be favorably resolved if there are more people along."

Kody shrugged. "We can keep an eye out for some."

At that moment, as if summoned, two dark unicorns trotted into view, heading toward the castle. They saw Kody and Zosi in the path, and paused.

"Hello, unicorns," Kody said.

Suddenly he saw a little picture of the two people meeting the two unicorns. A speech balloon appeared over the head of one unicorn. "Hello, humans."

Kody was taken aback. "Did you just answer me? Or was I imagining it?"

The picture reappeared. Now the speech balloon said, "Yes."

Then Zosi caught on. "They are projecting dreamlets! Because they can't talk with their regular mouths."

"True, human female," the balloon said. "We are Moonshine and Moonshadow, unicorn/night mare crossbreeds, and we inherit some abilities from each parent. We can phase out in darkness, heal injuries, purify springs, and yes, project little dreams."

"Thank you for that explanation," Kody said. "I am Kody, and my companion is Zosi." He did not add either Mundane or Zombie, uncertain what impression such terms would make. "We have just been to see the Good Magician, and are now on a Quest." Should he ask the unicorns to join them? He wasn't sure how Zosi would feel about it, or whether unicorns would make good Companions. He had really been thinking of human Companions.

"We are going there now," Moonshine said. "Not to see the Good Magician; we are friends of Dara Demoness."

"We wish you well," the balloon by Moonshadow said. Then the two unicorns trotted forward to the moat, ran across the water, and through the castle wall.

Kody exchanged a glance with Zosi. "I don't think they would have wanted to become Companions," he said.

"No," she agreed.

Another person was approaching the castle. Kody was coming to appreciate how busy it was. No wonder the Good Magician tried to set limits.

This one was a medium-age woman. "Hello," Kody said.

The woman bleated. Then she paused, looking embarrassed. "Sorry. I forgot what form I was in. I'm Annie Mal. I can become any animal." She demonstrated by becoming a sheep, then reappeared as human, clothes and all.

"Kody Mundane." He was concluding that it was best after all to establish his alien origin, so that people would know why he made social mistakes.

"Zosi Zombie." She was evidently coming to a similar conclusion about her nature. If that turned people off, well, it was best done at the outset.

"Verynicetomeetyouboth," Annie said rapidly. "I'llbeonmy way." She became a rabbit and bounded away.

Kody shook his head. "I guess a Mundane and a Zombie made her nervous."

"Yes. But if we want Companions, they will have to know."

"I agree. So maybe we had better continue to be open about our dark origins. So as to scare away folk before we get into things like Quests, if they're going to scare."

"Yes," she agreed unhappily.

She needed cheering. "But just so you know, I think you're a pretty girl and a nice person, Zosi. I'm even getting to like gray hair."

"Oh!" she said faintly. "I wish . . ."

"If it's anything I can help with, let me know."

"You're so nice to me," she said. "Even though you know I'm a zombie." She took a breath. "I wish . . . I could kiss you again."

Oops. That had not been the kind of thing he meant. But what could he do? "Okay." He took her in his arms and kissed her.

There was a soft explosion of something. She was surprisingly nice to kiss, but that wasn't really it.

"Oh look!" she explained as he let her go. "A heart!"

Now he saw it. A little red heart was orbiting them. "That came from us?"

She nodded, blushing. "It means we like each other."

So that, too, was literal, here in the magic land. There had been no heart when Princess Dawn kissed him, but there had been no prospect of romance there.

That made him pause. There was such a prospect here? That seemed unlikely. "Maybe we do," he agreed. "Though of course we won't be associating long."

"Yes." She was sad again, and the heart faded out.

Time to change the subject. "Now let's see what the chessboard offers." He brought the board out and unfolded it.

"I am not clear on exactly how it works," Zosi said. "All I see are check hers pieces. It's a naughty game."

"Those are there too. Can you play chess?"

She shook her gray curls. "Chess is too complicated for zombies. We don't have good minds."

"There is another set of images," he said. "We didn't go into that with Dara, as she already knew. You have to refocus your eyes to look through them and see the pictures beyond. Each square has a different one."

Zosi concentrated, frowning. "It's not working for me."

"Just keep trying. Once you catch it, you'll know how. I had practice with 3-D pictures in Mundania."

"With what?"

"Pictures that look flat until you refocus. Then you see them in three dimensions. They—" He broke off, because there was a commotion not far from the castle. In fact it was a female scream, and a loud squawking.

"A girl's in trouble!" Zosi said. "We have to help her."

"Of course." They ran together toward the sound.

Soon they saw it: a young woman floundering in a bog, while a winged monster flew toward her. It would reach her before they could, unfortunately.

"Hey!" Kody shouted. "Leave her alone!" Not that he thought it would do much good.

But the creature paused, glancing at him. Then it settled for a landing beside the woman. It put its huge eagle head down to her flailing body.

She flung her arms around its neck and hung on as the monster jerked back. It backed away, but she clung to it, her feet dragging.

Then Kody and Zosi arrived. He summoned a reverse wood chip, ready to flip it. And paused.

The monster was not attacking the girl. It was simply standing there while she sobbed into its feathers. "Is this normal?" Kody asked Zosi.

"I don't think so. That's a griffin; I can tell because its hide is the color of shoe polish."

"A griffin!" He recognized it now: a creature with the head and wings of an eagle, and the body of a lion. Like a greatly enlarged catbird.

"Normally it would dunk her in a clean pool, because they don't like dirty food, then eat her. Maybe we are distracting it."

The griffin looked at them and squawked negatively. Then its tail came around and rubbed against its own hide on the side. A word appeared: NO

"It understands us!" Kody said, amazed.

The tail moved again, finger-painting more letters in the polish. YES

"You weren't attacking the woman," Zosi said, as surprised as Kody was.

YES

"You were rescuing her," Kody said.

YES

Now the woman recovered some of her composure. She had blond hair, dark eyes, and European features. She was lithe and slimly built. "Yes. I was stuck in that awful blog and was getting overwhelmed by its opinionations. I had mistaken its nature and thought I could simply slog through it. That was a stupid mistake, and I hate making that kind, because I am very intelligent." She had a British accent. "Fortunately the griffin heard me scream and came to help."

Kody put it together. Not a bog, but a blog. Evidently such a mass of ignorant opinions that the woman had become disoriented and lost her poise. It seemed that such things happened in this weird realm. Actually they could happen in Mundania too; he had been stuck once in a public place with a radio blaring out phenomenally ignorant political verbiage and had soon felt ill.

"Let's exchange introductions," Zosi said. "I am Zosi Zombie."

The griffin shied away in horror.

"Not at the moment," Kody said quickly. "She is a living woman now. No rot."

The griffin relaxed. Then it painted more letters on its side.
ZAP

"Zap Griffin," Zosi said. "We are pleased to meet you, sir."
FEM

"Oh," Zosi said, embarrassed. "I didn't, er, look."

"Pleased," Kody echoed. He hadn't looked either. "I am Kody, from Mundania. I'm dreaming this."

They let that pass, maybe assuming he was speaking figuratively.

"I am the Maiden Yukay," the woman said. When the others, including the griffin, looked blank, she launched into her personal history. "I was delivered eighteen years ago to the Maiden Japan. I never knew my father, but he was said to be one of the three most intelligent men in Xanth at the time, which may be how he impressed my mother. She expected much of me, but was disappointed. I existed in my own perfect little world, unresponsive to speech, unable to speak myself until age six. These were symptoms of my magic talent, which is Precise Harmony with the Physical Universe, otherwise known as Zen."

"We have that in Mundania," Kody said, marveling at her self-description. Was it unusually candid, or delusional?

"Mother thought I was developmentally disabled," Yukay

continued. "But then she realized that I could perform any feat effortlessly, as long as I had never tried it before, and my mind was unfocused, or in a Zen state. So something I could do perfectly the first time, like accurately loosing an arrow at a moving target, I was unable to do again, making it seem like sheer luck. But if I deliberately went into the Zen state, I could do new things or variants of prior things. That made my talent seem less unreliable." She took a breath. "I am emotional, loyal, tenderhearted, and loving, but have been unable to function effectively in Xanth. So I elected to see the Good Magician, who I hope will tell me how to modify my behavior so as to become effective."

"Lotsa luck there," Kody murmured, remembering the famous obscurity of the Good Magician's Answers.

"But then, focusing on the castle, I waded into the blog and was bombarded by blathering ignorance. It was utterly awful! Fortunately you folk came to rescue me."

"If the Good Magician's Answer is like the one he gave us," Zosi said, "he will tell you to travel on a Quest, yours or someone else's, where you will find your Answer in due course."

Yukay sighed. "So I understand. I delayed coming here for some time for that very reason. But what else is there for me?"

"You might consider traveling with us," Kody said. "We are already on a Quest or two."

She gazed at him with her beautiful eyes. "There is something odd about the way you look at me."

"I see you as you are: a lovely young woman."

"That must be it," she agreed. "Others are revolted by my aspect. Ever since the Curse manifested."

"My Quest is to abolish that Curse," Kody said.

Yukay considered. "There's almost a certain nonsensical sense to that. Substituting one Quest for another, without the intercession of the Good Magician and his required year's Service or Equivalent. I must confess that abolishing the Curse is almost as important to me as becoming more effective. Without the Curse I hardly need to be effective; no one notices. But questions remain."

"I can think of one," Kody said. "Will our Quest provide you the Answer, or must it be your own similar Quest? And I can't answer."

"The other relates to your Quest companion," Yukay said. "She is a reasonably ugly woman, which means you see her as reasonably pretty. While I—" She paused. "How do you see me, Zosi?"

"Repulsively ugly."

"Precisely. Which means Kody sees me as outstandingly lovely. I am likely to divert his attention from you, men being superficial in that respect. Would you prefer that I not join your party?"

"Oh, that's all right," Zosi said. "I will revert to zombie status after this Quest. I'm not looking for any romantic association."

Not consciously, Kody thought. But unconsciously she was, well, hungry. That kiss had been potent, and there was the flying heart.

"Neither am I," Yukay said. "But sometimes these things happen unbidden."

"I am here on what might be considered a temporary visa," Kody said. "After the Quest is done, I will be gone. So I am not in the market either."

"Then it seems it is all right," Yukay concluded. "I will join your Quest, and assist in whatever ways I can." She smiled. "Though I confess knowing that Kody sees me as appealing does enhance my self-respect, despite the fact that I see him as a thoroughly homely man."

"Oh, thank you," Kody said. Because that was actually a compliment, in this context.

"Oh, I must look a sight," Yukay said. "Now that someone can see me, I mean." She produced a compact mirror and looked at her face. "My hair is all mussed!"

"It's lovely hair regardless," Kody reassured her.

"And my nose is smudged. And I seem to have lost my hankie." She walked to a nearby fabric bush and picked a fresh hankie. But it tugged out of her hand and flew away.

It passed Kody. He snagged it from the air and returned it to her. "Must be a hanky-panky," he said, feeling very gentlemanly. "It requires a very firm grip or it makes mischief."

She flashed him a smile. "Thank you." She took the hanky, now spelled with a y, with a very firm grip and made it behave as she erased the smudge. Then she combed her mussed hair. She had looked pretty before; now she was downright beautiful. When she was done she tucked the hanky into her purse, anchoring it securely. It tugged but could not escape, and soon resigned itself to its fate.

Kody realized belatedly that her name was a pun: Maiden Yukay, MADE IN THE UK. The United Kingdom, or Britain. She was the daughter of the Maiden Japan? This Land of Xanth seemed to be largely made of puns, regardless of how well they integrated with reality.

They turned to Zap. "I thank you again for coming to my rescue," Yukay said. "I want to be your friend."

The griffin nodded. YES

"I presume you were in the vicinity because you, also, are traveling to see the Good Magician."

The griffin swished her tail across her side. YES

"So you must have some question or problem you fear only the Good Magician can solve."

YES

"If I may inquire, what is it?"

The griffin could not answer with a yes or no, so Yukay adapted the game of Nineteen Questions to tease out the story. It seemed that Zap was once a lucky-go-happy griffin bouncing around the glens and rills of Xanth with little awareness of the future. Then she pounced on a juicy fresh rabbit.

But instead of coming loose from the ground when she grasped it in her talons, the rabbit swelled up into triple size, turned angry red, and blew smoke from its ears. "Unclaw me, beaksnoot!" it demanded.

Surprised, Zap flew higher with it.

The rabbit turned furious blue and grew fangs. "Are you hard of hearing, buffalo wings?" it festered.

Zap still flew upward, uncertain what to do about this nuisance.

The rabbit expanded into a full-sized demon. "Then be cursed, birdbrain! You will never eat a rabbit again, or any other meat. In fact I am foisting off on you a surplus soul I happen to have handy. Take that!" The demon made a throwing motion, and something invisible whomped into her body. Then the demon puffed into acrid smoke and dissipated.

It seemed the demon had been emulating a rabbit, and she had snatched it up, unawares. Now, suddenly, she had a soul. That was supposed to be a curse?

Soon enough it became clear that it was indeed a curse. She was unable to hurt anything, let alone kill an animal to eat. She became a vegetarian and something of a pacifist, seeking no quarrel with anything. Since griffins lived on fresh meat, this was a problem. She was in danger of starving to death. She had to forage to find vegetable swampmeat, which was awful stuff that made her constantly ill. She could no longer play games of kill-the-prey with her griffin playmates, which caused them to shun her. Her life was ruined. All because of that cursed soul.

So she decided to ask the Good Magician what to do about it. Was there a way to get rid of the soul? Then, when almost there, she had heard the Maiden Yukay scream, and had to fly to the rescue, because the soul made her do it. Now she was here, and it was time to be moving on, because the castle Challenges were probably awaiting her.

"Did it ever occur to you that you might actually be better off with a soul?" Yukay asked.

NO

"But many creatures are desperate to get souls," Zosi protested. "Only humans are guaranteed them."

YES But the griffin plainly remained unhappy.

Kody stepped into the dialogue. "As I understand it, the soul is responsible for conscience and appreciation of the finer things in life," he said. "In time you should come to value it."

MAYBE Zap agreed dubiously.

"It occurs to me that a fighting creature like a griffin might be a useful Companion to have on a Quest," Yukay said. "Even a pacifistic one."

"And our Quest might turn up something that helps," Zosi agreed. "If only other Companions who appreciate souls."

Kody saw the handwriting on the invisible wall. "Zap, why don't you join our Quest," he said. "At least it will save you a year of service to the Good Magician, as we hope to complete it in a few days."

?

"It's a double Quest," Kody explained. "To reverse the Curse that reverses appearance, and to find a way to restore zombies to Xanth before they are rendered extinct. These things might not mean much to regular griffins, but there are those who would sincerely appreciate their accomplishment."

"Support of such missions would be a decent thing," Yukay said. "The kind of thing to put a soul at rest."

Zap considered for a long moment, almost a moment and a half. YES

Kody wondered whether the griffin was being practical. That soul probably gave her fits when she ran afoul of its confusing strictures. Traveling with souled folk was bound to make that aspect easier. "Then it's agreed," he said.

Zap moved her tail. BUT I HAVE Then after a moment she wiped her side clear and started over. NOTHING TO She waited, giving them time to read it, then wiped it clear again. CONTRIBUTE

"You saved me from the dread Blog!" Yukay said. "Isn't that enough?"

NO

Kody stepped in. "You feel you are accepting the benefit of our company and Quest and don't want to be a drag. You want to contribute your share."

YES

Yukay glanced at him with sidelong respect. "You are sensitive to her feelings."

Kody shrugged. "I have had my own experiences with exclusion and inclusion."

"Haven't we all," Zosi said with feeling. Zombies were considered the lowest of the low, and Kody was sure they were normally excluded from polite society.

Yukay nodded. "Very well. Let's see what Zap has to offer." She faced the griffin. "Do you have any special abilities, apart from those natural to your kind, like flying?"

NO

Yukay did not give up. "Is there anything you're good at, even if it seems irrelevant?"

PUNS Zap wrote, embarrassed.

"You emit puns?" Yukay asked, wrinkling her nose.

NO

"You merely recognize them?"

YES

There was a silence.

Zosi came to the rescue. "It is the nature of Quests for Companions to be assembled seemingly randomly, but to turn out to have relevant abilities when the need arises. The abilities don't need to be grandiose, merely right for the occasion. It may be that there will come a time when quick pun recognition makes a difference."

"There may be a job for her at Caprice Castle," Kody said. "They are collecting puns there, trying to make Xanth safe for normal folk."

"Squawk," Zap said appreciatively.

"We could encounter Caprice," Kody said. "It travels wherever puns are found. I understand that pun duty is considered hard labor, and they have trouble holding on to workers."

I CAN DO IT

That seemed to suffice. The griffin now felt comfortable joining the Quest.

So now they were four. It was time to get moving.

"So where are we going?" Yukay inquired brightly.

"I . . . am still pondering that," Kody said, not caring to admit he had no idea. "Any suggestions?"

"Weren't we about to try the cheese board?" Zosi asked.

"Good idea." He brought it out. It had, it seemed, neatly folded itself and returned to his pocket when they heard Yukay's scream. "This is a dual purpose device. We can play games on it, like check hers and cheese. We can also travel by it. The key is to see the images, then touch the one that shows where we want to go."

Yukay and Zap looked blank.

"I haven't seen the images yet," Zosi said. "So we can all try together."

Kody set the board down on the ground and they all got down and pored over it. "You see the cheese pieces?"

"Squawk." That sounded affirmative.

"Yes," Yukay agreed. "After I saw the naughty check hers figures."

"Now fuzz your gaze somewhat. Try to look through it, at an object some distance beyond it, crazy as that sounds. You'll know it when you see it."

They all refocused, not seeing it.

"Like this," Kody said, doing it himself. The images leaped into focus.

There was a three-way exclamation. Suddenly they all were seeing it. It seemed that his focusing made it work for anyone else looking at the same time. Sixty-four little images.

"There's Castle Roogna!" Zosi said excitedly, pointing at a square with a picture of a fancy castle.

"Why, so it is," Yukay agreed. "I can even see the flags blowing in the wind."

"I'd like to stop at the Castle Roogna zombie graveyard, to let my friends know I'm working on it," Zosi said. "They'll be concerned."

That had not been a high priority for Kody. "Zombies get concerned?"

"Oh, yes, those with enough brains left. They guide the others whose brains have rotted out entirely. Now that I'm alive, my brain is much better."

"Um—"

She gave him a soulful look. "Please."

What could he do? "If it's okay with the others."

Zap was doubtful, but Yukay stroked her wing feathers. "You and I don't have to get close to them," she said reassuringly. "This is Zosi's business."

"Squawk," Zap agreed reluctantly.

"We can't all touch the picture simultaneously," Kody said. "But I think if we are all in contact with each other it should consider us as a group. We don't want anyone to get separated."

They crowded together, Kody holding hands with each of the women, and both of them firmly touching the griffin. "Now," Kody said to Zap, and she pecked the relevant square with her beak.

And they were there before Castle Roogna. It was massive, far larger than the Good Magician's Castle or Caprice Castle. Before them was the drawbridge leading over the moat. To one side was the orchard, with many luxurious trees.

"Well, now!"

Suddenly there were three infernally pretty princesses standing before them, in brown, green, and red dresses. All of them wore cute little crowns. "Harmony!" Kody exclaimed, recognizing the one in brown.

"Kody," she answered. "What are you doing here?"

"I'm on my Quest to save Xanth from the Curse. These are my Companions Zosi Zombie, the Maiden Yukay, and Zap Griffin."

"Zosi!" the green-dressed one said. Her hair was greenish blond, her eyes blue. "I hardly recognized you out of the graveyard. You're looking so healthy!"

"Princess Melody, I'm not healthy, I'm alive. I'm on a Quest to restore the zombie population of Xanth."

"Oh, that's good. We're almost out of zombies."

"And I know you, Yukay," the third princess said. Her green eyes contrasted with her red dress and hair.

"Yes, Princess Rhythm," Yukay agreed. "I decided to be a Companion."

"But we came here only so I could reassure my friends that I was on the Quest," Zosi said.

"I'm sure they are eager to hear your news. They are being called to action now. Bye."

All three were gone as suddenly as they had appeared. Zosi smiled. "Sometimes I think the princesses dismay visitors more than the zombies do. Still, the zombies have their ways. Once when they were annoyed, they staged a sit-down strike, leaving rotting pieces by the front gate."

Kody noted that now Zosi was speaking of the zombies in the third person. That suggested that she was getting used to being alive.

"They surely made their point," Yukay said, amused. "But what's this about being called to action?"

"We are about to find out," Kody said.

"I know better, but the Curse still affects me," Yukay said. "I know the three princesses are pretty, but to me they looked like young hags, and they must have seen me the same way."

"They, and you, all look pretty to me," Kody said. Then he was struck by a stray thought that happened to be passing. "How did they look to you, Zap?"

UGLY

"So the Curse affects you too, though you are not human. That's interesting."

"It affects our perception of the animals too," Yukay said. "How does Zap look to you, Kody?"

"Gorgeous. She's a magnificent creature."

"Squawk," Zap said, amused.

"To me she looks gnarled and blotchy."

UGLY Zap agreed, understanding perfectly.

"We really need to get this fixed," Zosi said.

"I don't want to be offensive," Kody said. "But there's something about zombies I don't understand. Do they really eat human brains, and if so, why?"

Zosi looked at him with horror. "You thought I wanted to eat your brain?"

"Not you, specifically," he said quickly. "You're alive. But can we trust your friends?"

"We don't eat brains!" Zosi said indignantly. "In fact we don't eat anything. That's why we're fading away."

"That's a relief. Maybe what I heard was wrong."

"There are other fantasy lands," Yukay said. "Maybe their zombies eat brains. Xanth zombies just drag about sloughing off pieces of themselves."

"That must be it," Kody said.

"I wouldn't eat you even if I were in zombie mode," Zosi said.

"I shouldn't have brought it up."

They walked to the graveyard in back. There was activity there. "Oh, no," Zosi said. "They are fighting off an attack, and there aren't enough of us to succeed."

The scene was strange. Half a dozen zombies were busy trying to move some sort of chain away from the castle, but there weren't enough of them to move all of it at once. Wherever they were not pushing, it was advancing. Progress was slow, but it was evident that in several more days it would cross the graveyard and encroach on the castle proper.

Kody focused, but could not clarify exactly what the chain was made of. First it seemed to be formed of mundane cigarettes, which didn't make much sense here. The zombies tried to push them away, but they emitted clouds of smoke that set the zombies to coughing. It seemed their lungs were not in good condition. One of them got a tattered if not actually rotten fan and used it to blow the smoke back. When it cleared the scene, there was something else looping across, flapping in the wind but not giving way because each piece was linked securely to the next. They looked like envelopes for letters. Another zombie fetched a big pair of rusty scissors and cut a link, and the letters blew away. Only to be replaced by what seemed to be loops of food. The zombies started getting hit by pies in their faces. But it all seemed to be part of the same general phenomenon. "Exactly what *is* that thing?" he asked.

A zombie overhead him. "Czhainzz!" it said.

"Chains?"

"Yezz."

Then Yukay caught on. "Chains," she agreed. "Chain smoking. Chain letters. Food chain."

"And when they balk one chain, another takes its place," Zosi said.

"Squawk."

They looked at Zap. On her side was the word YUKAY.

"But I have no idea," Yukay protested.

"Maybe I do," Kody said. "These are puns."

"Zombies are not good at puns," Zosi said. "It takes brains to handle them."

"And sometimes a cast-iron stomach," Yukay agreed. "I kept that hanky-panky mainly because I refuse to let it get the better of me."

"But Zap *is* good at puns," Kody said. "So we are armed, as it were."

Sure enough, Zap's side said FOOD CHAIN. She had caught on before Yukay did.

Meanwhile the zombies were still struggling ineffectively with the chains. When they tried to eat the food, not only did it do them no good, the chain changed to a group of prisoners chained together as they hacked weeds. The zombies couldn't get near without risking getting hacked themselves.

CHAIN GANG

But soon a new zombie roused from its grave: a zombie dragon. It reared up on two or three of its hind legs and breathed out a blast of blue fire.

The prisoners retreated. "Just as well," Zosi said. "Old Dragtail's fire has long since gone cold. That's why it's blue. They were lucky."

Now something else happened. The prisoners crashed into a tree loaded with pans. It was of course a pan-pipe tree, as Zap printed, but here near the zombie graveyard its pans were deformed. A pan dropped onto a row of zzz's that came from a sleeping man, waking him. The zzz's veered wildly, crossing out a section of the landscape before fading out. The man staggered onto a shiny new floor he had made, because he was a floor-ist, making footprints in the floor before it properly set. Now the zzz's were replaced by @#$%&!! and worse as he swore villainous bleeps at the damage. The ferocious interjections collided with a pile of window frames, and windows popped up, filled with salesmen who eagerly yammered their sales pitches. "Buy our Micro-Wave; its tiny puffs of air will blow bugs away!" one shouted. "And if that doesn't do it, our Mega-Wave will blow your whole house away!" "Do your robots have a bad case of corrosion?" another yelled. "Buy our anti-oxidant!"

Then a window banged into a sleeping animal, and it woke with a growl. It was a Bear Minimum, a small creature from Ursa Minor, and it was not pleased to be disturbed. It leaped at the window, smashing it into splinters and shards.

"What are we seeing?" Kody asked, amazed.

"I think it's another chain," Yukay said. "A Chain of Events."

Kody glanced at Zap, where those words were printed. He should have looked before asking. He groaned. "We have to get rid of it."

The zombies charged at the Bear. The Bear seemed fearless, but when it saw the oncoming rot it hurriedly retreated. Kody realized that this was the real advantage of the zombies: even savage animals and fearless warriors feared them, because of the rot. Zombies didn't have to eat brains to be frightful.

Then there appeared a line of men. They seemed to be officers in an army, with the lead one a lowly enlisted man and those following being of increasing rank right up to a six-star general.

"It's a Chain of Command," Kody murmured, seeing Zap's words.

Yukay stepped up to an officer about halfway along. "Hello,

sir," she said brightly. "I wonder if you—oops!" She had brought out the hanky, and it had tugged away from her hand and blown away on the wind.

Immediately the officer leaped out of the line and chased the hanky. Officers were by definition gentlemen, and could not let a lady be embarrassed. But it avoided him almost teasingly, dancing in the air before flying on. Soon both of them were out of sight.

Yukay faced the line. "One link of the Chain of Command has broken ranks and is lost," she said. "The chain is broken."

The other officers looked bewildered. Then they faded like dissipating demons. All the chains were broken.

"I don't know why I did that," Yukay said. "I wasn't even thinking."

"I believe we have just seen your talent in action," Kody said. "You did exactly the right thing, with no preparation."

She nodded. "I suppose I did. I couldn't have done it if I had thought about it."

"Here come the zombies," Zosi said.

"Um, yes," Kody agreed, a bit nervous despite Zosi's reassurance. He saw Zap and Yukay fidgeting the same way he was. None of them were eager to embrace a zombie, or even to shake hands.

Zosi went out to meet them. "Hello, Zam!" she said, hugging the male zombie who had first identified the chains for Kody. He was a cavernously gaunt figure with tattered clothing and sickly recessed eyeballs. "I am on the Quest! These are my Companions." She glanced back. "They are normals. You know what that means."

"Kheep our dishtance," Zam agreed. "But thanx for the helph." He had only two front teeth, complicating his speech.

"You're welcome," Yukay said primly.

Zosi moved on to the next. "Zuzan!" She hugged a female zombie whose straggling hair seemed to be falling out in spoiled hanks. Then the others. "Zeth! Zylvia! Zimon! Zamantha!" That was the lot. There were only six zombies, where the gravesites indicated there had been hundreds. They plainly needed reinforcements.

"I think zombies gradually wear out," Yukay murmured. "They

are forever shedding parts of themselves, and finally there's not enough of them left to function."

Kody had already concluded as much. "How did zombies get started?" he asked.

"There used to be the Zombie Master, at Castle Zombie. He made zombies by reviving dead people. But he retired twelve years ago, and since then no new zombies have been made. Now the castle is run by Breanna of the Black Wave and Justin Tree—he was a tree for decades—and they are very good, but they can't make new zombies. All they can do is assign the existing ones. So it seems it is a problem."

"A problem," Kody agreed. "I hope Zosi is able to come through for them."

"She's a nice girl. Maybe it will work out." But Yukay did not seem confident.

Soon Zosi returned. "I told them we would do our best," she said. "Now they can return to their graves and rest until the next threat comes. I hope we can solve the problem before then."

"We all hope so," Kody said.

They watched as the zombies returned to their scattered graves and sank into the soil. Then all was quiet.

The three princesses reappeared. "Well done," Melody said.

"We left it to you so Yukay could exercise her talent," Harmony added.

"Now we will entertain you for the night at Castle Roogna," Rhythm concluded. "Zap too."

"We'll show you the Magic Tapestry," Melody said.

"And all the other sights," Harmony continued.

"And introduce you to the Moat Monster," Rhythm concluded.

"That really isn't necessary," Yukay demurred.

"Because we're in charge while the elders are off setting up the Contest, and it's boring here," Melody said, starting another round of dialogue.

"But we have Quests to accomplish," Kody said, not liking the idea of delaying when time was surely short.

Princess Harmony produced a little harmonica and played a single note. "What did you say?" she asked.

"I said we'll be glad to be entertained," Kody said, surprising himself. He realized belatedly that the princesses had used magic on him. Also, that they tended to alternate talking, the three taking turns.

"That's what we thought you said," Princess Rhythm said.

"Never try to say no to a princess," Yukay murmured. "They don't understand the word."

So it seemed. He had inadvertently interrupted their round of dialogue, and they had promptly dealt with him. They looked like innocent girls, but he was aware that looks could be highly deceptive. They probably had histories that would make him wince.

"What contest is this?" Yukay inquired.

"We're not supposed to tell you," Melody said.

"Which is weird, because it has nothing to do with you," Harmony continued.

"So we're home alone, and want to know all about you," Rhythm concluded.

Kody saw the way of it. "We'll be happy to oblige."

"We were sure you would be," the three said together, laughing.

# 6
# ILLUSION FIELDS

I n the morning, thoroughly entertained, they set out again for zeroing in. Kody explained briefly how it worked. "I am immune to the Curse of Reversal. Zosi isn't. So we will go places, and rate our perceptions of other folk, and try to travel in the direction of the most extreme. That will be where the Bomb is."

"What about the zombies?" Yukay asked alertly.

"The Good Magician says I will find my answer in the course of helping him find his," Zosi said.

"And Zap and I hope to find ours in the same manner," Yukay said.

"It seems far-fetched, but that's the essence," Kody said. "Maybe you'd be better off going to the Good Magician after all."

She eyed him with that slightly disturbing appraisal. "And maybe not."

"Squawk," Zap agreed.

Kody wasn't sure what was on her mind, so he dismissed it from *his* mind. "We can check now, as this is a different place from where we last checked. Zosi, on our scale of one to ten, where do you see me now?"

"You're about as homely as before," Zosi said. "Maybe a two."

"What about me?" Yukay asked.

"Down near zero."

"Not surprising," Kody said quickly. "You are a very attractive woman."

"While I see you as a two, and Zosi as a four."

"I'm not as pretty as he is handsome," Zosi agreed a trifle wistfully.

"How about you?" Yukay asked Zap.

ZERO TWO FOUR

Kody laughed. "Same readout. At least we agree."

"We'd be better off with some disagreement," Yukay said. "To be sure we're not just being nice to get along. But it does seem like a valid reading."

"So this is similar to our last reading," Kody said. "Only maybe a bit more extreme. I think we need another reading."

"Yes," Zosi agreed. "We need big changes, not small ones."

Kody brought out the chessboard. He refused to think of it privately as a cheese board. "So where do we go next?"

"To get the best base for triangulation," Yukay said, "we should travel to a far edge of Xanth. Then to another far edge, in the form of a giant triangle."

"Which of these pictures shows a far edge?" Zosi asked, looking at the board.

There was the problem: no pictures were labeled. The scenes were varied, but they had little way to ascertain where they were.

"One of those is on the coast," Yukay said. "Castle Roogna is in the center, so that could be a fair distance."

"It will have to do," Kody agreed.

They gathered together and touched the coast picture. And they were there.

The incoming waves were silvery, and so was the sand. The plants farther in were silver. A silver crab scuttled past.

"The Silver Coast," Yukay said. "That's adjacent to the Gold

Coast. Beyond it will be the Copper Coast. Nothing much edible here."

Kory shrugged. "I hope you like peanut butter and jelly sandwiches."

"Fortunately we don't have to stay here long," Zosi said quickly.

They checked their perceptions, and concluded that the differential was about the same as before.

They checked the board again. "What about this one?" Zosi asked. "It looks nice."

It looked like nothing so much as a huge mud puddle to Kody, but he didn't argue. He just wanted to get a better differential. The others agreed.

But when they got there, Kody's perception turned out to be right. They sank almost waist-deep into a brown swamp.

"It's a sinkhole!" Kody said, alarmed.

"No, it's worse," Yukay said, wrinkling her nose. "It's a stink hole."

"Squawk!" If a beak could wrinkle, hers would have been corrugated.

"And griffins are notoriously wary of taint," Yukay said. "They won't touch spoiled meat. And she's too fouled to fly."

Now Kody smelled it. Putrid liquefied garbage. It seemed the smells were not reversed by the Curse. "Maybe I can help," he said. He conjured a reverse wood chip and flipped it into the brine.

It worked. Now the scent was of pristine perfume.

"But it's still garbage," Zosi said as they slogged to the bank. "We'd better clean it off. Before we go anywhere else."

The others agreed. "But where can we find clean water?" Kody asked.

They looked around. Not too far distant was a mountain, and it looked as if there was a river coursing down it. "There should be a pool at the base of that mount," Yukay said. "We'll have to cut cross-country to reach it, but do we have an alternative?"

"Is it safe?" Kody asked.

"By no means. Backwoods Xanth is dangerous."

"I will flip a chip at anything that seems dangerous," Kody said.

"Sometimes the worst dangers don't look like it."

"But what else can we do?" Zosi asked. "As a zombie this sort of thing never bothered me. But now that I'm alive, I detest it."

They set off, forging grimly toward the mountain. First Kody, then Zosi, then Yukay, then Zap as rear guard. The bog they had landed in soon gave way to dry sand, then regular dirt. Plants sprang up, and brush thickened. Kody spied a narrow path through the brush, and followed it. That was his mistake.

Because suddenly the path wasn't there. He stepped off a ledge and fell into a hole. Fortunately it was covered by turf so he didn't hurt himself as he landed on hands and knees. "Ooof!" he grunted belatedly.

"What happened?" Zosi asked, halting in place.

"I stepped into a hole I didn't see," Kody said, picking himself up.

"What hole?"

"This one." He looked down at his feet. And did a double-take.

His body was knee-deep in the ground. He could see his feet, but also the ground, two images occupying the same space. Yet he was sure his feet were not buried; they felt normal.

Yukay and Zap caught up. They looked.

"Oh, my," Yukay said.

"Squawk," Zap agreed.

"Have you any idea what I'm into?" Kody asked. "Because I don't."

"Illusion," Yukay said.

"Illusion?"

"More specifically, an illusion hole. Rather, a natural hole covered over by illusion. I haven't encountered it before, but I know it when I see it."

Kody lifted one leg and put it down half a step back the way he had come. It found lodging on a steep bank. Now it looked as if the ground covered it only ankle-deep. He lifted the other foot and found the regular ground. In most of a moment he was standing on the real ground again. Neither leg was dirty. "This is weird."

Yukay squatted beside him. She reached forward and down. Her hand passed through the ground and went below. "Definitely a hole. The level ground is the illusion."

"What's illusion doing here?" Kody asked.

"Illusion is all over Xanth," Yukay said, standing up again. "Small animals use it to conceal their existence from predators. Plants use it to prevent themselves from being eaten, or to make their flowers more beautiful. Women use it to make their faces pretty; it's called makeup. It's very useful."

"So some plant is covering this hole? Why?"

"It could be nickelpedes."

"Whats?" He had heard the term before, but couldn't quite place it.

"The larger cousin of centipedes. They gouge out nickel-sized chunks of flesh from folk they catch. Most folk are careful to avoid their pits. So they might use illusion."

Centipede. Nickelpede. More Xanth puns. "I did not get gouged," Kody said. Now he remembered: Zosi had encountered them before being zombied.

"And I did not get my hand chomped," Yukay said. "So it's not that. But something must have generated this illusion, for some purpose."

"Maybe there are other holes," Zosi said.

"Yes," Yukay said. "So we should take precautions."

"Like getting canes or poles to prod the ground ahead of us," Kody said. "I was lucky I didn't get hurt. I don't want to blunder into another hole."

"None of us do," Yukay agreed. She looked around. "Some of these saplings should do to make staffs."

Zosi took two cautious steps and reached for a sapling. Her hand passed through it. "Uh-oh."

"More illusion?" Yukay asked.

"Yes. I see it, but it's not there." Zosi swept her hand through the tree several times.

Zap walked carefully to a tree. She touched it with a wingtip. The wing passed through it without resistance. ILLUSION she printed, confirming it.

"This portends mischief," Yukay said. "The entire scene may be illusion. Why would anyone or anything take the trouble to do this?"

"*How* could anyone do this?" Zosi asked. "This may be a scene worthy of the Sorceress Iris."

"Iris?" Kody asked.

"King Emeritus Trent's wife," Yukay answered. "She was delivered a hundred and twelve years ago and became the most powerful mistress of illusion Xanth has seen. She was youthened nineteen years ago, and is still extant. She could have done this, and probably did, because magic talents are reluctant to repeat, especially the top-level ones. Assuming this is her handiwork, the question is why? Why would she bother to craft a scene in the middle of nowhere? She was never the frivolous kind."

"Maybe a new retirement retreat?" Zosi suggested.

"Possible," Yukay agreed. "We have not encountered hostile animals or plants. That would align."

"So are we intruding?" Kody asked. "I don't want to run afoul of a Sorceress." Or a capital D Demon, if that were the responsible party.

"I see no warning signs," Yukay said. "She could readily have made it clear this was reserved territory, if she wanted to."

"Let's assume the Sorceress did it," Kody said. "And did not post it. Could it be like a public park? For visitors to enjoy?"

"That is possible," Yukay agreed.

"In which case we don't need to vacate it, just get through it."

"So we can get ourselves clean," Yukay agreed.

"Then let's find some real saplings or fallen wood and try to make it on to that mountain pool beyond," Kody said.

The others agreed. They explored carefully, and did manage to find several sticks. Then they moved forward, each tapping the ground ahead to spot holes or obstacles.

Kody circled his hole and stepped forward. Soon he encountered an invisible boulder that he would have smacked into without the pole. The illusion had covered it over with the appearance of more level ground.

"You know, we might as well be blindfolded," he said. "Or proceeding through pitch black. We can't trust anything we see."

"Except each other," Yukay said. "So we had better keep our eyes open."

Progress was slow, but without mishaps, thanks to their caution. Then there was a sound ahead.

"Halloo! Can anybody hear me?" It was a man's voice.

"That's not illusion," Kody said. "Unless now it is doing sound too."

"Should we answer?" Zosi asked.

"Why not?" Kody said. "That will determine whether there's a real person there."

The others nodded, albeit slightly nervously.

Kody cupped his hands to his mouth. "Halloo! We hear you!"

"Oh great! Stay there. Let me join you, now that I have a direction."

"Right," Kody agreed.

They waited while the man approached with clumsy footsteps, running afoul of illusions. Soon he was visible, a tall, reasonably handsome blond.

"Oh, thank you!" the man said. "I hate being lost in this illusion, but I couldn't find my way out of it. I'm Ivan."

"Kody."

"Yukay."

"Zosi."

"Squawk."

"I was going to explore a lovely mountain I hadn't seen before, and I got caught in this mass of illusion and couldn't find my way out." Ivan shuddered. "I never was much concerned about illusion before, but I have a healthy respect for it now. Oh—my talent is making things fatter or thinner."

"Conjuring chips of reverse wood."

"Doing new things without thinking."

"Conjuring peanut butter and jelly sandwiches."

PAINTING WORDS

"I'm glad to meet all of you," Ivan said. "So do you know anything about this illusion?"

"No, we blundered into it just as you did," Kody said. "We've been picking our way through, going toward the same mountain. We think the Sorceress Iris must have made the illusion, but we don't know why."

"Well, if you will be kind enough to point out the way you came, I'll backtrack and escape it."

"That won't help," Kody said. "We first blundered into a stink hole, and fell into it by being conjured from elsewhere. So we don't know the way out."

"A stink hole," Ivan said. "I was trying not to remark on the odor."

"Thank you," Yukay said.

"Failing that, I suppose there is no way to go but forward. May I join you for that? It seems we all have a common mission: to escape the illusions."

"Welcome," Kody said. "We were headed for the mountain, though that too may be illusion." He realized belatedly that his reverse wood chip fix had worn off, so the smell was back.

"So if you try to go there, and get lost, you may find yourself out of the illusion," Ivan pointed out.

Kody laughed. "That hadn't occurred to us, but it may be so."

"Let me form a staff of my own," Ivan said. He felt around his feet and found a long straw.

"That isn't solid enough," Yukay said.

"You forget my talent." Ivan held up the straw, focusing on it. It thickened until it was a stout stick.

"That's a useful talent," Yukay said appreciatively. "Does it work the other way?"

"Yes, I can make fat things thin."

"What about people?"

"Them too," Ivan said. "I can also do parts of things, like making women's busts bigger. It makes me popular with some women."

"It surely does!" Yukay agreed. "So why aren't you making women happy?"

"There's more to a woman than her bust, whatever she may think," he answered seriously. "I wanted to get away from that attitude."

"You just made one excellent answer."

"Well, there's more to a man than muscle, too."

Yukay affected amazement. "There is?"

Ivan smiled. "I can see that we're going to get along."

Now Zosi had a question. "This pervasive illusion covers everything. Why is that straw—now a cane—visible?"

"Why, I'm not sure," Ivan said. "It was invisible until I picked it up."

"I think I have an answer," Yukay said. "The illusion is an overlay on whatever else is here. But it's passive; it doesn't affect new things. That's why we're visible; we came from outside after the illusion had been laid out. So we show up like footprints in new mud. When you found and moved the straw, it became in effect a new thing, and visible. Probably anything we move will become visible too."

"A trail!" Kody said. "We can make a trail! So we'll know where we have been, and will be able to find our way back to this spot."

"Let's try it," Ivan agreed. He scuffed the ground with his feet, and scuff marks appeared. "We're still lost, but maybe less lost than we were."

"That, oddly, sounds encouraging," Yukay said.

They resumed traveling, all of them tapping with the poles. That did save them some nasty collisions and falls. The scuffed trail appeared behind them. With growing confidence they made better progress, and maybe halfway reasonably soon enough, to be precise, they approached the mountain.

It was indeed illusion, as was the river pouring down it. They walked right through both river and mountain. "Bleep!" Yukay swore. "I did so want to get clean. I don't like being a stinker."

"There must be water somewhere," Zosi said.

"Squawk!"

They looked at Zap. On her side was written the word LISTEN.

They paused to listen. In the moderate medium distance was the sound of splashing. Water!

They made their way toward it. They came to the outskirts of a fine illusion palace surrounded by lovely gardens. In one garden was a fountain. The splashing sound was coming from there.

"Could it be a real fountain?" Yukay asked. "Concealed by the fake scenery?"

"Let's find out," Zosi said, forging toward it.

They walked through a surrounding illusion hedge and saw the fountain. It was in the middle of a pool. In the pool was a lovely nude young woman, splashing as she washed herself. She had blue eyes and lustrous blond/brown hair, in addition to remarkably aesthetic limbs and torso. Especially the torso.

Kody and Ivan both stared, Kody on the verge of freaking out. Only the lack of bra or panties saved his eyeballs from crystallizing. "Real or illusion?" Ivan whispered.

"Could be real," Kody said. "Because of the sound."

The woman heard him. She turned and looked. "Eeeeek!" she screamed, and disappeared.

"That was a five-E scream," Yukay said. "That kind is usually genuine."

"But she's gone," Kody said. "That suggests illusion."

"There's a ripple," Zosi said.

"Squawk!" They looked at Zap, who now had the word NAGA on her hide.

"A naga!" Yukay said. "That explains it. She turned into a snake and swam away underwater."

"What is a naga?" Kody asked.

"One of the crossbreeds of Xanth," Yukay said. "Half human, half snake. They can assume either form at will, or something in between. They can be friendly if they choose."

"I hope she's friendly," Ivan said. "She doesn't need any thinning or thickening."

"I'll say!" Kody agreed.

"Too bad I couldn't have glimpsed her before the Curse," Ivan said. "I'd have freaked blissfully out. As it is I can only recognize that she's a stunning beauty, while being sickened by the look of her."

Ah, yes: he saw beauty as ugly.

"You foolish boys stay here," Yukay said severely. "We girls will handle this." She knew that Kody was near freaking out. He was half bemused by the phenomenon. He had never been this way in Mundania.

Yukay, Zosi, and Zap walked to the pool. "Naga!" Yukay called. "We are friendly. Are you?"

A face appeared above the water. "Who are you?"

"We're a party on a Quest. We got lost in the illusion. Then we heard you."

"I'm on my own mission. I'm Naomi Naga."

"I'm Yukay. This is Zosi Zombie. And this is Zap Griffin."

"Zombie?" Her voice was sharp.

"She's alive for the duration of our Quest."

"What is your Quest?"

"Two Quests, actually. One is to locate the source of the Curse and turn it off. The other is to restore more zombies to Xanth, because they are becoming scarce."

"Who would want more zombies? They're almost as bad as rotten puns."

"They have their uses. Rotten puns don't."

"What about your menfolk? I saw them staring at me."

"They are Kody and Ivan. Kody sees things as they are."

"That's why he was staring!"

"That's why," Yukay agreed. "So if you're quite clean now, you had better cover up."

"I'll fetch my clothes." The head moved swiftly across the water. Kody saw now that it was on the body of a big snake. At the far side of the pool the snake slithered out of the water, became the nude woman, and picked up clothing waiting there. Soon Naomi was thoroughly decent, unfortunately.

"Our turn," Yukay said, and jumped into the water, clothing and all. So did Zosi. Zap joined them, spreading her wings and splashing them in the water.

In no more than a moment and a half the girls had doffed their clothing in the water and started rinsing it out. Now it was their bodies that threatened to freak Kody out, especially Yukay's.

Yukay looked across at him. "You can rinse too, Kody," she called. "Remember, we see you as ugly."

"But I see you as lovely," he called back.

"Oh, that's right. Too bad. You can wash, but face away from us."

Kody did that, and soon was rinsing his own clothing in the water, getting the stink off.

There was a ripple before him. Then Naomi's head appeared. "What's this about you seeing girls as lovely?"

"I thought you were dressed on the far bank!" he said, trying ineffectively to cover up.

"I was. But I changed again. Is it true?" She shifted back to woman form and inhaled.

Kody covered his eyes before his eyeballs popped their sockets. "Yes, it's true. Cover up!"

"I changed part way," she said. "You can look."

He looked. Now she was the snake with the human head. The naga form. "Thanks."

"How is it you are immune to the Curse? I thought it affected everyone in Xanth."

"It does. I'm from Mundania. And I'm not really here. I'm dreaming."

Naomi smiled. "Are you calling me a dream woman?"

"Yes, in more than one sense. But what I mean is that when I wake, I'll be gone from here. That may contribute to my immunity."

"That's intriguing." Now arms and breasts appeared below the head, while the rest of the body remained serpentine.

"Stop that!" he snapped.

"Oops; I let the change get sloppy." The snake torso reappeared up to the human head.

Had it really been carelessness? Kody had the distinct impression she was flirting with him. Unfortunately that made her even more appealing. He had never heard of a naga before, but was considerably intrigued. "Naomi, what's on your mind?"

"Good question," Yukay said. She and Zosi had come up behind him in the water.

He started to turn, saw their continued bareness, and turned back. Were they flirting with him too? If so, it was highly effective. All three of them had his full attention, or three-thirds of it.

"I am on my own mission, as I said," Naomi said. "Some miscreant is hunting and butchering naga folk for their hides."

"Their hides?" Yukay asked.

"Nagahide," Naomi agreed. "I have to stop it."

Kody groaned inwardly. There was a horrible pun there.

"I should think so," Yukay said. "But we have no knowledge of this."

"You're not a naga."

"True. Why were you flashing Kody?"

"I didn't believe he could be immune. How else could I check?"

"Fair point," Yukay agreed reluctantly. "Let's all get out of the water and get dressed and stay dressed."

"After your clothing dries?" Naomi asked mischievously.

Yukay paused. Evidently she hadn't thought of that.

"Do you ladies have a problem?"

They turned in the water. There, standing beside Ivan, was a solid, middle-aged man, roughly handsome. "OMG!" Yukay said. "That's King Emeritus Trent!"

"Who?" Kody asked. "I have heard that name before."

"Former king of Xanth, now retired," Yukay said, awed. "Queen Iris's husband."

"I must advise you that you are intruding on a private setting," King Trent said. "This is Illusion Fields."

The women, all of them, seemed to be too abashed to speak further. Maybe that had something to do with them being naked before a royal man. So it seemed it was up to Kody. "Elysian Fields? Paradise for the dead?"

"Illusion Fields," Trent said. "Our variation of that theme. A very pleasant place crafted by my wife."

"Sir, we blundered into it. All we want is to get out of it."

"You don't wish to enter the contest?"

"Princess Melody mentioned a contest but wouldn't tell us about it," Kody said. "We are sorry we got into it."

"Ah. You are the Curse party."

"Yes, sir. It's my Quest to locate and defuse it. We landed here by accident."

"Of course. I will help you on your way."

This was odd. "Sir, you know something of our situation?"

"Only that the princesses were to tell no one of the contest. Not even the Curse Questors. So you were not warned."

"So that was it," Yukay said. "We were not supposed to be distracted by it."

"Or we were supposed to blunder into it and find Ivan and Naomi," Zosi said.

That made both Kody and Yukay pause. So did Ivan and Naomi.

"I wasn't looking for a Quest," Ivan said. "I just wanted to see the mountain."

"Neither was I," Naomi said. "The illusion wasn't much of a danger to me, in my serpent form; I just slithered along. But it was confusing. When I encountered the pool I decided to swim and wash. Then those men peeked at me." Her blue eyes became stormy gray.

"Not by choice," Ivan said. "Your appearance made my stomach roil."

"I can't say the same," Kody said. "I don't think I've ever seen a lovelier woman's body. I couldn't help looking."

"Forgiven, both," Naomi said, the blue returning.

"We don't have to pick up every incidental person we encounter," Yukay said. A person who did not know better might have suspected she was slightly jealous of the luscious naga. "We can see them to the edge of Illusion Fields and they can be on their separate ways."

"Then again, my chances of identifying the naga poachers could be as good with a group as on my own," Naomi said. "I would be willing to contribute my share to your Quest efforts."

Kody kept his mouth shut, letting the girls settle this. He didn't trust himself to make a rational decision while on the verge of freaking out.

"And I have nothing better to do," Ivan said. "I'd love to join a Quest."

Yukay opened her mouth, but before she could organize her protest King Trent spoke. "Then that must have been the reason for the ban on publicity. To allow you to complete your roster for your Quests. Now that that has been accomplished, we shall announce the contest far and wide."

Yukay closed her mouth. What else could she do?

"Sir, this contest," Kody said. "Who is it for, and what is the prize?"

"It's a diversion during the Curse. The winners, one man and one woman, will be king and queen for a month here in Illusion Fields, the landscape and themselves rendered beautiful via additional illusion. They will be served by volunteer participants who will also be rendered beautiful for the duration." Trent's lips quirked. "That is to say, objectively ugly. But everything here will contribute to the appearance of beauty. It should be a marvelous occasion for all concerned, and a great relief from the Curse." He glanced at Kody. "We hope that before it finishes, you will have achieved your mission, and things will have returned to normal.

Folk have been getting rather edgy recently; we hope this alleviates it somewhat."

"We will do our best," Kody said. King Trent impressed him; the man was handsome and competent.

"I'm sure you will. Very well, I will see about providing you with a convenient route out of here. There is a hot pepper bush nearby; your griffin should be able to sniff it out under the illusion. That should help you dry your clothing."

"Thank you, sir," Kody said as Trent turned and walked away, soon disappearing into the illusion. Probably his wife had arranged to cover him.

Zap sniffed, and soon oriented on something on the bank. Kody, Yukay, and Zosi waded out of the pool while Naomi swam back for her clothes.

"Maybe we should, um, ignore bodies for the nonce," Yukay said. "Until we get dry and clothed."

"Agreed," Kody said.

Naked, they clustered around the hot pepper bush. Zap had touched and shaken it, and it was now visible, with a number of red peppers. They radiated intense heat. Ivan felt on the ground for fallen twigs and thickened them into useful frameworks to support clothing so that it could dry in the pepper heat. In a surprisingly brief time everything was dry and they were able to get dressed.

"That's a relief," Ivan murmured. "Much more nudity and I would have vomited."

Kody did not comment. He had studiously ignored Yukay and Zosi, but the reaction he feared was not vomiting. He, too, was relieved to see them clothed.

King Trent returned. "I have consulted with my wife, and she believes that a test run would be in order, to be sure we have the right degree of difficulty. Would you mind remaining here for the day, and departing tomorrow? We can provide you with food and a cabin for the night."

A glance circled around the group and landed on Kody. "We are amenable," he said. "What do we need to do?"

"There are two illusion tokens hidden in the set. One can be found only by a man, the other by a woman. They are small cardboard cutouts of a man and a woman. See if you can find them. If you cannot, we may have to hide them less deviously."

"Squawk?"

Trent smiled, having no difficulty understanding the question. "For this purpose, you will count as a man," he said. "To make two teams of three each." He looked around. "Are you ready?"

"We are ready," Kody said, not needing another circulating glance.

"Then behold."

Suddenly the scene changed. Now they stood in a fantastic garden, and a number of creatures were there. Some were petite dancing nymphs, others were huge lumbering ogres, and still others were dragons.

"All are real in their fashions," Trent explained. "None are dangerous. But they will not help you look."

Kody blinked. Because the nymphs were gnarled and ugly, the ogres handsome, and the dragons mixed. The trees were similarly mixed, ranging from aesthetic to ugly.

"Beautiful," Ivan breathed.

Kody looked where he was looking. It was at a hideous nymph. So the reversal still applied.

Or did it? Why coat the scene with illusion, if they had actors already looking the parts? "I need to check something," he said.

"You have a search strategy?"

"Maybe."

"I know it's illusion," Ivan said. "But I would love a pretext to get my hands on her."

Was it really illusion? There was one way to find out. Kody beckoned to the nymph. She smiled horrendously and came to him. "I am looking for something," he said. "It may be on you."

She shrugged. "I will neither help you nor hinder you."

"I will have to pat you down to search for it."

"Pat me," she agreed.

Kody put his hands on her shoulders, then her arms, then her body, groping her. She tolerated it without protest.

"Wow," Ivan murmured. "I may like this search."

Kody verified several things. One was that the body was solid, but not in the manner the illusion suggested. The nymph was conservatively clothed in reality, while her illusion costume was scanty and highly suggestive. But mainly, under the illusion, she was not malformed; she was a reasonably shapely young woman. Neither beautiful nor ugly, merely in the middle range. Probably a man who was reversed by the Curse, who felt her body, would think she was far better endowed than she was, because of the contribution of the illusion. The illusion was visual, not tactile, but sufficed.

Thus an ordinary girl was rendered by the Curse into an ugly one without changing her form, and by the illusion into an apparently ugly one that the Curse made seem beautiful. One kind of illusion countering another.

"No token on you," Kody said.

"I could have told you that," the nymph replied. "But then you would not have gotten such a good feel."

"It *was* a good feel," Kody agreed. "I apologize for putting you through that." She did not know that he was immune to the Curse, so assumed he had seen her lovely while feeling her. He was not about to correct that impression.

"No need. It was fun." She laughed. "If you want to do it again after the contest, look me up."

"I wouldn't recognize you without the illusion."

"Oh, he caught on," she muttered. "But seriously, I would never do this if I weren't concealed by illusion. It makes me a different creature." She walked away.

It certainly did, Kody reflected. The Curse and the illusion changed her appearance, and the contest allowed her to be uncharacteristically wanton. It was an interesting situation.

"This search has become more interesting," Ivan said.

"Go to it," Kody said.

Zap did not try to pat down people. Instead she checked out trees and objects, verifying what existed under the mask of illusion. Meanwhile the three female members of their party, observing what Kody had done, were groping males and ogres.

But there were hundreds of nymphs, ogres, dragons, and other actors. It would take days rather than hours to search them all.

Time passed without success. None of them found any tokens.

Kody realized that this needed some rethinking. If the tokens were not on the bodies of the actors or on the other objects, where were they? They had to be find-able, and maybe folk with the wit to devise new search strategies had a better chance. It would make sense to set up the contest that way, so that victory did not go to blind luck. Kody himself generally preferred to be thoughtful rather than proceeding blindly.

A bulb flashed over his head. The tokens might be on the bodies, but not where expected.

"Nymph!" Kody called.

She was standing nearby, having faded into the background after he searched her. "You want to grope me again? I am no more likely to yield your token than I was before."

"And no less likely."

She shrugged. "I think you just want more free feels."

"You're a sharp judge of character."

"Is it true that I feel different than I look?"

"Yes. Let me feel your purse." Because all women had purses even if they didn't show. That was so that they did not have to have bulky pockets ruining their contours.

She smiled. "Nothing there you'd want." She handed it over.

She was right. It contained only female things, no tokens.

Kody squatted before her. "Now your shoes."

"You're a foot fetishist!" But she lifted one foot, in the process flashing a good deal of illusion leg. Unfortunately the illusion made it an ugly leg, so the sight that could have freaked out a normal Xanth man merely made him avert his gaze.

She wore dainty slippers that felt exactly like what they looked like. Kody removed the slipper and ran his fingers inside. Nothing there. He put it back on her. "Now the other."

She put down her foot and lifted the other, showing even more leg, right up to the pantyline. That had to be deliberate. That meant there might be a reason. A regular man would have freaked out. Kody might have been seriously distracted, had the illusion not been counterproductive. As it was he had no trouble removing the slipper.

He felt inside it. There was something there. He slid it out. It was a thin cardboard image of a man, a paper doll. The token.

He nodded. Then he put it back in the slipper, and put the slipper back on her foot. "Thank you," he said, standing.

She gazed at him, astonished. "You found it! And you put it back!"

"I'm not a contestant, only testing. Thank you for your cooperation."

"And you didn't even feel me this time."

"You are disappointed?"

"Yes! You never would have gotten down to my shoe if you had let me distract you."

Now he was curious. "How far would you have let me go, while distracting me?"

"As far as you liked. As long as I kept my shoes on."

"You are dedicated."

"It's my job. Neither to help you nor hinder you, but to distract you."

"You did it well." He put his hands on her shoulders, brought her in to him, and kissed her. "Thank you."

"You're no ordinary man," she said as he turned her loose.

"Oh, she caught on," he muttered, smiling.

"Oh, bleep." She walked away.

Kody approached another nymph. "I must check your shoes."

She did not argue. She raised her foot for him, then her other foot, showing him just as much as the first one had.

There in her slipper was another token.

Kody sought Ivan. "You should check their shoes."

Ivan shrugged and asked a nymph to raise her foot. She obliged, providing him with a clear line of sight to her pantyline. He froze, freaked out. She put down her foot and walked away.

Kody snapped his fingers and Ivan came out of it. "What happened?"

"You saw too far up her leg. Sorry about that."

"I'll stick to torsos," Ivan said.

Kody went to Zosi. "Please, will you check a nymph's shoes for me?"

She obliged. The selected nymph lifted her leg, and Zosi saw everything but didn't react. Women were not freaked out by women's panties. She checked both slippers, but there was nothing there. "There was a point to this?" she asked.

"Yes. When I checked, there was a male token. Now we have verified that it exists only for men. We still have to locate the female token."

"We have looked everywhere with no luck."

"Where is the least likely place it would be?"

"In an ogre's mouth," she said, laughing.

"Try that."

"You're serious!"

"Yes. But you have to do it. I don't believe it will work for me."

She approached an ogre. He was about twelve feet tall and broad in proportion. He looked down at her, seeing mainly the gray curl at the top of her head. "Girl, curl," he rumbled appreciatively.

"Get your ugly face down here and open your mouth."

The ogre obliged, dropping to the ground with a thud and prying open the ragged crevasse of his mouth. His breath was like a wind from a garbage dump. But Zosi was a zombie at heart, and had no problem. There was a line of huge teeth. Zosi put both hands in and felt each tooth.

And found a token.

"I'll be knitted and darned," she said.

"Put it back and check another ogre," Kody said.

She did so, and found another token. "How did you know?"

"I pondered and figured it out. My token was in the slipper of a nymph. Any nymph."

"And she lifted her leg to give you her slipper."

"But I don't see such things as the rest of you do. I didn't freak."

"I could get to like you, if you weren't so ugly."

"You're not ugly, and I do like you."

"What, with Yukay and Naomi nearby?"

"I like all of you."

"So you have solved their puzzle. What do we do now?"

"We report to King Trent. What do you think about the difficulty of the puzzle?"

She considered. "There will be hundreds here tomorrow trying to solve it. A few of them may be original thinkers, like you. I think it's about right."

"So do I."

They rounded up the others. "Kody has found the tokens," Zosi announced. "Both of them really. For the man, in the slipper of a nymph, and he has to get past her lifted leg without freaking out to get it. For the woman, she has to peer into an ogre's mouth without retching. Only a few will do that. We think it's fair."

Yukay, Naomi, and Ivan considered. "We agree," Yukay said. "How about you, Zap?"

"Squawk."

"So we're all agreed. We'll tell King Trent when we see him."

Kody raised his voice. "King Trent, sir."

In a generous moment Trent appeared. "Yes?"

"We have solved the puzzle and believe it is fair. Most men won't think of nymph's slippers, and few of those who do will have the wit to avoid freaking out. Most women won't think of ogre's mouths, and fewer yet will go near them. But some will. The first of those will be your winners."

"Thank you," Trent said. "This way to your quarters for the night."

He ushered them to a nice cabin, big enough for six. "It is stocked; you should have no trouble."

They entered. Indeed, it was a very fancy cabin with five beds and a mound of straw for Zap. The central table was piled with delicious-looking food that was not illusion. It was evident that royalty knew how to provide for guests.

The three princesses appeared. "We're sorry we couldn't tell you about the contest," Melody said.

"But at least now you know why," Harmony added.

"We're glad you figured it out and got your group complete," Rhythm concluded.

"We understand," Kody said. "Thank you."

"Welcome," the three said together, and vanished.

"Let's eat," Yukay said. "Then take turns with the shower, ignoring bodies, as before." She glanced around. "Anyone have a problem with that?"

Kody might have, but decided not to make an issue. There had been problems enough to fill the day, and he just wanted to eat, clean up, and sleep.

# 7
# HADES

The way out was simple, once arranged: a white line originating where they stood showed a winding route, guaranteed safe, to the edge of Illusion Fields. It vanished behind them, being one-way. Soon they were back in Xanth-normal.

"Now we are out," Yukay said. "Anyone is free to go her own way."

Naomi eyed her with a cutting-edged glance. "And what do you mean by that?"

Yukay shrugged. "I was just making an observation."

"So anyone is free to go, or to remain with this Quest?"

"Yes, of course."

"Even if on occasion she accidentally flashes someone?" Naomi's blouse dropped down as her upper body became serpentine, but did not rise again as she restored her human form. Ivan turned away, repulsed. Kody turned away, fascinated.

"Even then," Yukay agreed tightly.

"Then I have nowhere else to go until I locate the nagahide poacher."

"And I have nowhere to go regardless," Ivan said.

"Then it seems we travel as a group," Yukay said, resigned. "Now we have to decide where to go."

Kody brought out the chessboard. "Anywhere far from here."

Naomi and Ivan soon learned to see the pictures. "Those places look pretty wild," Ivan said. "Except this one." He pointed at a mini-scene of a path leading to an elaborate castle.

"Don't touch it!" Yukay snapped.

"Why not?"

"It will take you there, alone, maybe with the chessboard along. Then the rest of us will be spiraled."

"Will be what?" Ivan asked.

"That's my cue!" The demoness Metria appeared. "Rotated, turned, spun, revolved, ratcheted, tightened—"

"Screwed?"

"Whatever," Metria agreed crossly. "What's going on here?"

"I was attempting to avoid a vulgar term," Yukay said.

"That's dull." The demoness faded out.

"It seems she is interested only in interesting things," Kody said.

"I won't touch the board," Ivan agreed. "But if we go anywhere, that looks nicer than the others."

Kody had to agree. "We don't want to get caught in a stink hole again."

"Why do we need to travel?" Ivan asked.

"We are trying to locate the source of the Curse," Kody explained. "I see things as they are; the rest of you see them reversed, or at least react to them that way. We believe the effect will be strongest near the source. So we need to orient on stronger effects."

"Ah, now I get it. So when Naomi flashes us with her bare bosom, you really are liking it."

That was an issue worth avoiding. "I see her as she is, yes."

"Well, I can't wait to turn off the Curse. I don't like being sickened when I know I should be freaking."

"None of us do," Yukay said. "Objectively I know you are both handsome men, but the sight of you repulses me."

"Which really complicates social interactions," Zosi said. "We all repel each other, except for Kody."

"So if we want to impress him," Naomi said, "all we need to do is choke down our revulsion and pretend to be turned on by him."

Still worth avoiding. "Let's try that castle," Kody said.

They gathered into a reasonably tight ball, and Zap pecked at the picture.

They stood on the path leading to the castle. But now that they were in the scene, they saw a good deal more than the picture had shown. The castle was more distant than it had appeared, and the path was narrower. It was also surrounded by weird scenery. Great gnarled trees seemed to be reaching for the path without quite touching it, and hungry-looking weeds jammed up against its edges.

"Where the hell are we?" Kody asked.

"You are close," Yukay said. "This looks very much like Hades."

"The abode of the dead?"

"Yes. The souls of people who die come here, where they are I think reeducated. They aren't allowed to depart for choicer realms until they are worthy of it, and some are very slow reformers. It is not a very nice place."

"Oh?" Ivan said. "That creature looks nice enough."

They looked. There was a lovely nymph in quite scanty apparel, beckoning enticingly. She did a slow dance with her hips, swirled her long dark hair around, and kicked up one nice bare leg. She smiled invitingly.

"Don't fall for it," Yukay said. "We must be on an enchanted path where the spirits can't reach us, so they will try to tempt us off it. But the moment any of us leaves the path, the protection is gone. I understand it's a lot easier to get into Hades than it is to get out of it."

"There is something else," Kody said. "That nymph looks luscious to me. She does to you too?"

"You bet," Ivan said.

"She looks lovely to me too," Naomi said.

"The mood reverse is not working here!" Yukay said.

They were all surprised. Then Zap figured it out. "Squawk!" On her side was printed OUTSIDE XANTH.

"That must be it," Yukay agreed. "Hades is its own domain. The Curse applies only to regular Xanth."

"So if we want to be free of it," Zosi said, "all we have to do is go to Hades."

They all laughed, including Zap's squawk. Then another glance circulated.

"No," Yukay finally said. "Only the dead go to Hades to stay. We don't want to die."

"We don't," Ivan agreed. "It is too high a price to pay to escape the Curse."

A handsome man appeared, opening his arms to the ladies. "Oh, my," Yukay breathed. "He *is* enticing."

And a male griffin, addressing himself to Zap. "Squawk," she said appreciatively.

Yukay bought herself up short, visibly. "Remember, crossing the line may be death. We do not want to do it. We need to get out of here before any of us forget that."

The others agreed, shuddering.

The dusky nymph before Ivan turned to face away from him. Was she going?

Then she caught the hem of her short skirt and lifted it.

"Cover your eyes!" Kody said, averting his own eyes.

Too late. Ivan had freaked as the nymph's panties showed.

Yukay went to him and put her hands over his eyes. Zosi snapped her fingers.

Ivan woke. "I must go to her," he said huskily.

"You'll do no such thing," Yukay said. "She's not worth dying for." She addressed the others. "As I said, we need to get out of here in a hurry."

Kody brought out the chessboard and focused. But something was wrong. "I can't see the pictures. Only the chess pieces."

"Take it over here, Zosi," Yukay said. Zosi went to hold her hands before Ivan's eyes so he could not see the infernal nymph, and Yukay came to look at the board. "Bleep!" she swore. "Hades has an interference pattern. We can't use it to get out. We'll have to follow the path."

"But first, let's check the divergence," Zosi said. "Oh, wait—we can't."

"We can't?" Yukay asked.

"Because now we're aligned."

"She's right," Kody said. "The rest of you are seeing things as I do. No divergence."

"Then it is *really* time to get out of here," Yukay said. "Before Hades pulls another fast one."

"Which way?" Kody asked.

"Away from the castle, I think," Yukay said. "The path must lead from outside Hades."

They followed it, keeping their eyes off the beckoning distractions on either side. Soon they came to a dark river. The path led up to it and stopped.

"Oh, bleep!" Yukay swore again. "The River Styx. We can't wade or swim across; there's Lethe water in it that will make us forget everything."

"Isn't there a ferry to cross the river?" Kody asked.

"Yes. But do you think the Ferryman will convey us *out*? I understand the Ferryman makes demands, especially of the ladies."

Kody sighed. "Then we'll have to try the castle."

"Maybe that's not so bad," Yukay said. "I just remembered: Princess Eve married the Demon Pluto and has a castle in Hades that caters to the living. She should help us."

"Chances are that's the castle we saw," Naomi said. "We have only to reverse our course."

"I hope it's that easy," Ivan said. "I have a bad feeling about this place."

"Squawk," Zap agreed.

They reversed course and walked along the path toward the

castle. They had less trouble now, as they were more proficient in not looking at the distractions.

Then the path divided into three. They were labeled Primrose, Good Intentions, and Eightfold. "Uh-oh," Ivan said. "I don't believe this split was here before."

"Squawk."

"I fear Hades is proactive," Yukay said. "If the temptations don't lure us astray, it tries something else."

"So which one goes to the castle?" Naomi asked. "And just where do the other two go?"

"I've done puzzles in Mundania," Kody said. "This isn't quite the same, but I suspect that whichever path we take will be the wrong one, and that finding our way back to the fork will not be easy. It puts me in mind of the shyster who puts a pea under one of three cups. I fear it will be a mistake to take any of these paths alone."

"I am not following you," Yukay said. "Your logic, I mean."

"Good thing you made that qualification," Naomi said. "You have been eying him all along, especially now that you can see him unreversed."

"And you haven't?"

"Uh, girls, maybe you should cool it," Ivan said. "It isn't as if you couldn't get the attention of another man if you tried."

The girls shared a significant glance. "The one who doesn't nab number one nabs number two?" Naomi asked.

"Why not?" Yukay answered.

They shook hands.

"Well, now we know where we stand," Ivan said to Kody. "Incidental prizes."

"So do you have a way to handle it?" Zosi asked. "The split, I mean."

Kody was glad for the reversion to the original problem. He was on the one hand flattered by the attention of the two pretty women, but also wary of it. "I think we should try all three paths simultaneously. That way Hades can't play hide-the-pea with us, to our detriment. One of the paths has to be it."

"We can form three teams," Yukay said. "But what happens to the two teams that go wrong?"

"When they realize they are wrong, they retreat to the fork, meet each other there, and take the right path, now knowing which one it is. The team on the right path remains in place, anchoring it, until rejoined by the others. Then we all proceed to the castle together."

The girls nodded. "That works for me," Naomi said.

"Then do me the honor of being my teammate," Yukay said.

"Gladly." They moved together to the one on the left, the Primrose Path.

"They have neatly fixed it so that neither gets to go with you," Ivan murmured. "No unfair advantage. An easy but temporary fix."

Which meant Kody would have to go with Ivan, Zap, or Zosi.

"Squawk," Zap said to Ivan.

"Okay," Ivan agreed, amused. They moved to the center path, Good Intentions. Kody saw that it was paved, with every block bearing its name.

"It seems we are the leftovers," Kody said to Zosi.

"I am sorry about that," she said.

"Don't be. I was trying to be humorous." They took the right-side path, Eightfold.

The three teams moved out, and soon lost sight of each other, as capering demons filled the spaces between paths.

This path, too, was paved. RIGHT VIEWS, RIGHT ASPIRATIONS, RIGHT SPEECH. "This is weird," Zosi said.

"I am not familiar with Oriental Mundane philosophy," Kody said. "But I believe the Eightfold Path is fundamental as advice on how to live a good life."

"Maybe I have not been alive enough to appreciate it properly."

They continued to read the blocks as they went. RIGHT CONDUCT, RIGHT LIVELIHOOD, RIGHT EFFORT. "Maybe it requires some study," he said.

RIGHT MINDFULNESS, RIGHT CONTEMPLATION. "Still, there's a certain appeal," she said. "I will try to do better."

"Better than what?"

"To be a better person. While I'm alive. I know I have not been doing very well."

"You have been doing well enough."

"I don't think so. The living folk don't make a big thing of it, but they don't want my company."

Tacit exclusion? Kody had encountered that himself in Mundania. "Why?"

"Because I am a zombie. I am alive now, but that's my background. That makes normal folk uncomfortable. It didn't bother me until I returned to life."

"Well, I'm not excluding you. I think you're a fine girl."

"Thank you," she said, seeming a bit uncertain.

"I mean, I know your origin. I wouldn't really care for you as a zombie. But for now you're a normal living girl, and your background doesn't bother me at all."

"And you're a normal man."

"I'm a Mundane who is dreaming."

"You are real to me."

She remained uncertain of her acceptance. Normal men were wary of her. He needed to prove he wasn't. "Zosi, you kissed me once. Now it's my turn." He put his arms around her, brought her close, and kissed her firmly on the mouth. She was surprisingly warm and accommodating. He had done it as a demonstration, but it felt like more.

"Thank you," she said. "I think I needed that."

Kody turned to resume walking, and saw a pair of sea creatures swimming toward them. They came up to the edge of the path, turned about, and used their flippers to draw up twin skirts Kody hadn't realized they were wearing. Then he found himself sitting on the path, and the creatures were gone.

"What happened?" he asked dazedly.

"You were panty-flashed by two man-a-tease that caught you off guard," Zosi said. "You freaked. I had to cover your eyes."

"And stop me from falling across the line," Kody said. "You saved me."

Her laugh was slightly strained. "Well, I had to, after you kissed me."

"Nevertheless, I am grateful."

They continued along the path. It led directly to the castle, which was a massive, forbidding structure atop a bleakly bare mountain. It had either a monstrous moat, or was somehow rising from a dreary lake despite its elevation. Fortunately the path had a thin causeway across the water to the main gate.

"We have found the right path," he said. "We'll wait for the others to join us."

"Yes."

There was a silence. "Are you being doubtful again?" he asked her.

"Not exactly."

"What does that mean?"

She closed her eyes and spoke as if forcing it out with great effort. "It means I'm getting a crush on you. I don't know how to handle it. Zombies don't have sieges of emotion."

"Oh, my."

"I shouldn't have told you," she said, alarmed. "Now you'll be wary of me too."

He took her hand. "It's not that, Zosi. I like you, and think you are a worthy person. But the moment my Quest is done, I will wake, and be gone from Xanth. You don't want to waste your emotion on a dreamer."

"And I'll be a full zombie again, and not care."

"We have no future together, regardless."

"No future," she agreed wistfully.

Kody discovered that he could not hurt her, even by being realistic. "But bleep it, as the saying goes here, we do have a present, however temporary it may be. We can make something of it."

She gazed at him longingly. "But Yukay and Naomi want you too. You don't want them mad at you."

"I don't," he agreed. "So I guess our present is right now, this minute, and not hereafter. Come here."

"Secret love?"

"I guess so, sneaky as that sounds."

"It will do." She came to him, and they embraced and kissed. Kody felt more than a little appreciation of her. She really was a nice girl, and they had a basis for understanding. And her kisses were remarkably sweet.

But then they had to separate, lest they be discovered. They forced the subject to innocuous things, and waited for the others.

In due course the others arrived. "Our path led to a dreadful gulf," Yukay reported. "Had we not been careful, we could have fallen in and been lost." The two women barely glanced at Zosi, and Kody, now sensitized, saw the truth of her concern. They hardly regarded her as a person, let alone competition.

"Ours led to a marvelous park where everyone wanted to help us," Ivan said. "They had the best intentions, but we would have had to step across the line to join them. Zap warned me back more than once."

"Squawk," the griffin agreed.

"So we outmaneuvered the devious path," Kody said. "Now we can tackle the castle."

They mounted the path to the formidable front gate. There was an armed guard. "Begone, intruders," he demanded.

"We would like to see Princess Eve," Yukay said.

"Wouldn't we all," the guard said derisively. "Now go away before I run you through and hurl you into the lake."

Kody considered the guard. He looked brutally competent. He probably could and would do as he threatened. This was, after all, Hades.

"Now I remember something else," Yukay said. "Only music fazes the minions of Hades. Anyone here a musician?"

"I'm not," Ivan said. "But maybe I can make a one-string guitar."

He fished in a pocket and found a loose thread. He focused on it and it became thicker, until it resembled a guitar string. Then he found a curved branch on the path and strung the string across it.

It did not look like much of anything, let alone a musical instrument.

"Anybody here know how to play a guitar?" Ivan inquired, holding it forth.

Yukay stepped up and took it. She put her left hand up where the string lay close to the wood, and pressed on it to adjust the tone. Her right hand plucked the string.

Loud, lovely music burst forth. "Stop!" the guard cried, putting his hands to his ears. "I can't stand it!"

"Then get the bleep out of our way," Naomi said. "We're coming in."

Just like that they were inside the castle.

Yukay handed the guitar back to Ivan. "Thank you."

"I had no idea you could play like that," he said.

"I can't. It's a one-shot thing."

"I don't understand."

"My talent is to do anything effortlessly as long as I never tried it before and don't think about it."

He shook his head. "It's some talent."

"Thank you. But I can't rely on it. I need to find a better way to manage my life, because I can't depend on my talent to lead me to fame and fortune."

"Well, hello!"

They looked. It was a dark and lovely princess. Kody could tell by her crown, and the fact that she looked just like Princess Dawn, apart from the hair and eyes. "Princess Eve, we presume," he said.

"Indeed. Who are you folk, and what brings you here to Hades?"

They hastily introduced themselves. "We were looking for a distant place to compare notes, for our Quest, and did not realize it was Hades," Kody said. "Then we had difficulty getting out of it, so hope you will help us."

"I will," Eve agreed. "But first I want to learn all about your Quest."

Soon they were seated in a very nice family room quite unlike the bleakness outside the castle, sampling refreshments. "So now Zosi is seeking a way to restore the zombie population of Xanth, and I am trying to zero in on the location of the source of the Curse. I realize that does not affect you here in Hades, but in Xanth proper it's quite a nuisance."

"Very little affects me here in Hades," Eve said. "My husband treats me well, and I have a fine son. But I must confess that I miss the excitement of Xanth life, even if it does mean watching out for dragons."

"But you have such a wonderful castle here," Yukay said.

"And one in Xanth," Eve agreed. "But I envy my sister Dawn."

"Envy her?" Yukay said. "But you're the Mistress of Hades."

"True. I married a Dwarf Demon for status, and got it. Dawn married a walking skeleton for love. She got the better deal."

"Surely you can visit her when you choose."

"Surely I can, and do. It only reminds me of the difference in our situations. Gone are the days when we were innocent girls teasing stray men." She smiled reminiscently. "She would flash her top, and I my bottom. Sometimes we reversed it. That really confused them." The upper section of her royal gown turned momentarily translucent, showing the shrouded outline of her breasts. Then the lower section, showing the outline of dark panties. Neither Ivan nor Kody quite freaked out, but both got a fair jolt. "But of course I don't do that anymore."

"Of course," Kody agreed faintly, knowing that she had deliberately pulled her punches.

"I must show off my son Plato," Eve continued. "He is three years old now, and his magic talent is manifesting. That's a problem."

"A problem?" Yukay asked.

"His talent is reanimating the dead. He constantly seeks dead things to bring back to life, but he is too young to do it right, and they can be pretty messy."

Kody got an idea, but held it back for the moment. "Yes, we must meet Plato."

Eve snapped her fingers, making a little spark. Soon a dusky demon maid brought a little boy. He had dark hair, like his mother, and a piercing gaze. "Say hello to our guests, Plato," Eve said.

"Aw, do I have to?"

Now it was her eyes that emitted the sparks. "Yes."

The child quickly fell in line. "Hello, Guests. Got any dead things?"

"Not at the moment," Kody said. "But maybe we can find some."

"Not in the house!" Eve said.

Kody realized there was a problem. Eve was in certain respects a normal housewife; she did not want stinking things in the house. Especially not-living ones. But the boy would need to practice properly to develop his talent.

Kody followed up on his idea. He realized that their seemingly coincidental arrival in Hades was nothing of the sort. They had solid reason to be here. "Plato, what do you animate?" he asked.

"Bugs," the boy replied. "Once a dead mouse I found."

"It was awful," Eve said. "The thing was old and rotten. When it started running around the kitchen floor I swept it up and dumped it in the garbage."

"It was a zombie mouse," Kody said.

"Yes. Sickening."

Zosi sat up straight. She opened her mouth.

"Could you take him outside, where animated dead mice would do no harm?" Kody asked Eve, preempting anything Zosi might say.

"Outside the castle is Hades. Everything is dead and active. Nothing for him to animate."

"I understand you have a castle in Xanth. You could have a maidservant take him outside."

"The last one freaked out so badly she refused to work there anymore. The same with the manservants." Eve smiled ruefully. "They say it's not the same as panty-freaks."

"Not at all the same," Ivan agreed.

Kody followed up on his notion. "But if you found a person in Xanth who did not freak at the notion, she could take Plato out for invaluable practice developing his talent."

"Oh, my, yes!" Eve agreed. "But who is there?"

"A zombie might do it."

"Absolutely not! I will not have a zombie tracking rot into my house. Anyway, Xanth is getting dangerously short of zombies. They would not be able to spare any."

"In the rush of introductions you may have missed something," Kody said. "Zosi is a zombie."

"No, she's a living woman. I can tell, because she's immune to my talent."

"She is a zombie, reanimated so she can try to solve the problem of diminishing zombies. Princess Eve, I believe your son could be the next Zombie Master."

Eve paused, assembling this in her mind. "Oh, my! I believe you are right. I think I didn't want to see it before. I mean, zombies?"

"It is surely a worthy talent," Kody said. "And severely needed in Xanth now. There will be an honored place for Plato, as there was for the former Zombie Master. All he needs is to grow up and perfect his talent. Zosi could even take him to visit Castle Zombie, where they would surely welcome him."

"You are right again, of course," Eve agreed. She looked at Zosi. "You would be willing to do this?"

Zosi's mouth worked unsuccessfully on several words before she got some that functioned. "I—I will return to being a full zombie when my Quest is done. The thought of remaining alive for an extended period appalls me."

"We could arrange for a very good life for you," Eve said persuasively. "As the nanny, no the governess, of a Demon prince you would have phenomenal authority and respect. No one would question you, and you would be welcome at any royal castle."

"I know," Zosi said. "But continued life would be torture for me. I just—just can't—"

"How about a trial run?" Kody said. "You could take the boy out in Xanth for a few hours, and we'll go with you. See how you feel about it then."

Zosi shook her head. "I don't think—"

"That such a trial will hurt," Yukay concluded for her. Yukay was smart enough to catch on to the issues at play. Zosi needed to be persuaded.

"Oh, that would be so nice!" Eve said. "I have an important social presentation this afternoon I must attend. It would be ideal if you took Plato today."

"Yes," Zosi said, looking woeful. It was obvious that she feared getting committed to something she did not want to commit to. Kody understood perfectly, but had to try to forge a compromise.

"I didn't mean for you to trust your son to us right now," Kody said. "You hardly know any of us."

Eve looked at him. "You're not from Xanth."

"No, I'm a dreamer from Mundania."

"Folk can generally be trusted in Xanth. I know it's different in Mundania."

"Yes," Kody agreed, privately amazed.

"Besides which, I heard from my sister Dawn during an interstice. She says you're all right."

Kody spread his hands. Dawn did know.

It was not long before they were back on the path, this time with a pass for the ferry across the river. Plato ran gleefully ahead, yelling "Booo!" at the apparitions. When he teased a horrific monster with a single finger, Zosi stepped in, cautioning him about manners. He frowned, but obeyed.

There were no splits in the path. Soon they reached the river. "Hey, Funnyman!" Plato called. "Get your fat barge over here!"

Zosi intervened, horrified. "You mean Ferryman. And it's not a barge, it's a raft."

"Yeah, sure," the boy agreed reluctantly.

The raft hove into view, poled by the dread Ferryman, the Dwarf

Demon Charon. They let Zosi handle it, as she was the one who would be doing this in future, if she decided to.

"Sir, we need to cross to Xanth," Zosi said politely. "The boy and I."

Charon eyed her with open lechery. "And what payment do you proffer, intriguing maiden?"

"I'm a zombie."

He looked at her more closely. "Why so you are, at least in spirit. I will have to double my price."

"What is your price?"

"One solid day and night passionate naked stork summoning."

"One clothed feel," she bargained.

"One day storking."

"One feel and one kiss."

"Done." He had evidently concluded that she was not going to yield more.

Zosi stepped up to the raft. She had plainly gained the terms she had aimed for. Charon embraced her and kissed her, also squeezing her bottom through her skirt.

"Yuck!" Plato said loudly.

"Stuff it, brat," Charon said.

"I'll stuff it up your—"

"Plato!" Zosi said.

"Nose," the boy finished under his breath. It was clear that he was willful but not stupid.

"Now we'll all cross," Zosi said.

"Nuh-uh. You bought passage only for you and the brat. They'll have to make their own payments."

"They have a pass."

"What pass?"

Kody showed the pass.

"Oh, bleep!" the Ferryman muttered.

They boarded the raft, and Charon started poling it across. "That pass covered the whole party, including you," Kody said to Zosi. "Why didn't you mention it before?"

"I've never been kissed by a Demon. Or felt. Zombies seldom get that kind of attention. I was curious."

"You minx! How was it?"

"I've had better." Half a smile hovered at the fringe of her mouth. "Not long ago."

She was learning, or remembering, how to be a girl. But would that mean she would decide to remain alive to mentor Plato?

They reached the other side of the river. "We shall be returning," Zosi told Charon.

"That pass is good for only one crossing," he said, eying Naomi.

"It's a season pass," Kody said.

"I don't honor those."

"I'll tell Mom," Plato said. "She'll tell Dad."

"But it will do for this time," Charon agreed.

"I'm hungry," Plato announced.

"Would you like a peanut butter and jelly sandwich?" Zosi asked.

"No! I want tsoda pop."

Zosi conjured a sandwich. "Try it."

"No!"

"Try it, or I'll kiss you. You know I can do it, because I just kissed Charon."

The boy opened his mouth angrily. The woman pursed her lips.

After a tense pause, Plato backed down. He took the sandwich and bit into it. "Hey! It tastes a little rotten. I like it."

They were getting along.

The path continued, leading away from the river. Soon it emerged from the gloom. There was Xanth in all its colors, complete, as it turned out, with a nest of puns.

Plato picked up a bell and shook it, but no sound came out. "Dumb bell," he said, dropping it.

"That is the point," Yukay said. "It doesn't make a sound when rung."

"I wonder where we are?" Ivan said, looking around.

"You are emerging from the path to Hades," a small snake in

the grass said. "It doesn't matter where in Xanth it is, because folk can go to Hades from anywhere."

"A talking snake!" Ivan said.

"Well, duh, you ignorant man," the snake said. "I'm not just any snake. I'm an asp. A smart asp."

A roil of smoke formed. "A smart what?"

"Cobra, viper, poison, serpent, reptile—" the snake said.

"Donkey?"

"Whatever," the asp said crossly.

"You silly asp!"

"Not half as silly as a demoness with a speech impediment," the snake said smugly.

"Metria, you got it backwards again," Kody said, smiling.

The demoness formed, wearing two long straps and nothing else. "It's a time of reversals."

"Cover up!" Yukay snapped. "There's a child present." Fortunately Zosi had already covered the little boy's eyes with her hands.

"Ooops! I'm wearing my gownless evening straps. Must've grabbed the wrong hanger." The straps fuzzed, and formed into a strapless evening gown.

"Aw, it's only a demoness," Plato complained as Zosi released his gaze.

Metria fuzzed again. In her place stood a cute little girl. "Woe Betide at your service," she said.

"A girl," Plato said witheringly.

"I know where there's dead things," Woe said.

Suddenly she had the boy's attention. "Where?"

"Here." She pointed to the ground between them. There lay a bloated dead frog.

"Great!" Plato picked up the frog, held it half a moment, then set it down. It gave a resonant croak and hopped clumsily away. It had become a zombie frog.

The adults exchanged glances. For once the demoness was helping.

"Regular practice like this, and he'll soon be competent," Yukay said.

"But it was a clumsy frog," Naomi said. "He'll need time to get it right."

"And a frog is far from a human being," Ivan said.

"And Xanth needs responsible zombies, not flesh-eating monsters," Kody said. "It will take years."

"Squawk," Zap agreed.

They looked at Zosi. "I just don't know," she said. "I just don't think I could stand staying alive that long."

"You can postpone your decision," Kody suggested. "You have shown that it is feasible, because the boy minds you. But that doesn't mean that you have to do it. Continue traveling with us while you think about it."

"Yes," she breathed gratefully.

"I think we're done here," Metria said, reappearing. "Woe Betide can have a play date another time. Now I must begone." She produced a pair of mirrors and spun them around. Smoke issued from them, forming a cloud around her. When it dissipated, she was gone.

"Squawk."

They looked at Zap. On her side were printed the words SMOKE & MIRRORS. It was another pun.

Zosi fetched Plato, who was playing with a small collection of zombie animals. "Time to go home," she said.

"Awww." But he looked tired, and was ready to go. He probably needed a nap, after the effort of animating the corpses. "Can I do it again tomorrow?"

"I'm not sure about tomorrow," Zosi said. "But sometime."

"Okay. Pick me up."

Zosi picked him up.

"Oh, almost forgot," Kody said. "How do things look to you folk?"

"You're not as ugly as usual," Yukay said.

"Neither are you," Kody said. The others agreed. "That means we are farther from the source of the Curse. We'll have to try another direction, after we return Plato."

The boy had already fallen asleep in Zosi's arms. "I must confess he's cute," she said. "And it is a nice talent."

"Does that mean—?" Yukay asked.

"No."

But maybe she was mellowing.

They started the trek back to Hades. They would have much to report to Princess Eve.

# 8
# DRAGON

Next morning, having had a good night as Princess Eve's guests, they navigated the path, Naomi gave Charon a K&F (kiss and feel) for passage across the river, and emerged in Xanth. Zosi was silent, feeling guilty for not agreeing to stay alive to be Plato's governess, but she had promised to think seriously about it. Kody suspected that what she lacked was some positive personal reason to counteract the chore of continued life, but he didn't know what such a reason could be.

Once they were clear of Hades, the chessboard worked again. They pondered the sixty-four little pictures, hoping to avoid the kind of mischief they had encountered before.

Yukay recognized one picture. "That's the Ever and Ever Glades," she said.

"The Everglades?" Kody asked.

"In Xanth they go on forever and ever, if you get lost in them," she explained. "Careless travelers can have a problem."

"We should not have a problem, as long as the board works, because we'll simply jump to our next site."

"It should work, since they are in Xanth proper."

They clustered together, and Zap pecked the picture.

Now they were on a broad, level plainlike swamp interspersed with islands of palm trees. Sure enough, it seemed to go on forever, whatever way they looked. It was hot; the sun beat down without interruption.

"In Mundania, the Everglades turned out to be a broad river," Kody said, remembering. "About two hundred miles wide and six inches deep, on average. Then they channelized one of the contributing rivers, and started to dry it up."

"The Demon Corps of Engineers did that here," Yukay said. "They took hold of the S's in the Kiss Mee River and pulled them straight, into L's, so that it became the Kill Mee River. It stopped being friendly and became hateful. Nobody could stand it, and finally they had to put the curves back in. Now it is good for honeymooners again."

"In Mundania that's Kissimmee," Kody said.

"Mundania does tend to be sloppy," she agreed.

"Now let's check our difference," he said. "You remain plain, not as bad as before."

"Same to you," she said. "So we are evidently farther away from the Bomb. That's progress, of a sort."

"Yes. If it's not to the south, it must be to the north."

"You folk can handle this without me," Zosi said. "I don't need to be here."

She was really feeling down. "I'll talk to her," Kody said.

"You do that while we stretch," Naomi said. She stretched, in the process showing off the fine points of her torso. Naturally Yukay then had to stretch too, and her points were just as fine.

But the display made Ivan turn away, repulsed. "Why couldn't you girls have done that while we were still in Hades?" he asked.

"Because you would have freaked out, ruining the effect," Naomi said.

"Let's go explore while we wait," Ivan said to Zap.

"Squawk," the griffin agreed, amused. She was neither freaked nor repulsed by human torsos, however pretty or ugly they might be.

Kody took Zosi by the hand and led her to a neighboring copse of palms. The palms, of course, were giant hands projecting from the ground, their fingers pointing to the sky. They sat down behind one, shielded from the gaze of the others. There was a little sign saying NO SMOKING. Kody smiled briefly, seeing it, then focused on his companion.

"Zosi, you have a right to make your own decision, whatever it is," he said. "You should not feel any guilt in that. I know I would hate to become a zombie, and I suspect that is the inverse of your feeling."

"I'm not used to guilt. I don't know how to handle it."

"Just abolish it. It is undeserved."

"I can't."

He took hold of her shoulders. "Zosi—"

She leaned forward and kissed him. Surprised, he took a moment to react. Then he kissed her back, emphatically.

"It's not just guilt," she said. "It's that if I live, I will have to live without you. I know you will be gone soon."

"Zosi, I can't stay in Xanth! I'm not even really here."

"I know." Tears streaked down her face.

Suddenly he was coming to know about guilt. He was a significant part of her unhappiness. She did not deserve it. "I'm sorry."

"Don't be," she said. "It's not your fault. It's my foolish inability to control my emotions, after not having any for so long."

"That inability is not limited to you. I—I have never felt about a girl the way I am coming to feel about you. If everything else were equal . . ." He trailed off, unable to formulate what he was feeling.

"What about Naomi and Yukay? They're prettier than I am."

"Yes, and they know it. I guess I prefer a girl I can believe in."

She gazed at him, her gray hair somehow making her look young and vulnerable. "What would you do right now, if you could do anything you wanted?"

"This." He kissed her again.

"Are you getting a crush on me?" she asked, amazed.

"I believe I am, foolish as it may be."

She smiled. "Then maybe there is hope."

"Zosi, any long-term relationship we might have is doomed. We both knew that from the outset."

"Yes. There is only the present. What else would you do now, if—"

He kissed her with burgeoning passion. In three-quarters of a moment they were lying on the ground, embraced, and his hands were hungrily exploring her body as the kiss continued. She matched him move for move, opening her blouse, drawing down her skirt.

There was a shriek.

They paused, mutually disheveled.

Then they saw the huge shape ascending into the sky, trailing streamers of smoke. It wasn't Zap. It was a dragon, carrying something.

There was another shriek. That something was Naomi!

They ran back toward their original site, tucking things in as they went. Yukay was there, in a dissipating cloud of smoke, also screaming. "The dragon! We didn't see it! It just swooped down, choked us in smoke, and grabbed Naomi!"

"I should have been more alert," Kody said.

"I shouldn't have distracted you," Zosi said.

"I should have grabbed her," Yukay said. "So we would be too heavy together for it to carry off."

Ivan and Zap came running back. "We should have been here!" he cried.

"Squawk!"

Guilt galore!

After another frenzied, useless moment, Kody hauled in his wits. "Maybe it's not too late to save her. How can we do it?"

"If we can find the dragon's nest, maybe we can attack," Ivan said. "Before the dragon—"

"Eats her," Yukay said succinctly.

"She's a naga," Zosi said. "Couldn't she change and get away?"

"Not while in the air; she would drop to her death. Not in the dragon's nest; that will be inaccessible and inescapable, regardless of her form."

Kody spoke to Zap. "Can you locate the dragon's nest?"

"Squawk!" Zap spread her wings and bounded into the air. Soon she was flying on the trail of the dragon, evidently sniffing its wake of smoke.

"Assuming she locates the nest," Kody said, "what can we do then?"

"Against a dragon that size? Feed it." Yukay grimaced. "With our bodies."

"Feed it," Kody repeated. "Zosi, how big can you make a sandwich?"

"Jumbo is my limit. I could conjure a number of them. But the dragon wouldn't eat them. Dragons eat live meat."

"But if we threw them into its mouth, down its throat, it might choke on them."

"It would take a hundred sandwiches all at once to make it choke," Yukay said. "Momentarily. Then it would blow them out on a wave of smoke."

"Suppose I put a chip of reverse wood in one?"

Yukay paused, considering. "Depends on the manner the sandwich reversed."

"Oops. I was thinking of it reversing the dragon somehow. But you're right; it would reverse the sandwich first."

"Still, Zap might deliver such a sandwich."

"Test one," Ivan suggested.

Zosi conjured a sandwich and set it down on the ground. Kody conjured a chip. He flipped the chip onto the sandwich. It bounced off, struck the ground, and splintered into dust.

Nothing happened to the sandwich.

"Squawk, as Zap would say," Ivan said.

Yukay looked at him. "You say it changed? You can smell it?"

"Yes. It's different."

Now Kody smelled it too. "Gasoline!" he said. He picked up the sandwich, carefully, and pulled it open. "Jellied gasoline! I had forgotten about that. Zosi can make them directly."

"What is that?" Ivan asked.

"An extremely dangerous and ugly weapon, in Mundania. They put it in bombs, and when they detonate they spray gasoline all around, and it burns the skin off any people nearby. It doesn't kill them immediately, just burns off their skin. Slow death by torture."

"I wouldn't much like Mundania," Yukay said, shuddering.

"But if that sandwich got tossed down the throat of the dragon . . ." Ivan said.

They looked at each other. "I think we've got our weapon," Kody said.

"Assuming Zap could deliver it," Yukay said.

Ivan shook his head. "Uh-oh."

"What?" Kody asked.

"I have come to know her somewhat," Ivan said. "Zap is a pacifist. She doesn't believe in killing. Not even dragons. That's her problem as a griffin."

"That's right!" Yukay agreed. "That soul she got really messes her up, in griffin terms. It makes her nice for us, but she's no fighter now."

"Scratch one notion," Kody agreed. "It also occurs to me that though it might work on a fire dragon, it probably wouldn't on a smoker. Not enough heat to detonate it, without a primer."

"We've got to think of something else," Yukay said.

Kody walked in a circle, concentrating. A bulb flashed over his head.

"What?" Ivan asked.

"When I was talking with Zosi I saw something."

Yukay frowned, her eyes flicking down toward her bosom. "I could have shown you more."

Zosi blushed. Kody would have preferred that she hadn't, as it tended to give away their activity. Yukay had made a shrewd guess.

"I saw a No Smoking sign. Given the way things tend to be literal in Xanth, could that be serious?"

Yukay considered it. "No Smoking—as in dragon breath? I don't know what it would mean in Mundania, but yes, that well might be its effect."

"So if we could deliver that sign to the dragon's nest, that might deprive it of its main weapon. Without actually hurting it, so Zap would not have to be concerned."

"That might be," Yukay said. "But Naomi would still be confined to the nest, and that dragon would still be formidable. We would need more."

"Could Zap carry my weight, flying? So I could get close and flip a chip at the dragon? That might turn it into a worm."

"She might. But you don't want to get smoked before you get there. And if you did, and flipped your chip, it still might reverse the dragon in some other way, like making it a fire breather instead of a smoker."

"Still, it may be our best chance. I'll fetch the sign." Kody headed off to the copse. Zosi did not go with him; she remained embarrassed. Still, that might be better than guilt.

He found the sign and brought it back. As he walked, he saw the griffin in the sky, returning. She had something in her beak. A piece of paper.

Zap landed about the same time as Kody got back. She presented the paper to him. He took it and found that it was a note.

To Whom It May Concern: If you want your sweet innocent girl back in that condition, bring a ransom of a bushel of diamonds to my nest before the day is out. Otherwise I will ravish her and then consume her as smoked meat. You will know when that happens by her piercing screams. Signed Dread Dragon.

PS—The goblins have bushels of diamonds, but I can't get into their mound. I hope for my captive's sake that you can. She looks delicious.

"It's a ransom note!" Kody exclaimed.

"That's a first," Yukay said. "Usually dragons eat first and talk after."

"How did you get the note, Zap?" Zosi asked the griffin.

It took a bit of dialogue, but they learned that when Zap approached the nest the dragon had signaled in Winged Monster Lingo to approach. It seemed that winged monsters had a policy of not interfering with each other unless absolutely necessary. This applied to all winged monsters, including flying centaurs and winged goblin girls, who did not regard the appellation as derogatory. Violation of the honor code could bring savage reprisals by the Winged Monster authorities, so as a general rule, one winged monster could trust another. So Zap had approached, and the dragon had given her the ransom note. Such a truce did not extend to non-winged monsters, so Naomi had no protection. Neither did the rest of them.

Kody was not comfortable with any of this. "What's it like, dealing with goblins?"

"Bad," Yukay said. "The girls are pretty and sweet, but the men are ugly, vicious, greedy, horny, and treacherous. Zosi and I would not dare to go near a goblin mound, and it wouldn't be safe for the rest of you either, for different reasons."

"Do they really have bushels of diamonds?"

"They could. But there's no price we could pay to get them legitimately. We would have to steal them or take them by force, and that would not be likely."

"Yet we shall have to try. We can't just leave Naomi to her dreadful fate."

Yukay shook her head. "We may not have a choice."

"There's always a choice," Kody said. "I will go talk with the goblins. Maybe they will be reasonable."

"You plainly have had no experience with goblins."

"Correct. Where is this goblin mound?"

"Squawk," Zap said, gesturing with a wing.

Now Kody saw a mound in the distance. The griffin must have spotted it by air. "Thank you." He nerved himself and started walking toward it.

"No!" Yukay, Zosi, and Ivan said together, and Zap squawked.

"I'd never forgive myself if I didn't at least try," Kody said, maintaining his pace.

The others hurried to accompany him. "At least formulate a plan of escape when it doesn't work," Yukay said. "So that you don't wind up in the goblin's cookpot."

"Well, I do have my reverse wood chips."

"Against one or two goblins those might work," she agreed. "Not against hundreds."

"So what do you recommend?"

"Cherries and pineapples."

"What, do they like fruit?"

"I keep forgetting that you really aren't from Xanth," Yukay said, frustrated. "Those are explosive fruits. Cherry bombs are small ones, and pineapples are larger ones. Lay down a barrage of those, and the goblins might show a little respect."

"Maybe sandwiches," Zosi said.

The others looked at her.

"With jellied gasoline."

"Oho!" Yukay said. "That just might do it. Let a few goblins get their heads blown off, and the others just might possibly begin to see reason."

"Squawk!" Zap protested.

"Look, Zap," Yukay said reasonably. "You know that goblins respect only unsubtle brute force. This may be that."

"Squawk."

"You're as oink-headed as Kody is," Ivan said. "You know she's right."

The griffin acknowledged that, but still did not like the violence.

"Maybe you should talk to her, Kody," Yukay said in a mock-serious tone. "You seem to have a touch."

Zosi blushed again.

Was that a challenge? He was beginning to recognize that it would be necessary to bargain from strength, whether with dragons or goblins, and a pacifist griffin would be a liability. "All right."

"Squawk?"

"Zap, I think you have a misapprehension about having a soul. Many souled folk are not pacifists and do not deplore violence.

What the soul contributes is the *capacity* for decency that is often unexploited. Consider the goblins: they are little humanoids, are they not? Therefore they have souls, no? But are they pacifists?"

Yukay and Ivan burst out laughing, and even Zosi smiled. He had made a point. "You want to be decent, and that's commendable. But you are a griffin. Decency in griffins should not have the same meaning it does in straight human folk, or in goblins. It would be more like the honor code of warriors. Like the Winged Monster code. Tough love."

"Squawk," Zap said thoughtfully.

"Violence with honor, when required," Kody continued. "The ability to kill or be killed, but never carelessly or treacherously. Only when it is called for to oppose indecency. Such as when goblins are about to rape an innocent maiden."

"Squawk," Zap agreed, suffering the revelation.

"Jellied gasoline sandwiches are weapons, to be used only in warfare. But if goblins attack and refuse to see reason, such weapons may be in order. We will try to negotiate honorably with the goblins. Only if we are met with dishonor will we resort to the sandwiches. With luck they won't be necessary." He smiled. "For one thing, we still have to figure out how to ignite them."

Zap nodded. She was reluctantly ready to go along.

"One detail you may have overlooked," Yukay said. "You speak of negotiation. To do that we have to have something the goblins want, and I don't mean our bodies for fun and food. What do we have to offer?"

She had him there. "You are too bleeping smart," Kody said, disgruntled. "I'm stumped. Do you have a suggestion?"

"Yes. I don't think it will work, goblins being what they are, but you are welcome to try. It is this: your mission to abolish the Curse will benefit goblins too. So they should try to facilitate it. We need to rescue Naomi to restore our party. So they should contribute their token bit. Like a bushel of diamonds."

"It's a notion," he agreed. "Zosi, if you will make some sandwiches, I'll add chips. And little stones that might strike sparks.

Maybe the combination will make them capable of detonation. So we'll have a defense mechanism if we need it."

"You'll need a bag," Yukay said. She removed her skirt.

"What are you doing?" Kody asked, taken aback.

"Making a bag." She snapped edges together, and held it out.

"But your legs!" They were great legs.

"Will nauseate goblins, same as the rest of us. Because of the Curse."

She was correct. But she was also perilously close to exposing her panties, barely covered by her shirt. Her reason made sense, but was she also using it as a pretext to flash him, knowing his immunity to the Curse? She might still have seduction in mind, unaware how serious he had gotten about Zosi.

"Too bad the Curse prevents you from flashing the goblins," he said. "To freak them out. That would be a useful weapon."

"Believe me, I and every pretty girl in Xanth truly misses that weapon."

"If I turned zombie, I would be ugly," Zosi said. "Then maybe I could freak out some."

"You could," Yukay said seriously. "But I think not ugly enough. Better not to risk it."

Zosi conjured a dozen sandwiches, and Kody flipped a dozen reverse wood chips into them, plus sharp-edged pebbles, and put them carefully into the bag. The odor of gasoline grew strong, but nothing exploded. Kody took the bag and carried it with a very gentle grip.

They resumed their walk toward the goblin mound. They came to a sign saying GODDAM GOBLINS. STRANGERS UNWELCOME.

Just so.

They came near the mound. It was swarming with goblins. The men were ugly runts with big heads and big feet. The women were like lovely dolls. But of course to each other they looked the opposite. "Bleep," Kody muttered. "I wish I could see them as others see them, if only for a moment."

"Try this," Yukay said, proffering her little mirror. "Maybe a Xanth mirror will show what Xanthians see."

He held up the mirror and angled it to reflect the mound and the goblins on it. And was amazed. Now the males were handsome creatures, and the females were little hags, even though their actual features were only reversed, not changed. That was how they looked to each other. "Thanks," he said, returning the mirror.

In half a moment the goblins spotted them. "Fresh meat!" one shouted. In the other half of the moment their party was ringed by male goblins.

"What the bleep are you bleeps doing here?" their leader demanded.

"Hello, Goddam Goblins," Kody said politely. "We are a party on a special Quest, and we need your help. We have come to negotiate for it."

"Har har har!" Several goblins actually fell over laughing. Only their appearance had been reversed, not their nature.

"Too bad your hags are so ugly," the leader said. "They won't even do for sport. But they should taste good enough."

"Aren't you even going to listen to my pitch?" Kody asked, nettled.

"Why should we? Your jokes are funny, but now we're hungry." He looked around. "Grab 'em. Get the pots hot. Get ropes to lasso the griffin before it flies off."

"But we've got sandwiches," Kody protested. "A whole bag full of them."

"Gimme those," the leader said, snatching the bag from his hand. He tore it open and pulled out a sandwich. "Smells great." He stuffed it in his mouth. In a quarter of a moment he had swallowed it, pretty much whole.

Nothing happened. Certainly no explosions.

The other goblins ripped into the bag, hauling out sandwiches and cramming them into their mouths. They evidently liked the gasoline taste. But why were they unaffected?

"Maybe the chips are touching the bread," Yukay murmured. "And not the goblins. Because of the way they eat."

Then the leader produced a bottle of brown liquid, probably boot rear, and swigged it as a chaser to his sandwich. The others followed suit. The leader let out a resounding belch.

Then he looked odd. So did the others. Kody wasn't sure exactly what had changed, but something had.

"They're reversing!" Yukay said. "They're looking ugly again."

Kody was glad she had defined it, because they looked the same to Kody. The oddness was in their expressions.

The goblins looked at each other. "We're back!" one exclaimed.

It seemed the reverse wood chips inside them were reversing the reversal of the Curse. Could this be an answer to the Curse?

But then there was a further change. It seemed the chips were gradually taking full effect. And what a change it was!

The brutish males were becoming petite females. Lovely little creatures.

"Aarrggh!" the leader cried, running madly away, as if he thought he could escape it. Soon the rest were doing the same.

"I'll be bleeped," Yukay murmured. "Reversal with a vengeance!"

"But it doesn't help us get the diamonds," Zosi said.

"I know it's the Curse," Ivan said. "But to me, handsome males became ugly hags. I can see why they're appalled."

"When two kinds of reversals interact, there can be interesting variations," Yukay said. "But Zosi is right: routing the goblins doesn't get us the diamonds. Kody never got a chance to present his rationale, and I doubt it would work anyway."

Kody nodded. "I fear getting the diamonds is not feasible. We'll have to come up with something else."

They walked away from the Goddam Goblin mound, disconsolate. Yukay spied a blanket bush and harvested a small light one to wrap around her as a replacement skirt. "Yes. But what else is there?"

"Squawk."

They looked at Zap. On her side was printed FEED DRAGON REVERSE WOOD?

"Now there's an idea," Yukay said. "After seeing what the chips did to the goblins, I wonder what it would do to the dragon."

"A fire dragon breathed ice," Kody said. "But how would smoke reverse?"

"Especially if there's a No Smoking sign," Yukay said.

"There are many ways it could reverse," Zosi said. "Any of them would probably set it back."

"She's right," Yukay said. "Kiss her, Kody."

Kody ignored that, being uncertain of her motive in saying it. Was she being sarcastic? Actually he had liked kissing Zosi. She was not as pretty as Yukay, but he felt more rapport with her. It was probably just as well that the dragon crisis had interrupted their continuation, as it was not something they might want to do when rational. "Could Zap carry me to the dragon's nest?"

"Squawk." NOT AS YOU ARE.

"But maybe if you were lighter," Yukay said. "Let me see if there's any lighter knot around here."

"Lighter knot?" Kody asked. "That's the heart of pine, that burns so fiercely it can be used to prime a fire."

"Maybe in Mundania." She was looking around.

Zap sniffed the air. "Squawk." She spread her wings and took off.

"She's sniffing out lighter knot!" Ivan said.

"I am getting to appreciate her increasingly," Yukay said. "Originally it was because she came to rescue me, but now I am learning her other qualities."

"So you're saying that rather than try to pay the ransom, I should go up to the dragon's nest and feed it chips of reverse wood."

"Yes. You can do battle with it in your fashion. After seeing what those chips can do, I believe you can prevail. I wouldn't recommend such action otherwise."

"You would let Naomi be eaten?"

"Not if I can find any way to rescue her. Sure, she's competition for your attention, but she has her own points and I am coming to like her. You will be gone the moment your Quest is done, but she'll still be around. I might want her as a friend."

"There is something about her," Ivan said. "I'm not sure she's anyone's friend."

"That's interesting. On what do you base that opinion?"

"It's just a feeling. Sure, if I could see her without the Curse I'd probably be smitten, same as with you, but there's something."

Yukay considered. "You're no good on this, Kody, because you see us as we are, physically, and are ripe for seduction. First one who gets a clear private panty flash at you will take you, at least for the nonce. You will see no evil in any of us."

"That's true," Kody agreed, taken aback by her candor. She was probably correct. He really liked Zosi, but other panties still had power.

She turned to Zosi. "What is your take on this?"

"The same," Zosi said. "She has her own agenda."

"So let's rescue her, then question her."

"Let's do that," Kody agreed.

Zap returned, carrying a fragment of wood in her beak.

Yukay picked it up. "Oho! That's lighter knot all right." She glanced at Kody. "Pick me up."

He put his hands on her elbows and heaved. She sailed up out of his grasp, over his head. Alarmed, he looked up, hoping to catch her before she fell.

Fingers snapped by his ear. He was standing, dazed, staring at nothing.

"Sorry about that," Yukay said. "You lifted me too hard, and then saw up under my skirt as it flared. Just like the check hers game. You freaked out."

Oh. He had indeed. Panty magic really was potent. Fortunately she had been light enough to handle the fall. "Too bad dragons don't freak."

"Now you know what lighter knot does. Try it yourself." She handed the wood to Kody.

He took it and immediately felt quite light on his feet. Could he actually weigh that much less?

"It's not your imagination," Yukay said. "I'll show you." She bent down, put her hands on his knees, and lifted. He came right up. "You really are lighter."

"I really am," he agreed.

"So now Zap can carry you to the dragon's nest."

"But the dragon's not just going to let me go there!"

"Zap can tell him you're there to negotiate."

"Negotiate with what? We have no diamonds."

"True. So maybe you can tell him you are there to fight him for possession of Naomi. Make it a challenge."

"Why should the dragon agree to fight me?"

"Pride. He would never live it down if he backed off from any challenge, especially one from a paltry human being."

There was a certain sense to that. But not enough. "And how can I fight it? I'm no warrior."

"With the reverse wood," she reminded him.

Kody considered. That might be feasible. "And if I lose?"

"You had better hope that you really are just a dream figure here. Otherwise the dragon will have a two-course dinner."

"And what will happen to my Quest?"

"Xanth will have to hope for some other hero to come and accomplish it."

"And what of the rest of us?" Zosi asked.

"Ivan and I will be free to do what we choose, hoping we have learned enough from this Quest to succeed better in life than before. You, Zosi, have the solution to your Quest in hand, if you care to do it."

Zosi stood there, slow tears forming. "Please succeed," she said.

Kody did not feel easy about any of this, but saw no other likely way to proceed. He tucked the lighter knot into a shirt pocket and buttoned it in. He tucked the No Smoking sign into another. "I will do it."

"Squawk." Zap stepped up, ready to carry him. She had of course been paying attention.

"I'm not a rider," Kody said. "You will have to help me stay on."

"Squawk."

He stood beside her. She was about the size of a pony. He gripped her feather mane and swung one leg up over her folded wing and back. His legs came down before her wings as he sat between them. "I guess I'm ready."

"Squawk." Zap walked a few paces, then broke into a run, then spread her wings and sprang into the air. She pumped harder and lifted. Soon they were well above the ground.

"This is something!" Kody said. "I've never flown like this."

"Squawk."

"Regardless how this works out, Zap, I want you to know I really appreciate your help. You don't say much, but you're always there when you're needed."

"Squawk."

"I hope that somehow this Quest enables you to find yourself the way you want to. Having a soul may be a burden to you, but it really makes you a nice person."

"Squawk."

"I think I'm beginning to understand you, Zap. You are saying that you have already accomplished some of what you seek. You look at yourself in a new way."

"Squawk."

"And that you never associated with human beings before, but you are coming to like us too, as we like you."

"Squawk."

"Yes, I understand that you don't want to fight the dragon, and not from any cowardice. You don't want to fight any winged monster."

"Squawk."

"And you won't have to. Just get me there, then back off and wait." Then he thought of something. "But I think I will need you to speak for me to the dragon. To tell him that I don't have diamonds, but I am challenging him to a duel."

"Squawk?"

"Yes, tell him I'm magically armed. If he doesn't want to fight me, then all he has to do is release Naomi, and not by dropping her to the distant ground. Tell him I'm not bluffing."

"Squawk," she agreed.

They came into sight of the nest. It was indeed on a lofty crag, inaccessible except by air. There was the dragon in it, and Naomi beside him.

"Squawk!" Zap called.

The dragon roared in response, blowing out a cloud of smoke.

"Tell him you're staying out of it. I need to join him in the nest. The moment I arrive, the fight is on."

"Squawk."

The dragon rose up and stood back, indicating the near edge of the nest. He certainly wasn't cowed.

Zap flew to the edge of the nest and hovered just above it. "You came!" Naomi cried gladly. Her clothing was in tatters, but she seemed to be all right.

Kody jumped down to the rim. As he did so, the dragon was inhaling, ready to suffocate him in smoke. But his hand was already in his pocket. As he landed he whipped out the No Smoking sign.

The dragon choked on his lungful. Smoke hissed out of his ears and from under his tail. He coughed, disappearing in a cloud of stifled smoke. Then it dissipated, leaving him spent and angry. Kody had scored the first point, but there was still a powerful opponent to deal with.

The dragon finally cleared his system and opened his mouth wide to chomp the man. Kody flipped in a chip, aiming for the throat to trigger an automatic swallow. This was the test: would it somehow disable the dragon?

The dragon swallowed. He paused. A pained expression crossed his snoot. Then he reached down with a claw, hooked a patch of white cloth, and lifted it up. He was capitulating.

"Suddenly he's a pacifist!" Naomi said in wonder.

Kody did not fully trust this. Even if the dragon wasn't faking, there was no guarantee how long the effect would last. "I reversed him. Now get on Zap and get out of here."

"Squawk."

The griffin glided in for a brief landing on the nest, with no opposition by the dragon. But instead of going to Zap, Naomi ran to Kody. She flung her arms around him and kissed him passionately. "You saved me!"

Tatters? Her clothing hardly existed! Everything she had, which was considerable, was pressed firmly against him. She was breathing, and that made it more so. It was electrifying.

He pried his mouth from hers. "Go!"

"Some other time," she murmured. She reached into his pocket, found the lighter knot, and took it. Of course she needed it, to make her weight low enough. He had forgotten that detail, but it seemed Zap had told her. Then she disengaged and got on the griffin. In most of a moment they were gone.

Kody was left alone with the dragon. If the chips were not really working, he was in trouble.

"You should have taken her," the dragon said. "I'd have waited. She was more than willing."

Kody's jaw dropped. "You can talk!"

"You thought I could write but couldn't talk?"

"I guess I didn't think about it," Kody admitted.

"Naomi and I had quite a little dialogue," Dread Dragon said. "She's a naga, you know. They're not covered by the Winged Monster convention, but sapient serpents are a related species and it would have been awkward to consume her. That put me in a difficult position. I had taken her for an ordinary maiden. I'm glad you rescued her."

Was this for real? "Why didn't you bring her safely back, then?"

"And admit my error? I would have become a laughingstock. No, she had to be duly rescued, and there's no need to mention the error, is there?"

"No need," Kody said, bemused. "So I'm not clear on some details. Are you really stifled by the No Smoking sign?"

Dread blew out a plume of smoke surrounded by several smoke rings. "Those signs are not directed at dragons."

"And did my reverse wood chip really stop you?"

"Yes. The one I swallowed has reversed my nature and rendered me into a pacifist. I think that effect will not last long, as I digest and nullify it, however."

"I can conjure other chips. It's my talent."

"Which I will blow away before they touch me."

"But if you try to eat me, I will conjure chips in your mouth."

"Unless I roast you in smoke first."

"I will reverse the smoke." That was a bluff, as he wasn't sure what a chip would do to smoke, but it was bound to do something.

Dread Dragon considered. "This promises to be an interesting contest."

"Or we can call it off and go our ways with mutual respect."

"Perhaps. Let's chat awhile first. I get little intellectual stimulation in my normal rounds."

"Until you digest the chip and become savage again?"

"Or until the griffin returns with the lighter knot to carry you away."

Kody concluded that chatting was in order. "I had no idea dragons were intelligent."

"Some are, some aren't, as with humanoids. It is not expedient to judge all by a single example." Dread looked at him at an angle, something he was able to do more readily than a humanoid might. "You do not strike me as an ordinary hero. For one thing you carry no sword."

Kody laughed. "I'm no warrior. I wouldn't know what to do with a sword."

"Yet you fascinate the humanoid females you encounter despite the Curse. Naomi is quite taken with you, and I gather she is not the only one."

"It may be because I am Mundane, and am dreaming this Xanth experience, and am not affected by the Curse. I see folk as they are physically, not reversed. There are comely women in my party, and

I appreciate them as such. That may turn them on. That effect may vanish once the Curse is removed and regular men can appreciate pretty girls again."

"You speak as if you know the Curse will be abolished."

"Well, it is my Quest to do that. Didn't Naomi tell you?"

"She did not."

"That's a curious omission."

"It is indeed," Dread agreed. "Had I known that, I would not have targeted you for consumption."

"You targeted me?"

"Not specifically. Your party appeared in the Ever and Ever Glades with several delicious-looking humanoids, so I decided to make something of it."

"What about the diamonds?"

"I really doubted you would be able to get them from the goblins."

"So it was a pretext?"

"And a device to keep your party here, so I could harvest them one by one."

"That seems unscrupulous."

"I am a dragon. Fresh meat does not appear every day. I must go after what I can get. The maidens appear ugly to me, but their meat remains tender, and that's what counts."

"You are affected by the Curse too?"

"I am. It has soured relations with my dragoness, through no inherent fault of hers. I can't stand to twine coils with her now. I would like to be rid of the Curse. So it seems I shall have to let you go also, unfortunately. But you should not trust other dragons."

"I shall try to be on better guard against your kind hereafter."

"However, you do have one thing I would like to get. Those reverse wood chips."

"I conjure them. That's my magic."

"But do they last after being conjured? Can they be stored?"

"I don't know."

"Because if I had a bag of them, I could find uses for them that could be more valuable to me than diamonds."

"Why should I conjure you a bag of chips?"

"Perhaps we can trade." Dread put a paw down into the straw of his nest and brought out a small object. "You should find this useful."

"What is it?"

"A magical sword. I can't use it, but it should work for you."

"It looks like a penknife."

"Try it."

Kody took it from the dragon's paw. It had a fairly stout handle, but the blade was barely two inches long. "Some sword!"

"Pretend I am about to chomp you, and all you have is that weapon."

Kody brought up the knife. Suddenly it was a good foot long. He made a feint with it, and it was two feet long. But still no heavier than the penknife.

"Illusion?" he asked.

"No. Try tapping it against my scales." The dragon presented his armored shoulder.

Kody tapped. The blade clanked against the shoulder, and a scale was dislodged. "Ooo, that smarts," Dread said, drawing back.

"But I barely touched you!"

"I repeat, it is magic. It expands to whatever size is appropriate, and it strikes with full force at the business end, while remaining feather light to the wielder. It's a good sword. An amateur could use it to good effect."

"I'm amateur, all right." Kody was intrigued. "You want to trade this fantastic weapon for a bag of reverse wood chips?"

"Yes. To trade an artifact I can't use, for one I can. Deal?"

"Deal!" Kody said. "Do you have a bag?"

The dragon scrounged in the straw and came up with a small bag. Kody conjured a chip and dropped it into the bag. He conjured another, and a third. Before long he had filled the bag with about twenty chips. They nestled comfortably, not reversing anything.

"That will do," Dread said, closing the bag.

"Don't you want to test them, to be sure they work?"

"I know they work. I can smell their magical power."

"Then it seems we have a deal." Kody put the little knife in a pocket.

"Our business is concluded," Dread agreed. "But I am curious. What is this business about dreaming?"

"I am Mundane. I am in a drugged sleep, and this is where my mind is for the moment. It is an interesting adventure."

"So probably if I had chomped you, you would have dissipated, being put out of your dream."

"That is my theory. I haven't cared to test it."

"You should make the most of it. Those girls will be happy to oblige you."

"I am trying to treat them like the responsible individuals they are."

"Naomi says you favor the zombie."

"Zosi is a *person*."

"So Naomi is right."

Was the dragon baiting him? "Naomi is right," he agreed.

"Here is my reasoning: you probably do not have long to remain in this realm. You could die or be awakened at any time. So you might as well indulge yourself while you can. You are unlikely to get such opportunities in drear Mundania."

"You proffer dragon logic. I am not a dragon." But the dragon was scoring.

"Even if the girls desire your indulgence, and will be frustrated if you depart leaving them unfulfilled? Whom does your abstinence benefit?"

Zap arrived. Kody was relieved, because the dragon's question was beyond his ability to answer. "If we ever meet again, let's not fight," Kody said.

"Agreed. You are an interesting, if deluded character."

Kody took the lighter knot and mounted the griffin. "Thank you."

They flew back to the others. Both Yukay and Zosi threw their arms around him and kissed him.

"That dragon makes a lot of sense, doesn't he?" Naomi remarked knowingly.

Too much sense. But Kody kept his mouth shut.

It was now late in the day. They feasted on peanut butter and jelly sandwiches and caught up on things. Kody showed the others the sword he had traded for, while the girls, sitting innocently cross-legged on the ground, showed him more than he was comfortable with.

"We have foraged for blankets," Yukay said. "But it may get cool at night. Choose any one or two of us to share a blanket with tonight."

There might be protection in numbers. "You and Zosi, each of us individually wrapped. We can lie together like logs."

"You are not being very sporting," Yukay complained. But they complied.

As darkness closed Kody had difficulty finding sleep. The dragon's words kept running through his mind. Was he being a fool? He would never have opportunity like this in Mundania.

They needed to get on with the mission.

# 9
# DEMO DERBY

In the morning Kody pried himself out from between the two women, whose body warmth had indeed lent comfort when the chill came. He saw that Naomi and Ivan had slept similarly wrapped beside Zap, whose larger mass had kept them warm. Zap foraged for food and found a nearby pie plant, so they didn't have to eat sandwiches for breakfast. And of course they washed up, Kody trying to tactfully avoid having the girls wash him.

Averting his gaze from the bare girls, Kody spied something he might not otherwise have noticed in the adjacent brush: it looked like an eyeball in a green globe on a stem. A plant of some sort. The eye seemed to be focusing on the girls. Could a plant have an urge to peep?

Zap saw him looking. "Squawk." On her side were the words EYE POD. Then: GOURD SEEDLING

Kody didn't get it, so let it be.

And he continued to wonder: was he being a fool? It seemed the girls had decided to cooperate with each other in encouraging him to select one of them for something more intimate than dialogue. Maybe after he was with one, it would be the turn of another, and finally the third. He was pretty sure he would enjoy being with any and all of them, in whatever manner they chose. So why did he still hesitate? Yet he did.

Then, clean and fed, they brought out the chessboard. Some of the little pictures had changed, but they could not identify any that showed the region of Xanth they wanted to go to. Several might be what they wanted, but there was no positive marker.

Then Kody spied one that interested him for another reason: it had cars. They looked like actual, genuine, Mundane vintage cars, the very kind he liked. It was only a hobby, but the prospect of checking out such vehicles in Xanth attracted him magnetically.

"I'd like to go there," he said, pointing.

Yukay wrinkled her nose. "It looks like Mundania!"

"Yes. Mundane cars. I like them."

"Let's vote on it." Yukay looked at Ivan. "Are you ready to go there?"

Ivan shrugged. "I've never seen a car. I'd like to see one."

She looked at Zap. "You, birdbrain?"

"Squawk," the griffin agreed. Zap was generally ready to go along with whatever the others wanted; it was part of her accommodation with her soul.

"Two votes for," Yukay said. "The remaining three will have to be earned."

"Earned?" Kody asked.

"One kiss buys one vote." The others nodded.

"Does this make sense to you?" Kody asked Ivan.

"Sure, if you can stand it. Why would you ever kiss them otherwise?" Ivan knew of Kody's immunity to the Curse, but had trouble relating to it in practice. To him the girls were hideous.

"Zap?"

"Squawk." On her side appeared the word SEDUCTION.

So the girls were really determined. Maybe they knew how the dragon's cynical appraisal had shaken him, and were capitalizing on it.

"One kiss," he agreed.

Yukay stepped up. She put her arms about him, drew him in close, and lifted her face. She kissed him deeply, her mouth partway open.

It did have effect. He felt as if he were floating. He could readily have drifted with her to some private scene and taken it further. He was halfway freaking out.

She stepped back, allowing him to recover. Then Naomi came forward. She took his hands and put them around her, just so, his hands on her sleek bottom. Then she kissed him, and tongued him. This time he did freak out, and found himself standing alone after she had withdrawn.

Finally it was Zosi. She did not demand an embrace. She merely stood on tiptoes and kissed him fleetingly on the lips. "I love you," she whispered as she withdrew.

He grabbed her and kissed her again, ardently. He couldn't help it.

"What does she have that we don't?" Naomi asked rhetorically.

"Bleep!" Yukay swore. "She trumped us."

She had indeed. Kody was more than ready to go with her and do anything she might want. Except for the fact that he knew he couldn't stay here in Xanth, so would be leading her into grief.

Once his head had cleared from the impact of the kisses, Kody returned to the chessboard. They gathered in close around Zap, and the griffin pecked the indicated picture.

They stood in what looked like a used car lot. Cars were all around them. Vintage 1970s vehicles in perfect condition. It was like a small slice of heaven.

"WELCOME TO PLANET DEMO DERBY," a loudspeaker voice blared. "DRIVERS CHOOSE YOUR CARS FOR THE BIG RACE. IT STARTS IN ONE HOUR."

Kody recoiled in horror. This was a demolition derby? With these fine cars?

"I think we've got a problem," Yukay said. "He's freaking out, and not from kisses or panties."

They led him to a shelter to the side. Zosi took his hands and gazed into his eyes. "What is it?" she inquired gently.

"It's a demolition race," he said. "They are going to destroy all these fine cars! They're classics of their types, but instead of preserving them—" He broke off, choking up.

"I think this is a Moon of Ida," Yukay said. "One devoted to a particular segment of human experience. In this case, Mundane cars of a certain vintage."

"A what?" Kody asked.

"There is an infinite string of worlds accessible only via Princess Ida," Yukay explained. "Each has its own nature, magic, rules. Some are very strange. This must be one of the stranger ones. We certainly don't have to stay here if you don't like it."

"I don't think I want to stay. The idea of wasting all these cars appalls me."

"Squawk."

They looked at Zap. CHECK AROUND

Kody nodded. "Yes. We may not stay here long, but we should check to see what else, if anything, it offers. One never knows."

Not far off the track there was something vaguely resembling a walrus, busy closing envelopes and boxes. Evidently there were things to be shipped elsewhere, like car parts. Zap saw him looking and squawked: SEAL.

Kody groaned. Sealing things. He moved on.

There was a shelter with a large screen. PRIZES: WINNER'S PICK. SUPER MUSCLE CAR. A picture flashed, showing what looked to be a half-million-dollar racing car. PILE OF GOLD COINS. Picture of the golden pile. AFFAIR WITH POLLY ESTER. A surpassingly luscious young woman in translucent plastic clothing and a come-hither-this-instant smile. ROBOT BOMB SNIFFER. A six-legged machine with an antenna.

The list continued, but Kody tuned it out. A bomb sniffer! Could that sniff out the Bomb that made the Curse, short-cutting their inefficient search? In that case he wanted to try it.

"What a babe!" Ivan murmured.

"What, that plastic slut?" Naomi asked.

"Just the clothing," Ivan said. "Her body is pure flesh."

"Squawk?"

"Sure, I see her as she is," Ivan said. "Sheer sex appeal." Then he did a double-take. "No Curse here!"

"No Curse," Yukay agreed. "This isn't Xanth. We aren't going to be able to do a divergence comparison, because we're all aligned. It's a wasted trip."

Kody realized that was true. He had been fascinated by seeing the cars, and messed up the reason for coming here.

Ivan looked at Yukay. "You're beautiful again. I hadn't noticed."

"Thank you. You're handsome."

"But you're interested in Kody, not me."

"True. He sees me as I am when the Curse is in force. You'll be turned off the moment we return to Xanth."

"Yes. So maybe I should try for Polly."

Yukay smiled cynically. "She can surely give you an artificially good time."

"Squawk!"

They looked at Zap. LAST PRIZE

Kody looked at the end of the list. PASS TO SOULED WINGED MONSTER ANNEX. That would certainly interest her, as she could probably be right at home there, no longer excluded by her kind.

"I need to enter that race," Kody said.

"For Polly?" Ivan asked.

"Squawk?"

"No, not for Polly or the Annex," he said. "I don't care about those. For the bomb sniffer."

"That does make sense," Yukay agreed. "That might enable you to complete your Quest in mere hours, instead of trudging around interminably with us."

Naomi and Zosi faced away, but not before he caught the glint of a tear at Zosi's eye.

That brought him up short. He discovered, now that he saw the prospect of an early conclusion, that he rather liked associating with them. Xanth was impossibly strange, but they had been buffering its wild impact. They had become familiar. Yukay with her ready explanations, Zosi with her niceness, Zap with her complete support. The group was, in its limited fashion, like a family. "Let me think about this."

"Of course," Yukay agreed.

They were always so decent about what might seem to them like his arbitrary decisions. That did not make him feel better.

Kody walked in a little circle, pondering. But his thoughts refused to settle. He did not know what he really wanted, or what to do about it.

"Squawk."

He looked at Zap. THREE CARS RACE

And there it was. Ivan wanted a prize. Zap wanted a prize. Kody wanted a prize. If they all entered the race, maybe one of them would win and get the prize he or she wanted. If it was not Kody, then that issue would be settled; he would continue searching the way they had been doing. If he did win—well, then he could ponder it further. Once again the griffin had come up with a plausible path.

"Zap, I'm going to kiss you," he said. He bent to kiss her on the beak, and she did not flinch away though she looked a little surprised. "Now let's work out the details."

They discussed it, and decided that Ivan would drive one car, with Naomi riding with him. Yukay would drive another, with Zap riding with her. And Kody would drive the third, with Zosi.

Then Kody gave them all lessons in driving, as none of them had done anything like this before. They all piled into a practice car and Kody drove it. "These are stick-shift vehicles," he said. "Automatic shifts exist, but control is better with stick in tight situations, so we'll leave the autos to other contestants. First you turn on the motor, like this." The key was already there. The motor came instantly to life. "Then you press this left-side floor pedal, the clutch. That disengages the motor. Then you use the gearshift to put it in first gear, and—"

He paused, because all of them were blank.

"Start over," he said, turning the motor off. He slid the driver's seat back. "Yukay, sit on my lap. I will guide your hands and feet."

Yukay sat on his lap. She was a marvelously supple lapful. He had her rest her feet on his, and her hands on his. "We start it this way."

Soon the car was moving. Then, suddenly, Yukay's body came to life. She pushed off his hands and feet and started competently driving it, complete with brakes and turn signals. It was her talent manifesting. "That's it!" he said. "You've got it. Just remember it. Can you do that?"

"I think so," she said. "The motions are automatic, once I've been through them. As long as I stay in the race, making it a single event."

"Go get your own car, and make space for Zap."

She did. "Now Ivan," Kody said. "I will ride beside you, and direct your hands and feet." He did, and after a few missteps Ivan began to get it.

"This is great!" Ivan said. "I like this machine."

"I think you have a natural talent for it. Now go practice with Naomi."

Now Kody looked for a car for himself. He selected one that he judged to be not the most powerful, but the most nimble. Maneuvering was likely to count more than velocity, in this deadly race. Zosi rode beside him, fascinated with the way he used his hands and feet to make the thing move back and forth and to the sides.

As the time of the race approached, they got together again. "Now the strategy," Kody said. "Only one car can win: the one that runs the full course without getting crashed out by others. So you will have to be constantly on guard. Every intersection is a chance for mischief. These cars are strongest with their bumpers, front and back; a side impact is likely to be lethal. So if you have to crash into another car, do it head-on. Make sure you have your seat belts on."

"Squawk." TEAM

Kody considered briefly. "Right again, Zap. We'll surely all do better if we operate as a team, running interference for each other. That means if you see an enemy car coming to ram one of us, you ram it first. If all three of our cars get through, then we can make it a straight race to the finish line to determine the winner. Remember, the course is marked by red banners, so when in doubt, follow them."

It was time for the race. They lined up with about seventeen other cars. Theirs were three black ones, a color other drivers did not seem to favor. A loud horn blew, and they were off.

Immediately other cars started swerving into each other, trying to knock them off the better tracks. The tracks themselves were a spaghetti pattern, winding about, crossing and recrossing each other. It was almost impossible to be sure of avoiding collisions.

Indeed, other cars were gleefully racing to the intersections, trying to catch each other broadside. One succeeded, and the victim car was not only pushed off the trail, it rolled over and finished on its roof. It was out of the race.

"Look," Zosi said.

There was a sign he had almost missed. MOUNTAIN ROUTE

"Now that's interesting," Kody said. "There is a red flag there, so it must go through. But it may be rough riding."

"No rougher than crashing."

"Right. Maybe easier to handle. I'll signal the others."

Ivan was just ahead of them. Kody honked, then put an arm out his window, pointing to the offshoot trail. Ivan could recognize him because of the color of his car. He saw Ivan nod.

He swerved to close on Yukay, and signaled her. She too nodded, and swerved her car in that direction. But another car was barreling through, aiming to catch her broadside as she made her turn.

Kody jammed his foot down on the gas pedal, angling to intercept the other car. He slewed into it, shoving it off the trail. Yukay escaped, but Kody's car was badly dented. Fortunately nothing vital had been bashed.

Then they were on the mountain trail. But three other cars had seen their maneuver, and swerved to take it too. A red one, a green one, and a blue one.

Kody knew how to handle that. He was third in their line of three. He took the center of the trail, blocking off the next pursuing car so that Ivan and Yukay could move ahead without having to watch their tails. When the red car tried to get around him, Kody moved across to block it again. It could not pass him. It fell back, frustrated.

Then, probably by sheer chance, the other two cars, green and blue, zoomed up side by side. He could block one, but not both. What to do?

But Yukay dropped back, taking her place beside Kody. Now they had a two-car block, and the trail was not wide enough for more.

Until the trail divided. The blue car peeled off and took the right trail, and Kody could not stop it without leaving the left trail vulnerable. The blue car forged ahead, unblocked.

Suddenly a car zoomed in from the side, on a cross trail Kody hadn't seen. It crashed into the side of the blue car, denting it in and almost breaking it in half. It was Ivan! He had looped back to help them.

After that other cars were not so eager to challenge them. They had the mountain trail to themselves. That did not mean the way was easy; the trail soon rose up into those mountains, and became a narrow cut in the side. They had to slow down to navigate it safely.

And more colored cars came up behind them, eager to smash bumpers. A bump on a curve could boost a car right off the ridge and send it rolling down the sleep slope. How could they handle this challenge?

Kody had an idea. He slowed his car, then brought it to a complete halt right in the middle of a curve. He could not be passed, and if anyone tried to bump him—

A purple car tried. It came charging up. Zosi put her arms over her head.

Just before the purple car struck, Kody let up on the clutch. He had kept the motor running. Now his car lurched forward and stalled. But it was enough; the purple car, unimpeded, missed his car and sailed off the ledge. It bounced down the mountain, turning end over end. Finally it landed in the water of the river below, and sank. It was out of the race.

Zosi peeked out from under her arms. "No crash?" she asked faintly.

"No crash," Kody agreed with satisfaction. *This time.*

He started the motor again and drove forward to catch up to the other black cars, which were waiting for him. The enemy cars seemed to have been cleared out of this section, so it was safe to move on. Kody continued as the third of the three.

"Keep an eye out behind," he told Zosi.

She turned around in her seat to peer back.

"No, use the rearview mirror."

She looked down at her bottom. "There's a mirror there?"

She had no familiarity with cars. Kody realized that he should have considered that before giving her technical instructions. "I'm sorry, Zosi. I didn't mean to confuse you. Look out the side window. There's a mirror mounted there. You can see behind us via that."

"Oh!" she said, surprised as she found it. "I can see everything! But it's moving backwards."

"That's the magic of reflection. Let me know the moment you see any car coming up behind us. That will allow me to pay full attention to what's ahead of us."

"Yes, I will do that."

He reached across and took her hand, squeezing it briefly. "Have you thought more about being the governess for little Plato?"

"I know I should do it," she said sadly. "But I just can't."

"You feel unqualified?"

"No, I think I could do it, and of course Eve would usually be there to set him straight if there was a problem."

"You dread living in Hades?"

"No. That's no worse than regular Xanth, for me."

"Living is that bad?"

"Not exactly."

Kody shook his head. "I don't see the appeal in being a zombie."

"Zombies don't have much feeling."

"Feeling?"

"Joy, sadness, excitement, anger, fear . . ." She trailed off.

"I heard that ellipsis. It means there's something you're not saying."

"Yes."

Kody might have been annoyed, but had learned patience with Zosi. "Something you'd rather not talk about?"

"Yes."

"Is it anything I might help you with?"

"Maybe."

Now his curiosity was growing. "Zosi, please. I don't like seeing you unhappy. Will you tell me what it is?"

"Yes," she said faintly.

That was his cue not to press it further. But his curiosity overruled his decency. "Tell me."

"Love."

It took him a moment to reorient. "That's the emotion you don't want to discuss?"

"Yes."

"What is so bad about love?"

"Nothing, I think. It's wonderful."

"Then why don't you want to talk about it?"

"You'll be mad."

"No, I won't."

"Annoyed."

With anyone else he would be verging on it. "Zosi, I promise not to be annoyed. What is it?"

She was silent. He glanced at her, and saw she was crying.

"Oh, Zosi, I'm sorry! I didn't mean to hurt your feelings. Only I'm not sure how I did that."

She just continued crying.

She needed to be held and comforted. But there was no place to park the car, and pausing here might not be safe anyway.

"Zosi, I'm sorry," he repeated. "I can't stop driving right now, but if you squeeze over toward me I'll put my arm around you."

"But you need it to drive the car."

"I can spare it for a while."

She managed to get close beside him without unfastening the seat belt. He put his right arm around her shoulders and drew her close.

Then, belatedly, it came to him. "You love me! And I can't stay."

Her tears accelerated.

"And you don't want to live if you can't be with me."

She put her face against his shoulder, soaking it.

"You'd rather be a zombie, because then it won't hurt so much."

"Zombies don't feel much love," she murmured.

"But if I could stay, then you wouldn't mind living so much."

"Yes."

Kody experienced a whirlpool of emotion. "I wish I could stay! So I could be with you. I think I love you, Zosi. But I can't stay. When this Quest concludes, I'll wake and be gone. I have no choice."

"Yes."

"I can't fault you for not wanting to live. They'll have to find some other person to governess Plato."

She continued silently crying.

"Zosi, I can't take my eyes off the trail. We'd run off the pavement. I want to kiss you, but I'd get freakish and we'd crash. Still, if you kiss me on the side of the face, that would be nice."

She lifted her head and kissed his cheek. It was nice.

That was all they could do. At least they understood each other.

After a while she returned to her seat and resumed looking behind them. Fortunately no cars were following.

The trail ascended across the mountain slope. They left the trees below and advanced through brushy reaches. They could see down into the neighboring valley, where trees clustered around a river; it was nice scenery.

But Kody distrusted this. There was bound to be something to interfere with their progress toward the end. Races didn't like to make it easy.

Then he spied it. The mountain rose up to a ridge, and the trail climbed on top of that ridge. There was a nervously narrow section high above the valleys on either side, with no guard rails. It was wide enough for a car, but only barely; any drift to either side would put a wheel over and stall the car right there, if it didn't tumble all the way down.

They drew up in a line before it and consulted. "We can make it," Ivan said. "Single file and very slow. But I don't trust it." He was echoing Kody's thought.

"Squawk." Zap spread her wings and took off. She flew above the trail, checking it. Soon she returned. "Squawk," she repeated, and on her side was printed GAP.

That was mischief. How could they navigate it if there was a gap? But Kody tried. "How big a gap?"

FIVE FEET

That just might be navigable at speed. "Is the near side higher than that far side?"

SLIGHTLY

"So we could hurdle it if we drove fast enough?"

YES

"But if we veer to either side landing, it's disaster," Kody concluded.

"Squawk," Zap agreed.

This was a challenge of nerves. "Probably we should turn back," Kody said.

"But I'm ready to do the jump," Ivan said.

"So am I," Yukay said.

"But if you try it and miss, you'll tumble down the slope to the valley and be out of the race at the very least, and lose your life at the most."

"Maybe not," Yukay said. "These vehicles are strongly built, and I suspect buttressed by magic, at least as far as the seat belts reach. Otherwise the contests would not have much repeat business. We probably put our cars at risk but not our lives."

Kody considered. That did make sense. "Well, if you're willing to gamble, so am I. Let's go for it. But maybe Zap should fly rather than weighing down Yukay's car for this."

The others agreed. Zap flew ahead, indicating where the gap was. Kody led the way this time, to give the following cars an indication how to handle it. The trail was narrow but firm, with good traction, and the car's steering was precise. This could be done.

He came up to where Zap hovered. That would be the gap. He accelerated carefully, building up enough speed but not too much. The cars behind paced him, being guided by him. He hit the gap and sailed across it, seeing that the mountain was about five feet below; it was not a total gulf. He landed and drove on; he had made it.

Almost immediately behind, Ivan jumped. He landed well, but one rear tire chipped the edge of the pavement. It crumbled down into the gap. But Ivan had made it.

Then came Yukay. She landed perfectly, but that fractured edge gave way, yanking the car askew. She went off to the side. The car went tumbling down the slope.

Zap dived after it. Kody couldn't stop, and neither could Ivan, but Zosi called out what she saw in the mirror. "The car hit a boulder and stopped partway down. Zap is landing by it. Zap's got Yukay! They are flying back up, following us."

"Zap must have hung on to the lighter knot," Kody said, relieved. "They are out of the race, but at least they're all right."

They drove on, and in due course the trail meandered back down the slope until they were on level ground amidst the trees. He drew to the side and stopped. Ivan parked beside him.

Zap came down to join them, and Yukay got off her back. "While Zap was carrying me, I saw cars lurking in ambush ahead," Yukay said. "You can't afford to ignore them."

That was important news. "Can we avoid them?" Kody asked.

"No. There's only one navigable trail leading from the mountain, and they are guarding it."

"Then we'll have to take them out."

They discussed it briefly, and decided to have Zap join Ivan and Naomi, riding in the backseat, while Yukay joined Kody and Zosi. If Zap had flown over the acorn tree, the lurking cars would know they had been spied, and no surprise retaliation would be feasible. Then they moved on.

Kody peered ahead, searching for the ambush, but couldn't see it. Without Yukay's warning, they would have been caught by surprise.

"Under that big acorn tree," Yukay said. "I made note of the spot. Two cars. They must be working together."

"As we are," Kody said. "It makes sense to team up to eliminate competition, then settle things among friends."

"It does," she agreed.

Kody put his arm out the window to signal Ivan. Then he proceeded toward the tree as if unconcerned.

As he approached it, a gray car lurched out, intent on collision. Kody was ready. He floored the accelerator, leaping forward. The gray car missed him by inches.

And got caught by Ivan following close behind. It wound up in the brush, out of commission.

Meanwhile Kody made a tight turn around the tree, throwing up dirt, almost freaking out Yukay. "That's how he drives," Zosi reassured her. Actually it wasn't how he normally drove, but this was a special situation.

Sure enough, the second car, a yellow one, was now revving up, ready to broadside Ivan before he got clear of the ruined gray car. Kody came at it crosswise, catching it at the rear and spinning it out of control. It fetched up against the trunk of the acorn tree.

But it was not yet out of commission. Its wheels churned up dirt as it got back into action. Kody backed away, not in position to engage with his bumper.

And Ivan caught it from the side, staving it in. This time it was dead.

They paused to compare notes. Both black cars had dents, but both remained fully functional. They had dealt with the ambush.

They resumed driving, following the flags.

"Why does this look familiar?" Yukay asked as she peered out the window.

Now Kody recognized it too. "We're coming back to the starting line! We got turned around."

"I don't think so. The route has been plainly marked throughout."

"It finishes where it starts," Zosi said.

That made sense. Every car had to run the course, but it was circular. So spectators could observe the start and the finish without moving.

But the race was hardly over. Only one car could survive to cross the finish line and take the prize. There were bound to be others waiting to intercept them.

And there were three other cars that had made the circuit by using the main trails. They were chasing each other in smaller circles, trying to crash them out. An orange car caught a white car broadside as Kody and Ivan came up, smashing it into oblivion. Kody saw the driver get out unharmed.

Now it was two against two. The orange car and a pink one reoriented to face the two approaching black cars. The orange one came straight at Kody. Would a head-on collision leave both cars intact, or wreck both? He could not be sure how strong the bumpers were. He didn't care to risk it, but the orange car was giving him little choice.

He swerved to the side, but the oncoming car swerved to match him. It wanted that collision! He swerved to the other side, and again the other matched him. He started to swerve a third time, then reversed before completing it. The other car had no time to correct before they slid past each other so closely that paint scraped.

"Hang on!" Kody muttered to the others. Then he threw the car into a turnaround skid and accelerated back the way he had just come. Yukay opened her mouth to scream, but Zosi, who evidently had stronger nerves, or maybe duller zombie nerves, cautioned her.

The orange car was just turning to come at him again, and was caught broadside by his surprise maneuver. It was finished.

But as Kody tried to pull away from it, the pink car caught him broadside, staving in his midsection. His car lost power; a key cable had been broken. He was out of the race.

But as the pink car disengaged, Ivan caught it broadside and sent it spinning. It slid to a halt and moved no more.

Ivan went on to cross the finish line, the winner. Kody and the others climbed out of their cars, all losers. But they had succeeded in promoting one of their own number to the victory. They assembled in the prize area.

"AND WHAT PRIZE DO YOU CHOOSE?" the loudspeaker asked. Kody saw Polly Ester, every bit as buxom in the flesh as in the poster, waiting expectantly.

"The robot bomb sniffer," Ivan said.

Kody felt his jaw dropping. What did Ivan want with that? Polly looked amazed, then angry. She had been snubbed.

Ivan took the sniffer and brought it to Kody. "This should help," he said.

"But you wanted the affair with Polly Ester!"

"I guess I'd rather have a woman who wants me for myself, instead of as a prize. My prize was selfish; yours is for the good of Xanth. I prefer to be more like you."

"I am impressed," Yukay said. "When the Quest is done, and the Curse is gone, and I am attractive to you, I will see about satisfying your selfish side."

"But you want Kody, not me!"

"Kody will be gone; you will still be around."

"And why do you think I'd want to be with you, after you ignored me so long?"

She stepped in to him and kissed him.

Ivan, visibly stunned, took a moment to reorient. "Asked and answered," he said. Yukay merely smiled, faintly. She had the power of any pretty girl, and knew it. She just hadn't seen fit to apply it to this particular target before.

"And you, Zap," Kody said. "That prize you want—"

"Squawk." It was negation.

"Let's find a lodge for the night," Naomi said. "The day is late and we're all tired. Tomorrow will be another day."

There were free accommodations for the contestants. They had dinner at a nice inn, and went to a well-appointed private log cabin for the night. Demo Derby was a good host.

Kody said nothing about his understanding with Zosi, fearing that it would only mess up the unity of the group. They slept in separate bunks, each person alone.

It took him some time to get to sleep. The situation bothered Kody increasingly. He had a Quest to fulfill, his only known purpose being here in this odd fantasy realm. He would be gone when it was done. He had no business getting emotional about any Xanth woman, whatever her nature. Certainly he should not be encouraging her. But he was, and was.

And that was only the beginning of his problem.

If there was a way out of it without hurting anyone, especially Zosi, he was unable to fathom it.

# 10
# ALTER EGO

In the morning, refreshed, they considered the big box
containing the Bomb Sniffer. On the side it said SOME
ASSEMBLY REQUIRED.

Kody groaned inwardly. He knew that that meant: a horrible
hassle. "I think we need a safe, quiet, comfortable place to focus
on this. Where can we go to find such a place?"

"Maybe the cheese board has something," Yukay said.

They looked at the chessboard. "Princess Dawn told me not to
depend on this," Kody said. "Lest it have a limited amount of invo-
cations, and not be usable when I need it. But I can't think of any
other way to progress."

"It has already shown us that the greatest divergence in perceptions is likely to be in panhandle Xanth," Yukay said. "We'll need
it to get away from this world, but once we're back in Xanth we can
trek overland if we have to."

"We're not making much progress anyway," Kody said.

"So let's go somewhere comfortable, and consider," Yukay said.
"Once we assemble the Bomb Sniffer, that may solve the problem."

They looked at the board. "Say!" Kody said. "There's Caprice
Castle!"

"I have heard of it," Yukay said.

"I was there soon after I arrived in Xanth. They were very kind to me, and helped me get oriented."

"So you want to visit there again?"

"I wouldn't mind."

"What is this castle?" Zosi asked. "I never heard of it."

"Few have," Yukay said. "It entered the mainstream scene only a few years ago. It was crafted by the Demon Pundit to collect and store surplus puns, so as to clean some of these annoying weeds out of Xanth. It travels randomly around the peninsula, having no permanent mooring; it simply fades out at one site and fades in at another. The original proprietor got seduced and corrupted by a scheming lady pun and was turned into a loathsome music monster as punishment. Then Picka Bone defeated the monster but also interceded for him, and he now serves Picka loyally, collecting puns. Picka married Princess Dawn, and they ride the castle, cleaning out nasty nests of puns wherever they find them. I understand Princess Harmony does volunteer service there, also courting her boyfriend while they work."

"She does," Kody agreed. "I met them. They are nice folk."

"So an ordinary person can't just go to Caprice Castle," Yukay concluded. "Because it isn't stationary. It is also choosy about whom it lets in. I'm surprised it is on that chessboard."

Now Kody was surprised too. "I never thought of that. I thought a castle meant civilization, so I went there. I'm glad I did."

"It may not have been entirely coincidence," Yukay said. "Xanth needed you for this Quest, so somehow arranged to provide you with what you needed to accomplish it."

"And now the Bomb Sniffer, thanks to Ivan."

Ivan laughed. "And here I thought I was doing the right thing on my own. You mean I was just part of a programmed grand plan?"

Yukay considered. "If the grand plan were that specific, it should have been able to set Kody up without involving the rest of us. More likely it provided you with the opportunity to do the right thing, and you took that opportunity, proving your mettle."

"And got your attention?"

"And got my attention," Yukay agreed. "This whole thing smacks suspiciously of a Demon contest."

"A what?"

"The capital D Demons, as contrasted with the relatively insignificant lowercase d demons, amuse themselves by making bets on obscure human events. They may set things up, then observe without interference while their human pawns act. I understand there was a Demon bet on whom Princess Harmony would choose to marry, at the time when half a dozen suitors were vying for her hand. Now I believe there is a bet on whether she will succeed in corralling the one she chose, after he turned her down."

"The fool turned down a lovely princess?" Ivan asked, astonished.

"He's from Mundania. He doesn't know any better."

"Oh, of course. Mundanes don't even believe in magic." Ivan glanced at Kody. "No offense."

Kody laughed. "None taken. I am the same kind of fool, at least outside this weird dream. But that reminds me: I have a magic sword. I traded with Dread Dragon to get it." He brought out the pocketknife, and saw the others repressing smiles. Then he shook it, and it expanded to full size. He chopped lightly at a chair leg, and the leg was cleanly cut off. The smiles faded. "So maybe that too was arranged," he concluded as he shrank the sword back to pocketknife size and put it away.

"Maybe it was," Yukay agreed, impressed.

"So this whole Quest could be the result of a Demon bet?" Ivan asked.

"It could be," Yukay said. "That is not to say that it is. We'll probably never know for sure. It is merely a possible explanation for seeming coincidences we encounter."

Kody mulled that over. It would explain a lot.

"Meanwhile we need to decide whether to go to Caprice Castle, or somewhere else," Naomi said.

"I'd love to see it in person," Yukay said.

"Let's vote on it," Kody suggested. "All in favor?"

Everyone agreed. It seemed they liked the idea of visiting this mysterious traveling castle.

They collected together, and Zap pecked the square. They stood before the front gate of Caprice Castle. They were definitely in Xanth, because Ivan was looking away from Yukay. She had become ugly to him.

A bell sounded. A dog barked. In about one and a third moments two young dogs charged out.

"Hello, Wolfe!" Kody called. "Hello, Rowena! Remember me? Kody Mundane?"

"Woof!" "Rowe!" Their tails were wagging. They remembered.

"I'm on my Quest. These are my Companions. We need a safe place for a few hours, and I was wondering—"

Princess Dawn appeared. "By all means, Kody." She stepped up to hug him briefly. She remained as alluring as ever.

Then she shook hands with Ivan. "That's a marvelous talent, Ivan. And it even works on people!"

"Uh, thanks." He was plainly daunted despite her phenomenal ugliness; her warmness had countered it to some extent.

Dawn hugged Zosi. "Oh, you poor thing! But with luck you won't have to be alive much longer."

"I don't know," Zosi said uncertainly. "Kody needs—"

"Oh, I see! You love him. That's awful."

"Yes."

Dawn moved on to Zap. "And you have a soul! That's a distressing burden. But if you can learn to live with it, there can be rewards."

"Squawk," Zap agreed doubtfully.

Then Yukay. "And your talent, too, is special, if only it weren't so unpredictable. But you have so many other fine qualities to compensate."

"Thank you."

Dawn hugged Naomi. "Oh, my!"

"There's something wrong? Are naga not allowed?"

"Not at all, dear. It's much worse." Dawn glanced around. "Come in, all of you. This will require some difficult discussion."

"Worse?" Naomi looked confused.

They followed Dawn into the castle, accompanied by the dogs. She settled them into chairs, and a nice rug for Zap. "We'll be glad to help you make progress in your Quest," she said to Kody. "But there's a problem you could not have anticipated. One of your number is a spy for your enemy."

All of them stared at her. "Spy?" Kody asked.

"Not knowingly. That's why it is difficult." Dawn turned to Naomi. "You are not a real person. You are a construct that will disintegrate within a month. You are being cruelly used to betray the one person you most want not to hurt."

"I don't understand," Naomi said. "I have no intention of betraying anyone, certainly not Kody. He rescued me from a dragon, surely saving me from ravishment and ugly death, at great risk to himself, and I really like him. You say I am going to perish anyway?"

"Yes. You are a kind of twin, an alter ego of the one who set off the Bomb. Her name is NoAmi, meaning no friend. You are her opposite in every way: lovely where she is ugly, nice where she is nasty, well-meaning where she is full of malice. Her opposite, but nevertheless animated by her life force. You share her soul. You were sent to intercept Kody and prevent him from locating the Bomb, so that it won't be turned off."

Kody kept silent. This was fascinating but alarming information. He saw the others keeping similarly mum.

"But I want to help him!" Naomi protested.

"Opposite to her design," Dawn agreed.

"But if I help him, how does that satisfy her?"

"In two ways. First, you would never have been suspected, because you do want to help him, and are falling in love with him."

"No! I am merely teasing him, as Yukay is. We're not serious."

Dawn merely looked at her.

"Falling in love," Naomi agreed faintly. "Maybe it started as teasing, but when he rescued me it got serious."

"I didn't know," Kody said. "I thought it was teasing."

"I'm still teasing," Yukay said. "She isn't. Neither is Zosi."

"But you know I can't stay!"

"That's why teasing is safe," Yukay said. "But sometimes it gets out of hand."

"This is part of the plot," Dawn said. "Naomi is designed as she is so she can literally seduce you away from your Quest. She had to fall for you, because you are unlikely to be fooled by an insincere schemer. When she was made, her mistress did not know that Zosi and Yukay would join you. You were still on the way to see the Good Magician. But she was made to be competitive in this respect, and she is. You have not seen her when she tries."

"Not anymore," Naomi said, pained. "I won't touch him now."

"You will have no choice," Dawn said. "You can't go against your nature."

Kody was not comfortable with this development. "What is the second way she is helping her evil alter ego?" he asked Dawn.

"She is a complete spy. Everything that Naomi sees or hears is being relayed to her mistress. Thus NoAmi knows all about your Quest."

Kody felt a chill. "Including this present interview?"

"No. She can't penetrate Caprice Castle, which has its own potent magic. But the moment you leave here, NoAmi will know everything in Naomi's memory, so it's only a temporary reprieve."

"Then I can't leave here!" Naomi said.

"You will have to, when Kody does. Remember the pain you felt when the dragon abducted you? It was not merely your fear of ravishment and death; it was that you were separated too far from Kody. You have to stay within range of him, or suffer unbearably."

"Then I'll just hunker down near him and do nothing to interfere with him."

Dawn shook her head. "No. You have not yet felt the compulsion to prevent him from finding the Bomb, because there has been no opportunity for him to do that yet, but when he does succeed on orienting on it, you will be compelled to act."

Naomi sank to the floor, sobbing. Kody got up, stepping toward her, wanting to comfort her, but stopped himself.

"Oh, do it," Yukay said. "She won't hurt you."

Kody looked at Dawn. "Am I . . . safe?"

"Here in Caprice Castle you are," Dawn said, understanding that it was not physical safety that concerned him. "Not outside it."

He went to Naomi, put his arms around her, and lifted her up to stand in his embrace. She turned in to him, still weeping. "I'm so sorry! I'm so sorry!" she wailed.

"So are we all," he said. "But we'll try to find a way around this."

"There is no way," she sobbed.

Then he became aware that she was too close to him. Her whole body was pressing into him, and it was a phenomenal body. It was turning him on embarrassingly. He realized that she was probably not conscious of it; the process was automatic. She simply was compelled to make her female nature score. As Dawn had said, she was equipped.

He tried to pull away, but she clung desperately. His attempt merely succeeded in snagging her blouse, drawing it open, baring a breast. As a naga whose clothing was awkward when she changed, she wore no underclothing, merely a simple outer shirt and skirt. The view was electric, making him want to see more.

He had to break this up without succumbing or hurting her or embarrassing the whole group. But how?

Then he got a notion. He conjured a reverse wood chip. He touched it to her bare shoulder.

Naomi froze an eighth of a moment. Then she drew away, covering up. "What am I doing?"

"It was just an accidental wardrobe malfunction," Kody said quickly. "My clothing snagged on yours. I apologize."

She glanced at him, now away from the chip and no longer emotionally reversed. She fully understood what had happened. "No need to apologize." Literally true.

Kody returned to his chair. "I fear we have some things to figure out before we get to the Bomb Sniffer," he said.

The others nodded grimly.

"All of you are of course welcome to stay here at Caprice Castle until this matter is resolved," Dawn said. "Naomi must remain inside, which means Kody should also, lest he cause her avoidable pain. In fact, the closer the two of you are together, the less pain she will feel. Do you wish to share a room?"

"No!" Naomi cried in emotional agony.

"I agree," Kody said. "That would be asking for trouble."

"Here is the logic," Dawn said. "She must make every effort to stop you from reaching the Bomb. One obvious way would be to seduce you, make you love her, and voluntarily give up the mission for her sake. She is motivated to try that first. It might be better to give her that opportunity than to force an alternative."

"Alternative?" Kody asked.

"She might have to try to kill you."

He considered that. It did make sense. If she loved him she would not want to kill him, and would suffer grievously if she had to do it, but if she had no alternative, she would have to make the attempt. Kody was not sure he could be killed, here in Xanth, but the equivalent might be simply to end the dream and send him home to Mundania. In any event, it would end the Quest, which would give victory to NoAmi. It might be better to buy time by giving Naomi the chance to seduce him if she could.

Except for one thing. He was already close to loving Zosi. That might protect him. But how would Zosi feel about letting Naomi try to seduce him? Zosi was already in serious doubt about continuing her living state. If that pushed her over the edge, and she returned to zombie status, her Quest to restore the zombies would end in failure, or at least be long delayed.

"Put it to a vote," Yukay suggested.

At least that would eliminate the difficult decision for him. "Do you want to vote?" he asked the group.

A glance circled around, eliciting nods. They were ready.

"Then vote, the four of you," Kody said. "Naomi and I won't vote, of course."

"I will call the roll," Yukay said. "Should Naomi room with Kody, whatever that may lead to. Ivan?"

"No," Ivan said. "He can see her as she is. I saw her that way in Hades and on Demo. She's a knockout. She'll seduce him."

"One nay," Yukay said. "Zap?"

"Squawk." It was affirmative.

"One nay, one yea," Yukay said. "Tie vote. I will abstain, so that it can't conclude as a tie. That leaves it to Zosi. Zosi?"

"Yes," Zosi whispered.

Kody stared at her, astonished. "But that means—"

"She must have her chance to accomplish her mission," Zosi said. "We all deserve that. She must win you or lose you."

"But what if she wins me?" Kody asked, appalled. "She's no incompetent creature. She's one bleep of a lot of woman, as Ivan says. I can't be sure I can hold out against her." He glanced at Dawn. "When she tries."

"I don't want to try," Naomi said tearfully. "Because I don't think you can resist me, when I try."

"Then we all lose, including you, Kody, because you will give up your Quest," Zosi said. "But we will have our answer."

Yukay too was surprised. "I thought you would vote no, Zosi. You love him yourself. That's why I cleared the way for you. Are you sure?"

"Thank you," Zosi said. "I am sure."

Yukay spread her hands. "Then so be it. The motion is carried, two to one. Kody rooms with Naomi."

"I think you have put me in the lion's den," Kody muttered.

"Not the lion," Dawn said. "The naga. That's more formidable."

"I would rather have roomed with Zosi."

Now Zosi smiled, faintly. "All you have to do is resist her. Then it will be my turn." She paused thoughtfully. "Or even if you don't."

"If I don't what?"

"If you don't succeed in resisting her. I would rather have a small leftover part of you, than none. I will always be yours to claim, on any basis."

"Zosi, no!"

"She truly loves you," Dawn said. "She would rather see you happy with another woman, than unhappy with her. She may lose you, but you can't lose her."

"I don't want to be happy with another woman!"

"We have here what I believe is called a situation," Yukay said. "A kind of triangle, wherein none of the participants want to play it out the likely way, yet all are bound to do so anyway. Someone is going to be hurt. Maybe all of you." She looked at Dawn. "Can't they simply refuse to participate?"

"And proceed as before, as if they have learned nothing?" Dawn asked. "That would mean that NoAmi would continue to know exactly what Kody is doing, and be able to balk it by means of her choosing."

Yukay sighed. "I suppose then it does have to be played out."

"It does," Ivan agreed. "What use to get the Bomb Sniffer if she can counter it regardless?"

"Squawk," Zap agreed.

"So it seems you do have to settle things with Naomi," Dawn said.

"I hate this," Kody said.

But that night he shared a room with Naomi. He donned a bathrobe, ready to take a shower. But she blocked his way.

"There is an easy way for you to handle this," she said as she undressed and stood beautifully naked. "Take your magic sword and cut off my head. I will die immediately and you will have no further problem. Except for a bit of blood to clean off the floor."

"I couldn't do that," he protested.

"Get your knife-sword. It's right there in your pants pocket on the chair. Take it out and use it."

"I am supposed to kill a lovely woman who wants only to make out with me? And live with my conscience thereafter?"

"I am your enemy. I seek to destroy your Quest and leave all of Xanth under the Curse. That's why you need to destroy me. Now, before I get close to you and subvert your resolve."

"You are not my enemy! You are an innocent person co-opted to mess me up. You don't want to do it. You don't deserve death."

"Believe me, Kody, I am dangerous to you. Don't temporize any longer. Do it now. That's the quickest and cleanest way, messy as it may be for the moment."

"No. I couldn't murder someone even if I wanted to, and I don't want to."

"Kody, please," she begged. "I want what you want. To save Xanth. This is the best way."

"I can't do it."

"Oh, Kody, you are being a fool. I love you for it, but this is disaster." She put her face in her hands. She was crying.

He went to her and embraced her. She was phenomenally soft.

"Don't let my tears get to you," she said. "That's an infamous female ploy. Push me away while you still can."

It was already too late for that. "There has to be another way."

"Any other way is doom! I can't help myself." She nestled against him, somehow inside the bathrobe with him, then straightened up and kissed him wetly. "You should never have let me touch you."

She was probably correct. But the idea of coldly killing her appalled him. "But we shall each sleep alone."

She stood close against him. She caught his hands and put them behind her back, then down to rest on her bottom. That contact transformed his awareness of her. Her warm bare bosom pressed against his chest, working its own transformation. "We shall sleep together," she said. "But we won't sleep."

He tried to back away, but she followed him step for step. He came up against the bed and fell backward, and she fell forward, on him. She kissed him.

"No," he said. But the word lacked force.

"Yes," she said, and her word had immense force.

Then he thought of Zosi. It was as if she were standing there watching them, a tear trickling from the corner of her eye. She had voted to put them together, but she had hoped he would be able to resist the naga's blandishments. She was about to be excruciatingly disappointed.

He could not do that to her.

That changed him in another manner. It was as though clothing appeared between him and Naomi. He still found her infernally attractive, but he was no longer captive to her allure. They could be friends, but not lovers.

"Something changed," Naomi said.

"I remembered Zosi."

"And you love her," she agreed. "I think that's the only shield you could have raised against me."

"I don't hate you, Naomi. Had things been otherwise maybe I could have loved you. But you came on the scene too late."

"I'm glad."

"Glad?"

"Kody, you know I am not doing what I want to, but what I have to. I want you to be rid of me, and to succeed in your Quest. And yes, to love Zosi, who surely deserves it."

"I'm going to break her heart when I leave Xanth. I hate that."

"Then don't wait any longer with her. The moment this night is done, go to her and love her. Don't waste any more time."

"This is the advice of an enemy agent?"

"I was sent by your enemy, but I am not your enemy."

"I apologize. Of course you aren't."

"We are all in difficult positions. At least I can sleep with you for a while."

"But—"

"Literally." She kissed him, then rested her head on his shoulder and closed her eyes. In moments she was sleeping.

Oh. Sleeping as in sleeping. He relaxed and closed his own eyes. He was in effect naked, with a lovely naked woman against him, but now the fatigue of sustained effort caught up, and he slept too.

He woke later in the night. Naomi was gone. Had she given up, or merely repaired to the bathroom?

Then he heard the hissing. Something was in the room, and it wasn't a bare woman. It sounded more like a dragon. He strained to see in the gloom, but couldn't make out any details of anything.

The hiss grew louder. It was coming toward him! Somehow a reptile had gotten into the castle, into the room, and was attacking. It must have dispatched Naomi already and was coming for him.

Kody conjured a reverse wood chip and flipped it at the thing. But he heard the whoosh as it blew the chip away, untouched. It knew about his talent!

The chip landed on the soft quilt on the edge of the bed. The quilt reversed into a hard bed of nails. Then the chip fell to the floor and bounced under the bed, apparently losing power. The quilt reverted to softness.

Both Kody and the unseen attacker were momentarily distracted by the transformation. Then he heard it advancing again.

He flung out his arm, casting for the chair beside the bed. There were his trousers. He foraged frantically for the knife in the pocket. He found it, and gripped it.

There was a third hiss. Now he saw it: the head of a huge serpent. Its jaws gaped as it oriented on him. Then it plunged at him.

He whipped the knife around, expanding to the sword. He put it up to block the striking serpent. The head came down above it, but the blade caught the neck and cut deeply into it. Blood spilled out as the serpent collapsed.

Then it changed. Naomi lay there, half on the bed, bleeding from a deep cut at the base of her neck. She was a naga, a serpent-woman. He had forgotten. "I'm done for!" she gasped.

"Naomi! Why?"

"Just kiss me, please."

He dropped the sword and put his face to hers. He kissed her, but even as he did, he felt the life go out of her. She lay in her own pooling blood.

Then others were in the room with him. "I slew her," Kody said brokenly. "I didn't mean to."

"She made you do it," Dawn said. "That was her design."

"Made me?" But of course she had.

"There were only three likely outcomes of her required mission," Dawn said. "Seduction and corruption of you, or her death, or yours. She chose her own."

"But I refused to kill her!"

"So she tricked you. Perhaps that was best."

"She attacked me! I had to defend myself. Luckily I found my sword in time. But I didn't realize—"

"Good thing she didn't remember the sword," Yukay said. "She could have stolen it and rendered you helpless."

"But she did remember! She knew exactly where it was. She told me."

"And yet she didn't hide it before she attacked you?"

"She didn't," he agreed.

"How did you become aware of her?" Dawn asked.

"She hissed. Three times."

"She did not have to do that. She could have been silent. She wanted you to hear." Dawn paused. "And when she struck, how fast was it?"

"Not so fast I couldn't counter with the sword."

"A naga can strike with lightning speed."

Kody put it together. "She left the sword alone. She hissed to warn me. She struck slowly. She didn't want to kill me. She wanted me to kill her."

"She loved you, in her fashion," Dawn said. "She wanted you to live, and to succeed in your Quest. She knew you couldn't do that as long as she was with you. So she did what she had to do, to free you of her."

"Love is like that," Zosi said.

"And I didn't even let her seduce me," Kody said, stricken anew. "Oh, Naomi! I'm sorry!"

"We must vacate this room, so the castle can clean it up," Dawn said. "I don't think you should be alone tonight, Kody. You should be with someone."

"I will share," Zosi said.

Kody found himself emotionally balked. In half a moment he realized why. "The last person I shared with, who loved me, is dead by my hand. I don't dare be with you, Zosi. Not right now."

Zosi nodded, understanding.

"Then share with me," Yukay said. "I am intrigued by you, I care for you, I flirt with you, but I don't love you, so I'm safe."

"You are safe," he agreed, hoping he wasn't being cruel.

She led him to her room, where he cleaned off the spattered blood on him, changed, and lay down. She lay beside him. "I will leave you alone, if you wish. Or I will hold you and try to comfort you. I have no design but to help you get through this horror."

"Hold me," he agreed.

She put her arms about him and drew him in. He lay with his face against her soft bosom, and he cried.

One part of him observed with a certain bemusement. He had never before been with a woman in this manner, either. It was a revelation. Her embrace really was shielding him from the immediate horror of his guilt.

Fortunately he did not dream of the horror. Maybe her silent consoling was responsible for that, too. He realized that Yukay was a good woman in ways he had not before appreciated.

He woke in the morning, still in her comforting embrace. "Did you get any sleep?" he asked, belatedly guilty for his selfishness.

"I got enough," Yukay said. "Your need was greater than mine. Fortunately my talent enabled me to do what needed to be done, without thinking about it."

"You did," he agreed. "I feel somewhat better now. Not so close to the gulf."

"You face another gulf with Zosi."

"Zosi! Did I hurt her by refusing to be with her?"

"No. She knew you feared for her safety. She knows you love her."

"I think I do. But when this Quest is done, I will leave her. I will have no choice. That tears me up."

"I know it does. All I can say is that sometimes things don't work out the way we expect."

"This is all a dream! I can't stay in it forever."

"It is not a dream to us. I don't know the answer. But one may come."

Kody did not argue with her. What possible answer could there be, that would not hurt someone?

They got up, and in due course joined the others. There was Zosi, looking forlorn. Kody knew she would have preferred to be the one to comfort him, but that she also knew why she couldn't.

He went to her and swept her into his embrace. He kissed her. No words needed to be said.

"We need to bury the body," Dawn said. "We can handle it without your participation if you prefer, or we can hold a small service."

"The service," Kody said immediately. The others agreed.

Naomi's body was on a wheeled cart, covered by a shroud. Picka Bone hauled it out, and the two children, Piton and Data, walked sedately behind it. Kody, Yukay, Ivan, and Zap followed. They moved out of the castle proper, to its central court, and from there to a garden in back.

But when they left the castle, something happened. Smoke seemed to be coming from under the shroud. Picka lifted it and stood surprised.

The body was dissolving into dust. Soon that blew away, and the cart was empty.

"She was a temporary construct," Dawn said. "When she ceased to be animated, she disintegrated."

Somehow that did not make Kody feel better. "May we have the service anyway?"

"Of course."

They stood around the cart. Then Kody was moved to speak. "Oh, Naomi, you were sent to be my enemy, but I know you weren't. You sacrificed your life so that I could continue my Quest. I am sorry I couldn't find a better way to handle it. I just didn't understand enough, soon enough. I hope that if there is a Heaven in this magic land, that you are in it now. I—" But he was unable to continue, choked up.

"She did have half a soul," Dawn said. "So she does have an Afterlife. I'm sure by her sacrifice she earned her place in Heaven."

"And what of the other half of her?" Ivan asked. "The original, who sent Naomi to her doom instead of doing her own dirty work, who continues to live, and to maintain the Bomb's Curse on Xanth?"

"Squawk."

They looked at Zap. On her side was printed HELL.

"NoAmi has earned her place in Hell," Yukay agreed.

"Hell," Zosi agreed.

Kody experienced a wave of resolution. If Naomi had deserved love, NoAmi deserved hate. "And I will do my best to send her there!"

The others nodded grimly. Now the Quest was not merely to improve things for the ordinary folk of Xanth. It was for vengeance.

# 11
# BOMB SNIFFER

T hey got to work on the Bomb Sniffer immediately. Their Quest party was joined by the children and the puppies. When they opened the box, it turned out to consist of myriad small packages containing wheels, screws, panels, wires, and obscure fixtures. There were detailed instructions, but they were so dense as to be opaque.

"Well, it is a robot," Yukay said.

"What's a science thing like a robot doing in a fantasy land like Xanth?" Kody asked, frustrated.

"Robots are part of Xanth," Yukay said. "There was a considerable battle a few years ago, to prevent the robots from taking over Xanth. The few that are left are reasonably well behaved."

"Then maybe we should get one of them to help us put this thing together."

"Great idea," Ivan said.

"I was being facetious."

"But it does make sense," Yukay said. "If anyone knows how to assemble a robot, it's another robot. At one time they had whole robot factories. Maybe Princess Dawn knows one."

The children and puppies dashed off to find Dawn. And in

barely a moment and three-quarters, she was there. "Yes, as it happens I do know a person who can help. His name is Cyrus Cyborg."

"A cyborg?" Kody asked. "Isn't that a human/machine combination?"

"Yes. His parents were Roland Robot and Hanna Barbarian."

"A robot and a barbarian woman? That must have been quite a story."

"It was. So is Cyrus's association with Princess Rhythm."

"I remember that," Yukay said. "It was quite a scandal."

"Princess Rhythm," Kody said. "She's one of the three seventeen-year-old princesses we have encountered. Isn't she entitled to a romance?"

"She was twelve at the time," Yukay said. "She used an aging spell to add a decade to her life, making her twenty-two for an hour at a time, but not everyone believed that was proper. However, in the course of that romance, she did work with her sisters to save Xanth from conquest by Ragna Roc, so her folks were lenient."

"I see," Kody said, though he was not at all sure he did. There was evidently more to this fantasy land than he was ever likely to explore.

"At any rate," Dawn said, "I'm sure Rhythm will be glad to lead Caprice Castle to Counter Xanth, where Cyrus is exiled."

The machine-man was exiled, but his girlfriend could visit him? Kody wondered whether her folks knew about that, but it was surely best not to remark on it. "That's good," he said.

Soon Rhythm showed up, quite similar to Harmony, only with red hair and dress, and green eyes, as he remembered. "Sure, I can lead you to Cyrus." She glanced at Dawn. "Only . . ."

"Off the record," Dawn agreed with a smile. "Your folks need not know."

"Next year when I'm eighteen, I'll marry him. Then no one can tell us no."

"No one," Dawn agreed. "No one was able to stop me from marrying a walking skeleton, either."

So the several princesses knew what was going on, and kept

the secret, in the conspiracy of youth. So would Kody and his companions.

"We are there," Dawn said.

"In Counter Xanth?" Yukay asked, surprised.

"Yes."

"But we haven't gone anywhere!"

"Look out the window."

They looked out. The entire landscape had changed. Now it was weird.

"So Caprice Castle faded out and faded in, and we're there," Yukay said in wonder. "I never felt a thing."

"That is the nature of it," Dawn agreed. "Now we don't want to go outside, because we are unused to the type of reversals that exist here. But that's no problem; Cyrus will come in."

"I'll fetch him," Rhythm said, and vanished, literally.

"Those three princesses," Kody said. "I understood that no person had more than one magic talent in Xanth, but they seem to have many."

"They are general-purpose Sorceresses," Dawn explained. "Whatever they sing and play together can become real. They have sung up a number of spot spells they can call on at need. Rhythm just used one of them. She's the drummer; her talent is drumming things real. But with a prepared spell she merely thinks the drumbeat and accomplishes it."

"I'm impressed," Kody said.

"Sorceresses are impressive, however young and innocent they may choose to appear," Yukay said. "It is best for the rest of us never to forget it."

Kody knew that was a serious warning.

"Even so, the triplets are special," Dawn said. "Each is a Sorceress in her own right, but when two of them get together their power is squared, and when all three focus, it is cubed. When they took on Ragna Roc, who had similar power, nothing seemed to be happening, but the very blocks of his castle melted from the force of the warring magics."

Very serious. Even the Sorceress Princess Dawn was evidently careful not to annoy the triplets.

Rhythm reappeared. This time a man was beside her. He looked distinctly ordinary, but there was a slightly mechanical slant to him, as if he was partly made of metal. This had to be Cyrus.

"They have a Robot Bomb Sniffer in a box," Rhythm said. "Some Assembly Required."

"Which means that no one in his right mind can do it," Cyrus said with a knowledgeable smile.

"Fortunately Cyrus has never been in his right mind," Rhythm said fondly.

"I fell in love with you," Cyrus retorted.

"Which proves it."

"Touché," he agreed. He examined the spread contents of the box. "First, we'll just ignore the instructions; they are never much good, being written by angry elves in Mundania who want to be sure that no one else has any fun."

"I like this man," Kody murmured to Zosi.

Cyrus began putting parts together, and Rhythm helped him, seeming to know what he needed when. "We'll need a small supply of dry firewood."

"Firewood?" Kody asked, surprised.

Cyrus glanced at him. "You have not had experience with robots?"

"Not with magic ones."

"Ah. They burn wood."

Wood-burning robots!

"We'll fetch some," Piton and Data said together. They dashed out, accompanied by the pups.

"If I may ask," Kody said, "how did you first get together with Rhythm? I understand she was only twelve at the time."

"I'm not sure I'm supposed to tell. I got banished for it."

"*I'll* tell," Rhythm said. "They can't banish *me*. Cyrus is a playwright. He's good at it. I was part of the troupe. I admired his ability. I got a girlish crush on him."

"Girls do," Yukay said.

"I got him alone and told him. But he brushed me off. 'You're a child!' he told me, as if I didn't know. So I was a girl scorned."

Cyrus smiled as they worked. "Later I learned the three rules of romance: never scorn a woman, even a young one. Or a princess. Especially a Sorceress."

"Three strikes," Kody agreed.

"So I invoked a spell to make me twenty-two for an hour, busted out of my clothing, put my arms around him, and leaped into a love spring." Rhythm smiled reminiscently. "That fixed him. That hour left him passionately in love with a woman who wouldn't exist for ten years."

"It has been only five years," Cyrus said. "But you resemble her a lot."

"Are you flirting with me?" she asked archly.

"If I say no, will you feel scorned?"

"Yes."

"Then I wouldn't dare."

Rhythm frowned prettily. "Are you going to kiss me?"

Cyrus looked around as if nervous. "Will anyone tell?"

"No," Dawn said.

Cyrus stood up and kissed Rhythm. They made a lovely couple, and were obviously deeply in love. Little hearts radiated out and circled around them.

"Later I learned it wasn't really a love spring," Cyrus said as the hearts cleared. "But it was too late."

"It was too late the moment I got my crush," Rhythm said as they went back to work. "I was going to cast my spell on you one way or another."

They continued assembling the robot, which was rapidly taking shape as a doglike device with small wheels for feet and an antenna for a nose.

"Are you going to kiss me?" Zosi asked Kody, taking his hand. "Even if there's not a love spring here?"

Kody was discovering the joys of flirting for himself. "Will you feel scorned if I don't?"

"I may."

"Will anyone tell?"

"Yes," Dawn said with a straight face. The others laughed. They knew he had no way out.

Kody embraced her. She was delightful to hold and kiss, and he could no longer pretend he didn't love her. And when it ended, there were the little hearts.

But his time in Xanth remained limited. Where would their love be when he was recalled to Mundania? That haunted him. He had killed Naomi physically. Was he destined to kill Zosi emotionally?

"It's done," Cyrus announced, standing back from the assembled robot. "Now we need the fuel to animate it. Once it has a fire in its belly, it will come alive, as it were."

Kody realized that life could be hard to define, in a land where even inanimate things could have feelings.

The children and dogs returned, hauling a bundle of dry sticks. Maybe they had been waiting for the announcement.

Cyrus opened a door in the sniffer's side, revealing a metallic cavity. He put in several sticks and some dry moss. Then Rhythm snapped her fingers, making a spark, and the moss caught fire. She blew on it, and it blazed up through the sticks. She shut the door. Smoke came out of the sniffer's rear end. Then its head section lifted and looked around. "Woof!" it said.

"Woof!" Wolfe and Rowena answered together, and the two children clapped their little hands. The sniffer was functional.

"This is Kody Mundane," Cyrus said, indicating Kody. "He is your master. He will take care of you and tell you what to sniff."

The sniffer's head turned to gaze at Kody. That was all.

"It understands human speech?" Kody asked.

"Yes. This model is unable to talk, but its brain unit is fully equipped to understand. It will be operative as long as you maintain its fire. The fire generates smoke and steam to do the work."

"That's science!"

"Which is the form of magic Mundania uses," Cyrus agreed. "Give it a directive."

"The Bomb," Kody said. "Find the Bomb."

Immediately the sniffer was scrambling for the door.

"Not yet!" Kody said hastily. "Right now, just stop and point your nose toward it."

The robot stopped. It sniffed the air. Then its nose pointed directly toward Princess Dawn.

"Believe me, I am not the one you seek," Dawn said, laughing.

"I think I have it," Yukay said. "You did not sufficiently define 'Bomb.' Princess Dawn is one of the most beautiful women in Xanth. The fact that most folk see her as ugly right now does not change the underlying fact."

"A bombshell," Kody breathed.

"A type of bomb, to be sure," Cyrus agreed.

And things tended to be literal in Xanth. "A more, um, functional Bomb," Kody said. "One that affects people."

The robot sniffed the air again. Then it pointed to Cyrus.

"I'm not a bomb," Cyrus protested.

"Maybe you are," Rhythm said. "Remember that last play you wrote? The one that did not do well?"

"It bombed," Cyrus agreed ruefully. "It affected many people negatively."

Kody cast about for a better description. "We don't know exactly how the Bomb works. Maybe it affects the air, diffusing throughout Xanth."

The sniffer walked to the corner of the room. There was a little device emitting sweet-smelling mist.

"That's our aerosol bomb," Dawn said.

"Let me try something," Yukay said. She rummaged in her purse and brought out what looked like a tube of lipstick. She applied it to her lips.

The robot turned to face her, its nose pointing to her face.

"Squawk!" Zap exclaimed.

"Lip bomb," Zosi echoed.

"Don't you mean lip balm?" Kody asked. "I heard the variant spelling, but it doesn't make sense."

Yukay glanced at Zosi. "May I?"

"Do it," Zosi agreed, seeming to suppress a laugh.

Yukay approached Kody. "Brace yourself," she said. "This will blow you away." Then she kissed him.

It was like a concussion grenade detonating. Kody picked himself up off the floor across the room. "What happened?" he asked dazedly. He wasn't hurt, but the impact had been considerable.

"She kissed you with the lip bomb," Zosi explained. "It blew you away."

Another pun. "It blew me away," he agreed.

"I believe we are done here," Cyrus said.

"Thank you so much for your help," Kody said. "I doubt we could have assembled it without your expertise."

"You are welcome. It was a pleasure meeting you. I hope you succeed in saving Xanth."

Then Rhythm took Cyrus's arm, and the two of them vanished.

"You are welcome to stay here in Caprice Castle," Dawn said. "But you may prefer to get out in regular Xanth, where you can remain in one place, and practice with the sniffer. You will want to understand it well before you actually zero in on the Bomb."

That did make sense. "Then I think it is time for us to depart," Kody said. "With our thanks."

"It has been a pleasure," Dawn said. "Especially because I know you see me as I am. I do grow tired of seeing men turn ill with disgust when they look at me."

"We shall do our best to abate the Curse," Kody said.

"I'm sure you will," she agreed. "Now Caprice will drop you off in the area you prefer. Where would that be?"

"Panhandle Xanth," Kody said promptly. "We have determined that the Bomb is most likely there."

"You may exit now, then. But beware; my reading of Naomi indicated that her other ego is a vicious creature. A naga, but opposite in personality. She will not give warning or strike slowly. Be constantly on guard."

"We'll try to be," Kody agreed.

They left the castle, which now nestled in a pleasantly rolling landscape behind a beach and ocean shore.

"Now I think we need three things," Yukay said. "Practice, a safe place for the night, and a clearer understanding of interpersonal relationships."

"I think Zosi and I are an, um, item," Kody said.

"Which leaves Ivan for me," Yukay said. "That will do."

"It will?" Ivan asked. "I know you're pretty in real life, but right now you don't appeal to me at all."

"Let's experiment a bit." She turned to Kody. "You won't mind a small delay while we sort this out?"

Kody was curious what she had in mind. "I won't mind."

"Then flip me a chip."

He conjured a chip and flipped it to her. Yukay caught it. Nothing happened.

Then she spoke. "Thanks for nothing, you ignorant Mundane. I thought those chips were real. This is useless."

"Yukay—" Zosi began, upset.

"Stay out of this, you refugee from the graveyard. It's a wonder you're not dropping stinking clods all around."

"Squawk!"

"You too, birdbrain. This is none of your business."

Ivan shook his head. "Now you're as ugly verbally as you are physically."

"Yeah, meat-face? You're no prize yourself. What did I ever think I saw in you, you lousy loser?"

Kody thought of something. "Ditch the chip!"

"You bet, chip-faker." She threw the chip to the ground, where it struck a star-shaped flower. The flower glowed brightly, swelled up, pulled a pistol, and started firing wildly around, so that they all had to duck.

Then the chip dropped to the ground, fell into a crack, and was lost.

Yukay stared after it. "That chip converted a star jasmine flower into a shooting star," she said. "It was potent after all."

"It was," Kody agreed. "When you held it, it reversed your normally pleasant nature, and made you into a grouch."

"So it did," she agreed, chagrined. "I insulted everyone. I take it all back; I didn't mean any of it."

"Reverse wood reverses in different ways," Kody said. "I never know exactly what to expect."

"I wanted it to reverse my appearance," Yukay said. "Not my nature."

"Let me try it," Ivan said. "The Curse affects the seer, not the seen. Maybe a chip would make me appreciate you."

"You're right," Yukay said. "It's how you see me that I want to change."

Ivan held out his hand, and Kody flipped a chip to it. Ivan caught it. "Oh, gee," he said bashfully. "I wouldn't know what to do with a girl, if—" He cut off, blushing.

"Instead of bold, you're shy," Yukay said. "Drop the chip."

Ivan did, taking care to drop it on bare ground, not a flower. "That was weird," he said. "I bleeping well *would* know what to do with a girl, if I had one."

"Does a chip always reverse the same way for the same person?" Zosi asked.

"I don't know," Kody admitted. "I haven't experimented all that much."

"Maybe you should," Yukay said. "Because it may be your main weapon against NoAmi, when you face her. You need to know what the potentials are, and be ready to follow up on any of them." She took a breath. "Now flip me another."

"Are you sure? I don't know that they *don't* act the same way on the same person or creature."

"We need to verify this, one way or another. Flip."

"You have courage." He flipped her another chip.

She caught it. And changed drastically. She had been lovely; now she was hideous.

"Oh, ugh!" Kody said. "You're a hag!"

"You're beautiful!" Ivan said.

"You are," Zosi agreed.

Yukay looked at Zap. "Squawk," the griffin agreed.

She looked back at Ivan. "You actually want to hold me, kiss me, et cetera?"

"I sure do! You're luscious."

Yukay brought out her little mirror and gazed at her face. "I do look lovely, don't I! But that means I am really ugly. Kody sees the truth; he knows."

"But with the goblins your mirror wasn't the same," Kody said.

"Yes, it was. Try it." She handed him the mirror.

He held it up and angled it so he could see her face. It was beautiful. "Oh, that's right, it reflects what Xanthians see." He handed it back, and she was ugly again.

"Who cares?" Ivan asked. "I'm ready if you are."

"Hold off," Yukay said. "I'm not sure I am, at least not right this minute. We're still experimenting. This means that the effect is not necessarily the same."

"It is a different chip," Kody said. "Maybe the nature of the reversal is with the particular chip I conjure, and they're not all the same."

"That must be it," Yukay said. "Let me save this one for future reference." She popped it in her purse, which did not seem to change. Was it because it was inanimate? Kody remembered how the quilt had become a bed of nails. Maybe the feathers were organic, so were affected. At any rate, Yukay herself returned to her natural state, causing the others to look away. "Maybe you should flip Ivan another."

"Sure," Ivan said, holding out his hand.

Kody flipped him another chip. He held it and gazed at Yukay. "You lovely creature," he breathed.

"You see me as beautiful? Check the others."

Ivan looked at the others. "Zosi's cute," he said. "Zap's a handsome griffin. Kody's a handsome man."

"It's reversing the Curse!" Zosi exclaimed.

"That's what we want," Yukay agreed. "But how do the rest of you see things?"

"You're still ugly," Zosi said.

"Squawk," Zap agreed.

"And I see everyone as ugly," Yukay said. "So it is affecting only Ivan's perception. Still, that's a giant step. If everyone had such a chip, the Curse would be gone."

"Except that Kody won't be staying in Xanth," Zosi said. "And we don't know how long the chips will last."

"Too limited," Yukay agreed. "Even if he stayed, he'd have to spend all his time doing nothing but conjuring piles of chips. Better to fix it the old-fashioned way: by eliminating the Bomb." She glanced at Ivan. "But save that chip. You can use it tonight. In the darkness I'll pretend you're handsome."

Ivan nodded. He found a kerchief and wrapped the chip, and put it in a pocket.

Kody was satisfied. They had learned a lot.

"Now let's try for the safe place for the night," Yukay said. "We can use it as a base for operations, relaxing between efforts."

"Efforts?" Kody asked.

"Fully understanding the sniffer and orienting on the Bomb will likely take several efforts. Things are seldom as simple as they may appear from a distance."

She was probably right. "Night place," he agreed.

They looked around. There was a path leading from the beach into the deep woods. "Where would a path lead, except to a residence?" Kody asked.

The others laughed. "Never trust an innocent path," Yukay said. "It well might lead to a tangle tree."

"What kind of tree?"

"It's a good thing you have Companions. Otherwise you'd be dead by now."

"Squawk."

Yukay looked at Zap. "This nice path does lead to a tangler? Then we'd better show Kody."

They followed the path, Zap leading the way, the sniffer puffing along behind. It went to a large green tree with branches that drooped so deeply that they almost looked like tentacles. Ivan picked up a stone and threw it at the tree.

The tentacles whipped around to catch the rock. Then, disgusted, they dropped it to the ground. But in that moment of disarray Kody had caught a glimpse of the trunk of the tree. It had a big gnarled mouth coated with what looked like dried blood, and there was a pile of broken bones beside it.

"Now I think I know what a tangle tree is," Kody said soberly. "I would have blundered into it, alone."

They walked back to the beach. "Let's see if the sniffer can help," Yukay said.

Kody looked at the sniffer, which was pacing them while emitting balls of smoke. "It sniffs only bombs," he reminded her.

"There are different kinds of bombs," she reminded him in turn. "We just have to think of an appropriate one."

"What about when you're bombed out?" Ivan asked. "And need a place to sleep it off?"

"I wonder. Kody, why don't you try that?"

This was so far-fetched as to be ludicrous. But he humored her. "Sniffer, can you sniff out a safe place for several bombed-out folk to find shelter?"

The sniffer perked up. It sniffed the air and rotated its antenna. Then it belched out another ball of smoke and started walking on its rollers. Kody noted how it really did walk, and the wheels enabled each leg to move forward after touching the ground, to provide further progress. It was actually fairly efficient.

They followed it along the beach. It seemed to know where it was going. The walk took some time, and the day was getting late. It strolled/rolled right up to—

A sleeping cat.

They stood and looked at the feline. "This is for bombed-out folk?" Kody asked.

The base of the sun dipped below the upper foliage of the trees.

Darkness was closing. They had, it seemed, wasted their time on this foolishness, and now would be caught out in the open for the night.

The cat woke. It stretched. Then it changed. It expanded hugely, causing them to step back, startled. It became the size of a house.

"A house cat!" Zosi exclaimed.

A pun! Yet there was the house, its door somewhat mouthlike, complete with side whiskers, its windows eyelike with vertical slits of light from the interior, its tail curled up to make a bushy thatch-like roof. It looked quite peaceful and perfect for shelter.

Ivan opened the door and entered. There was no protest, so the others followed. The inside seemed to be well appointed, with a couch and table in the main room and beds in the two bedrooms. There was even a bathroom and a kitchenette, though no food except for a pitcher of clear water.

"We will feast on sandwiches," Yukay said.

They did. Zosi conjured a fine assortment of peanut butter and jelly sandwiches with no hint of gasoline smell.

"Now we sleep," Yukay said. "Zap, I trust you will guard the door so that we get no unwelcome nocturnal visitations. Ivan and I will take one bedroom, Kody and Zosi the other." She looked at Ivan. "Whose chip do we use: mine or yours? We can't use both together, as the reversals would cancel out."

"Mine," Ivan said. "That way we're actually normal. That's better."

"That's better," she agreed.

Kody looked at Zosi. "Oh, yes, I'm willing," she agreed.

There was a beeping sound. They all looked around.

"Squawk."

They looked at Zap. On her side was printed SNIFFER LOW.

"The robot!"

Yukay exclaimed, "We forgot about it. Of course it needs more fuel."

"Squawk," Zap agreed, and bounded out of the house. Soon she was back with a beakful of dry branch.

Ivan took the branch and broke it into smaller sticks. Then he kneeled and opened the robot's side door. Only glowing coals remained inside. He fed in the sticks and watched as they blazed up. Then he shut the door. "But we'll need to keep an eye on it," he said. "I don't know if that will last the night."

"Squawk."

"You'll handle it? Good enough." Ivan stood up. "Where were we?"

Yukay took his arm. "Dig out your chip. We have a date."

"But don't you still see me as ugly?"

"Women are more sensible than men. We judge by more than mere appearance. When you sacrificed your hot date with Polly Ester for the good of the Quest, I saw that there was more to you than looks."

"Well, I didn't do it to impress you. It was just the right thing."

"Precisely. Anyway, as I said, it will be dark." She drew him on into the bedroom and shut the door behind them.

Kody did not inquire why, if darkness sufficed to nullify the Curse, they had not done it before.

Zosi took Kody's arm. "Our turn."

"But you see me as ugly too."

"Yukay already answered that." She drew him to the other bedroom. "Good night, Zap and Sniffer."

"Squawk."

The robot beeped. Zosi's mouth fell open. "It acknowledged!"

"It may be more of a machine than we realized," Kody agreed. And realized that the Bomb Sniffer now had a name. It was a person machine.

Alone together in the bedroom, Zosi was suddenly shy. "I assumed you would like to be with me tonight. Maybe I presumed too much, and you are just being polite. If so, I apologize. Sometimes I get carried away. So if—"

He cut her off with a kiss. Then they lay on the bed clothed, embraced, and talked.

"Zosi, you know how mixed up I am about Naomi. I treated her

politely but distantly, yet she gave her life for me. I know it's foolish, but I can't help fearing that it could be similar with you. Because I can't stay here in Xanth. I don't think it's right to lead you
on, when we have no future."

"You said you didn't even let her seduce you. Would you have,
if you had known she was about to die for you?"

"Yes, I think I would have. I didn't love her, but maybe it would
have reduced the unfairness of the situation."

"Yet you plan to leave without doing it with me?"

That hurt. "Zosi, in Mundania we usually don't do it without
the expectation of a larger commitment. I can't make that commitment."

"Just as I can't make the commitment to stay alive long enough
to governess Plato and solve the zombie problem. I'm as bad as
you are."

She was actually trying to make him feel better about it! "To
make it worse, the way I resisted Naomi's seduction was to think of
you. Of my love for you. It would have been a betrayal of you."

"And the reason I remained on your Quest was that I couldn't
bear to be away from you. Being near you is my main reason for
being willing to remain alive. I betrayed my own quest because of
personal weakness."

"Oh, Zosi!" he said, anguished. "I didn't realize."

"Not your fault," she said quickly.

"Or yours. We're both victims of hopeless love."

They kissed again. This time there was fire.

After that things proceeded on their own course, not allowing
any further dialogue to get in the way. In one moment they were
embracing and kissing. In the next they were both nude. In another
they were embracing and kissing again, more intimately than before. The room was filled with little floating, glowing hearts. Then
came the finale that blasted the hearts away and left them both
happily exhausted.

"Oh, Kody, I would tutor Plato forever if I could just come home
at night to you."

"I don't want to leave Xanth. I want to stay with you."

"And we can't," she said, her tears flowing.

"We can't," he agreed, his tears joining hers. They were united in their frustration about not being able to unite.

But this was not the past or the future. This was the present. There was nothing between them but passion.

They slept between bouts of love. It was a busy night.

In the morning Zosi's eyes suddenly went wide open. "The stork!"

"The what?"

"We signaled the stork. What will we do if it brings a baby?"

"Storks don't bring babies! That's just a fantasy told to children."

"Yes, they do. This is Xanth, a fantasy land. When people do the signaling ritual, as we did several times, they bring babies. They're not very efficient; it takes about nine months. Suppose the stork brings me a baby and you're gone and I'm not alive? I never thought of that last night."

Kody realized that in this magic realm some significant details really were different. What was a fairy tale in Mundania was literal here. "You were distracted." It was a gentle understatement.

She was not consoled. "We couldn't have made it any plainer. But the storks don't always deliver. I'll just have to hope they lose the order this time. That poor baby!"

He had no answer. So he kissed her. That seemed to suffice.

They cleaned up, dressed, and went out to join the others. Ivan and Yukay emerged at about the same time, Ivan putting away his chip. Zosi and Yukay exchanged a look that covered the whole situation and then some, so that no questions were necessary. They had just proved that they knew all about entertaining men.

"Squawk."

"The house!" Yukay agreed. "By day it returns to feline form. We need to get out."

They got out. The house shrank back into the cat.

"Thank you for the night's lodging," Zosi said to the cat. "It was very nice."

The cat opened one eye and gazed at her. Zosi blushed. Of course the cat knew all about the events of the night. Then it went to sleep.

"I wonder what dreams it has?" Ivan murmured.

"What dreams could it have, wilder than the reality?" Yukay asked rhetorically.

Kody just hoped they were not of having guests who did not leave in time, and got caught inside and digested.

They foraged for breakfast, finding a pie tree nearby, together with milkweed pods filled with fresh milk. Zap found more dry wood to re-stoke Sniffer. Kody was still getting used to the way Xanth provided for its residents. It seemed that no one really had to work. But everyone had to be on constant lookout for magical dangers, like dragons and tangle trees. On the whole, he preferred Mundania, work and all.

"Now let's try to make Sniffer locate one more thing, so we are sure we know how it works," Yukay said briskly. "I thought of another kind of bomb."

"Bombe," Zosi agreed.

That glance had really communicated!

The men looked blank.

"Bombe," Yukay explained. It was pronounced the same, but Kody heard the different spelling. "An eye scream dessert. See if Sniffer can find one."

"Find a bombe," Kody told Sniffer. He hoped the robot had a better idea of it than he did.

The robot puffed out smoke and started moving. They followed, alert for dangers along the way. Soon they came to a literal candyland. The rocks were chocolate, lollipops grew from the ground, the trees were covered with candy balls, and Ivan harvested a walking stick that was a sugar cane made of solid sugar. This was a child's delight, but they knew better than to stuff themselves with sweets.

And there was the bombe, a round dish of ice cream—eye

scream, Kody corrected himself—holding another kind of eye scream inside. In the shape of an eyeball, of course. This time they indulged themselves and ate it. It was sinfully delicious.

The sniffer had pretty well proved itself.

# 12
# GHOST

"One last thing we should do, before we move on," Yukay said. "We need to calibrate our two kinds of Bomb locators to be sure they align. Then we'll be sure we know what we're doing."

"Calibrate?" Kody asked.

"You can tell how close we are, but not specific direction. Sniffer can tell what direction, but not proximity. We need to know both, so we don't make any mistake or walk into any ugly surprises."

"Good point. The three of you and Zap all look perfectly normal to me."

Yukay looked around. "Zosi looks a degree uglier than she used to. Ivan looks a shade more brutish. And you, Kody, are stomach-turning loathsome."

"That suggests we are closer, as we expected." Kody looked at Ivan. "How do you see the rest of us?"

"If I hadn't had the chip, I would have vomited on Yukay when she touched me last night. Zosi's no prize either. And Yukay's right: you are loathsome, worse than before."

"And you, Zosi?"

"It's a good thing it was dark last night, in the bedroom, or I might have retched. Ivan's not a lot better, and Yukay is the crone of crones." She smiled. "But I never judged you by your appearance. I love you for other things."

Kody had to smile. "So we are agreed: the contrast is stronger than it was. So we are closer to the Bomb. But we still don't know how close. It could be several days' walk away, or several minutes'. We need a better measure."

"Squawk." On the griffin's side was the word PERSPECTIVE.

"You're a genius!" Kody said. "That's magic that works in both Xanth and Mundania."

"But how do we apply it?" Yukay asked.

"We move sidewise and triangulate."

But the faces of the others were blank. This was not magic they understood.

"I will demonstrate," Kody said. "Um, I think I will need a compass. But maybe I can make do with the sun and shadows."

They still looked blank.

"Zap, you stand here, with your back to the sun," Kody said. "See where your shadow points: pretty much west. So I take my position due west of you, so your shadow points right toward me."

"This is weird magic," Ivan muttered.

"Now I will travel crosswise, going north," Kody said, walking a few paces. "And sight on Zap again. And lo: she's no longer aligned with her shadow. The angle is different. I can tell by that that she's about as far away from me as the distance I just walked north. I am triangulating: sighting along two sides of a triangle. From those two sightings I can tell about how far away something is."

"But you can see Zap without all that," Ivan protested.

"But I can't see the Bomb. But the same technique will work on that. We can get an approximation today, and know how near or far from it we are."

It took awhile, but finally they came to understand the magic of perspective and triangulation and agreed that it should work.

They did a sighting based on Sniffer's pointing and judged its direction. "Just about due west," Kody said.

Then they marched north a distance and sighted again. It was still pretty much west. "That means it's not too close yet," Kody said.

They went farther north, to take another sighting. And something bothered Kody. There was a bit of clouding at the edge of his vision that disappeared when he looked directly at it. Was he having a vision problem? He dismissed it and walked on.

He saw a vague shape. It reminded him of something, or rather someone. Was his imagination playing tricks on him?

Then he got a better glimpse. "Naomi!" he exclaimed.

The others looked at him. "Is that guilt getting to you again?" Yukay asked.

"Maybe. I thought I saw her. And of course that's impossible, because—"

"Because she's dead," Yukay finished. "But it's not impossible. You could be seeing her ghost."

Kody paused. "Are ghosts literal too, in Xanth?"

"Oh, yes. If a person dies and can't make it immediately to Heaven, Hell, or somewhere else, s/he may hang around the place where s/he died."

S/he? "This isn't that place."

"But you are the one who killed her. That will do."

"She's haunting me?"

"Not necessarily. She liked you, and maybe that emotion survives her death and keeps her close. Maybe she still has something to tell you."

"I have something to tell *her*: I'm supremely sorry about killing her."

"I'm sure she already knows that."

"So what does she want with me?"

"You'll have to talk with her and find out."

Kody shook his head. "I'm not used to this kind of dealing."

"Don't be negative. It might be important. Remember, she was the alter ego crafted by the enemy. She could know things."

Kody resumed walking. The apparition became stronger. It was as though the ghost were still zeroing in on him, somewhat the way he was trying to zero in on the Bomb. What did she have on her vaporous mind?

When they reached another reasonable distance north, they stopped for another sighting. This time the direction was a little south of west. "Still not really close," Kody said. "I think we have at least another day's walk ahead of us."

*You do.*

Kody looked around. "What?" Then he saw the ghost. She remained translucently faint, but it was definitely Naomi. "Did you just speak to me?"

"No," the others said almost together.

"Be quiet," Yukay said. "He's trying to communicate with the ghost of Naomi."

"Squawk."

Kody looked at Zap. "You're aware of her too?"

"Squawk." And on her side appeared the words YOU DO.

"You heard her too!"

The griffin nodded.

"Then maybe she can manifest to all of us," Kody said. "Not just to me." That was oddly reassuring.

*I'll try.*

"Folks," Kody said. "She says she'll try. Maybe if you all try to tune in, you'll see or hear her."

The others, who of course believed in ghosts, concentrated.

"I'm beginning to see her," Zosi said. "Oops, she's naked."

"She was when she died," Kody said. "That must lock her into that state."

"Fortunately she looks ugly."

"Not to me," Kody said. "She's beautiful."

"So death has not reversed the Curse," Zosi said. "That's unkind."

"But it makes sense," Yukay said. "We have established that the Curse affects the viewer, not the viewee. So she looks the same as she did in life, and we see her as we did before."

"I'm seeing her," Ivan said. "As ugly as ever."

"Yet for me, as pretty as ever," Kody said. "It's a good thing she's not wearing panties; I'd freak out. As it is, I feel a little giddy."

"Try your chip, Ivan," Yukay said.

"Good idea." Ivan unwrapped his chip of reverse wood and held it in his hand. He looked at the shimmering image again. And promptly stiffened into a freak.

"Without bra or panties," Yukay said. "That's potent." She went to Ivan, held a handkerchief before his face to block off the image, and snapped her fingers.

"Huh?" he said, shaking his head.

"Put away your chip. You can't handle her nude image. You freaked out."

Ivan wrapped and pocketed his chip. Now he was out of danger.

Gradually Naomi became clearer, until she was like an animated glass statue, visible but not yet lifelike.

Now Zosi took the initiative, perhaps because as a lifelong zombie she had a greater familiarity with the dead. She went to hug the ghost, putting her arms carefully around the form without impinging. "We're sorry you died. We're glad to see you back. But why have you come?"

*You need my help.*

"We need your help," Zosi repeated. "In what way?"

*NoAmi is vicious. She'll kill you if you let her. You're not ready to face her.*

"Let's find a place we can be comfortable," Yukay said. "Then we can talk with Naomi at our leisure. We can sure benefit from what she has to tell us."

They cast about. Soon Zap discovered a sandalwood tree, with sandals hanging from its branches. Under those branches it was quite pleasant, as the tree maintained an environment that would not rot or warp its offerings. They found a blanket tree, harvested several large blankets, and suspended them from the branches to form a crude enclosure. It wasn't as nice as the house cat had been, but would do.

"We're depending on you, Zap, to sniff out any dangers before they reach us," Yukay said. "Because we may be distracted, communicating with Naomi."

"Squawk."

"Is that feasible?" Yukay turned to the others. "She says Sniffer could help with that."

Kody faced the robot. "We fear bombers. That is, folk or animals who might come to bomb or otherwise harm us. Can you be alert for them?"

"Beep."

"Thank you," Yukay said. "We do appreciate your effort."

Kody, bemused, did not comment. The wood-burning robot hound was becoming increasingly like a person. It was probably the ambient magic of Xanth.

"Now, Naomi," Yukay said. "Is there any one of us you can most readily communicate with, to make it easier?"

*Kody.*

"That makes sense. Then he can channel you."

Kody picked up on it. "First let me repeat: I am extremely sorry I killed you, Naomi. I didn't mean to do it, and would have avoided it if I had been more alert."

The figure thickened before him. She leaned forward and kissed him on the mouth. He felt the faint touch.

*I know. I tricked you into it. The guilt is mine. I wish I could have loved you, Kody, without hurting Zosi. But that was not to be.* She shrugged. *Now all I can do is flash you.*

He smiled. "Not to much effect. You have no panties."

*I have dream panties.* She reached into the air and picked something out of it. It was a green panty. She put it to her middle and it formed around her, along with a matching green bra. Then she turned in place, showing her pantied bottom and bra-ed bosom.

Fingers snapped at his ear. "Snap out of it, Kody," Yukay said.

"I freaked out," he said dazedly.

"You sure did," Ivan said. "I saw the panties, but they sure didn't freak me out."

"They would have if you'd been touching your chip," Yukay said.

"Bleep! I missed my chance."

"All right, Naomi," Zosi said severely. "You made your point. Now are you here to help us or hinder us?"

*To help you,* the ghost said. She giggled naughtily. *But that certainly was fun.* She no longer wore the green undies and was safely nude again.

"How can you help us?" Yukay asked.

*I can scout for you, warning you of nearby dangers. I can tell you what NoAmi is doing so she can't ambush you.*

Yukay nodded. "That would help."

*But there is more.*

"More?" Yukay asked suspiciously. It was obvious that she had not been much amused by the green panties prank.

*There is a community of ghosts I have contacted. For one reason or another they can't go to Heaven or Hell, and are stuck here in Xanth with nothing to do. They are willing to help too. You can't see or hear them, but I could relay their news.*

"Their news?"

*They could multiply the scouting twenty-fold. I don't think any living creature could match what they could do.*

"A community of ghosts," Yukay repeated thoughtfully. "Helping us locate NoAmi without her knowing. That would help a lot."

*But they have a price.*

"There's always a price," Yukay agreed, annoyed. "But what could ghosts want that we could provide?"

*A house of their own, so they would no longer have to wander.*

"They can't just take over an existing house and haunt it?"

*No. They don't want to make trouble for the living folk. They want to reside where they can be safe and useful, as accepted citizens. They can't build their own house, of course, being immaterial; they must take over an existing one.*

"That's a tall order," Kody murmured. "Most living folk don't much like haunts."

"Exactly," Yukay said. "Do they have anywhere in mind?"

*No. But if we could find them a suitable house, they would be glad to trade their favors for it.* Naomi smiled. *That is, scouting, spying, keeping us informed. That sort of thing.*

"Some living folk might like flashing by the pretty ghosts," Ivan said. Yukay spared him a brief glare.

"The gourd," Zosi said.

"The gourd?" Kody asked.

"That's a daytime access to the dream realm," Zosi explained. "The hypno-gourd. Usually the first thing a visitor sees there is the Haunted House."

*Ideal!* Naomi said. *They are here with me, and they heard. But they don't know whether the Night Stallion would let them be there.*

"The Night Stallion?" Kody asked.

"Pause here," Yukay said. "We have some explaining to do."

*Of course.*

Yukay faced Kody. "Here in Xanth there are a number of connecting realms, such as the Moons of Ida that we saw with Demo Derby, and Counter Xanth where Cyrus is exiled, and islands that come and go on their own schedules. The dream realm is another major one. Night mares carry bad dreams to sleepers who deserve them, to tweak their inferior consciences and encourage them to be better people in the future, if only to avoid worse dreams thereafter. Those dreams are crafted carefully in the dream realm, each designed for a particular sleeper; it's a very serious business. There are a number of crews who act in those dreams, such as the walking skeletons. Princess Dawn's husband Picka Bone is the son of Marrow Bones, who left the dream realm and became real. There is a kind of access to the dream realm via the peepholes of the gourds; folk who gaze into those holes enter that realm mentally while their bodies lie unconscious outside. So they are dreaming, but they have control where they go, to a degree. There is the Haunted House setting that greets most newcomers. This formidable realm is governed by the Night Stallion. He alone can grant permission for the ghosts to move into the Haunted House. So to make our deal with the ghosts, we need to talk with him."

"I see," Kody said. This was wild, but not significantly worse than other aspects of Xanth he had encountered.

*Kody is the dreamer,* Naomi said. *He might be able to do it.*

"I am the dreamer," Kody agreed. "This provides me with a certain interest in dreams. I think I would like to meet this night scallion."

"Stallion," Yukay said quickly. "Do not fool with his name."

"I just thought he might know his onions."

No one laughed. "He is Trojan, the horse of a different color," Yukay said.

"I think we could use the ghosts' help," Kody said. "So let me go meet Trojan. Maybe he will be reasonable."

"Reasonable by his definition may not be reasonable by ours," Yukay said darkly. "I think we had all better come along."

"So I won't screw up?"

"Exactly."

Well, he had asked.

*I'll come too,* Naomi thought. *I want to check out that haunted house anyway.*

"Then we'll need to find about six gourds," Yukay said.

"Squawk."

"You can sniff them out? Go to it. We'll bring them back here."

Zap moved off. Yukay and Ivan went with her.

"I wonder," Kody said. "From your description, a gourd is a kind of mind bomb. Sniffer?"

The robot put out a puff of smoke and started moving. Kody followed, and Zosi went with him. Soon it came to a patch of gourds. "That's it!" Zosi said.

*Yes, it is,* Naomi agreed.

They harvested three ripe gourds and brought them back to where they had started from. From the other direction came Zap, with Ivan carrying one and Yukay with one. They had five gourds.

"We're missing one," Kody said.

"We need one person to mount guard over the unconscious bodies," Yukay said. "To prevent molestation, and to break the connection after an hour so we don't get locked in."

"Once you're in, you can't get out on your own," Zosi explained. "Someone has to break your eye connection."

Oh. "Who is staying behind?"

"I will," Ivan said. "The gourd realm gives me the creeps. Anyway, I can keep Sniffer stoked, too."

"Good enough," Yukay agreed. "Now we will each take a gourd, lie down comfortably, and peer into the peephole. We'll need to hold hands or whatever, to be sure we all arrive in the same place."

This did not make a lot of sense to Kody, but he didn't argue. He lay down as they did, including Zap, with his gourd before him. Then he reached out to take Zosi's hand on one side, and the ghost's hand on the other, trusting that Naomi would maintain the contact. She in turn reached out to touch one of Zap's paws, and Zap's other paw was taken by Yukay, who in turn took Zosi's other hand. Then, more or less together, they lowered their heads to gaze into their peepholes.

Curious, Kody delayed slightly. He saw the others go seemingly unconscious as their eyes connected. Then he oriented on his own peephole.

He stood in a gloomy fall setting, with gaunt acorn trees surrounding a rickety gate in turn surrounding a rickety old house lurking under a rickety greenish full moon. There seemed to be an ill-kept graveyard behind it. There were faint lights in the cracked windows of the house. It certainly looked forbidding.

"All present?" Yukay asked. "We don't have to maintain contact here; we're in. But we don't want to get separated from each other either. This is not a fun place to be lost in."

"Squawk," Zap agreed for all of them.

Yukay did a double-take. "I just realized: the Curse is not in force here. You look handsome, Kody."

"Thank you," Kody said indifferently. "You all look the same to me."

"Dream on. And you, Naomi, look real."

"I suppose ghosts do, in the dream realm," Naomi said, pleased. "I wonder if I feel real too?"

"You just want a pretext to smooch Kody."

"Of course." She approached Kody. "Do I feel real to you?"

"I'm not sure." So here in Xanth's dream realm she could talk naturally.

"Well, you have to touch me." She took his hand and set it on her bare bottom. His vision blurred, but he didn't quite freak out.

"You feel real," he agreed.

"Are you sure?" She stepped into him, pressed her bare upper body close, and kissed him. It was one hot smooch.

"Yes," he said somewhat breathlessly.

"I didn't see little hearts. Maybe the contact wasn't firm enough. Maybe I should try a gourd apology for my presumption."

"All *right*," Zosi snapped.

Naomi withdrew, smiling obscurely.

Faintly nettled, Kody took hold of Zosi and kissed her. Little hearts flew out. When they separated, the obscure smile had somehow migrated to Zosi's face.

Then he remembered another obscurity. "What's a gourd apology?"

"I will be happy to demonstrate," Naomi said.

"You will *not*," Zosi said severely.

"I will explain," Yukay said quickly. "A gourd apology is an expression of regret in the form of a kiss. If that isn't effective, the apologizer tries again, with more feeling. If that still doesn't do it, s/he makes a phenomenal effort. Normally gourd apologies are effective, especially when rendered by comely young women."

"Oh. Now I understand." He also understood why Zosi did not want Naomi making one to him, whatever the pretext.

"Now the most practical route to the interior is through the haunted house," Yukay said. "But I'm not sure of the route to the Night Stallion."

"Squawk."

"That so?" Yukay asked, surprised. "He will come to us, once he's sure we are serious? Then let's get serious." She turned, opened the rickety gate, and marched toward the house. The others followed her.

There was a huge ornate knocker on the decrepit door. Yukay lifted it and let it fall. It punched a hole in the door, and fragments of rotten wood rained down.

They waited, but nothing happened. Finally Yukay put her hand on the doorknob and turned it. It came out in her hand, leaving another hole. "Bleep!" she swore.

"Just pull it open," Zosi suggested.

Yukay put her fingers in the doorknob hole and pulled, and the door fell off its rusted-out hinges and crashed to the ground beside them.

"I think the maintenance has been neglected," Kody said, keeping a straight face.

"I think Trojan is toying with us," Yukay muttered. "He knows we're here."

A sheetlike ghost appeared in the doorway. "Booo!" it cried.

"Oh, go stuff it up your pillowcase," Yukay snapped, and walked in, passing through the ghost. The ghost looked annoyed as it faded out.

They faced a gloomy hall. There was a clomping sound as a pair of body-less shoes tramped toward them.

"Maybe I can handle this," Kody said. He reached down, picked up the shoes, and put them on his own feet in place of his regular shoes. "Now take us to your master," he said.

The shoes struggled to get free of his feet, but couldn't. So they walked on into the house. Kody, sensitive to their impetus, walked with them. No other spooks manifested; they had evidently gotten the word.

They walked right on through the house and into the graveyard behind. "Where are the zombies?" Yukay asked. "There are supposed to be zombies."

"There's a shortage of zombies all over," Zosi reminded her. "That's my mission." Then she clouded up.

Kody, realizing that she had been reminded of her own di-
lemma, put an arm around her shoulders and squeezed. She leaned
into him appreciatively.

The shoes took them on through the graveyard and to a high
fence that evidently marked the next setting. It seemed the shoes
wanted to get this done with so they could get off his alien feet.

There was a stile surmounting the fence. The shoes guided
Kody onto the stile and over the fence. He held on carefully, dis-
trusting this, but there were no problems. Then he held the stile
firmly in place so Yukay could cross next. As she swung her leg
over the top he got a glimpse up under her skirt; fortunately he was
able to jam his eyes shut before her panties freaked him out.

"I'm down," she said, amused. "You can look now."

He opened his eyes. "Did you do that on purpose?"

"Of course. How else was I to get over the fence?"

That wasn't exactly the answer he had sought.

Naomi appeared, walking through the fence. She looked solid
here, but evidently retained her ghostly nature. "You may have
chosen Zosi, but we still have flashing rights, when we can do it by
seeming accident. Isn't it similar in Mundania?"

"Maybe."

Zosi came over, managing to do it without exposing anything
beyond her knees. Finally Zap flew over.

Now they surveyed the setting ahead of them. It was a vast sea
of oil, with a tiny white-sand beach and roiling storm clouds beyond. There was a small rowboat almost at their feet.

"I don't get it," Yukay said. "Xanth doesn't have seas of oil."

Kody remembered something. "A few years back there was a
bad oil spill in the Gulf of Mexico, from a blown well below. It
took months to shut off the flow, and they were afraid it would
wash up on the shores and ruin the tourist trade. They never did get
it cleaned up completely. I don't think the executives responsible
were ever brought to justice."

"Some bad dreams do get exported to Mundania," Yukay said.
"Though I don't see exactly how this relates."

"Ho there!" someone called from the side. It was a goblin. "You must be the actor for this scene. You look Mundane."

"I am Mundane," Kody said. "However—"

"Good enough. Get in that boat."

"But I'm no actor!"

"I don't care what you are, you slacker! Get moving!" the goblin snapped. "We're low on time. This bad dream is scheduled for delivery tonight."

Now Kody saw other goblins, one carrying a portable movie camera.

"Don't make a wave," Yukay murmured. "We're trying to get along here."

Kody found himself getting into the rowboat, mainly by the urging of his shoes. Maybe they were getting back at him for preempting them. The goblin immediately pushed it out to sea. The wind was rising, bringing the storm rapidly closer, yet the tiny craft was going away from shore.

He grabbed the oars, trying to get the boat back to the beach. He saw the camera goblin orienting on him. He rowed, but didn't have the hang of it, and the boat merely spun around.

Then the storm was upon him. The waves of oil became mountainous, lifting him high, then sucking him down into a trough. It was vaguely like a roller coaster, but more scary because there was no track to hold him in place. Oil leaked into the boat, soaking his clothes.

A fierce splash of oil smacked the boat, snapping off both oars. Then another wave picked it up, hauled it high into the sky, and hurled it and him into the awful depths.

Kody screamed.

"Cut!" the goblin chief yelled from somewhere.

The oil melted away. Kody found himself standing on a level floor, not even wet. "What?" he asked, confused.

"It's a good take. Thanks," the goblin said. "That guilty exec's really going to get it tonight. Go on to your next scene." He and the camera goblin hurried away, doubtless going to *their* next scene.

"I think you just starred in a spot dream intended for a guilty Mundane," Yukay said. "Of course when the night mare delivers it, they'll substitute the exec for you. You just marked the place so they could film it."

"Glad I could be of service," Kody said with a certain edge.

"In fact you did well, and we appreciate it," a new voice said.

They turned to discover a magnificent dark stallion who scintillated luminescently. The girls, including Zap, wore expressions of awe.

"Trojan, I presume?" Kody said, not nearly as impressed by the talking horse.

"Well, I do know my onions."

Uh-oh. "You heard my humor."

"Indeed. I enjoy humor. Your performance here was hilarious."

So the horse was teasing him back. "We came here to ask a favor."

"Of course. The haunted house. And your nude ghost naga will surely make a fetching addition to it."

Naomi blushed. Kody hadn't realized that a ghost could do that.

"However, I am thinking of an exchange of favors."

Uh-oh again. "Of what nature?" Kody asked.

"A bit of background. As you know, our night mares deliver bad dreams to deserving sleepers. But they are limited to darkness. Some evil-minded miscreants have taken to sleeping by day, so that the mares can't reach them. In this manner they think to escape dream justice. That is annoying."

"I appreciate that," Kody said.

"We need to shield the mares from the rigors of day. So that they can reach those vexing perverts and do their duty by them."

"Such as making a guilty oil executive dream of drowning in an oilstorm?"

"Actually that particular exec is reachable by night. The Demon Earth requested the dream, and we honor it as a courtesy. But there are others as guilty in their fashions, who are escaping justice. The principle is similar."

There was something about this nightmare justice that Kody liked. "How can I help?"

"There is a shield in the form of a cape that will protect my mares from the rigors of daylight," Trojan said. "It is out of my reach, but not out of yours."

"Where?"

"Caprice Castle. They mistook it for a pun and stored it deep in their dungeon."

"You are unable to visit Caprice?"

"Unable to transport a physical shield. It needs to be moved to my stall at Cape Can, where I will be able to make dream copies of it for my mares."

"And if I move that cape to Can, you will allow the ghosts to occupy the haunted house?"

"That's the deal," Trojan said.

"Then I'll do it." Kody looked at Naomi. "Tell your friends."

"As soon as I get out of here," Naomi agreed, pleased.

"You may depart now," the stallion said, glancing at her. He breathed out a jet of vapor. A cloud formed around her, and she vanished.

That impressed Kody. The Night Stallion was able to eject a dreamer from this dream realm, even when her eye was still locked on the peephole of the gourd.

Trojan turned back to Kody. "I like you. Therefore I will proffer some lagniappe. A token gift." A piece of paper appeared in his mouth. "Take it."

"Without looking in your mouth?"

"Hilarious!" The stallion blew the paper at Kody. It struck his forehead, but when he reached to catch it, it was gone.

"I'm not sure I understand," Kody said cautiously. Was the creature having more fun with him?

"It is inside your head," Trojan explained. "A pass to dream."

"I'm already dreaming."

"Indeed. This will enable you to return here at will, from Mundania, for a few hours at a time, when you are sleeping there."

"Uh, thank you," Kody said, not wishing to disparage what might be a well-meant gift. It was bad enough being in a dream here, without entering a dream within a dream.

"Now begone," Trojan said. He breathed out more vapor.

And abruptly they were back in Xanth, their heads lifted from the gourds.

*The ghosts are overjoyed,* Naomi reported. She was back to thought speech.

"But I still have to do my part," Kody said. "That means returning to Caprice Castle and talking with them there, then locating this Cape Can Trojan mentioned."

"There's something you should know," Ivan said. "Caprice Castle landed nearby while you were in the gourd." He pointed. Kody saw the turrets of the castle beyond the trees.

"It's eerie the way that castle knows where to be," Yukay said.

"It's magic," Kody said shortly.

They made their way to the castle, which had evidently found a sufficiently wide clear spot to settle onto. They approached the front gate.

There was barking, and the two puppies charged out, tails wagging. Soon Princess Dawn and the children joined them. "There must be a reason the castle came here," she said. "We thought it traveled mostly randomly, but this isn't random."

"It's not," Kody agreed. Then he explained about the shield cape.

"But we have no idea where that might be," Dawn protested. "We have so many puns stashed away, it's like a noodle in a haystack."

Noodle? Kody let it pass. "Maybe we can help." He addressed Sniffer. "We need to find a magic cape, a shield so the night mares don't get bombed when they try to work by day."

Sniffer put out a ball of smoke and moved forward into the castle. They followed. The robot went to the dungeon, sniffing avidly. It pointed at a huge box.

"There must be three hundred puns wedged into that box," Dawn said.

"Let Sniffer look," Kody said.

Dawn lifted the lid, revealing a jammed jumble of items. Kody picked up the robot and set it on top. The sniffer sniffed again, then started digging. Soon it disappeared into the pile. Only an uneasy turbulence and puffs of smoke revealed its presence.

Then it came up again, material caught in its doglike jaws. "Is that the cape?" Kody asked.

"Beep."

Kody took the cape. It was cellophane-light and translucent. On its hem was the word SHIELD. That was the one they wanted.

"Thank you," Kody said to Dawn. "Now we'll depart and make our way to Cape Can, wherever that may be."

"No need," Dawn said. "We're there."

He had for the moment forgotten how readily the castle traveled. When they looked out, there was a town consisting of buildings resembling big cans. A sign said CAPE CAN AVERAL.

Kody stifled a groan. "Now we need to find the Night Stallion's stall."

"It's here," Dawn said. Sure enough, the closest big can was actually a deserted stall.

Kody carried the cape out and down to the stall. He set it on the bed of hay there. Could that be all there was to it?

There was a small gust of wind. A cloud formed over the cape. When the cloud dissipated, the cape was gone.

Kody returned to the castle. "It seems the delivery has been completed," he said. "But I must say, this is suspiciously easy."

"Caprice is sensitive to important things in Xanth," Dawn said. "I think it quietly makes friends where it can. The Night Stallion is an excellent friend to have."

*It certainly is,* Naomi thought. *The ghosts are already moving into the haunted house, where nice rooms have been reserved for them.*

"That house didn't look big enough for another twenty ghosts," Kody said.

*It is,* Naomi reassured him. *You are thinking in Mundane terms, where physical things occupy physical space.*

"I was doing that," Kody agreed. He took a breath. "Now we need to resume our Quest for the Bomb."

"Caprice will leave you where it picked you up," Dawn said.

"Then we had better get to it."

"In the morning," Dawn said. "Today and tonight you can relax here. We enjoy your company." She glanced at Naomi. "Yours too, though to me you are just a wisp of mist."

*You are generous.*

It was a nice afternoon and evening, and Kody did appreciate the chance to relax. He also appreciated sharing a room with Zosi, now that they had broken the ice. But still the problem of his return to Mundania loomed. When he would have to leave her.

"Somehow maybe things will work out for the best," Zosi murmured hopefully. But she hardly seemed confident.

The morning came. Refreshed, they bid Dawn and the children and pups farewell and exited the castle again, and were right where they had boarded it in the panhandle. Reasonably close to the Bomb. They were on their own from this point on. That made Kody nervous.

Zosi took his hand. That banished the nervousness.

# 13
# TRAP

Sniffer went to work with vigor, puffing out little balls of smoke as it sniffed out the Bomb. The others followed, occasionally detouring around nuisances like sting thistles and stink horns that Sniffer didn't notice.

Zosi passed a weedlike plant that suddenly reached out to snag her legs. Kody went to her rescue, and another plant caught hold of him.

"Back off," Yukay said. "That's a catch her and a catch him. You just have to avoid them if you don't want to get all entangled."

Kody had just about given up groaning at puns. He helped Zosi back off. But then another plant heaved Zosi up and threw her a short distance. When Kody went there, it threw him similarly. They landed on the ground together, unhurt but annoyed.

"You two just don't have enough experience in the Xanth wilderness," Yukay said. "That's a pitch her plant, and a pitch him plant."

"We are partners in ignorance," Kody said to Zosi. "You were a zombie too long, and I was a Mundane."

"That's why we need Companions," she said.

"I heard that especially dangerous talents are sent to Mundania, where magic is suppressed," Ivan said. "If that got messed up, it would take more than zombies and Mundanes to fix it."

"It would," Kody agreed. "Most Mundanes don't believe in magic, so they'd have a real problem."

"Most Xanthians don't believe in science," Yukay said. "So we'd have a similar problem if dangerous science things got sent here."

That brought Kody up short. "The Bomb that's Cursing Xanth—could that be from Mundania? It does seem to be using the science concept of radiation, affecting all Xanth to varying degrees."

"So they sent a Mundane to deal with it?" Yukay asked. "That makes uncomfortable sense."

"Except that I'm not a Bomb specialist. If it doesn't have an On/Off switch, I'll be as incompetent as any Xanthian."

Yukay smiled. "Let's hope it has that switch."

They moved on. But then the way became so clogged with brambles that they needed to protect their legs. "We need a good heavy-trousers bush," Yukay said.

*The ghosts know of one nearby,* Naomi thought. *This way.*

They backtracked and found a side path leading to a pond. A dolphinlike creature swam in it, but shied away the moment they approached.

"That looks like a liquidator," Yukay said. "They consort only with aquatics."

Liquid dater. To be sure.

In the pool floated several pairs of jeans. *This is a jean pool,* Naomi thought. *But there's a problem.*

"There's always a problem," Yukay muttered.

*Anyone who wears these jeans has a change in their genes to make them different. At least for a while, until the jeans get broken in.*

"That's risky," Yukay said. "Maybe we should keep looking."

*There is nothing else within range.*

"Bleep! Then we'll have to risk it."

"I wish we could just buy what we need," Kody grumbled. "That would be easier."

"Except that we don't use money in Xanth," Yukay said. "But if you have a reality check, that might do."

This time Kody did groan.

They fished out four pairs of jeans, and Kody, Yukay, Ivan, and Zosi put them on wet. They fit each person snugly, rapidly drying into shape. Kody noticed that the girls looked remarkably fetching in theirs, with their bottoms tightly outlined, though Ivan averted his gaze in disgust.

Then he noticed more. Yukay normally had blond hair and dark eyes; now her hair was reddish, her eyes bright. She was normally slim with a nice upper configuration; now her butt was full, her bosom less so. Zosi normally had gray hair and gray eyes; now both were brown. Ivan was lean and handsome; now he was less so on both counts. And Kody himself seemed to have lost several inches in height.

Gene pool. Naomi had warned them.

Their genes had changed when they donned the jeans. Not greatly, perhaps because the pool was dilute, but enough. With luck and the Curse, maybe the others would not notice.

"My bust! My butt!" Yukay exclaimed with horror.

She had noticed.

"I can fix that," Ivan said. He pointed to her bosom. It expanded about three sizes. He pointed to her bottom. It shrank similarly.

"Thank you," Yukay said tightly. She undid her top button to alleviate some of the tightness. The jeans still accommodated her perfectly; that seemed to be part of their magic. "I will keep your talent in mind for the future, Ivan."

"Hmm," Zosi murmured. She remained slender throughout.

Ivan pointed to her bosom. It expanded a size. Kody had liked her the way she was, but had to admit this looked good too. He now appreciated more personally why Ivan's thickening/thinning talent was appealing to the ladies.

"Look at those," Yukay said. There was a boot tree with pairs of steel-toed boots. "Those would really enable us to forge ahead." She harvested a pair and put them on. Then she made a face. "Uh-oh."

"What?" Ivan asked.

"I felt them tugging at my toes. I believe these are not steel-toed, but steal-toed. They will steal my toes if I wear them too long." She hauled them off.

They returned to the bramble patch. It was thicker than ever, having had extra time to marshal its forces. But their new jeans were up to the challenge. They forged through without getting scratched.

Soon the brambles gave it up as a bad job and faded back. The way opened into what appeared to be a small golf course, with several tees for the balls. But a group of people were using them instead for small cups of tea. They seemed to be having a little tee-tea party.

"Conservative golfers," Yukay murmured. "We don't want to mess with them. They don't like outside interference in their business."

They moved on past, and the tee partiers ignored them.

Just beyond the golf course was a small pavilion. A sign said IS YOUR LIFE DULL? ENTER FOR THE CURE.

Kody smiled. "I'm curious what they think the cure is. A funny picture?" He stepped up to it.

"Squawk!" Zap cried warningly.

"No!" Zosi cried. "It's a trap!" She flung herself into it ahead of him.

There was a flash and a whiff of brimstone as she disappeared.

Kody stood stunned. "It destroyed her!" he said.

"Maybe not," Yukay said. "Naomi, can you find out?"

The ghost vanished.

Kody leaned against a post, reeling. "She sacrificed herself for me. Just as Naomi did."

"She loved you," Yukay said. "As Naomi did. But there's hope."

Naomi returned. *We canvassed the area and found it. It was a trap meant for Kody. NoAmi is now aware of our approach, after losing track of us when I died. She seduced a man who had a special spell, and got him to plant it along our route. It transported*

*Zosi to an ancient sacrificial dragon-feeding station. It's not normally used for that anymore, but dragons do check it out every so often, just in case. A big fire breather is heading there now. She's doomed.*

"The hell!" Kody swore, and the posts of the pavilion turned black with scorch. Somehow his irate expression had gotten past the bleep censorship. "I'll take out that dragon, and cut it to little pieces if it touches her."

*No,* Naomi thought. *The dragon is on the path between us and the station. If it spies us going there, it will rush to toast her first.*

"Then some other route. I must get there first."

*There is a back way. But it's dangerous.*

"Who cares? Show me the way."

*You need to get beyond the station and come back to it without the dragon seeing you.*

"Squawk."

"You'll carry me?" Kody said. "Good enough."

"But not high in the air," Yukay cautioned. "You must not be seen by any dragon."

*I will guide you along a low route. The station is atop a hill, and Zap can't carry you there from any direction without being visible. But the back path will get you there without visibility.*

"Good enough." Kody went to Zap and found the lighter knot she carried. "Carry on," he said to the others. "I will bring her back."

He mounted her, catching hold of the heavy feathers of her mane. She bounded forward, spread her wings, and took off. She looped around to gain height, rose above the treetops to orient, then angled back down into a section of smaller trees so that she could fly below the level of the tops of the larger trees. She knew what she was doing.

"You warned me also," Kody said as he rode. "But you weren't close enough to block me from entering that pavilion trap."

"Squawk," she agreed.

"You joined us because you want to find out how to manage with the liability of having a soul. I don't see it as a liability at all.

You've been a fine Companion and a really useful assistant in times of need. Such as right now. I don't know how I would manage without your help."

"Squawk," she said appreciatively.

"I'd be happy to have you with me after this Quest is done. But I won't be here, regardless how it turns out. So all I can do is wish you good hunting and a good companion. There must be one somewhere."

Zap didn't answer. Maybe his wish for her was unrealistic. Another souled griffin?

*We'll look out for one,* Naomi thought.

He had forgotten that the ghost was showing the way; she was invisible unless he looked for her. Now he saw that she was floating just ahead of them, stroking with her arms as if swimming, kicking her bare legs, displaying everything in motion. She was flashing him again!

"I think you could have seduced me if you'd really tried," he murmured subvocally. "But you didn't, did you, any more than you really tried to kill me."

*I want you to succeed in your Quest.*

That was answer enough.

They circled the round hill and came down for a landing in a cozy glen. Kody dismounted and looked around. Ahead of him was the thickly forested base of the hill.

*There is a path,* Naomi thought. *But it is hard to see, and dangerous. Also, it is single-use.*

"Single use?"

*When one person uses it, it is used up. No others can follow. The person who uses it can't follow it back. It no longer exists, until the next day, when it re-forms.*

"I never heard of a path like that."

*Fortunately ghosts don't count as users, so I was able to explore it without destroying it. It begins here.* She indicated a spot where no path was obvious.

Kody turned to Zap. "It seems I won't be returning this way, regardless of the outcome. So you don't need to wait for me. You might as well fly back to rejoin Yukay and Ivan."

"Squawk." But Zap did not move. Maybe she planned to wait awhile, just in case.

Kody stepped up to the forest where Naomi stood. There, beyond her, was a small vague path that wasn't visible from any distance. He put a foot on it, and more became evident just ahead. So it was working.

He paused, turned, and looked back. There was nothing except dense forest. Not only was there no path, there was no place *for* a path. The trees and brush had closed in as if never disturbed. So in Xanth, a one-use path was exactly that, magically.

He looked forward, and the path was there, along with Naomi. *Now you know.*

"Now I know," he agreed.

*In Xanth, one-way routes are just that.* She turned, presenting him with her bare bottom by no coincidence, and stepped forward. She seemed to be having more fun teasing him in death than she had in life.

The path climbed the slope, finding its tenuous way through the thick growth. Even going the right way, with his ghost guide, he had to look carefully to find it. That might be one reason it wasn't used much.

He followed it through a patch of onions. Jangly music played as he passed them, startling him. *Those are rap scallions, loud but harmless,* Naomi thought.

He should have known that they wouldn't be garden-variety plants.

Then he passed through a patch of melonlike plants that made an awful smell. *Mel odious,* the ghost explained.

"Thanks for letting me know," he muttered, wrinkling his nose. He moved on.

Naomi paused. *Here is a hazard. A nickelpede nest we can't avoid.*

"I can't simply step around it?"

*If you step off the path to the side, you won't find it again.*

That made unfortunate sense. So he would have to walk through the nest. Kody remembered the pun on centipede. A nickelpede might be five times as big. Apart from being spooky in the manner of a big insect, what was the problem with it? He didn't remember.

*Do not fool with them. Do not let them get on you. They will gouge out nickel-sized scoops of your flesh.*

Oh. They were like biting ants or stinging scorpions. Kody conjured a reverse wood chip.

Now he saw the nest. It swarmed with big bugs. They had many legs and lobsterlike pincers. Certainly he did not want them swarming over him. He saw them lurking alertly, just waiting for him to give them a foot up.

There was no way around the nest. It filled the path, and the brush closed in tightly to either side. It was too broad for him to jump over. He had to put his foot in it. Who had made this path, the nickelpedes, to trap unwary hikers?

Kody hoped he had a nasty surprise for them.

He flipped the chip into the center of the nest. The bugs swarmed aggressively over it. And backed away, seeming confused, no longer aggressive.

Ha! The chip had reversed their nature, making them timid. Kody set his foot down beside it, and no nickelpede attacked. He dropped another chip ahead, and stepped there, and still the bugs hung back. A third step, and he was able to return to the debugged path. His talent had enabled him to pass unscathed.

Then he got a notion. It wasn't enough to light a bulb over his head, but it would do. He dug out a handkerchief, formed it into a little bag, put a chip in it, then kneeled and reached into the nest. He picked up a passive nickelpede and put it in with the chip. Then he got another, and another, until he had the impromptu bag filled with half a dozen. The chip kept the vicious little creatures torpid. He tucked the bag into a pocket. "Never can tell when a nasty biting bug might be useful," he explained to Naomi.

*It will take more than nickelpedes to stop that dragon.*

"Undoubtedly," he agreed.

They continued up the hill, the path winding quietly around trees and rocks to find its own special route. It seemed to like shaded spots with moss. It had its own personality. Kody rather liked it, though he was wary of its tricks. But if it was for the nickelpedes, why did it continue beyond the nest?

*Another hazard,* Naomi thought. *Tangle tree.*

Kody looked. There was a big tree with the hanging green tentacles, the same kind they had shown him before. "Avoidable?" he asked.

*No.*

He saw that the path led right under the tree, right past its massive trunk. Unlike the other tree, this one was not in a glade, but in a tight crevice between boulders; there was no way to bypass it without going around the boulders, and they buttressed deep cracks in the ground in which sinister-looking vines lurked. The tangle tree had set up shop in the one route past the boulders. Or the path had been designed to benefit the tangler.

"I don't suppose I can reason with it?"

*Tanglers don't reason much. They just grab and chomp.*

Nevertheless, Kody decided to try. "Tangle Tree, I need to pass by you on my way to the top of the hill. I bear you no malice. Will you let me pass in peace?"

A ripple shook the tree. It was almost as if it were laughing.

"I don't want to fight you, but if I have to, I do have weapons," Kody said. "I ask again: will you let me pass?"

This time the tree shook so hard its dangling tentacles writhed.

"I will give you a small demonstration. Here is one of my weapons." He conjured a chip and flipped it at the tree. It struck a tentacle and clung there. The tentacle became a normal wooden branch with brown bark and green leaves. It had been reversed from magic to mundane.

The branch rocked as if stung. It shook off the chip, shuddered, and slowly reverted to its tentacular nature. It did not look happy.

"Now will you be reasonable?" Kody asked.

Three tentacles lashed out, reaching for him. But Kody had taken care to stand just beyond their likely range. Their tips snapped like whips, making sharp reports.

*I told you.*

"Then so be it," Kody said grimly. "This is war." He really would have preferred to pass in peace, or to desert the path, but the thought of Zosi getting toasted and chomped by a dragon galvanized him to action. He could afford no more delay.

He conjured another chip and flipped it at the tree. But a tentacle picked up a bone from beneath the canopy and used it to bat the chip away. He flipped another, and again it was batted away. The tree was evidently a fast learner, and had figured out how to nullify the chips. The monsters of Xanth might be ravening, but they were not necessarily stupid.

Kody pondered briefly. Then he brought out his bag of nickelpedes. He loosened the tie and flipped the bag at the tree. The bone struck it, but the handkerchief merely unwound and wrapped around the implement, spilling its chip and the nickelpedes across several adjacent tentacles. The chip dropped to the ground, but the nickelpedes, freed from its influence, caught on to the tentacles. The bugs were in a bad mood. In a quarter moment they were clamping with their pincers, gouging out nickel-sized chunks of green.

*Beautiful! I never thought of that.*

There was a sound like wind whistling through bare branches. The tree felt that! The tentacles writhed, catching at bugs. But the nickelpedes intercepted incoming tentacles with their pincers, and gouged them too. Nickelpedes were like the tangler in one respect: they weren't reasonable.

Now, while the tangler was distracted, Kody advanced, flipping chips as he went. They struck potentially dangerous tentacles and rendered them into harmless branches.

But the tree was not completely out of it. There were hundreds of tentacles, and more were orienting on him. He could not flip chips fast enough to nullify them all. One wrapped around his left arm, stopping the flipping and almost hauling him off his feet. The tree might have been distracted, but now it was focusing on the main threat, which was Kody. He was in trouble.

He drew his sword. At first it was the little knife. The tree evidently could see. It paused for a moment, shaking with mirth, contemptuous of such a little bark sticker. It whipped out another tentacle to catch Kody's right arm.

Kody swung at the tentacle. The full length of the sword manifested. He lopped off the terminal two feet. Thick green ichor leaked out as the tree pulled back its injured member.

Then three more tentacles launched at him. Kody swung the sword in a vicious arc, severing them all. Then he moved forward, chopping as he went, severing all tentacles that came within reach.

He came to the thick trunk. There was the great gnarly mouth, stained with blood. It had several ragged barklike teeth. The tree normally caught its prey and fed it into that mouth to be chomped. Presumably digestion occurred underground, in the roots. Kody swung at the mouth and lopped off the upper teeth. Then he moved on, still swinging.

But the tree had had enough. No more tentacles reached for him. He emerged beyond it, unscathed. He paused.

"I did warn you," he said. "Maybe next time a person tries to be reasonable, you will consider it."

The tree merely shuddered and writhed. Had it learned its lesson? He might never know.

*That was probably the only way,* Naomi thought. *Brute force is all they understand.*

They moved on up the path. It came to the top of the hill and ended, its job done. "Thank you, path," Kody said. He could have sworn that it wriggled with pleasure as it faded out. So it seemed it was not the lackey of nickelpedes or tangle trees; the monsters had merely colonized it for feeding convenience.

There was Zosi! She was chained to a boulder in the center of the knoll, her head hanging, her hair across her face in a disconsolate gray mass. Had she given up hope? "Zosi!"

Her head lifted. "Kody!" she cried gladly. "You came! And Naomi!"

*I led him in.*

He ran across to her. "Of course I came! How could I let you die? After you sacrificed yourself for me?"

She smiled bravely. "If I died, I'd revert to zombie. I wouldn't taste very good to the dragon."

Then he reached her. He kissed her repeatedly. "Oh, Zosi!"

"I love this passion," she said. "But you are wasting time. Can you free me before the dragon comes?"

Kody took stock. She was manacled on wrists and ankles, and chained to eyelets embedded in the stone. Would the sword sever the chains? He feared that the attempt would only ruin the sword. It would be better to pry the manacles open. But that would take time.

There was a roar.

*The dragon!*

Kody whirled. There was the monster, charging up the hill, exhaling fire. It was unlikely to be any more reasonable than the tangle tree. Still, he had to try.

He walked several paces forward and took his stance in front of Zosi. "Dragon, let this woman be. Go away and let me free her. She is not for you."

The dragon never paused. It continued its charge.

*That courtly streak may be the death of you,* Naomi thought loudly.

"Yes," Zosi said. "But I love that in him."

Kody drew his sword. "Last warning, dragon! Give over! Depart! Let this maiden be. Else I must smite you."

*This is not an educated dragon,* Naomi warned. *Not like the one you saved me from. You can't reason with it.*

The dragon paused only long enough to inhale hugely. That was mischief.

Kody hurled a chip at it. The chip struck its snoot just as it was starting to exhale. The emerging fire turned to ice, clogging the exit.

*Beware! It's going to blow!*

There was a titter from Zosi. Bad as her situation was, she was still amused.

The fire backed up inside. The dragon swelled up like a balloon, its eyes turned bright red, and flames shot out of its ears. It was definitely not amused.

Then the chip fell aside, the clog dissolved, and the flame jetted out and into the ground, gouging a smoking hole. The dragon coughed, clearing its channel, then started to inhale again.

Kody flipped another chip. But this time the dragon aimed its snoot at the chip and shot out a small jet of fire that caught the chip in midair, toasted it, and sent the charred ash to the ground. This dragon might not be educated, but it was cunning.

*I hate a smart dragon!*

So did Kody. What was he to do now?

He flipped another chip. Then, as the dragon's snoot whipped around to toast it, he flipped another, this one at its eyes. And a third, at its near ear.

The first chip got toasted, but the other two scored. The dragon's eye became a potato, and its ear a corn stalk. Kody wasn't sure of the precise nature of the reversals, but they did mess up the dragon. Potato eye? Ear of corn? Did the chips have a sense of humor?

Then the dragon breathed out a veritable wall of flame, surrounding itself in fire. No more chips could get through, and the creature's sight and hearing were probably recovering. Move and countermove, and the dragon was hardly intimidated, let alone defeated. More was required.

Kody charged, swinging the sword. He held up a chip and forged right through the firewall, making it turn to ice in his vicinity. Then he was beside the dragon. "Take that!" he cried, and clove it on the tail.

The sword sliced through the tail and cut it off. The severed part twisted on its own, like the tail of a snake, but he knew it was harmless. He whirled and went for the dragon's head.

The dragon came to meet him, puffing out jets of fire. Kody held his chip out with his left hand as he dodged to the side. Ice coated his arm. Then the dragon's head swung at his hand and knocked the chip away. The snoot aimed for him like the sooty muzzle of the flamethrower it was.

Kody put both hands on the hilt of his sword and smashed it down on that snoot. His grip was wrong, and he struck with the flat, possibly bruising but not cutting the dragon's nose. The dragon shook the blade off and inhaled.

This time he dodged to the side, got the sword straight, and chopped as hard as he could at the dragon's relatively thin neck. The sword cut through the scales and dug into the flesh below. Blood oozed out. The dragon recoiled, then opened his mouth wide and struck teeth first.

But Kody was already dodging again. He swung the sword like an ax, cutting at the same place as before. A scale flew out like a chip of wood, and more blood flowed.

The dragon's head whipped around, jaws gaping, fire jetting. But Kody was moving again, getting clear of the trajectory. He chopped once more, at the same spot. This time the blade dug deep into the softer flesh of the interior. Blood spurted—and smoke came out.

He had cut through to the windpipe! Now the dragon tried to withdraw, but Kody did not trust that. He chopped once more, and opened the cut deeper. This time he must have severed a nerve, because the head abruptly dropped to the ground.

Kody chopped once more, and finally managed to sever the head completely. Smoke poured out of the neck, but the dragon was effectively dead.

*You did it! You killed it!*

So he had. Kody relaxed, his berserk fury fading. He had done what he had to do, but now it sickened him.

*More dragons are coming!*

Oh, no! He couldn't go through that again. He had to free Zosi and get her out of here.

He ran back to her. Again he pondered the chains. Could the sword sever them? It was magic, but he feared not impervious. He needed a better way.

"Try the reverse wood," Zosi said.

Genius! He conjured a chip and touched it to a manacle. The thing sprang open, freeing her hand. He tried the other, and it too opened. Then he got down and touched an ankle manacle, but nothing happened.

*You've used up the power of one chip. Conjure a new one!*

Good idea. He threw away the chip and conjured a new one. This one worked, and soon both Zosi's legs were free.

*The dragon!*

He looked. The next dragon was coming up the hill. It looked just as big and dangerous as the first. He looked at the route he had taken to get here, but there was now no path here, just impenetrable forest. Was there no escape?

Then a shape flew down from above. It was Zap! "Take her away!" Kody called.

"Not without you!" Zosi protested.

"Zap can't carry both of us."

"Then you go. You must complete your Quest."

"The hell!"

"Squawk!"

*You're right, Zap. The main path may be defensible. The dragons can come only one at a time.*

"But I have only the one sword," Kody protested. "And I'm tired. Better that Zosi goes."

"No," Zosi said. "I'll stay and fight with you. With sandwich bombs."

Zap was already going to the narrow portion of the trail to challenge the first dragon. This was a smoker, which would require a different defense. Kody and Zosi hurried to join the griffin.

"You don't have to fight for us, if it violates your principles," Kody told Zap. "You've done enough already, carrying me to the hill, and being ready to carry one of us to safety."

"Squawk."

The essence, succinctly expressed, was that the griffin now understood that fighting for a good cause, such as protecting her friends, did not violate her conscience. She was not going to let Zosi or Kody get eaten.

The smoker came up the path, encountered Zap, and paused. It blew out a puff of smoke in the form of a question mark.

*One of the ghosts is a dragon,* Naomi thought. *He says that's a question: "Why is a griffin interfering in dragon business?"*

"Squawk!"

*Zap responds that these are her friends.*

The dragon puffed again. *"Well, they are both tasty morsels, the rightful prey of dragons. So get out of the way if you don't want to get smoked."*

"Squawk!"

*The dragon responds, "I'm a land dragon. I am not part of the winged monster protocol. I don't have to honor your stupid preferences. Now clear out, birdbrain, before I get annoyed."*

"Squawk!"

*"Yes, I know griffins can fight. But not as well as dragons. You are overmatched, featherhead, even if you lack the wit to know it."*

Zap reared up on her hind feet, claws extended, beak to the dexter side, rampant. It was a fighting stance. She was not as large as the dragon, but this was impressive.

The dragon puffed out one more ball of smoke.

*"Oh, yeah? Then taste this!"*

The dragon inhaled. But Zap didn't wait on the exhalation. She lurched forward, batting at the dragon's snout with both forepaws while pecking at its left eye with her beak. She was surprisingly fast. It was evident that what she lacked in size she made up for in speed.

The dragon jerked back, barely saving its eye, while smoke barreled out of its mouth, surrounding them both.

Kody wasn't sure what to do. He wanted to help Zap, but couldn't see either her or the dragon. He did not dare chop into that smoke with his sword, lest he strike his friend. Neither could he risk a reverse wood chip. So he just had to stand back and wait for the smoke to clear.

It slowly dissipated. The dragon had drawn back, surprised by the attack. But now it was angry. It charged forward, jaws gaping.

Kody flipped a chip into that open orifice.

Suddenly the wide-open mouth was a tightly closed mouth, its position reversed. The chip remained inside; the dragon couldn't open to spit it out. Nor could it blast out much smoke. It seemed that it did not use its nostrils to release smoke, just its mouth. Neither could it bite. It had been deprived of its main weapons.

Zap took a menacing step forward. "Squawk!"

*Oh, what a nasty term!*

The dragon, thoroughly nullified, turned around and ran away.

But another dragon was already coming to the fore, and Kody saw others behind it. It seemed that the news of the chained sacrificial maiden had spread, attracting predators from all around. First come, first served.

A bulb flashed over Kody's head. The maiden!

But before he could act on his inspiration, the next dragon was upon them. This was a different species, squat and low, not emitting fire, smoke, or steam. That made it dangerous because they did not know what to expect.

Zosi conjured a huge sandwich that reeked of gasoline. She heaved it at the dragon. The dragon chomped it without thinking, and it detonated. The blast sent peanut butter and pieces of dragon flying in three and a half directions.

That made the next dragon pause, assessing the situation. It was becoming evident that there was no easy prey here.

Now Kody raised his voice. "Dragons!" he yelled. "Hear me! Your attack is pointless. There's no helpless maiden chained for sacrifice! She escaped! Look at the post! It's empty!"

Several heads turned to gaze at the empty post. The main

attraction was gone. They did not make the connection to the sandwich woman. Then the dragons turned about and walked away. It
had been that simple. After they had had to fight three of them, and
kill two.

*They really are departing. You will be able to use that path
once they clear it.*

Now Kody took hold of Zosi. He enfolded her, his emotion
overflowing. "I couldn't let you go!"

And now she collapsed into tears. "I thought I was doomed!"

"NoAmi set that trap for me. You took it instead."

"I had to. You have to complete your Quest."

"And you don't have to complete yours?"

"I should, but that means staying alive. That's funny, isn't it? I
was afraid of getting killed, but I don't want to live anyway. Not
without you."

"Zosi, if I could stay here and be with you, I would." He noticed irreverently that her appearance had largely reverted to natural; the jeans were losing their effect, and her hair had turned gray
as before. "But I know my dream will end when my Quest is complete. Short of deserting my Quest—"

"No! You must complete it!"

"And so our love is doomed."

"Forever doomed," she agreed faintly.

"Esrever doom," he said. "I thought that was just an ordinary
phrase spelled backwards. But it seems to be literal."

"Squawk."

"She's right," Zosi said. "We have to return to the others."

*We ghosts have reassured them about your safety,* Naomi
thought. *They were concerned.*

"Tell them we're on our way," Kody said.

"Or will be soon," Zosi said.

He looked at her questioningly.

"Zap will guard us from chance predators," she said. Then she
kissed him so ardently that he could no longer miss her meaning.
He had rescued her, she was grateful, but it was more than that.

She wanted all of him she could get, right now, because they both knew there was no reasonable prospect of a future together.

"Soon," he agreed. They were out in the open, but it didn't concern them. Love was all that mattered at the moment.

*Bleep! I'm so jealous!*

"Then this one is in honor of you," Kody said. "For enabling me to rescue her."

*Actually, that recognition does help. I did not die in vain.*

# 14
# BOGEYMAN

Yukay hugged them both. "We were so afraid we had lost both of you, and we could do nothing."

"We survived, thanks to Zap and Naomi," Kody said.

*But beware. NoAmi still plots against you, and I fear she knows where you are.*

"How so?" Yukay asked.

*I am her twin. I am dead, but I am feeling a tug. She may be tracking me again. Maybe I should go far away.*

"No," Kody said. "If she tracks you, she tracks you. We'll close on her soon regardless. Then it won't make much of a difference."

*Thank you. I value your presence.*

"Tell your ghost friends to keep alert. We don't want to walk into any more traps."

*They are watching. But NoAmi does things indirectly, and they can't track her communications, just her actual body.*

"And we will orient on that body," Kody said. "Maybe tomorrow we'll catch her."

They found an old caterpillar tent and used that for the night.

Kody lay with Zosi, just holding her close. "I need to complete my Quest as soon as I can," he said. "To be sure that I do accomplish it. But that will mean the end of my association with you. That's the irony of the situation."

"I know. And I must help you all I can, even if it means losing you sooner."

"Oh, Zosi! You are being so noble about this."

"I wouldn't be, if I thought I had any real choice."

She was probably right. She was being honest and realistic rather than noble. She was no paragon, just an ordinary woman, regardless of her past. He loved her exactly the way she was.

In the morning they fired up Sniffer and started off, knowing their quarry was close. The ghosts reported that NoAmi remained where she was, almost as if waiting for them. That was odd.

It started uneventfully. They saw an impolite shape flying over the trees, pursued by a worse-looking one. "Flying buttress," Yukay observed disdainfully. "Followed by the male of the species, the flying butt. I wish they would keep their obscene antics out of the sky."

Then they came to a circle of giant ears mounted in the ground. "Look! An earring!" Yukay exclaimed. "They perform oracles for passing folk." She stepped into the circle. "What will our luck be today?" she asked.

The ears wilted and lay flat on the ground. "Uh-oh," Ivan said.

"That's a bad sign," Yukay agreed. "It means we'll have bad luck today."

Kody could have lived without that news, but he remained silent.

Then they were intercepted by a crying young woman. "Please, please," she said. "Are yew the man with the reverse wood chips? I need yewr help right away!"

"But I'm on a Quest," Kody said. "I can't take incidental time off."

"It's a child!" she said. "A little boy. The Bogeyman's got him.

I can't save him because I am knot his mother, but I can knot just let him bee eaten!"

"Eaten!"

"That's what the Bogeyman does. He eats children. It's horrible. Please, yew must help!"

There was something about her accent that he found odd, but now was not the time to be distracted by irrelevant things. He looked at Yukay.

"Of course we'll help," Yukay said, and Zosi agreed. "But it can be hard to make the Bogeyman back off once he captures a child."

"I thought if I could get some reverse wood, that wood reverse it and free the boy. Please, there is little time."

"Show us the way," Yukay said.

The young woman hurried north. They followed. Kody noticed incidentally that she was shapely, and she wore what appeared to be a little crown. Could she actually be a princess? That seemed unlikely.

"We should get acquainted," Yukay said as she paced the woman. "I am the Maiden Yukay, this is Zosi Zombie, this is Ivan Human, Zap Griffin, and you are right: Kody Mundane, with the chips."

"I am Wenda Woodwife." She paused. "More formally, Princess Wenda Charming, because my husband is a prince. But I dew knot worry about that, just the children. I can knot have any of my own, so I adopt those in need, and that is working well. It is rewarding."

"And you speak with the forest dialect!" Yukay said.

"I dew," Wenda agreed. "I wood knot try to conceal my origin; I am proud of it, though some say it is unprincessly."

"Princessly is what princessly does," Yukay said. "You adopt needy children? That is wonderful!"

"Yes. Those with infirmities that make others knot want them. They especially need support and love."

"More than wonderful," Zosi murmured.

Kody found this interesting, but remained conscious that it was a diversion from his Quest. "How did you come across this lost child?"

"I was visiting forest friends, when I heard the cry of a lost child," Wenda explained. "I can hear a child in trouble anywhere in Xanth; it is a special talent my friend Eris gave me. Also the ability to get there swiftly, to rescue the child, and take it home with me if that is called for. It is how I find the children in need. So I came immediately. But I was too late; the Bogeyman reached him first. The Bogeyman thought I was his mother, and I did knot deny it, because otherwise he wood have eaten the child right away, and anyway I might adopt the boy if he needed it, and truly become his mother. But the Bogeyman made demands I wood knot honor, and I had to tell him I had to pause to consider. But he will knot wait long."

"I thought the Bogeyman was just a scare story to make children behave," Kody said.

Both women, and Zosi, turned on him. "Not in Xanth," Yukay said. "The Bogeyman is all too real, and dangerous. Many children are lost every year to his awful appetite."

"But there are rules," Zosi said. "He can't take just any lost child."

"That's right," Yukay said. "The mother has to give him to the Bogeyman. Then when the Bogeyman comes and she's sorry, she has to deal with him alone. But he doesn't readily give up the child. She has to buy it from him, and that can be a price she doesn't want to pay."

"I can imagine," Kody said dryly.

"So I invoked another gift from my friend Eris, which is to locate the nearest source of help. That is yew with yewr special chips."

"This friend Eris must be very special," Kody said.

"She is. I could knot dew any of this without her."

"But why would a mother give her child to the Bogeyman, if she didn't want to be rid of the child?" Ivan asked.

"In a fit of temper," Yukay said. "Children can be horribly

trying at times, pushing mothers over the edge. Then they can threaten the child with the Bogeyman. They don't really mean it, but technically they may say it. Then the Bogeyman comes, and they're sorry, but it's too late."

"That must have happened this time," Wenda said. "I wood knot say it to my own children, but sometimes I've been tempted."

"Your adopted children," Yukay said.

Wenda looked at her. "Dew yew mean there is a distinction?"

"No, of course not," Yukay said quickly.

The more he learned of this, the less Kody liked it. "I think I need to know, if I am to help. Exactly what did the Bogeyman demand of you, to give up the child?"

"I dew knot want to say," Wenda said.

"It's ugly," Yukay said. "Best not to ask."

"But there might be some way of handling it," Kody said. "If I knew exactly what to reverse."

Yukay sighed. "Then I will tell you. Traditionally the Bogeyman gives the mother a choice from three similarly repulsive payments. The first is to be his mistress for a month. She must sneak out, not telling her husband, for an hour every night to cater to the lust of the Bogeyman. He is said to be an ugly lover, demanding unspeakably obscene things, who leaves a woman feeling forever unclean thereafter. The second is to give up enough of her blood, flesh, and bone for him to eat to make up for what he would have had from the child. This will leave her seriously ill, and take a long time to recover, and she can't tell her family what happened. The third is to bring him another child of similar size to eat, either another of her own or of another woman's family; she must steal that child and never speak of it thereafter."

"And if she refuses to do any of these," Zosi said with a shudder, "he will simply eat her child, biting off the arms and legs, then the head, and finishing with the body. She must watch it happen."

"I understand most mothers take the first option," Yukay said. "Rather than let their child die. But it demeans them horribly."

"I could knot," Wenda said. "Eris wood know, and bee disappointed in me. I fear what she might dew."

"This is one ugly creature!" Kody said, appalled. "I would simply kill him."

"You can't," Yukay said. "The Bogeyman is immortal, and protected by magical law; no mortal person can even try to kill him. He has to be dealt with on his own terms."

"Then how will a reverse wood chip help?"

"I am knot sure," Wenda said. "All I know is that when I sought help, I was brought to yew. So there must bee a way."

Which left it up to Kody. Would it be like fighting a dragon, using chips to reverse the fire or smoke? Somehow he doubted it. What needed reversing was the whole situation, and he wasn't sure chips could do that.

Then, suddenly, they came to the scene. There was the little boy, wailing in the bottom of the pit. And there was the Bogeyman, a horrendous, vaguely manlike figure with a scaly body, a ratlike head, and soulless white eyes. He looked the epitome of evil, and Kody knew at a glance that there would be no placating this monster. His terms had to be met, or he would eat the child; it was that simple.

Or was it? Something was nagging the fringe of Kody's mind. There was a wrongness here that went beyond the ugliness of the creature or of the situation. But Kody couldn't quite pin it down.

"Squawk!" It was an exclamation of recognition.

Then Zosi cried out. "That's Plato! Eve's son!"

Kody had not really looked at the child before. Now he did. She was right: this was the boy with the talent of reanimating the dead. The one Zosi was supposed to mentor, if she decided to live long enough to do it. How had he come here?

Well, he would ask. "Plato, remember us? We visited your mother a few days ago. Zosi Zombie took care of you for a few hours while your mother was at a meeting."

The boy ceased bawling and looked at them. "Take me home!" he said.

The Bogeyman made a menacing gesture. He was standing right behind the boy; he could snatch him up and bite off his head before any of them could get there.

"In a moment," Kody said. "First we need to know how you got here." He was stalling, hoping for an insight into the solution to the larger problem.

Plato was not bashful about it. "I heard something. I sneaked out. I found a dead thing. I made it live. Then I found another dead thing. I made it live too. I kept finding dead things. It was great! Then I fell into this pit and this monster came and said he was going to eat me. So I screamed for help, and Wenda came. The monster told her something I didn't understand, and she went away. Now take me home!"

Kody looked at the Bogeyman. "Isn't that entrapment? You lured the boy here with pieces of meat. His mother didn't give him to you at all!"

Now the Bogeyman spoke. His tone was growly gruff. "He is legally mine. He is a naughty child who sneaked out against orders. I will eat him. Unless I get my price."

"And what is your price?"

The Bogeyman gave him a straight look. "Give up your Quest."

That was a shock. "You know who I am?"

"I don't care who you are. That is my price."

Kody was outraged. "You snatched this innocent child in order to make me give up my Quest for the good of Xanth? That can't be legitimate."

"Then I will eat the child."

Kody drew his sword. "Then I will cut off your head."

The Bogeyman laughed. "You can't hurt me."

"He's right," Yukay said. "The Bogeyman is invulnerable. We have to deal on his terms."

"I don't see it that way."

"Please," Zosi said desperately. "I will pay his price. I can't let the boy be eaten."

"I'll be damned if I'll let you pay that price," Kody said.

Wenda stepped forward. "I am the one who must pay it. I refused before, but I can knot let my friend's child suffer." She walked on into the pit, sliding down the steep slope.

The Bogeyman grabbed her. "Well now! That's more like it. You're one delicious morsel of a woman." One gross hand reached into her blouse.

"She's not the boy's mother!" Kody called.

The Bogeyman paused. "Not?"

"He is the son of Princess Eve," Kody said. "How is it that you didn't know that?"

"Then bring Eve to me," the creature said. "Or pay my price yourself." But he didn't let go of Wenda.

Another person appeared at the edge of the pit. She was absolutely beautiful, but she wasn't Princess Eve. "Wenda, you are in trouble!" she said.

"Eris!" Wenda replied. "I did knot want yew to get involved!"

Eris. That was Wenda's talented friend. "Who are you?" Kody asked her.

The women looked at him, and he felt the shock of unfathomably enormous impact. It was like a cushioned sledgehammer. "I am the Demoness Eris, come to rescue my friend from distress."

"She's a Dwarf Demoness!" Yukay cried. "A creature beyond any we know! Do not annoy her!"

Kody might have argued the point, but that single glance had shaken him. This was indeed a creature of immense power. "I meant no offense, lady."

"You have no authority in Xanth, Eris!" the Bogeyman called. "Begone!"

The Demoness considered. "I will return," she said, and vanished.

Now Kody addressed the Bogeyman. "You're a fake! You're not the real Bogeyman! The real one would have known that Wenda Woodwife was not the boy's mother. And he would not have had to lure the boy here with a trail of dead meat. You're an impostor, and I can deal with you myself."

"I am new to this region, but no impostor," the thing said. "I merely don't yet know all the families here. That will be remedied in time."

Could that be correct? Kody wasn't sure. He hefted his sword.

Eris reappeared. Beside her Princess Eve also appeared. Beside Eve was another sinister man. "Not so fast, dreamer," the man said to Kody.

"With all due respect, sir, who are you?" Kody asked.

"He is my husband," Eve said. "Dwarf Demon Pluto. Plato's father."

Kody was silent, overwhelmed by the extraordinary ramifications this situation had taken on. Another Dwarf Demon? He sheathed the sword.

Then yet another figure appeared. This was a dragon with the head of a donkey. The creature was so ludicrous that Kody had to stifle a laugh. Had this business dissolved entirely into farce?

"No," Yukay said, answering his unspoken question. "That is the Demon Xanth. The ruler of this land."

Kody was glad he hadn't laughed. Why a powerful Demon should go about in such a form he couldn't guess, but evidently rank had its privileges. It seemed that each Demon had a finger in this particular pie. Why weren't they acting to abate the menace of the Bogeyman? The thing might or might not be a fake, but he still was a threat to the woman and the child.

Then a fourth Demon appeared. Kody could tell by the aura of power. These things were assuming human (or dragon-ass) form, but their intense magic radiated out regardless.

"And the Demon Earth," Yukay said in awe. "What an assembly!"

"Who has jurisdiction here?" Eris asked. "I do not believe this creature is from Xanth."

"It is not," the Demon Pluto said. "It was somehow imported from some other magic realm."

"There are rumors of it in my realm," Demon Earth said. "But it is not my creature."

That explained the Bogeyman's unfamiliarity with the region. He had been operating elsewhere.

"I'm not waiting for you freaks to make up your minds," the Bogeyman said. "I'm taking what's mine." He swept up the child and tightened his grip on Wenda.

Kody charged before he even realized he was going to. So did Ivan, Yukay, and Zosi, and Zap made a huge leap over all of their heads in an arc aiming for the Bogeyman.

And the scene froze, catching them all in motion like a flash photograph. They were stationary, and the griffin was stopped in midair. The Bogeyman too was frozen, along with Wenda and Plato. Kody realized that this was the spell of the Demons, who had magic in a league beyond any mortals knew.

"I claim jurisdiction because my friend Wenda Woodwife Charming is threatened," Eris said.

"I claim jurisdiction because my son Plato is threatened," Pluto said.

"I claim jurisdiction because the domain is mine," Xanth said. It seemed he could speak when he chose to, despite his asinine head.

"I claim jurisdiction because the protagonist, Kody Mundane, is mine, and is threatened," Earth said. That made Kody take note: so the Demon of his own world was involved in this. That confirmed what the Night Stallion had said about honoring requests for dreams. Kody was another dream.

"Then it seems we are at an impasse," Eris said. "We need a decision on jurisdiction before we can deal with this situation."

"The mortal woman, the Maiden Yukay, is reasonably sensible and objective," Xanth said. "Let her decide."

"Agreed," the other three said together.

Yukay, in the middle of their running group, spoke without moving. "Each of you has a valid claim, a personal involvement. This would not be happening without the setting in the Land of

Xanth, Demon Pluto has a right to protect his son, Demoness Eris has a right to protect her friend, and Demon Earth—you sponsored Kody? How could that be, here in Xanth's domain?"

"I made a deal with Demon Xanth," Demon Earth replied. "He knew there was Demon-level interference in his domain, but did not know who was responsible. He needed an exterior investigator who would not reveal that he was searching for the miscreant Demon. One who would be immune to the effect of the Bomb. I provided that person in the form of a dream. Physical folk can be tracked, but not dream folk."

"But then is Kody really at risk? Won't he simply emerge from the dream if anything happens to him here?"

"If he dies here, he dies in Mundania. That provides him motive to make his best effort."

Indeed, Kody thought sourly.

Yukay might have nodded, though she did not move. "Then he is at risk. Your claim is as valid as the others. I am unable to choose between them."

"Is there another reasonably objective and sensible mortal?" Pluto asked.

"The man Ivan has no direct ties to the woman or the child at present risk," Xanth said.

"Agreed," the other three said. Kody realized that their spoken words must be only part of their total communication.

"What would each of you do with the Bogeyman, if you had jurisdiction?" Ivan asked without moving.

"I would put him in a vise and squeeze him until all his information relating to his appearance and action here in my domain emerged," the Demon Xanth said. "Thereafter I might treat him unkindly, depending on my mood."

"I would take him to my domain of Hades and make him the servant-man of my son, on pain of losing a finger or toe any time he balked," the Demon Pluto said.

"I would take him to my domain, the chill planet Eris, and

slowly freeze off that member with which he threatened my friend," the Demoness Eris said.

"I would take him to my domain of Mundania and throw him into a prison for incorrigible rapists and child molesters, and let them have their way with him forever after," the Demon Earth said.

Kody realized that the Demons were serious. They had the power and the ill will, and they did not fool around with wrongdoers.

"These are all worthy punishments," Ivan said. "I am unable to choose between them."

"Is there another reasonably objective mortal present?" Demon Earth asked.

"The griffin, being nonhuman and possessing a soul, is about as fair-minded as any," Demon Xanth said.

"Agreed," the other three said.

"Squawk."

"Good point," Demon Xanth said. "Technically, the mother has to give the child to the Bogeyman."

"I did not!" Princess Eve said hotly. "I would never do that."

"I will replay the sequence," Demon Pluto said. "It occurred in our vacation residence in Xanth, Castle Windswept, an hour ago."

The scene appeared inside the castle. Princess Eve, dark eyed, dark haired, and breathtakingly lovely as ever, was hurrying to make arrangements for the reception of a royal visitor. Plato was playing with something he had dug out from the garbage. It looked like half a squashed toad. In a moment he had animated it. The thing leaped just as Eve was carrying a vase of flowers to the family room table, and she almost stepped on it. "Eeeek!" she screamed. "Plato, I've told you a hundred times, not in the house!"

"Ninety-seven times," the boy corrected her amiably.

"Take it out! If you don't behave, the Bogeyman may get you." She shook her head. "What would Princess Wenda think if that rotten thing jumped into her lap? She'd never agree to take you for a play date with her youngest!"

"Don't want a play date with a girl," Plato said truculently.

Eve made a gesture as of tearing her hair out in handfuls. "Oh, I wish Zosi were here to governess you. She'd make you appreciate the value of girls."

"Never."

"Remember, she's a zombie."

Plato reconsidered. "Yeah. She's fun."

Eve looked at the squirming dead toad in his hand. *"Now."*

The boy knew better than to argue further. He took the undead toad out and let it go. Then he saw another dead thing lying in the grass not far away. He went to it and animated it. Then he saw another farther from the castle. He continued walking and animating, paying no attention where he was going.

The sequence ended. "Now we have the answer," Pluto said. "She did not give him to the Bogeyman. He lured my son away without cause."

"But she did mention the Bogeyman," Demon Earth said.

"She said 'may.' That's supposition, not permission."

"It's a technicality. It was a definite threat."

Demon Xanth glanced at Zap. "Verdict?"

"Squawk."

"More indecision," Demoness Eris said.

"We need another suggestion," Demon Xanth said.

"Squawk."

"Now that will do," Demon Earth said.

"Let them settle it themselves while we watch," Demoness Eris agreed.

"And wager on the outcome," Demon Pluto said.

"So be it," Demon Xanth said.

Then the motion of the group of them resumed. Zap got there first, striking with beak and talons. The Bogeyman dropped the boy and let go of Wenda, who caught Plato before he hit the ground. He fended off the griffin and poised a fist to strike back. Obviously he was neither afraid nor weak.

Kody was next. He caught the poised arm and hauled it back. It felt like a two-by-four rather than flesh and bone. Indeed, this creature was tough.

The Bogeyman turned on him, poising the other fist.

Zosi caught it. The stroke hauled her along, but was slowed enough to allow Kody to dodge out of its way.

Even with his arms encumbered, the monster was far from helpless. The Bogeyman's face came up to Kody's face. His ratlike mouth opened wide, wider than any mortal man could manage, showing horrendous pointed yellow teeth. He lunged at Kody's face, those teeth snapping. But Kody, getting belatedly smart, flipped a chip into that gaping orifice.

The face paused. Then the mouth snapped shut, as had happened with the dragon, its impetus reversed. The Bogeyman couldn't bite his head off.

Ivan dived for the creature's legs. He hauled them up, and the Bogeyman was toppled to the ground. But still he fought with demonic strength. Kody feared the creature would not tire, and would overcome them all before long.

Kody let go and drew his sword. He chopped at the thing's exposed arm. The sword dug in slightly. He chopped again, but again made little progress. Two-by-four? More like concrete! The thing was truly invulnerable.

Through it all the four Demons watched impassively. They did not help or intervene; they merely waited. Kody realized that this was part of their nature: to let mortals sort things out without interference, to settle some obscure wager. It was their way of randomizing the decision.

"I think we have a problem," Ivan said.

"I'm not going to let this freak eat the child," Kody said. "Or molest Princess Wenda. There has to be a way."

"There is no way," the Bogeyman said, speaking through his shut mouth. "Soon you will all be mine."

Kody pondered. The Bogeyman's body was odd in several ways, apart from its ugliness and invulnerability. It looked almost as if it had been assembled piecemeal, like Frankenstein's monster. Then he got a notion. It wasn't sufficient to light a bulb, but it was worth trying, just in case.

He took hold of the creature's arm again, holding it firmly. He still had the strength to do that, at least briefly. Then he flipped a chip at the shoulder joint.

And the arm came off. The chip had reversed the connection.

Well, now. Kody kicked the arm away from the body. It rolled and stopped, flexing at the elbow joint, like a severed serpent's tail. Then he oriented on the other arm. In a moment he had reversed its fastening too. Then the two legs. The thing was now largely helpless. Still invulnerable in whole or in parts, but unable to move.

"What about the head?" Yukay asked.

"Don't you dare!" the Bogeyman said.

Kody flipped a chip at the neck. It disengaged and the head rolled free. "Bleep!" it swore. "When I get myself back together, I will make you utterly sorry! All of you!"

"Then we had better see that he never gets back together," Yukay said. "How can we best do that?"

They considered, and decided that they should bury each part by itself, far from the others. "I can dew it," Wenda said. "One by one."

Kody handed her an arm, which still flexed on its own, its fingers clenching spasmodically. That gave him the creeps, but he didn't say so. Wenda took it and disappeared, doing her traveling thing.

"We can bury the torso right here," Yukay said. "That's apart from the limbs and head."

"I will get together again," the head said grimly. "In time."

"Maybe in several centuries," Yukay said. "If we don't find a way to destroy your parts first."

"My maker will come and make you sorry."

"Oh? And who is your maker?"

But now the head was silent. That was too bad, because it could have been highly significant information. It occurred to Kody that the same person or thing that had sent the Bogeyman could have sent the Bomb.

They used the legs as spades and dug in the ground. The work was slow, but steady. Wenda returned and took the other arm for distant burial. Then she returned for one leg, and the other. Finally, as they were ready to bury the body, she came for the head.

"You'll never get away with this, woodbottom," the head said.

"One more chance, before I throw yew into the sea for the krakens to play with," Wenda said evenly. "Who sent yew here to consume innocent children?"

The head was silent.

Wenda took it and disappeared. The others dropped the torso into the hole and used their hands to push the dirt in over it.

"The issue has been settled," Demon Xanth said. "The Bogey-man did not get the boy."

Princess Eve ran to swoop up her son. "Oh, that scene re-minded me," she said. "About that play date—"

"Of course," Wenda said. "My little girl loves ooky things. That's why she was unadoptable."

"She does?" Plato asked.

"She sticks her fingers in and licks them off," Wenda said. "Ugh! I've told her a hundred times it's unprincessly, but she keeps doing it."

Plato looked at her.

"Well, maybe only ninety-seven times," Wenda confessed. But the boy was satisfied: the play date might be worthwhile after all.

Princess Eve looked at Zosi. "That scene also reminded me—"

Zosi burst into tears.

"She's working on it," Kody said quickly, putting his arm around Zosi. "First she wants to be sure I succeed in my Quest."

Princess Eve gave them both a long, thoughtful look. Her talent was knowing anything about nonliving things, but she seemed to be getting a fair notion of their case. "We hope you do too."

"Meanwhile, I won the wager," Demon Pluto said. "One per-cent of a status point from each of you."

"Agreed," the three others said morosely.

"You bet on our son's life?" Princess Eve asked her husband sharply.

"It is the Demon way."

"Not when it's your son. Give those points back!"

"But dear—"

"*Now.*" There was that in her tone that brooked no denial, even by a Demon.

The Demon Pluto made a resigned gesture with one hand. The three other Demons snapped their fractional points out of the air, smiling.

"Lady Eve, we like you," the Demon Earth said.

"You'd like me less if you had married me," Eve said bluntly. Demon Pluto nodded faintly.

They laughed together, including Demoness Eris. Then all four Demons disappeared. Their scene was done.

"Thank yew so much for helping me save the boy," Wenda said to Kody and the others. "I wood have been in bad trouble without yew."

"You're welcome," Kody said.

"It was nice to meet you again," Princess Eve said. "I really appreciate what you did."

"You're welcome," Kody repeated.

"This way to Castle Windswept," Princess Eve said, and she and Princess Wenda started walking, each of them holding a hand of the boy. Soon they were gone.

"Wow," Ivan said. "I understand Demons are so powerful that a sequence like this occupies only one percent of their attention."

"Which accounts for that one percent of a status point," Yukay said.

"Yet even so, Demon Pluto's mortal wife bosses him around."

"That is universal, in marriage," Yukay said. "See that you remember it."

"Warning taken." He shook his head. "I know in real life she's a beauty. I saw her in Hades. But with the Curse it's hard to imagine how Eve could impress Pluto."

"Demons are immune, I think," Yukay said. "They have their own domains where it doesn't apply. Meanwhile, what an experience we just had: four Demons came on the scene and interacted with us directly. I rather doubt that has ever happened before in Xanth."

"And provided me with significant information about my presence here and the nature of the challenge," Kody said. "Is it a foreign Demon responsible for the Curse?"

"That seems likely, now," Yukay said. "I suppose it could be one of the four we just saw, but I find that hard to believe. They came across to me as essentially people, unimaginably powerful, but still people at heart. Maybe it's because they married mortals, and got half souls. A soul makes a huge difference."

"Squawk," Zap agreed.

"They married mortals?" Kody asked.

Yukay counted them off on her fingers. "Pluto married Eve, as we saw. Eris married Jumper Spider, who had acquired a soul. Xanth married Chlorine, a mortal girl. And Earth—um, I don't think he married, actually, but he had a serous interest in a mortal woman. About the only other Demon who has seriously interacted with the Land of Xanth is Fornax, from whom we got Counter Xanth." She paused thoughtfully. "Her nose might be out of joint about that."

"Fornax? Isn't that a stellar system?"

"A foreign galaxy. One with reversed substance. But to Demons physical things are only real estate. Still, I wonder."

"Assume it is Fornax," Kody said. "Who wants to get back at Demon Xanth in a way that can't be traced directly to her. Does that make sense?"

"Too much sense," Yukay said. "I think we had better assume that that is what we are up against: a vengeful Demon who must act indirectly."

"Wouldn't the other Demons catch on?"

"Surely so. But they can't make an accusation without proof."

"Or investigate too openly," Ivan said. "Demon protocols."

"Thus I was brought on the scene," Kody said. "To do the impossible."

Yukay smiled. "Consider it a challenge."

Kody was dreadfully sure that this was exactly the case.

# 15
# NoAmi

W hat do you think?" Kody asked Zap.

"Squawk?" On her side was a question mark.

"I think you may be the most objective member of our party," Kody said. "You came up with points the Demons considered valid, and showed the way to dealing with the Bogeyman. So now I want your input on how we should proceed."

"Squawk." And on her side was the word NOAMI.

"We should deal with NoAmi first? Then what?"

"Squawk." FORNAX.

"And you have a way for mortals to deal with a capital D Demon?"

"Squawk," she said affirmatively.

Now everyone focused on the griffin. "What is it?" Yukay asked.

"Squawk." MAKE HER ACT OPENLY.

Yukay nodded. "Because this is Xanth, and any open interference would be an infraction of the Demon wager rules that the Demon Xanth can deal with. We just have to trick her, or taunt her into using her powers openly in Xanth, thus violating Demon protocols." She took a breath. "There's one small problem, though."

"We'll be dead," Kody said.

"That's the problem," Yukay agreed.

"Squawk." NAOMI

"Ask Naomi, who is already dead," Yukay agreed.

*I am here. I stayed out of sight during the fight with the Bogey-man because the Demons could have seen me and asked questions. But I can tell you: being dead is no picnic. The frustration of being aware but helpless to act is enormous.*

"But you and the other ghosts have helped us considerably," Yukay said.

*Because you can see and hear me. Few ghosts retain close enough contact with living friends to communicate effectively with them, and it took me some time to accomplish it. Don't risk it.*

"So we're better off not dying," Kody said dryly.

*Yes.*

"That means we should tackle NoAmi and the Bomb first, as Zap said," Yukay said. "Then with the Curse lifted, we can see to Fornax. If we die then, at least we will have accomplished our Quest, and maybe made the Demoness act openly."

"Small comfort," Ivan said.

"I will try to make it up to you before we die."

"Thank you," he said, as dryly.

"So how can we deal with NoAmi?" Kody asked.

*Just reach her and kill her before she can come up with anything else to throw at us.*

"How far away is she now?" Yukay asked.

*About half a day's walk.*

Kody nodded. "Let's make camp here and sleep."

"But the day is only half over," Yukay protested.

"So we can travel by night, and come across her before morning."

"By surprise," Yukay said appreciatively.

"Squawk."

*She's right. If my evil alter ego sees you sleeping early, she'll know what you plan.*

"Good point," Kody agreed. "Then suppose we travel today, and camp before we reach her. Only it will be a mock camp, while we plow on in darkness to ambush her. We'll lose some sleep, but we can catch up on that after we've dealt with No."

*That might work,* Naomi agreed.

They fired up Sniffer and moved west. They passed a configuration that looked rather like a female torso with an arm lifted. A man was digging in the armpit.

"Hello, stranger," Kody said. "What's up?"

"Her right arm," the man replied.

Kody forced a smile. "I mean, what are you doing?"

"I am mining for gemstones," the man said. "Here in the nymph lodes."

"Jewel the Nymph plants assorted gems around Xanth for others to find," Yukay explained. "The nymph lodes."

Kody eyed the earthen torso. "Looks more like lymph nodes to me." Then he got the pun. "Ouch!"

"I love the way you keep getting caught by routine Xanth puns," Yukay said. "You have such a refreshing innocence."

Foolishly irritated, Kody snapped back, "I love the way you flash me with your torn blouse."

She glanced down. "I do need to change clothing. We all do, after that fight with the Bogeyman. We had better look for a place to wash and change."

She was such a good sport that he was immediately sorry. "I apologize for looking."

"Don't. I'll flash you more when I change."

They came to a streamlet. Beside it was a bush growing somewhat old-looking clothes. Yukay and Zosi stripped and washed, showing everything, but Kody kept his eyes only on Zosi.

"I think you're cheating," Yukay complained.

"I don't think so," Zosi said.

"I dare you girls to do this again after the Bomb is off," Ivan said, forcing himself to look briefly.

"Squawk," Zap said, appreciating the interplay.

"It won't make a difference to me," Kody said. "Zosi is the only woman I want to see."

Then Naomi flashed him.

"Bleep," Zosi said. He seldom heard her swear.

"Remember, she's untouchable," he murmured.

*Unfortunately true,* Naomi agreed. *Zosi, would you deny me one of the few pleasures I have left?*

Zosi relented. "No."

They dried and donned the replacement clothes, which were at least intact. "Suddenly I feel demoralized," Yukay said.

"So do I," Zosi said.

"Because you flashed us and we didn't react?" Ivan asked. "That's not your fault. I'm sure your magic is still there."

"I don't think that's it," Yukay said. "The Curse has been in place for days and I didn't feel depressed. Frustrated, but not depressed. Now I'm depressed."

"So am I," Zosi said.

"And your man really appreciates you," Yukay said. "That hasn't changed. So you have no reason to be depressed."

"Except that he can't stay," Zosi said.

Yukay reconsidered. "True. That *is* depressing."

Ivan and Kody stripped and washed. Neither woman looked at either of them. They could handle the men clothed, but their ugliness was simply too much when they were bare by daylight.

"I forgot my chip!" Ivan said. "I could have used it and seen them both!"

*Poor boy,* Naomi thought, amused. *Such a naughty chance, and you missed it.*

"Maybe next time," Kody said.

"Squawk," Zap agreed, also amused.

*Use your chip now, and I will flash you.*

"You don't count, ghost. You're always bare."

Even Sniffer seemed amused, puffing out little heart-shaped smoke balls.

They finished and harvested their own new clothing while Zap took her turn washing. The griffin had really gotten dirty, and the water of the river turned solid brown before she was through. That was why she had courteously waited until last.

Then Kody felt oddly disgruntled. His mood had been reasonably upbeat, but now it was downbeat, as though he had run afoul of significantly bad news. His Quest seemed largely unaccomplishable. How could he ever defeat NoAmi and turn off the Bomb? He had no idea how to accomplish it.

"Bleep, I'm worn out," Ivan said. "What's the point?"

"Squawk."

They all looked at Zap. Her side said CLOTHES.

"We all turned negative after donning these clothes," Yukay said. "They must be careworn clothes, the kind worn by the Lady Care I heard about. Nothing bad happened to a person as long as he or she walked with Care. But what happened to all that badness she fended off? It could have stayed with her clothes; after she was through with them they were careworn. This bush picked up on the type and grows them."

Kody refrained from groaning at the pun. They all stripped off their clothing, and this time Ivan remembered his chip and was very pleased. Until Yukay harvested fresh new panties from a pantree and put them on, catching him by surprise. Then, while Ivan remained freaked out, they foraged for and harvested better clothing. They were ready to move on.

They also harvested pies and milk pods and had a late-afternoon meal. "Why don't we just camp right here for the night?" Yukay asked. "We can harvest tent halves and pitch tents and get some real rest before moving on tomorrow."

"I'm for that," Ivan agreed, holding his chip.

They made two tents, and got into them by nightfall. But instead of sleeping in them, they quietly crawled out, leaving them unoccupied.

Sniffer led them on to the west. Naomi and the ghosts guided them around bad sections, and Zap remained alert without flying so that she too was largely out of sight. Progress was slow, in the dark, but the ghosts assured them that they were now quite close.

*We're there,* Naomi thought.

The five of them paused, gazing at the scene ahead. Kody wasn't sure what he had expected, if anything, but not this. It was a beautiful garden, its trees softly illuminated, with statues, hedges, fountains, and a lovely central pavilion. Within the pavilion was a soft bed, and on the bed a woman lay.

*She's not asleep.*

So they could not pounce on NoAmi by surprise. She had fathomed their coming and was posing as vulnerable to lure them in.

"She must have guards," Kody murmured. "Where are they?"

*They are the statues. They will let you pass unchallenged, but will animate the moment she calls them.*

Ah. Another cunning trap. "Then let's nullify them."

Kody advanced on the nearest statue, which was of a man holding a long spear. The man did not move, but Kody could tell that he was indeed alive and conscious, merely playing the part of a statue. In the relative darkness it was effective, and might have fooled Kody had he not been warned.

Kody touched a chip to the guard, tucking it into his hair. There was no apparent change, but now the man's alertness had been reversed to sleeping in place.

Kody went to another and did the same thing. Then a third, and a fourth. There were six guards in all, circling the pavilion. Now all of them slumbered in place. He had, he hoped, neatly reversed the trap.

"Stay back," Kody told the others. "You too, Sniffer. Keep watch. I don't want to be surprised while I'm dealing with NoAmi."

"We are watching," Zosi said.

Kody walked up to the lighted pavilion. It was richly decorated and furnished. He saw that tent flaps could be dropped down to enclose it, rendering it abruptly private. NoAmi might do that when entertaining a man.

He came to the bed and stood gazing down at the supposedly

sleeping woman. She was not old, but was the ugliest crone he had seen. Which, thanks to the Curse, made her seem like the loveliest woman in Xanth. She had evidently used that appearance to fascinate many men, gleaning their favors and getting them to do her dirty work.

"I think you know who I am, NoAmi," he said.

NoAmi opened her eyes, no longer feigning sleep. She smiled languidly, and moved slightly so that her robe fell open. Unfortunately for her, her torso was singularly unappealing. Now Kody understood better why Ivan turned away when seeing the bodies of attractive women. They were like this, for him. "I have been expecting you, Kody Mundane." She glanced beyond him. "And you too, alter ego."

*You sent me to my death.*

"I sent you to track Kody. I can't help it if you bungled it."

The ghost was silent.

Kody was not pleased by the exchange. "My business can be simply accomplished. Give me the Bomb so that I can turn it off."

"In due course. Abide with me here for a time." Her robe fell farther open. She wore no slip or bra. She really needed both.

*It won't work. You can't seduce him. He's not reversed like the others.*

"Hardly," Kody said, referring to NoAmi's invitation. "I am trying to conclude my business with you amicably. It's an effort."

"Indeed." She shifted her position again, and the rest of her body came into view. She did wear panties, and she was flashing him with them. They would have freaked him out instantly, had they been on a full, firm bottom, but as it was they merely disgusted him.

"The Bomb," he repeated.

"So it really is true, as my doting alter ego says: you are not affected by the Curse."

"It is true, you grotesque hag," he agreed. "Stop stalling."

She snapped her fingers, summoning the guards.

Kody waited.

After about a moment and a half she realized that there was no response from the guards. *He nullified them with chips,* Naomi thought, pleased.

NoAmi was unruffled. "You are less stupid than I thought."

"I should hope so, you wretched witch. Now shall we get on with it?"

NoAmi sighed. "I tried to make nice. This is the thanks I get for it?"

"You tried to deceive me. You tried to kill my friends. You have thrown all Xanth into misery. I am fed up with you. Now I mean to end it, amicably if at all possible, inimically if necessary."

"Aren't you even interested in my side of it?"

Kody feigned surprise. "You have a side?"

"Naomi and I were delivered as twins conjoined by sharing one organ: the soul. She got most of it, I but a little. That made her beautiful and nice, and the opposite for me. But it gave me one surpassing advantage."

*True.*

Now Kody was curious. "What advantage?"

"She was unable to hurt people, or to practice malign deception. She was ineffective, being badly inhibited by decency. I, in contrast, had no difficulty doing whatever I deemed necessary, unrestrained by the paltry bit of the soul I possessed. So naturally I dominated our association."

*Alas, true. I could not deny her imperatives, though they appalled me.*

Kody thought of Zap Griffin, handicapped among her own kind by her soul. "This shows why you governed your alter ego. That much is true in Mundania too: the one who cares less governs the relationship. It does not make the case for using the Bomb to render other women into hags."

"I was the ugliest woman in Xanth. No one would give me a chance. I was doomed to inferiority and obscurity, regardless of my other qualities. Does that seem fair to you?"

"No, actually," Kody said, surprised by her candor.

"So when I happened upon the Bomb, and turned it on, and discovered its effect, can you blame me for leaving it on? It completely changed my life for the better."

"And changed every other person's life for the worse."

"Not entirely. Ugly folk are now handsome and beautiful folk, and they are quite satisfied to be so. They are getting the benefits of appearance, just as I am, without sacrificing their underlying nature. If it was fair to have all the good things accrue to the best-looking people before, regardless of their other merits, is it not similarly fair now that the people have changed?"

For a moment Kody could not answer. She did seem to have a case.

*Oh, Kody, don't let her merciless logic daunt you.*

NoAmi pounced, verbally. "So why don't you simply give up this foolish Quest and let things sort themselves out naturally?"

Kody shook his head. "I am not ready to do that. How did you find the Bomb?"

"I was just meandering my desultory way, mourning my lack of an interesting life, when I heard a mental voice murmuring, 'Come to me.' So I followed it, and in due course discovered the Bomb sitting amidst ancient ruins. This was the source of the mental voice. Now it said, 'Turn me on.' I said, 'Why?' and it said, 'Because I will fulfill your fondest desire.' I said, 'I doubt it.' It said, 'Try me and see.' So, being curious, I turned it on. And it ushered in the Blessing."

"The Curse."

"Not to me."

Kody pondered briefly. "Weren't you suspicious of such a windfall? Didn't it occur to you that you could pay a price?"

"What price? My life has improved a hundredfold since I turned on the Bomb."

"Like maybe selling your soul?"

She laughed. "You believe in that garbage? I never had most of my soul anyway."

"I'm Mundane. I don't believe in magic. Not until I entered the dream that is Xanth. It's a marvelous adventure, but I will pay a price."

"What price?"

Suddenly he was wary. This creature had acted without conscience. If she knew that he loved Zosi she might try to kill her. "This fantastic land has grown on me. I will be sorry to leave it, never to return."

"And lose your zombie girlfriend?"

So she already knew. "That, too."

*She knows everything. She tracked you throughout, via me. She can tune in on my larger share of our soul far more readily than I can tune in to her tiny share. I told you you should send me away.*

"A soul is not a bleeping liability!" Kody snapped.

"She actually believes that," NoAmi said scornfully.

*I do,* Naomi agreed sadly.

"With respect to your zombie paramour, you are missing the most significant aspect." NoAmi smiled, waiting for his retort.

He had to make it. "Leave Zosi out of this."

"You strike me as an intelligent man, but sometimes you're an idiot."

"Surely true. Do you have a specific in mind?"

"I do. Consider that dream pass the Night Stallion gave you."

So she knew about that too! "You have been tracking me more closely than I thought." Actually Naomi had joined his party for that reason, so he shouldn't have been surprised. NoAmi seemed to be better prepared for this encounter than he was, ironically. How could he be letting her put him on the defensive?

"Of course I have, since you're the one designated to deny me my dream. How could I stop you, if I didn't know what you were up to?"

"You say I am being stupid about the Night Stallion's pass?"

"You assumed it meant you could enter his dream realm. Why

would you need a pass for that, when you can do it via any peep-hole gourd?"

"Good point," Kody said, grudgingly impressed.

"That pass is obviously far more significant. It will admit you to your dream realm of Xanth, from Mundania, any time you invoke it."

Kody stared at her. "I'll be bleeped!"

*Oh my! I never thought of that.*

"So you can visit your rotten zombie creature, after you go home. Just for a few hours at a time, which should be enough. What more does a man want with a woman, after the first hour?"

"You are being extremely cynical."

"I learned cynicism in my prior life, the ugly one."

"But I believe you are correct," Kody conceded. "The end of my Quest does not have to be the end of my romantic life here."

"Exactly. In fact you don't have to complete your Quest at all."

"I think I do. Too many people have put their faith in me."

"I was afraid you would see it that way. You have followed an honorable course throughout."

"I can't say the same for you."

"In war we do what we must."

"Though many others suffer?"

"There is always suffering when a regime changes."

"Maybe so. But the original Xanth regime does not need to change."

She gazed at him pensively. "What loyalty do you have to a dream realm made up mostly of egregious puns?"

"My loyalty is to my companions and those who trust me to complete my Quest. It's a matter of honor."

"Honor," she repeated thoughtfully. "You do seem to have it. Pity."

Kody shrugged. "I do what I feel is right. It's that simple."

"The girls are all smitten with you despite the Blessing. You could have had Yukay or Naomi. Instead you chose the least of them, the zombie."

Her repeated references to Zosi were not complimentary. Kody repressed his annoyance. She was probably baiting him. "It wasn't a deliberate thing. It just gradually happened."

"And then you killed Naomi."

"You set me up for that!" he retorted. "Her death is on your head."

"She is my alter ego, my better half. I did not want her to die. I wanted her to seduce you and nullify you. Why couldn't you simply have taken what she offered?"

"Because she was obliged to make me give up my Quest. I did not want to kill her. She forced my hand."

*I did,* Naomi thought.

NoAmi changed the subject. "I must confess that becoming beautiful is not all that I had wanted it to be. I can take just about any man I want, and I have taken many. But all they want is one thing, that first hour." She grimaced. "That first ten minutes, for some. They have no interest in my mind or my ambition, only in my body. That soon becomes wearisome."

"You can readily give up that shallow appeal."

NoAmi shook her head. "That would be terminally wearisome. No, I mean to keep my appeal. I merely need to orient on a better grade of man." She eyed him appraisingly. "It is too bad you are not interested."

"I see you as you are," he reminded her.

"Had you wanted beauty, Yukay was available," she reminded him. "And Naomi."

"I meant your personality. You are a cynical, ruthless, virtually conscienceless creature I would not care to associate with regardless of your physical appearance." He shook his head. "What I can't fathom is why Naomi, who was all the nice things you aren't, went along, soul or no soul. I have a soul, and I won't cater to you. She knew your nature. Why did she do your bidding?"

NoAmi smiled hideously. "She did not realize until she died that she had any choice. So I got control, being the more practical one."

*True. I was a fool.*

"The more ruthless one," Kody said. "Because of your lack of soul."

"Choose the terminology you prefer. I am able to do what needs to be done. She isn't."

*I wasn't. I could now, but it's too late.*

"I, too, mean to do what needs to be done. That is to turn off the Bomb."

NoAmi sighed. "Well, I tried to make nice. Now go your way. You shall not have the Bomb."

"I tried too. Now I will have to take it without your cooperation."

"You are a fool. I could have killed you at any time."

"Why didn't you?"

"Because my alter ego, foolish as she is, nevertheless has good taste in men. Her love for you transfers somewhat to me. I would far prefer to seduce you and win you than to kill you. As long as I think there is a chance, I will let you live."

"Naomi had a chance. You don't."

"So I may yet have to kill you," she said with apparently sincere regret.

She knew he would not be staying here, so she had to be thinking short term. "Or I you. I am constitutionally unable to attack a person unprovoked, but the moment you try it, I will try to destroy you."

"Love or death," she agreed, unalarmed.

Kody left the pavilion. He would far rather have completed his Quest amicably.

*That did not go well.*

"She's a tough one," he agreed.

*I had not realized that any of my emotion transferred to her.*

"You may have done me more good than you knew. I thought she would attack; now I see why she didn't. But it may not take her long to understand that she can't win me."

*When she does, she'll be terribly dangerous.*

Day had brightened around them. Kody returned to the others. "She won't give up the Bomb. Now it's up to Sniffer."

"Sniffer is ready," Ivan said.

"So are we all," Yukay agreed.

"Squawk."

Zosi just took his hand and squeezed it.

"Hello, handsome."

They turned. It was NoAmi, who had followed him here.

*Oh, bleep! I should have watched her.*

Which meant NoAmi had overheard his last remark. This was mischief.

"What a gorgeous creature!" Ivan said.

"The Curse strikes again," Yukay muttered. "She is breathlessly beautiful."

"Come to me," NoAmi said to Ivan.

Ivan took a step, plainly dazzled. Then he took something from a pocket and held it. His demeanor changed. "No thanks."

"The chip!" Yukay breathed, delighted. "It reverses his vision of her, just as it does his vision of me. He sees her as she is."

"Then it is war," NoAmi said, turning away. In two or three moments more or less she was gone.

"She sure was luscious," Ivan said. "But I knew she was no good."

"She was so lovely that even I wanted to believe she was good," Yukay said. "Beauty can have that effect."

"Which is another reason I was chosen for the Quest," Kody said. "Not for whatever other qualities I may have, but for my immunity."

"Maybe," Yukay said. "Your other qualities do help."

Sniffer moved away from the pavilion. It found a path and followed it. They could tell by its attitude that the Bomb was close.

*NoAmi is still lurking.*

"Let her lurk," Kody muttered.

Then something shot across the path from the side. It smacked into Sniffer and knocked it off the path and into a dark place they hadn't seen. It slithered on into the brush and disappeared.

"That was NoAmi, in her serpent form," Yukay said. "She pushed Sniffer into a hole."

They gazed into the hole. It was too deep and narrow for Kody to reach into to recover the robot. Sniffer was helplessly stuck there. NoAmi had struck with elegant simplicity to stop them from finding the Bomb.

"We'll have to dig Sniffer out," Kody said.

They looked around, and found sticks they could use to start inefficiently digging. Kody got on it while the others spread out, searching for something better.

*Look out!*

Then the serpent reappeared. It neither hissed nor gave any other warning. Suddenly it was launching toward Kody, jaws gaping. There was no doubt of its identity: this was a truly ugly creature. NoAmi had waited for her chance, again, catching him alone. He didn't even have time to draw his sword.

All he could do was flip a chip of reverse wood into that gaping maw as it came for him. Then the snout struck him on the chest and knocked him backward.

Both Kody and the naga paused, anticipating the effect of the chip. But there seemed to be no effect. After a moment the head drew back as the serpent recovered her position, getting ready to strike again.

Now Kody drew his sword. He knew from prior experience that it could be effective where the chips were not. As the head lifted, so did the sword.

Then he suffered a moment of déjà vu. This was so like the scene when he had killed Naomi. That unnerved him.

He knew he needed to kill NoAmi and be done with her. But he hated the very idea of slaying the naga again. He had said his soul did not stop him from doing what was right, but maybe it did make him hesitate.

Still she did not attack. She seemed confused. Had the chip had some effect, if only indigestion?

Then he became aware of two things. The ghost Naomi was no longer present; he had become somewhat attuned, and her sudden absence left a psychic gap. And the serpent was turning beautiful.

He was not much of a judge of serpent beauty, but there was no doubt of it.

Yet how could this be? There was no beauty in NoAmi.

Unless somehow the chip had reversed them.

"Naomi!" he said. "Change!"

The serpent looked confused, but obeyed the voice of command. She became the woman. She sat on the ground, looking dizzy. She was naked, but none of them cared about that at the moment.

And it was Naomi.

The others returned, attracted by the commotion.

"Squawk!"

"What is this?" Yukay asked.

"It's Naomi!" Zosi said.

"But she's dead!"

"Not anymore, I think," Kody said.

"What happened?" Ivan asked.

"NoAmi attacked. I flipped a chip. I think it made the two alter egos exchange hosts. NoAmi must be the ghost, now."

"Then where is that ghost?" Yukay asked.

"The two shared one soul," Kody said, working it out. "Naomi had most of it. That's what made her nice. NoAmi had only a little of it. That's what made her nasty. It must take a lot of soul to manifest to living folk, even when other connections are strong. NoAmi doesn't have enough soul to manifest. She may be here, but unable to contact us."

"What would she have to say to us, that we would want to hear?" Yukay asked. "My concern is, can she recover the body? We don't want that."

Kody got down beside Naomi. "Are you in control?" he asked.

"Kody," she said. "Kiss me."

He smiled. "Naomi, you're not dying. I did not just kill you. You are no longer a ghost. You are alive again."

She looked around dazedly. "Can that be so?"

"Maybe you had better kiss her after all," Yukay said. "Zosi permitting."

Kody glanced at Zosi. She nodded.

He put his mouth to Naomi's mouth. She remained naked, but this was not a romantic ploy. He kissed her.

She fainted.

"I think we have seen what you Mundanes would call a miracle," Yukay said. "The dead have returned to life."

"But will it last?" Zosi asked.

"She swallowed the chip," Kody said. "If her system digests it, and it becomes part of her, maybe the effect will last."

"Her beauty is certainly gone," Ivan said. "That NoAmi might have been bad, but she was almost blindingly pretty."

"Or it's like the flip of a switch," Yukay said. "Once the change is made, it stays made. NoAmi might try to take back the body, but her bit of soul would not be able to dislodge Naomi's larger portion, now that she has possession."

"Let's hope so," Zosi said. "I like Naomi."

"Even though she has a thing for Kody?"

"It means she has good taste."

They laughed, though it was more relief than humor. "If she turns pretty again," Kody told Ivan, "let us know instantly."

"Got it," Ivan agreed.

Then Yukay and Zosi got to work finding and putting clothes on her, while the men and Zap returned their attention to Sniffer.

"I can do that," Naomi said.

"You don't need to dig," Kody said. "Just rest."

"No, I mean I can fetch Sniffer out more readily. Hold my tail." She changed into her serpent form, sliding out of her new clothing. She slithered to the hole and down into it, headfirst.

Kody jumped to grab her tail. He held it as the rest of her disappeared in the hole. He was faintly surprised at how firmly singular it was, instead of the two legs she had before; sometime he would have to watch more closely as she converted, to see exactly what changed how.

After a moment the tail wriggled in his grasp. He hauled it up, and slowly the serpent emerged. Her jaws had hold of one of

Sniffer's hind wheels; she was dragging the little robot up. She did not let go until all of her was out and Sniffer was safely back on the ground.

Ivan came to tend Sniffer, putting in more sticks, checking the slightly bent antenna. "No real damage done," he reported.

Yukay and Zosi checked Naomi similarly as she changed back to human form, and re-dressed her. Then, reorganized, they followed Sniffer toward the Bomb.

Sniffer came to a great gnarly old beer-barrel tree, its foliage thin and worn, its beer long since tapped and gone. It was just a hollow shell. It reminded Kody of one of the African baobab trees.

"Inside here?" Kody asked.

Sniffer beeped negatively.

"In the foliage," Yukay said.

They looked up, but didn't see it.

"Boost me up," Yukay told Ivan. "I'll find it."

Ivan heaved her up, one hand on her bottom, obviously not turned on. Unless he held his chip, he had no appreciation of her body. She scrambled up into the foliage. In a moment they heard her yell. "I've got it, I think."

Soon she was down with the object. It looked to Kody like nothing so much as a television remote control unit. But it pulsed with power. Could this really be it? The fabulous Bomb that they had scoured all Xanth for?

"It seems to be set on Button Number One," Yukay said. "Can we simply turn it off?"

Kody took it, but found no power switch. There was only what resembled a channel-changing button. So he depressed that.

"Squawk!"

"Oh, my!" Ivan breathed.

Yukay turned to him. "What do you see?"

"A beautiful woman."

Yukay turned to Zosi. "True?"

"True," Zosi said.

"Then we have done it! We have turned off the Bomb!"

"But I didn't turn it off," Kody protested. "The power light remains on. I think I merely changed the station."

"Station?" Yukay asked.

"The setting. I think it is now doing something else."

"But the Curse is gone," Ivan said.

"I don't trust this," Kody said. "I want to know exactly what it is doing now."

"Squawk."

Kody looked at Zap. "You have an idea?"

GERM

"I don't understand. Don't get me wrong, Zap, I'm sure you have something in mind, but I need more information."

"Play Nineteen Questions," Yukay suggested. "We'll run it down."

They did. Yukay was good at it. It turned out that Zap had very fine eyesight. So fine that she could even see floating germs in the air. Some of them lived quite rapidly, so that it was possible to see them evolving. And they were evolving backward.

Now they understood. The Bomb had shifted its reversal magic to a new venue. Now it was making living things live backward. All of them were getting younger, rather than older.

"But this is great!" Yukay said. "We won't have to see ourselves grow old and wrinkled. We can return to the prime of our youth."

"And zombies," Zosi said. "If they live backwards too, they will be healing rather than constantly sloughing off parts of themselves. This can solve my Quest!"

Kody shook his head. "Where does it stop? When you return to childhood, and finally get undelivered by the stork?"

Yukay closed her eyes in seeming pain. "Bleep! That's no good either."

"This device must be from the Demoness Fornax," Kody said. "Whose association you said is reversed substance. That's what I call contra-terrene matter. CT, SeeTee. Antimatter. The exact opposite of normal matter. Naturally her creations reverse things. This is a gift horse we are going to have to look in the mouth. I doubt we can afford to allow it to run on any setting."

"We must destroy it," Yukay agreed grimly. "And I'll bet it is indestructible."

Kody turned the device over. On the bottom was a panel. He slid the panel aside. Beneath it was a flashing red button. "I think it has a self-destruct button."

"Squawk!"

"I take your point," Kody said. "A device this powerful must have a huge amount of energy. When it destroys itself, there may be an explosion that takes out whoever pushes the button, plus a good bit of surrounding landscape." He slid the panel shut. "I think we need to think about this."

The others nodded. This could be no casual decision.

# 16
# BOMB

"At least let's try some other settings," Yukay said. "Just in case there's one we like."

"How do the rest of you feel about that?" Kody asked.

"Why not?" Ivan asked.

"Squawk," Zap agreed.

"Yes," Zosi agreed faintly.

"Should I vote?" Naomi asked. "I did betray you."

"You did not betray us," Yukay said. "You sacrificed your life to stop from doing that. Now you have it back. You are one of us."

Naomi looked at the others. They nodded. She looked directly at Zosi. "You know I have a thing for Kody. I can't help it. I want to flash him, and, you know. So maybe I should go away."

"We've been through this before," Zosi said. "Stay."

"But—"

"If you keep arguing, I'll tell him to kiss you."

The others laughed. "Let's *all* flash him," Yukay said, hoisting her skirt. "Panties galore!"

Kody looked away and scrunched his eyes shut. In one and a half moments, when he judged it was safe, he opened them again.

Three skirts were just dropping back into place. Ivan stood frozen; he had not blinked in time. He had not yet completely adjusted to the disappearance of the Curse, so was careless where he looked.

"Which one of us got him?" Yukay asked.

"Does it matter?" Zosi asked in turn.

"Yes! By rights it should be me."

"I think it was. He's facing you."

"So he is." Yukay went up to Ivan and snapped her fingers. "Wake!"

Ivan woke. "Huh?"

"Caught you looking," Yukay said.

Then Naomi nodded too. "Then I vote yes."

So they were agreed. Kody pushed the switch.

Nothing seemed to happen. But of course none of them trusted that. They simply needed to figure out what the change was. What had been reversed?

"Kody," Yukay said after three-quarters of a moment. "You're holding the Bomb. Shouldn't Naomi have it?"

Kody was surprised by this, as it seemed to relate to nothing. "Why?"

"She's the leader of the Quest, isn't she? So she should have it."

"I suppose I am," Naomi said. "I hadn't realized it before."

"But just moments ago, you were uncertain whether you even belonged in the Quest," Kody said.

"Moments ago I was evidently confused," Naomi said.

"Squawk."

They looked at Zap. REVERSAL

"It reversed the leadership!" Yukay exclaimed. "Putting the least certain one in charge."

"Did it also demote Kody?" Zosi asked.

"No," Kody said. "But I am immune to the effects of the Bomb."

"And this must be happening throughout Xanth," Yukay said. "The king must be at the bottom, and the lowliest laborer will be king. I don't think that's wise."

Kody pushed the switch again.

"Oh, I'm glad that's over," Naomi said. "I had no idea how to be a leader."

"But what effect is it having now?" Yukay asked.

"And why did I ever think I liked Kody?" Naomi asked. "He totally turns me off."

"I agree," Zosi said. "I hate him."

Kody felt his jaw dropping. "Zosi—"

"Don't touch me!" she snapped.

"Squawk!"

"OMG!" Yukay said, employing an unXanthly interjection. "You're right, Zap. It reversed feeling! Making friends enemies, and lovers into haters."

Kody quickly touched the switch again.

"Oh, Kody, I'm sorry!" Zosi said. "I don't know what came over me!"

"You love him most," Yukay said. "The reversal made you hate him most."

"Don't go back to that one!" Zosi said tearfully.

"I can't. The button seems only to go forward. If we find a setting we like, we can stay on it, or maybe loop back to it."

Yukay looked around. "I never noticed before how ugly this landscape is."

"Revolting," Naomi agreed.

"Squawk."

"Right, Zap," Ivan said. "Xanth is a garbage dump."

"Now it's reversing scenic appreciation," Yukay said. "This was a lovely region before the switch."

Kody considered. "The landscape looks the same to me as ever. But of course I'm no judge, being immune. It strikes me that this Bomb setting is less onerous than the others have been. Maybe we should leave it here for now."

"I wonder why it's called the Bomb?" Yukay asked. "So far it hasn't exploded."

"I seems more like an aerosol bomb," Kody said. "Diffusing its poisons into the environment, accomplishing its purpose more subtly."

"And exactly what *is* its purpose?" Naomi asked.

"I see it as a Demon plot," Yukay said. "Or more likely a Demon game, a wager of some sort. Toss in this disruptive thing and watch the ants scurry around trying to deal with it. Did you notice how we had four actual Demons show up together, besides the Bogeyman, and not one of them ever mentioned the Bomb or the Curse? Probably because that is for us to deal with, to settle their bet."

"And the Quest put in the hands of the one person immune to the Bomb's effect," Naomi said. "That can't be pure chance."

"It can't be," Yukay agreed. "So he can't be corrupted by it. Not only is he immune, he isn't staying here. So he just wants to get the job done and go home."

"I do," Kody agreed. "Except that after coming to know the group of you, especially Zosi, I'm not so eager to go home yet. I don't believe I ever associated with women in this manner before."

"What, only as sex objects?" Yukay asked.

"No, not at all," Kody said, nettled. "I didn't mean it that way."

"Squawk."

He looked at Zap. TEASING. Oh. The griffin sometimes seemed to be more alert to human nuances than the humans were.

"It's the way of the Quest," Yukay said. "An unlikely group of folk get together, and by the time they're done, they're fast friends, and some even marry. We'll always be friends, even if we never see each other again."

Zosi did not comment, but her tears started flowing.

"Oh, Zosi!" Kody said. "The end of the Quest is not necessarily the end of our association. NoAmi pointed out that the dream pass the Night Stallion gave me must be to let me re-enter *this* dream, to visit Xanth for a few hours when I sleep in Mundania. So I can see you again."

Zosi was speechless, so Ivan spoke. "Can this be trusted? No-Ami was our enemy."

"She was your enemy," Naomi agreed. "But she was not a liar. I know that much about her. Anyway, it's just conjecture. It does seem to make sense."

"She was using it as a reason for me to give up the Quest," Kody said. "That I could return without completing it."

"Oh, Kody!" Zosi said, coming to him. "That gives me reason to stay alive."

Which in turn would enable the completion of *her* Quest, as she governessed young Plato until he could make new zombies. It did indeed make sense. But mainly, it meant he could be with her regularly, if only a few hours at a time. That was enormously better than losing her forever.

"It occurs to me," Kody said, "that not only was my selection artful, but that the tools I needed to accomplish my Quest were also rather conveniently put in my hands. The chessboard, for example, and the sword, and of course my magic talent. To make sure it was possible. So the Demon wager would be fair. I was set up for this in every detail."

"The way of the Quest," Yukay repeated. "Demons set these things up, then watch them play out without interference."

But he still intended to complete it. Obviously just stopping the Curse was not enough; he had to find a way to permanently nullify the Bomb.

"So I think I need to use that self-destruct switch," Kody said. "But I fear it will blow me up when I do. What I don't know is whether that will represent the completion of my mission, so that I'll wake in Mundania, or whether it will mean I die here in Xanth, and therefore in my Mundane body too. Regardless, I think we need to find some real estate that can be spared, so that no one else gets hurt."

"That is an unkind uncertainty," Yukay said. "We'll be with you, of course."

"No, I don't want you with me at that point," Kody said. "I want to be sure the rest of you survive, even if I don't."

"I don't want to survive if you don't," Zosi said.

"Here is the equation," Kody said. "I see it as a fifty-fifty gamble whether detonating the Bomb will kill me or merely send me back to Mundania. So if I set it off alone, I still have an even chance to visit you later. But if you are with me, and you get killed, I will have nothing to return to, even if I survive. I don't want you with me then."

"He's got a case," Yukay said.

"Squawk," Zap agreed.

Zosi struggled, then agreed. "But if you don't return, I will revert to being a zombie. Then it won't hurt so much."

"So where can I take this thing to blow it up?" Kody asked.

"Let's consider," Yukay said. "There may be some isolated spot in Xanth that will do. But I don't think we should risk that unless we have to. What about one of the Moons of Ida? Not Demo Derby, but somewhere else. There must be a barren moon somewhere along that chain."

"If we can get to it," Naomi said. "Is it pictured in the chess set?"

Kody brought out the board. "All I see is Demo Derby."

"They won't allow it," Ivan said. "They crash cars, but they won't want to maybe crash their whole world."

"What about a sometime island?" Naomi asked.

"A what?" Kody asked.

"There are islands off the coast of Xanth that are there only sometimes. If you happen to be there when one manifests, you can cross over to it. If there were a small barren island, that might be good. Set off the Bomb when the island is out of contact with Xanth."

Kody looked at the chessboard. "I see no island."

"Bleep! Then how about Counter Xanth?"

"That reverses everything," Naomi said. "It might reverse the detonation. That might not be healthy."

"The dream realm?" Zosi asked.

"Would the Night Stallion appreciate that?" Kody asked. "He gives me a pass, I bring in a Bomb?"

"Trojan might not be amused," Yukay agreed.

Kody was still looking at the chessboard. He saw what looked like a planetoid orbiting in deep space. "How about this one?"

The others clustered around. "That looks desolate," Yukay agreed. "But there may not be air there for us to breathe."

"Would the board have a site that is lethal?" Kody asked.

"Probably not, if it is meant for human use," Yukay said. "So it's a gamble, but maybe not much of one."

"If we go there, and it is lethal, and we die there," Zosi said, "will that leave the Bomb where it can't bother Xanth?"

"It might," Yukay said. "Or we might take the Bomb there and leave it, well clear of Xanth."

"Let's try it," Kody said.

They gathered around the chessboard, touching each other, with Ivan holding Sniffer, and Zap pecked the picture. Immediately they were there, and there was air to breathe. It was indeed a planetoid, uninhabited, far from anywhere. It seemed ideal.

"Uh-oh," Kody said. "I see Sniffer, but—"

"What?" Yukay asked.

"The Bomb didn't make it here."

"**BLEEP!!**" Yukay swore in bold capitals with double exclamation points.

"I hope I can find the way back," Kody said, peering at the pictures.

"No need."

They turned to see a lovely woman with a Demon glow. She was a Demoness.

"Don't tell me, let me guess," Yukay said. "Demoness Fornax."

"You are astute," Fornax agreed. "Come into my parlor." She made a sweeping gesture, and the parlor formed around them: a phenomenal palace. There were fantastic plants growing under arches, and assorted gems sparkled on every surface, and a table was laid out with a sumptuous banquet. "Serve yourselves," Fornax said, indicating the luxurious chairs by the table. "Buffet style. I assure you it is not poisonous."

"Am I confused?" Kody asked as he took a piece of cake. The

others did the same, including Zap, who found a nice leg of raw meat, and Sniffer, who found some really nice dry aromatic wood. "I thought Demons were not allowed to take direct action in Demon games."

"You are confused," Fornax agreed. "It depends on the game. In this case I set the Bomb in Xanth and have not touched it since, or interfered in any way with the mortals who are participating. But we are not in Xanth now. We are in my home galaxy of Fornax, hundreds of thousands of light-years from Xanth."

"Hundreds of thousands of light-years!" Kody said incredulously between sips of excellent multicolored wine. "But we traveled here instantly. That's not possible."

"You are from a Science realm," Fornax said. "Your silly limitations do not apply here. Demons are not bound by them anyway."

"Oh." That was all the comment he could muster at the moment. He sat in a plush chair, nibbling on excellent nuts.

"As long as you remained in Xanth, I could not intervene without forfeiting my stake in the game. But you, of your own volition, departed from Xanth and came to my realm of CT matter. Here I am free to dialogue with you without violating any of the rules that govern you in Xanth."

"What realm?" Yukay asked.

"CT," Kody repeated tightly. "Contra-terrene. Antimatter. The opposite of our type of matter. You know of it, but don't want to believe it. Contact between the two types makes both instantly explode in total conversion of mass into energy. There's no other explosion like it."

"Except that I am shielding you from that conversion," Fornax said. "Because it is not in my interest to destroy you. I want to acquaint you with certain things."

"Such as why you planted the Bomb?" Kody asked.

"That I have already answered. What I want you to know is that you do not have to destroy the Bomb; it is merely a token, an artifact serving as the focus. You can bury it in the ground where no one else will find it, and be done with it."

"But it will still be affecting Xanth," Kody said, "making lovely landscapes seem ugly to the people."

"Yes, but that's minor. They will get used to it. What counts is how you will benefit."

"Benefit?"

"You can come here with your paramour," Fornax said, glancing at Zosi. "Who can be given the power to generate zombies by the mere touch of her hands, immediately solving the problem of the current shortage. Between times you can make continuous love, your every need attended to. Or if you tire of her, I will accommodate you myself, and guarantee your rapture." She glowed, her dress melting away to reveal a matchless female form.

Kody didn't need to glance at Zosi. "No thanks. I prefer to remain with my friends."

"They are welcome too." Fornax made a gesture, and a large serpent slithered forward. Then he transformed into an impressively endowed man. "Nolan Naga is eager for compatible company, having been long away from his own kind."

Naomi looked at Nolan, and it was plain she was impressed.

Fornax made another gesture, and a male griffin appeared. "Germane Griffin is also lonely, isolated from his own kind by the inadvertent acquisition of a soul. He thinks you are a very fine-looking griffiness and he would like to know you better, Zap."

Zap was also visibly impressed.

"And the pair of you, Ivan and Yukay, can have your own kingdom here, in every manner the equal of anything you might ever achieve in Xanth."

"You're a Demoness," Yukay said. "With powers such as we can't even dream of. You already have all the kingdoms and powers you want. Why are you bothering with us? We are no more than gnats on your horizon."

Fornax smiled indulgently. "Gnats? You flatter yourself. You are a thousand times less than that. But I will answer. I am doing it to win a full Demon point. There is nothing you are equipped to imagine that can approach the value of that to me. All this that I offer you is inconsequential to me. All that matters is that invaluable status point."

"Oh, I see," Yukay said. "Status is the only currency that Demons value."

"Correct, apart from a few foolish relationships, such as marriage to royal mortals. So I am offering this package of benefits, in return for one simple thing: bury the Bomb and depart. Are you interested, Kody Mundane?"

"Intrigued," Kody agreed. "And I hate to deny such gifts for my companions. But no, I do not accept this deal."

"I will enhance it. You can have an entire harem of exquisitely beautiful and highly obliging young women."

Kody smiled. "There may be one or two things you don't know about me. I'm not particularly susceptible to bribes, and in any event I will not be remaining in the fantasy realm. I am here only in a dream, and soon I will wake and it will be over. So there is nothing you can offer me for the longer term; I would be unable to accept it even if I wanted it."

Fornax considered him thoughtfully. "I see you were an artful choice for this Quest."

"So it seems," Kody agreed. "The other Demons must have known you would try to corrupt me."

"Of course. But there are ways and ways. For instance, have you considered the welfare of your friends? If you detonate the Bomb, all of them will be blown up too, unless they are far away from you. Is that your desire?"

"No! But we're looking for a safe place to do it. I can go there alone."

"And if you do, and destroy yourself in the process, what of Zosi? She does not wish to live without you."

That was his problem. Kody knew he could do what he had to do. But to torment Zosi in the process? That was beyond him.

"Here is an option you may not have considered," Fornax continued. "You do not need to keep the Bomb yourself. It belongs to whoever is holding it. You can give it to any one of your friends, or to an enemy, and be done with it. You could give it to Zap, and it could make her the queen of griffins, with any male of her choice. You could give it to Yukay, and exploring its ramifications could give meaning to the rest of her life." She paused. "Or you could give it to Zosi, and it could make her happy as she completes her own Quest. There is a setting for that."

Zosi was on that. "It can reverse happiness? So that I would become happy with life, while happy folk become miserable?"

"That would not bother you," Fornax said. "You would still be happy."

Zosi shuddered. "It's not the kind of happiness I care for."

"You are a foolish girl."

Kody reached out, took Zosi's hand, and squeezed it, signaling his approval of her attitude.

"So your choices are three," Fornax concluded, speaking to Kody. "You can blow yourself and your friends to smithereens. You can give the Bomb to someone else. Or you can bury it where it will not be found. In due course you will wake in Mundania, and at that point the Demon game will be over and a victor decided, depending on your decision. You will never know which Demon wins, so it is of no concern to you. Do you understand?"

"Oh, yes," Kody said grimly. "I'm a tiny ant, or a mere germ on an ant, and the bet is which way I will turn. None of you Demons really cares about the welfare of mortal folk like us."

"Nicely put," Fornax agreed. "Now are there any further temptations I can ply you with, or are we done here?"

"We're done here," Kody said.

And they were back in Xanth, where they had been, gazing at the chessboard. Kody felt the Bomb in his pocket, where it had been. It seemed that no time had passed. Demons were good at freezing time.

Kody folded the board. "I think we have some things to consider," he said.

"No, we don't," Yukay said.

"But those other options—"

"We don't need them," Naomi said.

"But—"

"We know you'll do the right thing, whatever it is," Ivan said.

"But—"

"Squawk."

"Beep." Sniffer emitted an agreeing puff of smoke.

Kody looked helplessly at the only one who had not spoken.

"I love you," Zosi said.

"That's beside the point."

"No, it isn't," Yukay said. "You love her. You'll do what's best for her. That will be what's best for Xanth. Then you'll go home."

"Bleep!" Kody swore. "I need better advice than that. What good are the lot of you if you won't help me think?"

"You need it in words of one syllable?" Yukay asked.

"Yes!"

Yukay looked at each of the others in turn.

"Get by your self," Naomi said.

"Blow the Bomb," Ivan said.

"Hope you can come back," Zosi said.

"Squawk." SOON

And there it was. If destroying the Bomb completed his Quest, he would wake in Mundania, with the dream pass that would enable him to visit the land of Xanth again. To see all of them. Especially Zosi. If it did not, he would be dead, but Xanth would still be saved.

They were right. There was nothing to discuss.

Kody shook his head. "I thought maybe there would be a huge dramatic crisis, dragons charging, empires clashing, magic running riot, scary wizards invoking hell-fire. You know, fantasy adventure climax. This is sort of anticlimactic."

"You have to do it," Yukay said. "Because none of the rest of us can. We would lack the courage, even if we were dreaming."

"We still have to find a suitable place," Kody said. "Soon."

Then a bulb flashed over his head. "I'll be bleeped! It's obvious."

"That's nice," Yukay said.

Kody lifted his arm as if hailing a passing taxi. "Caprice Castle! We need you."

And there before them the castle formed, quietly filling the space.

They walked up to the front gate. It opened and two little skeletons dashed out, accompanied by two puppies: Piton and Data. Wolfe and Rowena. In half a moment the visitors were getting hugged, licked, and nose-sniffed. It was as if they had been expected.

"Tell your folks we'd like to stay the night, then have a little ceremony of termination tomorrow morning, attended by anyone interested," Kody said. "Caprice will know where."

"Caprice does," Data said. "We were waiting."

"We knew when Mommy got pretty again," Piton said.

That did seem to explain it. Of course all Xanth had been immediately affected. They knew the Bomb had been possessed, if not turned completely off.

They were ushered inside, where they were royally feted. The hosts, Picka and Dawn, were interested to learn all of their adventures, and impressed with news of the appearances of four Demons, and then a fifth.

"We are in doubt about how much damage the Bomb will do when destroyed," Kody concluded. "So I will do that alone, in a safe place."

"Where is that?" Picka asked.

"In the Void. It is where I first arrived in Xanth. I was merely slow to take the hint."

"Perfect," Picka agreed. "Nothing that crosses that boundary returns, except in extremely rare and peculiar circumstances."

"I will invite my sister here, so she can check the Bomb," Dawn said.

"Thank you, Dawn," Eve said, appearing from a shadow. Kody realized that the sisters had close rapport, and they were Sorceresses with special powers. Eve probably had a magic pass that took her straight to Caprice Castle.

Plato was along too. He ran to join Zosi, one of the few adults he seemed to like; her zombie heritage really counted. That and the fact that he knew she would let him animate any dead things he wanted to.

Eve came to Kody and took the Bomb. "This is not just any old bomb," she said. "This is a New, Clear Bomb, with enormous energy. Detonating it will release all that energy at once, and that will vaporize everything within a hundred paces. Indeed, it should be handled carefully." She dropped it into Kody's lap, making him jump. That was her way of teasing him; she was not really being careless.

"I thought it might be something like that," Kody said, putting the Bomb away.

"Thank you for resetting it," Eve said. "Now when I visit Xanth I don't look like a hag."

"You never looked like a hag to me."

Eve smiled. "Of course."

Zosi was with him for the night. She was very soft and warm and close. "Oh, Kody, I'm so afraid!"

"You know I can't stay," he reminded her. "But if I win, you also know I will return to visit you."

"That will give me reason to live," she said seriously. "And to governess Plato and guide him into making new zombies. I know Princess Rhythm is satisfied to visit Cyrus intermittently, and Princess Harmony spends some time away from Bryce Mundane. If they can do it, I can do it with you. But if you lose—"

"Then you will be free to do what you choose."

"I hope you win," she said fervently. "Even if it means you have Mundane girlfriends."

"There will be no girlfriends in Mundania," he said firmly. "You are the only woman I will ever love." It was the absolute truth.

"Oh, Kody!" Little hearts radiated from her.

Then the Adult Conspiracy closed in to censor out the rest of their interaction, as there were three naughty children trying to sneak a peek under the closed door. There was a muffled "Peep!" which was as close as a child could get to a bad word.

In the morning they exited Caprice Castle, which was parked not far from the event horizon of the Void. The scenery was gruesome, but if all went according to plan, that would not be the case much longer.

They all lined up before that dread shimmering line of no return. The others looked at Kody. He was evidently expected to say something. He turned just before the line and faced them.

As it turned out, he did have something to say. "Whatever happens to me, I want you members of my Quest to know that I sincerely appreciate your support and friendship, and hope to see you again. Meanwhile, there are two items I can't take with me to Mundania. Ivan, I want you to have my sword; call it a return for the way you helped me to get Sniffer and locate the Bomb."

"Uh, thank you," Ivan said, taken aback.

"And Yukay, I'd like you to have the chessboard. I know you like to travel, and this will help."

"Why, thank you, Kody," she said, and kissed him.

"I know some of you Companions agreed to join my Quest out of simple good-heartedness, and because you had nothing better to do at the moment. You can of course go your separate ways now. But I want to remind you that Caprice Castle is in need of pun collectors, and I'm sure you will be welcome there if you wish to stay."

"Oh yes," Dawn said. "Hunting puns is considered hard labor, and few can continue long before their minds rot. But we'll sincerely appreciate any time any of you can give us."

Yukay and Ivan exchanged a glance, and so did Zap and Naomi. They were seriously considering it. Zap was good at puns; this was ideal for her. Naomi would be well positioned to meet many new people, both human and animal. Zosi of course would be at Castle Windswept governessing Plato, who was already possessively holding her hand.

"And you, Sniffer," Kody said. "Cyrus Cyborg should be able

to adjust your setting so you can sniff out puns. I'm sure Zap and the others will be glad to be sure you always have plenty of wood to burn."

"And if Sniffer gets tired of that," Eve said, "then welcome to come play with Plato in Hades."

Plato looked at the doglike machine, interested. Sniffer puffed out an agreeable ball of smoke. They would get along.

Kody was ready to turn and step across the line. But he paused. There was an urgency infusing him, something else he had to do. He had to—to give Zosi the Bomb.

What?

*Give Zosi the Bomb. It will make her happy.*

That could not be his thought! He had already decided to make Zosi happy by returning to visit her, using the Night Stallion's pass. If he possibly could. He knew she did not want the Bomb, but would not be able to destroy it if she had it. She was depending on him to take it forever out of her reach.

*Give Zosi the Bomb.* The urgency was intense.

Kody fought it. But slowly his mouth was opening to say the words he did not want to say, and his hand was reaching into his pocket to fetch out the Bomb. It was as though some other power was controlling his body, making him a marionette. He was trying to resist it, but it was slowly gaining.

"Squawk!"

"You're right, Zap!" Naomi said. "He's being attacked by an evil ghost!"

The griffin and the woman came to Kody. "Squawk!"

"Right again! That's NoAmi, my sinister alter ego! I'd know her anywhere."

Kody, still forced, brought out the Bomb and started to speak. "Zosi—"

"Squawk!" Zap said, drowning him out while Naomi grabbed his arm.

"Look at that!" Ivan cried. "On Zap!"

"It says Fornax!" Yukay exclaimed. "She's acting through No-Ami Ghost to make Kody give Zosi the Bomb!"

"That will mess up the Quest," Ivan said.

"Pluto." That was Eve's voice, not loud, but in the tone her husband heeded.

And the Dwarf Demon Pluto was there. Suddenly Kody froze, unable to move or speak. In fact the whole assembly was in stasis.

"Demoness Fornax influence verified," Pluto said. "Earth, Xanth, your turn."

The two other Demons appeared. Only the Demoness Eris was missing.

"I am here, Kody," Eris murmured in his ear. "My friends are affected too. But I can only observe, this time."

"Pluto, we return your partial status points," Xanth said. "You secured our coming victory." Then all four Demons vanished.

Suddenly Kody was free again, along with the others, and the ghost attack was gone. They had handled it, Demon fashion. His Quest was done.

Then why was he still here? He realized that the Demons had not said he was finished, only that their victory had been secured. Maybe the outcome depended on his deciding that for himself. After all, he still held the Bomb, and the landscape still looked wretched to the others. It was his Quest to win or lose.

So Kody's role was not yet finished. Not quite. He still had to dispose of the Bomb. He saw the others waiting as if watching a play. He saw the tear in Zosi's eye. She knew he had to do it, yet feared the outcome, as he did.

"I will return, Zosi," he murmured, and knew that she heard him, because her mouth formed a third of a brave smile.

Kody turned around, holding the Bomb, and stepped quickly across the event horizon. There was no shock, no flash of light, no horrendous fall into a yawning chasm. Merely an uneventful crossing of the line.

He stood in an unremarkable landscape, neither better nor

worse than the one he had left. Behind him the line shimmered. He knew he could not pass it again; crossing was strictly one way.

He walked forward, feeling the increasing pull of the Void, the Region from which nothing returned. When he felt he had enough distance, just in case the Bomb was even more powerful than they had thought, he lifted it, slid aside the back panel, and gazed at the bright red button.

Did he really want to do this? Was he about to commit suicide? That fifty-fifty chance of survival suddenly seemed excruciatingly weak. Was it to be Esrever, the reversal, or Doom?

The bleep with it! This was his fantasy destiny. He would meet it with seeming courage. He punched the button.

Kody woke in the Mundane hospital bed. "It's Esrever!" he exclaimed gladly.

Immediately an alarm sounded. "He's coming out of the coma!" a nurse said. Kody recognized her as the one who had first told him of his accident. "But he's still incoherent."

That was what she thought. He had in his fashion won the gamble. His future was settling into place, here in Mundania and there in the dream realm of Xanth. Glorious!

A doctor appeared, the same one who had sent him into supposed oblivion. "All is well, Mr. Kody," he said. "You have been out for several days, completely unconscious. But the operation was a success and you'll be fine." He walked away before Kody could comment.

Completely unconscious? How little they knew!

"Your friend Joshua is on his way here," the nurse said. "He was really concerned for you."

"Just what happened to me?" Kody asked her. "Did I get hit by a rogue cement truck? What kind of surgery did I have?" But the nurse was already moving on to the next patient. Par for the hospital course. Everybody knew about the details of his case except the patient. Well, Joshua would surely tell him.

Kody saw that he was definitely back in the real world. His

amazing dream was over. But he felt the dream pass in his mind and knew he could invoke it when he chose. His life in Mundania was totally different, but he knew that when he was ready he would return to the fantasy dream, Esrever, not Doom. To his friends there. To the magic. To the ludicrous puns. For a few hours at a time.

And to Zosi.

# Author's Note

This is #37 in the Xanth series of novels. The next one, slated to be titled *Board Stiff,* will complete the alphabet in Xanths. Will the series go beyond that? That depends on how well reader interest holds up. The publishing industry is suffering a seismic quake as electronic books pass paper books in sales, and I think no one knows for sure what the future holds. I am getting my books published both ways as much as I can, so as not to lose a sizable portion of my readership. Negotiations with publishers have been fierce; I hired a high-powered lawyer to represent my case that those rights are mine to assign.

I had my seventy-seventh birthday AwGhost 6, 2011, which I celebrated by staying home and getting my work done. At this age birthdays are not the novelties they were in youth. No, no birthday cake; I am keeping my weight down. Next day I wrote five hundred words of notes for *Esrever Doom,* as I got serious about starting the novel. Next week when I was doing my morning exercise run, my right foot snagged on something and suddenly my face was on the pavement. I made it home okay, but my face, hands, and knees were awash in blood. My wife helped clean me up. Fortunately the scrapes were superficial; no bones broken or bent. But I did wonder whether it had been a mistake to turn seventy-seven.

Three days later, on the 15th, I started writing text on the novel. It went well. But then, on the 28th, I fell again. This time it was Sunday morning. I was on the scooter I use to go out to fetch the morning newspapers on days when I'm not running. It's the kind you push with your foot, an adult version with sixteen-inch wheels. I did not see a fallen branch, and in a moment I was on the pavement again, the scooter beyond me, the branch behind me. I was wearing a helmet and goggles, so didn't hurt my face this time, but I did crunch down on my left shoulder. I climbed to my feet, in pain, my left arm inoperative. My wife took me to the emergency room, the same one I had taken her to when she fell last year, where they took about twenty X-rays of my shoulder. They determined that no bones were broken, my collarbone was intact, but a couple of ribs might have hairline fractures. No surgery needed, and I was good to go home. That was a relief.

I can now report that even a bruised shoulder and a hairline rib fracture can be plenty incapacitating. I couldn't cough, and heaven forbid that I should have to sneeze; pain was instant and awful. For about sixty years I had eaten with my left hand; I'm right-handed, but on a whim in high school switched for that one thing, and it stuck. Well, now I had to eat right-handed. I couldn't get into or out of a regular shirt. I couldn't lie down to sleep; for two weeks I sat up in my study easy chair for that. And of course I couldn't maintain my exercise schedule. I exercise seriously for my health, not pleasure, and believe I am healthier than the average man my age; I hated being so limited.

But I did manage to maintain normal life in other respects. I make meals, wash dishes, and make beds, since my wife can no longer stand on her feet long enough to do such things; I continued, slowly, very carefully. I couldn't run, but could walk, so I walked. Each time it was faster, as I healed. I started jogging, faster, and within a month I was running again, and working out with my hand weights. The hardest recovery was my archery: I could not come close to drawing a fifty-five-pound pull bow, let alone do it with an arrow nocked. But I kept trying, and one day I was able to draw the left-hand bow once. The right-hand bow recovery was slower. This might seem odd, since it was my left shoulder I had injured; my right side was fine. But what I discovered was that it was easier for my left hand to pull than to push. So I could pull on the left bow, but to do the right bow I had to hold it with my left hand, and the pressure was inward on the left shoulder. No way! But eventually I got there too, and was able to build up slowly, and finally resume archery, albeit rather clumsily at first. My target-hitting scores were abysmal, but that's no change from before. I do it for arm muscle, not accuracy.

How did this affect my writing? Not as much as you might think. I found that if I rested the heel of my left hand on the base of the computer keyboard, I could reach the keys with my fingers. I was severely slowed by the time spent at the hospital, and taking daytime naps, and my typing was not speedy, but I did do it. The main limitation is imagination rather than typing speed, and my mind was fine. (Pause here for the sardonic laughter of my cri-tics to fade. As you surely know, a cri-tic is an obnoxious bug that hates everything.) The day before the fall I typed twenty-one hundred words of text; the day after, one hundred. It remained low for a week, one hundred to three hundred words a day. But on the eighth day following the fall, it was twenty-one hundred again, and it con-tinued at one to two thousand words a day. So I was still in busi-ness.

One other complication was my computer: I had shifted to a new distribution of Linux, Fedora, and liked it. But it did not have Courier, the fixed-character font that has been the standard for writers for decades, and I had to shift to a proportional character font. The thing about a fixed font is that you can calculate exactly how much space a manuscript will take when published. Publish-ers need to know that, so they can judge how many pages they'll need. It would be unfortunate if they allotted 300 pages for the book, and it ran 305 pages and the ending was chopped off. No, they don't actually operate that way, usually, but you can appreciate my point. The computer wordage count doesn't do that; each word is equal, and "a" is equal to "antidisestablishmentarianism" in that reckoning. I'm not sure what kind of a headache this manuscript will be for my publisher, but I couldn't help it. It's a nuisance for me too, because I write to a certain wordage, and computer count simply does not match calculated count. I wish there could be computer programmers who are also writers, so that they would understand such things. But it has long since been evident that if I want the perfect computer system for a writer, I will have to design it myself. Maybe someday, if I live long enough and don't fall and hit my head too hard.

Apart from such concerns, my mundane life is nothing special. I'm a reasonably ordinary guy living on my little tree farm with one exploitable talent: writing. I don't go flying to all parts of the world to research for my books, I stay quietly home. I don't have a luscious woman in every city, I stay with my wife of fifty-five years. I tease her that she was nineteen when I married her, but she didn't stay that age. Sigh. Between novels I may spend a few days pigging out on videos I lacked the time to watch while writing, and catching up on accumulated science and news magazines. I'm a writaholic; when I'm in a project, other things tend to slide. In short, I'm dull. Now you know. If you still doubt, then visit my www.hipiers.com Web site, where I do a monthly blog-type column, provide information about my other novels (I do write more than Xanth), let readers know when there are movie or TV prospects for my books (so far there have been many prospects but nothing has actually made it to the big or little screen), and maintain an ongoing survey of electronic publishers that aspiring writers may want to check. Just trying to do my bit for the world, while I last and it lasts.

As usual, I had more ideas from readers than I could accommodate. I hate using an excellent notion as a throwaway scenelet, but sometimes have to. Some I have marked for the next Xanth novel, so as to try to do justice to them there. Suggestions kept coming in while I was writing the novel; I noted them down, but couldn't keep feeding them into ongoing scenes, so they must wait for the next. It's like bailing out your boat in a thunderstorm; catching up completely is impossible without magic. Some ideas relate to characters who didn't fit into this novel; they'll get their turns in due course, I trust. Readers are great for suggesting super-phenomenal magician-class talents for great protagonists, but the sneaky truth is that ordinary folk with ordinary talents make for better stories. You may have noticed that the central cast of characters this time are way beneath Magician-level magic. Thus they can never be quite certain they will surmount ordinary challenges, and they may mess up the attempt, just the way any of us would. Kody doesn't know until the very end whether he will win or lose, and then it's clear he won't be a king or billionaire or famous celebrity. He will just disappear into the nonentity from which he came, and few in Mundania will ever know or care about his dream life. That's the fate most of us face. Welcome to dreary reality.

Here, at any rate, are the credits for this novel, and I hope I didn't foul any up this time. They are in approximate order of appearance, except for being grouped when more than one is from one person. Sometimes I don't have a complete name, so I use what I have; e-mails can be obscure about identities. Leading off with one about me: Chris Ceranskiy sent an anagram based on my name: Horny Panties. Now we know why in Xanth girls freak out boys with naughty panty flashes. I couldn't help it; it was in my name.

Kody—Joshua Harrelson; catbird, barrel of crackers, robots with corrosion, path paved with Good Intentions, Primrose Path, re-seeding hairline—Robert; the Time Being—Jessi Rha; Griff the Hipporoc—Shauneci Switzer; vices—Cal Humrich; Sniper Harpy—ippikiokami; melon-collie gourd dog—Robert Lecrone

(there was a straight melon collie in *Pet Peeve*); Frank 'n Stein—
Eileen DuClos; crab grass, storm front, cashews, something that
goes bump in the night—Darrel Jones; Novel-tea—Nathan Theri-
ault; ass-et—Tina Yu; gravi-tree—Gavin; Demon Ceased—Kevin
Swearengin; D Mension gives other demons length, width, depth;
Talent of Ida's child: converting lies to truths; mining in the nymph
lodes; Eye Pod as hypno-gourd seedling—Misty Zaebst; talent of
persuasion—Brant; sidehill hoofer—Dean Howell; Hadi the Ali-
cenagon, boot rear float—Harli; egg plant, chains, tee party—Tim
Bruening; gin rummy, Annie Mal—Jeff Stephens; tough cookies—
Ben; Senior Citizen Ship—Thomas Pharrer; Mother Ship, Father
Ship, etc., reality check—William Roper.

The ability to call fish, Nymph Ophelia Maniac, Intella-
Giant—David D'Champ; prose and cons, oil wave ruining Xanth
shore—Aaron Jackson; CAT scan—mb ; Philip fills things up—
Phil Giles; Nora Nosnoora, I M Bigbucks, Xanth running low on
zombies, zombie sit-down strike, names of Woofer/Rachel's pups,
house cat, flying buttress—Mary Rashford; Onomatopoeia—Tia
Adams; heir guitar/heir band—Olivia Davis; panty shield—Andrew
and Amber Pilon; Burnice from Burnsville—Nathan Machelski;
Aqua-fir, sandalwood tree—Thomas Pfarrer; curse of losing memories for lies, Micro-Wave, Mega-Wave, catch her, catch him, pitch
her, pitch him—Athena-Lee Maynard; Barbar and Barbara—Kellie
Madyda; Moonshine and Moonshadow—Nadia Edwards.

The Maiden Yukay—Andrew Fine; Zap Griffin—Noele
Ashbarry; pan-pipe trees, crossed zzz's—Nadia Edwards; floorist—
Jessy Galletley; pop-up windows—Jacob Buehler; Bear
Minimum—Jon Conyers; Ivan—Ian; Naomi, Nagahide—Naomi
Blose; seal closing envelopes—Shyan Simpson; man-a-tease—Fe-
licia Sible; dumb bell, smart asp, gownless evening straps, smoke
and mirrors—Joanie Evans; shooting star—Shyan Simpson; sugar
cane walking stick—Kerry Garrigan; dangerous talents sent to
Mundania—Laura Kwon Anderson; jean pool—Kyle Bernelle;
liquidator—John Cochrane; steal-toed boots—Emilio Valdovinos;

rap scallions, mel odious—Lou Nelson; earrings—Mark A. Davis; Bogeyman—Clayton Overstreet; careworn clothes demoralize the wearer—Mark A. Davis.

And I hope you enjoyed the novel. There should be another next year.